About the

USA Today bestseller **Michelle Celmer** is the author of more than forty books for Mills & Boon. You can usually find her in her office with her laptop loving the fact that she gets to work in her pyjamas. Michelle loves to hear from her readers! Visit Michelle on Facebook at Michelle Celmer Author, or email at michelle@michellecelmer.com

Cathy Williams is a great believer in the power of perseverance as she had never written anything before her writing career. From the starting point of zero, she has now fulfilled her ambition to pursue this most enjoyable of careers. She would encourage any would-be writer to have faith and go for it! She derives inspiration from the tropical island of Trinidad and from the peaceful countryside of middle England. Cathy lives in Warwickshire her family.

Stefanie London is a *USA Today* bestselling author of contemporary romance. Her books have been called 'genuinely entertaining and memorable' by *Booklist,* and her writing praised as 'elegant, descriptive and delectable' by *RT* Magazine. Originally from Australia, she now lives in Toronto with her very own hero and is doing her best to travel the world. She frequently indulges her passions for lipstick, good coffee, books and anything zombie related.

Tempted by the Tycoon:

Tempted by the Tycoon:
The Ultimate Seduction

MICHELLE CELMER

CATHY WILLIAMS

STEFANIE LONDON

MILLS & BOON

First Published in Great Britain 2023
by Mills & Boon, an imprint of HarperCollins*Publishers* Ltd,
1 London Bridge Street, London, SE1 9GF

www.harpercollins.co.uk

HarperCollins*Publishers*
Macken House, 39/40 Mayor Street Upper,
Dublin 1, D01 C9W8, Ireland

Tempted By The Tycoon: The Ultimate Seduction © 2023 Harlequin Enterprises ULC.

Virgin Princess, Tycoon's Temptation © 2010 Michelle Celmer
The Tycoon's Ultimate Conquest © 2018 Cathy Williams
The Tycoon's Stowaway © 2015 Harlequin Enterprises ULC.

Special thanks and acknowledgement are given to Stefanie London for her contribution to the *Sydney's Most Eligible...*series.

ISBN: 978-0-263-31875-3

MIX
Paper | Supporting
responsible forestry
FSC™ C007454

This book is produced from independently certified FSC™ paper
to ensure responsible forest management.

For more information visit: www.harpercollins.co.uk/green

Printed and Bound in the UK using 100% Renewable electricity at
CPI Group (UK) Ltd, Croydon, CR0 4YY

VIRGIN PRINCESS, TYCOON'S TEMPTATION

MICHELLE CELMER

To my grandson, Cameron James Ronald

One

A genuine believer in fate and fairy tale romances, Princess Louisa Josephine Elisabeth Alexander knew that if she was patient, the man of her dreams would eventually come along. And as their eyes met across the crowded ballroom, beneath a canopy of red and white twinkling lights, shimmering silver tulle and pink, white and red heart-shaped balloons, she could swear she felt the earth move.

She just knew he was the one.

Her family would probably remind her that she'd felt that way about men before. Aaron would tease her and call her a hopeless romantic. Chris, the oldest, would just sigh and shake his head, as if to say, "Here we go again." Her twin sister Anne would probably sneer and call her naive. But this time it was different. Louisa was sure of it. She could *feel* it, like a cosmic tug at her soul.

He was the most intriguing, handsome and *tallest*

man—by several inches—at the charity event, which was what drew her attention to him in the first place. With raven hair, a warm olive complexion and striking features, he was impossible to miss.

Was he an Italian businessman, or a Mediterranean prince? Whoever he was, he was rich and powerful. She could tell by the quality of his clothing and the way he carried himself. Most people knew better than to openly stare at a member of the royal family, but this man gazed intently at her with dark, deep-set eyes, as though they already knew one another. Which she was sure they didn't. She definitely would have remembered him. Maybe he didn't realize she was royalty, although she would imagine the diamond encrusted tiara tucked within her upswept hair would be a dead giveaway.

Another woman might have waited for him to make the first move, or manufactured a scenario in which their paths accidentally crossed, but Louisa didn't believe in playing games. Much to the chagrin of her overly protective siblings. The youngest member of the royal family by a mere five minutes, and labeled as too trusting, Louisa was treated like a child. But contrary to what her family believed, not everyone was interested in her money and title, and those who were, were fairly easy to recognize.

She set her empty champagne glass on a passing server's tray and headed in his direction, the full skirt of her gown—in her customary shade of pink—swishing soundlessly as she crossed the floor. Never once did his eyes leave hers. As she approached, he finally lowered his gaze and bowed his head, saying in a voice as deep as it was smooth, "Her Highness is enchanting tonight."

Not a half-bad opening line, and he spoke with a

dialect not unlike her own. Almost definitely from Thomas Isle, so why didn't she recognize him? "You seem to have me at a disadvantage," she said. "You obviously know me, but I don't recall ever meeting you."

Most people, especially a stranger, would have at least offered an apology for staring, but this man didn't look like the type who apologized for *anything*. "That's because we've never met," he answered.

"I suppose that would explain it," she said with a smile.

Face-to-face, he was a little older than she'd guessed. Mid-thirties maybe—ten years or so her senior—but she preferred men who were older and more experienced. He was also much larger than she thought. The top of her head barely reached his chin. It wasn't just his height that was so imposing, either. He was big all over, and she would bet that not an ounce of it was fat. Even through his attire, he seemed to have the chiseled physique of a gladiator. She couldn't help noticing that he wasn't wearing a wedding ring.

This was, without a doubt, *fate*.

She offered a hand to shake. "Princess Louisa Josephine Elisabeth Alexander."

"That's quite a mouthful," he said, but she could see by the playful grin that he was teasing her.

He took her hand, cradled it within his ridiculously large palm, lifted it to his mouth and brushed a very gentle kiss across her skin. Did the ground beneath her feet just give a vigorous jolt, or was that her heart?

"And you are…?" she asked.

"Honored to meet you, Your Highness."

Either he had no grasp of etiquette, or he was being deliberately obtuse. "You have a name?"

His wry smile said he was teasing her again and she felt her heart flutter. "Garrett Sutherland," he said.

Sutherland? Why did that sound so familiar? Then it hit her. She had heard her brother speak of him from time to time, a landowner with holdings so vast they nearly matched those of the royal family. Mr. Sutherland was not only one of the richest men in the country, but also the most mysterious and elusive. He never attended social gatherings, and other than an occasional business meeting, kept largely to himself.

Definitely not the kind of man who would need her money.

"Mr. Sutherland," she said. "Your reputation precedes you. It's a pleasure to finally make your acquaintance."

"The pleasure is all mine, Your Highness. As you probably know, I don't normally attend events such as these, but when I heard the proceeds would benefit cardiac research, for your father's sake at the very least, I knew I had to make an appearance."

A testament to what a kind and caring man he must be, she thought. Someone she would very much like to get to know better.

His gaze left hers briefly to search the room. "I haven't seen the King tonight. Is he well?"

"Very well, under the circumstances. He wanted to make an appearance but he has strict orders from his doctor not to appear in public."

Louisa's father, the King of Thomas Isle, suffered from heart disease and had spent the past nine months on a portable bypass machine designed to give his heart an opportunity to heal and eventually work on its own again. Louisa took pride in the fact that it had been her idea to hold a charity ball in his honor. Usually her family wrote off her ideas as silly and idealistic, but for the first time in her life, they seemed to take her seriously. Although, when she had asked to be given the responsibility of planning the affair, they had hired a team of professionals instead. Baby steps, she figured. One of these days they would see that she wasn't the frail flower they made her out to be.

Across the ballroom the orchestra began playing her favorite waltz. "Would you care to dance, Mr. Sutherland?"

He arched one dark brow curiously. Most women would wait for the man to make the first move, but she wasn't most women. Besides, this was destiny. What could be the harm in moving things along a bit?

"I would be honored, Your Highness."

He held out his arm, and she slipped hers through it. As he led her through clusters of guests toward the dance floor, she half expected one of her overprotective siblings to cut them off at the pass, but Chris and his wife Melissa, enormously pregnant with triplets, were acting as host and hostess in their parents' absence. Aaron was glued to the side of his new wife, Olivia, a scientist who, when she wasn't in her lab buried in research, felt like a fish out of water.

Louisa searched out her sister Anne, surprised to find her talking to the Prime Minister's son, Samuel Baldwin, who Louisa knew for a fact was not on Anne's list of favorite people.

Not a single member of her family was paying attention to her. Louisa could hardly fathom that she was about to dance with a man without *someone* grilling him beforehand. He took her in his arms and twirled her across the floor, and they were blissfully alone—save for the hundred or so other couples dancing. But as he drew her close and gazed into her eyes, there was no one but them.

He held her scandalously close for a first dance—by royal standards anyhow—but it was like magic, the way their bodies fit and how they moved in perfect sync. The way he never stopped gazing into her eyes, as though they were a window into her soul. His were black and bottomless and as mysterious as the man. He smelled delicious, too. Spicy and clean. His hair looked so soft she wanted to run her fingers through it and she was dying to know how his lips would taste, even though she felt instinctively they would be as delicious as the rest of him.

When the song ended and a slower number began, he pulled her closer, until she was tucked firmly against the warmth of his body. Two songs turned to three, then four.

Neither spoke. Words seemed unnecessary. His eyes and the curve of his smile told her exactly what he was thinking and feeling. Only when the orchestra stopped to take a break did he reluctantly let go. He led her from the dance floor, and she was only vaguely aware that people were staring at her. At them. They probably wondered who this dark mysterious man was dancing with the Princess. Were they an item? She would bet that people could tell just by looking at them that they were destined to be together.

"Would you care to take a stroll on the patio?" she asked.

He gestured to the French doors leading out into the garden. "After you, Your Highness."

The air had chilled with the setting sun and a cool, salty ocean breeze blew in from the bluff. With the exception of the guards positioned at either side of the garden entrance, they were alone.

"Beautiful night," Garrett said, gazing up at the star-filled sky.

"It is," she agreed. June had always been her favorite month, when the world was alive with color and new life. What better time to meet the man of her dreams? Her soul mate.

"Tell me about yourself, Mr. Sutherland."

He turned to her and smiled. "What would you like to know?"

Anything. *Everything.* "You live on Thomas Isle?"

"Since the day I was born. I was raised just outside the village of Varie on the other side of the island."

The village to which he referred could only be described as quaint. Definitely not where you would expect to find a family of excessive means. Not that it mattered to her where he came from. Only that he was here now, with her. "What do your parents do?"

"My father was a farmer, my mother a seamstress. They're both retired now and living in England with my brother and his family."

It was difficult to fathom that such a wealthy and shrewd businessman was raised with such modest means. He had obviously done quite well for himself.

"How many siblings do you have?" she asked.

"Three brothers."

"Younger? Older?"

"I'm the eldest."

She wished, if only for a day or two, she could know what that felt like. To not be coddled and treated like a child. To be the person everyone turned to for guidance and advice.

A chilly breeze blew in from the bluff and Louisa shivered, rubbing warmth into her bare arms. They should go back inside before she caught a cold—with her father's condition it was important that everyone in the family stay healthy—but she relished this time alone with him.

"You're cold," he said.

"A little," she admitted, sure that he would suggest they head back in, but instead he removed his tux jacket and draped it over her shoulders, surrounding her in the toasty warmth of his body and the spicy sent of his cologne. What she really wanted, what she *longed* for, was for him to pull her into his arms and kiss her. She already knew that his lips would be firm but gentle, his mouth delicious. Heaven knows she had played the scene over in her mind a million times since adolescence, what the perfect kiss would be like, yet no man had ever measured up to the fantasy. Garrett would, she was sure of it. Even if she had to make the first move.

She was contemplating doing just that when a figure appeared in the open doorway. She turned to find that, watching them, with a stern look on his face, was her oldest brother, Chris.

"Mr. Sutherland," he said. "I'm so pleased to see that you've finally accepted an invitation to celebrate with us."

Garrett bowed his head and said, "Your Highness."

Chris stepped forward and shook his hand, but there was an undertone of tension in his voice, in his stance.

Did he dislike Garrett? Mistrust him? Or maybe he was just being his usual protective self.

"I see you've met the Princess," he said.

"She's a lovely woman," Garrett replied. "Although I fear I may have monopolized her time."

Chris shot her a sharp look. "She does have duties."

As princess it was her responsibility to socialize with *all* the guests, especially in her parents' absence, and duty was duty.

Another time and place. Definitely.

"Give me a minute, please," she asked her brother.

He grudgingly nodded and told Mr. Sutherland, "Enjoy your evening." Then he walked away.

Louisa smiled apologetically. "I'm sorry if he seemed rude. He's a little protective of me. My entire family is."

His smile was understanding. "If I had a sister so lovely, I would be, too."

"I suppose I should go back inside and mingle with the other guests."

His look said he shared her disappointment. "I understand, Your Highness."

She took off his jacket and handed it back to him. "I was wondering if you might like to be my guest for dinner at the castle."

A smile spread across his beautiful mouth. "I would like that very much."

"Are you free this coming Friday?"

"If not, I'll clear my schedule."

"We dine at seven sharp, but you can come a little early. Say, six-thirty?"

"I'll be there." He reached for her hand, brushing

another gentle kiss across her bare skin. "Good night, Your Highness."

He flashed her one last sizzling grin, then turned and walked back inside. She watched him go until he was swallowed up by the crowd, knowing that the next six days, until she saw him again, when she could gaze into the dark and hypnotizing depths of his eyes, would be the longest in her life.

Two

Garrett sipped champagne and strolled the perimeter of the ballroom, eyes on the object of his latest fascination. Everything was going exactly as planned.

"That was quite a performance," someone said from behind him, and he turned to see Weston Banes, his best friend and business manager, smiling wryly.

He pasted on an innocent look. "Who said it was a performance?"

Wes shot him a knowing look. He had worked with Garrett since he bought his first parcel of land ten years ago. He knew better than anyone that Garrett would have never attended the ball without some ulterior motive.

"I've hit a brick wall," Garrett told him.

Wes frowned. "I don't follow you."

"I now own every available parcel of commercial land that doesn't belong to the royal family, so there's only one thing left for me to do."

"What's that?"

"Take control of the royal family's land, as well."

A slow smile spread across Wes's face. "And the only way to do that is to marry into the family."

"Exactly." He had two choices, Princess Anne, who he'd commonly heard referred to as *The Shrew,* or Princess Louisa, the sweet, innocent and gullible twin. It was pretty much a no-brainer. Although, considering the way she'd looked at him, as responsive as she was to his touch, he wondered if she wasn't as sweet and innocent as her reputation claimed.

Wes shook his head. "This is ruthless, even for you. Anything to pad the portfolio, I guess."

This wasn't about money. He already had more than he could ever spend. This was about power and control. To marry the Princess, the monarchy would first have to assign him a title—most likely Duke—then he would be considered royalty. The son of a farmer and a seamstress becoming one of the most powerful men in the country. Who would have imagined? If he played his cards right, which he always did, someday he would control the entire island.

"We can discuss the details later," Garrett told him. "I wouldn't mind your input, seeing how this involves you, as well."

"This is really something coming from the man who swore he would never get married or have children," Wes said.

Garrett shrugged. "Sometimes a man has to make sacrifices."

"So, how did it go?"

"Quite well."

"If that's true, then why are you here, and she's way over there?"

His smile was a smug one. "Because I already got what I came for."

"I'm afraid to ask what that was."

Garrett chuckled. "Get your mind out of the gutter. I'm talking about an invitation to dinner at the castle."

His brows rose. "Seriously?"

"This Friday at six-thirty."

"Damn." He shook his head in disbelief. "You're good."

He shrugged. "It's a gift. Women can't resist my charm. Just ask your wife."

Wes turned to see Tia, his wife of five years, standing with a throng of society women near the bar. "I should probably intervene before she drinks her weight in champagne and I have to carry her out of here."

"You need to let her out more," Garrett joked.

"I wish," Wes said. Despite considerable means, Tia was the kind of nervous new mother who believed no one could care for their child as well as she and Wes, but he worked ridiculous hours and because of that she didn't get out very often. In fact, this was the first public function they had attended since Will's birth three months ago.

"Join us?" Wes asked, gesturing in his spouse's direction.

Garrett gave one last glance to the Princess, who was deep in conversation with a group of heads of state, then nodded and followed Wes to the bar. He already had a game plan in place. What he would say to her and what he wouldn't, when they would share their first kiss. The trick with a woman like her was to take it very slow.

He had little doubt that in no time, probably next Friday, he would have her eating out of the palm of his hand.

Louisa had been right.

It had been a murderously *long* week waiting for Friday to arrive, and when it finally did, the day seemed to stretch on for weeks. Finally, when she thought she couldn't stand another second of waiting, at six-thirty on the dot, a shiny black convertible sports car pulled up in front of the castle and Garrett unfolded himself from inside.

She watched from the library, surprised that someone of his means didn't have a driver, and wondering how such a big man fit into such a tiny vehicle. Maybe someday he would take her for a drive in it. With her bodyguards following close behind of course, because no member of the royal family was allowed to leave the castle unescorted. Especially not since the threats began late last summer.

Louisa peeked out from behind the curtain, watching as Garrett walked to the door. He looked so handsome and distinguished in a dark gray, pinstripe suit. And *tall*. She'd almost forgotten just how big he was.

Her brother Chris hadn't been happy about the short notice when she'd informed him this morning that she had invited Garrett for dinner. She knew though that if she'd told him sooner, the family would have teased and harassed her mercilessly all week.

As it was, everyone had managed to get their digs in this afternoon. Chris of course questioned Garrett's motives, as though no man would appreciate her for anything but her money and connections. Aaron voiced concern about the age difference—which, as Louisa had guessed, was just over ten years. Anne, who had been particularly cranky since the ball, warned her that a man like Garrett Sutherland was way out of her league and only interested in one thing. Louisa would love to know how Anne knew that when she didn't even know Garrett. Even her parents, who had been relying on Chris's judgment lately, were reserving their opinion. She wished, just this once, that everyone would mind their own business.

When Chris married an illegitimate princess, everyone just had to smile and go along with it for the good of the country, and when Aaron announced that he was going to marry an American scientist, an orphan who had not even a trace of royal blood, barely anyone voiced an objection. So what was the big deal about Louisa dating a rich and successful businessman?

She had checked up on him this week, purely out of curiosity of course, and though she hadn't been able to find too much information, none of it had been negative.

She was sure, though, that since her announcement this morning, Chris had ordered Randall Jenkins, their head of security, to dig up all the information he could find on Garrett. Louisa wasn't worried. She knew instinctively that he was a good person because she was an excellent judge of character.

The bell rang and she scurried over to the sofa to wait while Geoffrey, their butler, let Garrett in. She sat on the edge of the cushion and smoothed the wrinkles from the skirt of her pale pink sleeveless sundress, her heart pounding so hard it felt as though it might beat right through her chest.

Under normal circumstances she would have worn something a bit more conservative, like a business suit, for a dinner guest, but this was a first date and she wanted to look her best. Make a good first impression.

It seemed to take a millennium before the library door opened and Garrett strolled into the room. She rose to her feet to greet him.

Garrett wore his confidence like a badge of honor. So different from the cocky young royals she'd been introduced to in the past, who reeked of wealth and entitlement, as though their name alone afforded them everything their greedy and spoiled hearts desired.

Louisa and her siblings had been raised with wealth and privilege, but taught not to take anything for granted. Life, they had learned, especially since their father's illness, was fragile, and family was what mattered above all else.

Maybe it was wishful thinking, but she had the distinct feeling Garrett shared those values.

When he saw her standing there, a gorgeous smile curled his lips. He bowed his head and said, "Your Highness, a pleasure to see you again."

"I'm so glad you could make it," she replied, even though she'd never had a single doubt that he would show. What had happened between them on the dance floor had been magical and she was certain that they were destined to be together. Besides, his assistant had phoned hers this morning to confirm.

"Would you care for a drink, sir?" Geoffrey offered.

"Scotch, please," Garrett said, and his manners made Louisa smile. There was nothing she despised more than a man who treated the hired help with disrespect.

Especially Geoffrey, who had been with them since before Louisa was born and almost single-handedly kept the household running like clockwork.

"White wine, Your Highness?" Geoffrey asked her.

She nodded. "That would be lovely, thank you."

She gestured to the sofa and told Garrett, "Please, make yourself comfortable."

He settled onto the cushion, looking remarkably relaxed, as though he dined with royalty on a daily basis, when she knew for a fact that the charity ball had been the first time he had visited the castle under social circumstances. She sat at the opposite end, all but crawling out of her skin with excitement. When their drinks were poured, Geoffrey excused himself and they were *finally* alone. No family breathing down her neck, no bodyguards watching their every move.

"I was looking forward to my parents meeting you, but unfortunately they won't be joining us this evening."

"Your father isn't well?" he asked, looking concerned.

"He's going in for a procedure soon and has to stay in tip-top shape. The fewer people he's exposed to, the less likely he is to contract illnesses. His immune system is already compromised by the heart pump."

"Another time," he said. Was that his way of suggesting that he wanted to see her again? Not that she ever doubted he would. This was destiny.

It was still nice to hear the words out loud, to know what he was thinking.

"I'll warn you that tonight might feel more like the Spanish Inquisition than a dinner," she told him.

Garrett smiled. "I expected as much. I have nothing to hide."

"I Googled you," she admitted.

Her honesty seemed to surprise him. "Did you?"

"Earlier this week, although I didn't find much."

"There isn't much to find. I am a simple man, Your Highness. What some may even consider...boring."

She seriously doubted that. Everything about him intrigued her. He was so dark and serious, yet his smile was warm and inviting. She liked the way his eyes crinkled slightly in the corners when he smiled, and the hint of a dimple that dented his left cheek.

She opened her mouth to tell him that she would never consider a man like him boring, but before she could get the words out, her family appeared in the doorway. The entire lot of them.

Fantastic bloody timing. God forbid they let her have a little time alone with the man she planned to marry.

As everyone piled into the room, Garrett rose and Louisa stood to make the introductions.

"Garrett, I believe you already know my brothers, Prince Christian and Prince Aaron."

"A pleasure to see you again." Garrett bowed his head, then accepted a firm and brusque shake from each of them. Very businesslike, but with an undertone of possessiveness, a silent notification that he was being carefully assessed.

"This is my sister-in-law, Princess Melissa," Louisa said.

"Just Melissa," she added in the southern drawl she had adopted while living in the States. She shook his hand firmly and with purpose. For a southern belle, she didn't have a delicate or demure bone in her body. "It's a pleasure to finally meet you, Mr. Sutherland. I've heard so much about you."

"Please call me Garrett," he said. "I understand you're expecting. Congratulations."

"Kind of tough to miss at this point," she joked, laying a hand on her very swollen middle.

"I understand it will be soon."

"They prefer I make it to thirty-six weeks, so the babies' lungs have enough time to mature. Preterm labor is a possibility with multiples, but I can hardly imagine another month of this. I feel like an elephant."

"I've always believed there's nothing more beautiful than an expectant mother," Garrett said with genuine sincerity.

Melissa grinned widely and Louisa knew that he'd instantly won her over.

Aaron stepped forward and said, "This is my wife, Princess Olivia."

Liv smiled shyly, still unaccustomed to her role as a royal. A botanical geneticist, she was reserved and studious and would much rather be in her basement lab studying plant DNA than interacting with people. But she shook Garrett's hand and said, "Nice to meet you."

Anne, not waiting to be introduced, stepped forward and announced, "I'm Anne." She stuck out her hand, shaking Garrett's so firmly that Louisa worried she might challenge him to an arm wrestle.

What was her problem?

If Anne had been expecting a negative reaction from her confrontational introduction, she got the opposite.

"A pleasure to meet you, Your Highness," Garrett said with a smile, the picture of grace and etiquette, and Louisa all but beamed with pride. The situation couldn't be more tense or uncomfortable, yet he'd handled it with ease.

"I'll admit I was surprised when Louisa informed us this morning that you were joining us for dinner," Chris said, and Louisa wanted to punch him. Garrett had to be wondering why she would wait until this morning to tell them. She didn't want him to get the wrong idea, to think that she was ashamed of him or uncertain of her invitation.

Instead of appearing insulted, Garrett looked her way and flashed her that adorable, dimpled smile. "And I was a bit surprised when she asked." His eyes locked on hers with a look so warm and delicious she almost melted. "I could hardly believe I was lucky enough to draw the attention of the most beautiful woman in the room."

The honesty of his words and the admiration in his eyes warmed her from the inside out. The fact that he would speak so openly of his feelings for her, especially in front of her family, made her want to throw her arms around his neck and kiss him. But who wanted an audience for their first kiss?

Geoffrey appeared in the study door and announced, "Dinner is ready."

Melissa held out her arm for Chris to take. "Shall we?"

"Go ahead without me. I'd like to have a private word with our guest."

Louisa's heart nearly stopped. Why did Chris need to see him alone? She prayed he wouldn't say something embarrassing, or try to scare Garrett off. But if she made a fuss, it might only make things worse.

At Melissa's look of hesitance he added, "We'll only be a minute."

Louisa flashed Garrett an apologetic look, but he

just smiled, looking totally at ease as Melissa ushered everyone from the room.

With any luck, Garrett wouldn't decide that pursuing a princess was just too much hassle and bring an end to their first date before it even began.

Three

And so it begins, Garrett thought as the rest of the family walked, or in Melissa's case, waddled, from the room, leaving only himself and Prince Christian. He wondered if, had he been a royal, the Prince would feel this chat was necessary.

Well, it wouldn't be long before Garrett had a royal title, garnering him all of the respect he had earned. Though time wasn't an issue, he would still push for a quick engagement. The sooner they were married and settled, the sooner he could relax and begin enjoying all the fruits of his labor.

"Under normal circumstances it would be the King having this conversation with you," Chris said.

But the King wasn't well enough, so Garrett was stuck with the Crown Prince instead. He hadn't yet decided if that was a good or a bad thing. "I understand."

The Prince gestured to the sofa, and after Garrett

sat, Chris took a seat in the armchair across from him. "As a precaution, I had a thorough background check performed on you."

He had anticipated that, and as he had told Princess Louisa, he had nothing to hide. "Did they find anything interesting?"

"Actually, they didn't find much of anything at all. Though ruthless in your business practices, as far as I can tell you've always kept it legal and ethical, and you seem to be a fair employer. You donate a percentage of your income to worthwhile charities—most having to do with education for the underprivileged—and as far as any brushes with the law, you've never had so much as a parking ticket."

"You sound surprised."

"I would expect that a man so elusive might have something to hide."

"I certainly don't mean to be elusive," he said. "I simply lead an uncomplicated life. My work is my passion."

"It shows. Your accomplishments are quite impressive."

"Thank you."

The Prince paused for a second, as though he was uncomfortable with what he planned to say next. "While I see no clear reason to be concerned, I'm obligated to ask, on the King's behalf, what your intentions are regarding Princess Louisa."

It seemed ridiculous to Garrett that, at twenty-seven years old, Louisa wasn't allowed to make her own decisions regarding who she wanted to see socially. "Her Highness invited me to dinner and I accepted," he said.

The simplicity of his answer seemed to surprise the Prince. "That's it?"

"I admit I find your sister quite fascinating."

"Louisa is…special."

He said that as though that was an impediment, and Garrett felt an odd dash of defensiveness in her honor. Which was a little ridiculous considering he barely knew her.

"I've never met anyone quite like her," he told the Prince.

"She tends to be a bit naive when it comes to the opposite sex. Men have taken advantage of that."

Maybe if her family stopped sheltering her, she would learn not to be so gullible. However, that particular trait was working in his favor, so he could hardly complain. "Rest assured, I have nothing but the utmost respect for the Princess. I pride myself on being a very honorable man. I would never do anything to compromise her principles."

"I'm glad to hear it," Chris said. "But of course I will have to discuss the matter with the King."

"Of course, Your Highness."

The shadow of a smile cracked the serious expression. "We've known each other a long time, Garrett. Call me Chris."

With that request Garrett knew he was as good as in. Chris needing to speak with his father was merely a formality at this point. "I'm very much looking forward to getting to know you better," Garrett told him.

"As am I." Chris paused, his expression darkening, and said, "However, if you did take advantage of my sister, the consequences would be…unfortunate."

The fact that Garrett didn't even flinch seemed to

impress Chris. Still, Garrett was going to have to be very cautious while he courted Louisa.

Chris rose from his chair and said, "Shall we join the others?"

Garrett stood and followed him to the dining room. The first course was just being served, and as soon as they entered the room, Louisa shot from her seat and gestured him to the empty chair beside her.

When they were seated again, she leaned close to him and whispered, "I'm so sorry he did that. I hope he wasn't too hard on you."

He gave her a reassuring smile. "Not at all."

If he thought the worst was over, he realized quickly that it had only begun. He barely had a chance to taste his soup before Anne launched into the inquisition portion of the meal.

"I understand your father was a farmer," she said, her tone suggesting that made him inferior somehow.

It had only been a matter of time before someone broached the subject of his humble beginnings, but he wasn't ashamed of his past. He was instead very proud of his accomplishments. Although for the life of him he never understood why his parents hadn't strived to better themselves. Why they settled for a life barely a step above poverty when they could have done so much more for themselves and their sons.

"All of his life," Garrett told her. "My earliest memories are of working beside him in the fields."

"Yet you didn't follow in his footsteps," Anne noted, her words sounding an awful lot like an accusation. Much the way his father had sounded when Garrett had informed him that he planned to leave the island to attend college.

"No, I didn't. I wanted an education."

"How did your father feel about that?"

"Anne," Louisa said, plainly embarrassed by her sister's behavior.

"What?" Anne asked, her innocent look too manufactured to be genuine. He wasn't sure if she was jealous of Louisa, or simply being difficult because she could. If there was one thing Garrett knew for sure, he'd definitely chosen the right sister. Had he picked Anne, he would be asking for a life of misery.

"Stop being so nosy," Louisa said.

Anne shrugged. "How else can we get to know Mr. Sutherland?"

"Please call me Garrett," he told Anne. "And in answer to your question, my father wasn't at all happy with me. He expected me to take over the farm when he retired. I wanted to do something more with my life."

"Which you certainly have," Chris said, and maybe Garrett was imagining things, but he almost sounded impressed.

"If there's one thing I've learned," Garrett said, "it's that you can't live your life to please other people." He glanced over at Louisa, catching her eye for emphasis. "You have to follow your heart."

"I believe that, too," Olivia said. She reached over and placed a hand on her husband's arm. "Aaron is starting back to school in the fall. Premed."

"I'd heard that," Garrett said. He made it his business to know everything about his stiffest competition. Aaron's leaving the family business would create the convenient opening he required to insinuate himself inside.

"He's going to be a brilliant doctor," Olivia said,

beaming with pride. She was a plain woman, very young and unassuming, but pretty when she smiled... and quite the brilliant scientist from what he understood. The previous autumn, an unidentifiable blight potentially threatened all the crops on the island. The effects would have been devastating on the export trade, the main source of income for the country, and Olivia had been hired by the royal family to find an eco-friendly cure.

"I've heard that your own brilliance saved the livelihood of every landowner in the country," Garrett told her. "Myself included."

Olivia grinned shyly and blushed. It would seem that he had won over at least three-quarters of the females at the table. Anne seemed a lost cause at this point. Chris and Aaron, he wasn't sure about, but it looked promising. Now it was time for a change of subject, and he'd done his research.

"I understand you spent quite a lot of time in the States," Garrett said to Melissa.

"I was born on Morgan Isle but raised in New Orleans," she told him.

"A lovely city," he commented.

"You've been there?"

He nodded. "Several times in fact. For business. Terrible what happened during Katrina."

"It was. I started a foundation to fund the rehabilitation of the city."

"I had no idea. I'd love to make a donation."

Melissa smiled. "That would be lovely, thank you."

"I'll have a check sent round next week."

"What other places have you visited?" Louisa asked him, and they launched into a conversation about traveling abroad, and everyone's favorite vacation spot.

Garrett was pleasantly surprised to find that, with the exception of Anne, they were a friendly bunch, and not nearly as uptight as he'd expected. The tone of the conversation was not unlike those of his youth, when his family gathered for supper. In fact, by the time dessert was served, Garrett realized that he was actually enjoying himself.

Louisa didn't say much, but instead spent most of her time gazing up at him, seemingly mesmerized by every word that passed his lips.

After dinner, Chris pushed back from the table and asked Garrett, "Up for a friendly game of poker? We play every Friday evening."

Before he could answer, Louisa said, "Garrett and I are taking a walk in the garden." Which he took as his clue to decline their offer, when the truth was he would much rather play cards than take a leisurely stroll, but securing his position with Louisa took precedence for now.

"Maybe some other time," he told Chris.

"Of course." Chris turned to Louisa, his expression serious, and said, "Not too far, and I want you inside before sundown."

"I know," Louisa replied, sounding exasperated, and Garrett didn't blame her. He knew her family kept a tight grip on the reins, but telling a woman of twenty-seven that she couldn't stay out past dark bordered on the absurd.

Louisa slipped her arm through his and smiled up at him. "Ready?"

He thanked her family for dinner, then let Louisa lead him through the castle and out onto a patio that opened up into acres of lush flower gardens. The evening was a warm one, but a cool breeze blew in from the bluff.

She kept a firm grip on his arm as they started down the path, as though she feared the instant they were in the clear he might run for his life.

"I'm really sorry about my family," she said, looking apologetic. "As you probably noticed, they treat me like a child."

"They are quite...*protective*."

"It's humiliating. They think I'm naive."

Maybe they weren't so far off the mark, he thought wryly. She was unsophisticated enough to fall for his charms without question or doubt. Not that he would ever mistreat her, or compromise her honor. She would never suffer as his wife.

"I'm sure they mean well," he told her. "I imagine it would be much worse if they didn't care at all."

"I guess you're right," she conceded. "But since the threats started they've been a lot worse than usual. They think everyone I meet is a spy or something."

"I had seen something on the news about the security being breached in your father's hospital suite in London. I understand no one was able to identify the suspect from the surveillance footage."

"He calls himself the Gingerbread Man."

"Seriously?"

"Strange, I know. It started last summer with e-mail. He hacked into our computer system and sent threatening messages to us from our own accounts. They were all twisted versions of nursery rhymes."

"Nursery rhymes?" That didn't sound very threatening to him.

"Mine said, 'I love you, a bushel and a peck. A bushel

and a peck, and a noose around your neck. With a noose around your neck, you will drop into a heap. You'll drop into a heap and forever you will sleep.'" She looked up at him with a wry smile and said, "I memorized it."

On second thought, that was rather ominous. "What were the others?"

"I don't remember them word for word, but the common theme was burning alive."

Ouch. No wonder the family was being so cautious.

"At first we thought it was just an elaborate prank, until he managed to slip through castle security and get on the grounds. They think he scaled the bluff."

That explained the seemingly excessive security the night of the ball. "Was anyone harmed?"

"No, but he left a note. It said, 'Run, run, as fast as you can. You can't catch me. I'm the Gingerbread Man.' That's how we learned his name. We haven't heard anything from him lately, but that doesn't mean he's stopped. Things will be quiet for a while, then just when we think that he's given up, he'll leave another note somewhere or send an untraceable e-mail. He sent a gift basket full of rotten fruit for New Year's, then he sent flowers for Melissa and Chris congratulating them on the pregnancy. *Weeks* before the official announcement was made. He even knew that they were having triplets."

"Sounds like someone on the inside."

"We thought so, too, but everyone checked out."

At least her family's protectiveness made a bit more sense now. He just hoped it didn't interfere with his plans. It could be difficult courting a woman who wasn't allowed to leave her home.

"Enough about my family drama," she said, waving

the subject away like a pesky insect. "What is your family like?"

"Simple," he said, then quickly added, "Not intellectually. But they prefer to live a...*humble* lifestyle." One that didn't include him.

"What do your brothers do?"

"Two own a business together in England. They sell farming equipment. My youngest brother is something of a...wanderer. Last I heard he was working a cattle ranch in Scotland."

"I'd like to meet them," she said, with an eagerness that surprised him. "Maybe they could all come to the castle for a visit."

Considering he was trying to impress the royal family, that probably wouldn't be wise. "I'm not so sure that would be a good idea."

She frowned. "You're not ashamed of them?"

Once again, her directness surprised him. "I'm afraid it's quite the opposite."

Her eyes widened. "They're ashamed of *you?*"

"Maybe not ashamed, but they're not very pleased with the path I chose."

"How is that possible? Look how well you've done. All that you've accomplished. How can they not be proud?"

He'd asked himself that same question a million times, but had long ago given up trying to understand their reasoning. He no longer cared what they thought of him. "It's...complicated."

She patted his arm. "Well, I think you're amazing. The instant I saw you I knew you were special."

He could see that she truly meant it, and in an odd way he wished he could say the same of her. He was sure that Louisa was very special in her own right, and maybe someday he would learn to appreciate that.

"Tell me the truth," she said. "Did my family scare you off?"

He could see by her expression that she was genuinely concerned, but he was a man on a mission. It would take a lot more than a grilling by her siblings to get in his way.

He gave her arm a squeeze. "Absolutely not."

Her smile was one of relief. "Good. Because I really like you, Garrett."

Never had he met a woman so forward with her feelings, so willing to put herself out on a limb. He liked that about her, and at the same time it made him uncomfortable. He was taught by his father that showing affection made a man weak. If he loved his sons, his father never once said so.

But Garrett had the feeling that if he was going to make this relationship work, he was going to have to learn to be more open with his feelings. At least until he had a royal title and Louisa had a ring on her finger.

He smiled and said, "The feeling is mutual, Your Highness."

Four

Louisa gazed up at Garrett, looking so sweet and innocent. So...*pure*. He felt almost guilty for deceiving her.

"I think at this point it would be all right for you to call me Louisa," she said.

"All right, Louisa."

"Can we speak frankly?"

"Is there ever a time when you don't?"

Her cheeks blushed a charming shade of pink and she bit her lip. "Sorry. I have this terrible habit of saying everything that's on my mind. It drives everyone crazy."

"Don't apologize. It's a welcome change. Most women play games." Unless this was some sort of game she was playing. But his instincts told him that she didn't have a manipulative bone in her body.

"You should know that I'm not looking for a temporary

relationship. I want to settle down and have a family."
She stopped walking and looked up at him. "I need to
know that you feel the same. That you're not just playing
the field."

"I'm thirty-seven years old, Louisa. I think I've played
the field long enough."

"In that case, there's something else I should probably
mention."

Why did he sense that he wasn't going to like this?

"We should talk about children."

She certainly didn't pull any punches, although oddly,
he was finding that he liked that about her. "What about
them?"

"I want a big family."

He narrowed his eyes at her. "How big?"

The grip on his arm tightened, as though she was
worried he might try to make a run for it. "At least six
kids. Maybe more."

For a second he thought she might be joking, or testing
him, then he realized that she was dead serious.

Six kids? Bloody hell, no wonder she was still single.
Who in this day and age wanted that many children?
He'd never felt the desire or need to have one child, much
less half a dozen of them! Marrying a royal, he knew at
least one heir would be expected. Maybe two. But *six?*

Despite his strong feelings on the matter, he could
see by her expression that this was not a negotiable point
for Louisa and he chose his next words very carefully.
"I'll admit that I've never given any thought to having a
family that large, but anything is possible."

A bright and relieved smile lit her entire face and he
felt an undeniable flicker of guilt, which he promptly
shook off. This was business. Once they were married,

he would lay down the law and insist that two children at most would be plenty and she would eventually learn to live with that. Or maybe, after the first child or two, she would change her mind anyway. He'd seen the way his parents struggled with a large family, the emotional roller coaster rides. Who would want to subject themselves to that?

Louisa gazed up at him, a dreamy look on her face. "It would be okay if you kissed me now," she said, then added, "If you want to."

Oh, he wanted to. So much that it surprised him a little. The idea had been to wait until their second date before he kissed her, to draw out the anticipation. Did she intend to derail each one of his carefully laid plans? "Are you sure that's what you want?" he asked.

"Just because my family treats me like a child, that doesn't mean I am one."

There was nothing childish about her, which she proved by not even waiting for him to make the first move. Instead, she reached up, slid her hands behind his neck, pulled him down to her level and kissed him. Her lips were soft but insistent, and she smelled fantastic. Delicate and feminine.

Though he had intended to keep it brief, to take things slowly, he felt himself being drawn closer, as though pulled by an invisible rope anchored somewhere deep inside his chest. His arms went around her and when his fingers brushed her bare back, what felt like an electric shock arced through his fingers. Louisa must have felt it, too, because she whimpered and curled her fingers into the hair at his nape. He felt her tongue, slick and warm against the seam of his lips and he knew he had to taste her, and when he did, she was as sweet as candy.

He was aware that this was moving too far, too fast, but as she leaned in closer, pressing her body against his, he felt helpless to stop her. Never had the simple act of kissing a woman aroused him so thoroughly, but Louisa seemed to put her heart and soul, her entire being, into it.

To him, self-control was a virtue, but Louisa seemed to know exactly which buttons to push. Not at all what he would have expected from a woman rumored to be so sweet and innocent. Which had him believing that she really wasn't so sweet and innocent after all.

Her hands slipped down his shoulders and inside his jacket. She stroked his chest through his shirt and that was all he could take. He broke the kiss, breathless and bewildered, his heart hammering like mad.

Louisa expelled a soft shudder of breath and rested her head against his chest. "Now *that* was a kiss."

He couldn't exactly argue. Although the whole point of this visit had been to prove to her family that his intentions were pure, yet here he was, practically mauling her out in the open, where anyone could see. If someone *was* watching, he hoped they hadn't failed to notice that she'd made the first move and he'd been the one to put on the brakes.

She nuzzled her face to his chest, her breath warm through his shirt. He curled his hands into fists, to keep from tangling them through her hair, from drawing her head back and kissing her again. He wanted to taste her lips and her throat, nibble at her ears. He wanted to put his hands all over her.

"It probably isn't proper to say this," Louisa said, "but I can't wait to see you naked."

Bloody hell. He backed away and held her at arm's

length, before he did something really stupid like drag her into the bushes and have his way with her. "Do you ever *not* say what's on your mind?"

"I just gave you the censored version," she answered with an impish grin. "Would you like to know what I'm really thinking?"

Of course he would, but this was not the time or place. "I'll use my imagination." He glanced up at the darkening sky and said, "It's getting late. I should get you back inside."

"Lest I turn into a pumpkin," she said with a sigh and took his hand, as naturally as if they had known each other for years, and they walked down the path toward the castle.

"I had a good time tonight," he said.

"Me, too. Although I get the feeling that I'm not quite what you expected."

"No, you're not. You're more intriguing and compelling than I could have imagined."

As she smiled up at him, he realized that was probably the most honest thing he'd said all night.

Louisa stood in the study, watching as Garrett's car zipped down the drive, until the glow of his taillights disappeared past the front gate.

She sighed and rested her forehead against the cool glass. This had been, by far, one of the best nights of her life. Kissing Garrett had been…magical. Even if she had been the one to make the first move. Later, when he had kissed her goodbye, it was so sweet and tender she nearly melted into a puddle on the oriental rug.

He was definitely the one.

"He's using you."

Louisa whipped around to find Anne leaning in the study doorway, arms folded across her chest, her typical grumpy self. Typical for the last week or so, anyway.

"Why would you think that?" she asked.

"Because that's what men like him do. They use women like us. They feed us lies, then toss us aside like trash."

Louisa knew that, like herself, Anne hadn't had the best luck with men, but that reasoning was harsh, even for her. "Are you okay, Anne?"

"He's going to hurt you."

Louisa shook her head. "Garrett is different."

"How do you know that?"

"How do *you* know that he isn't?"

Anne sighed and shook her head, as though she pitied her poor, naive sister. Louisa would have been upset, but she knew that attacking her was Anne's way of working through her own anger. Not that she didn't get a little tired of being her sister's punching bag.

"I can take care of myself," Louisa told her.

Anne shrugged, as though she didn't care one way or another. Which she must, or she wouldn't have said anything in the first place. "Don't say I didn't warn you."

"Did something happen to you?" Louisa asked, and she could swear she saw a flicker of pain before Anne carefully smothered it with a look of annoyance.

"You think that just because I don't like Garrett, something is wrong with *me?*"

"You can talk to me, Anne. I want to help."

"You're the one who needs help if you think that man really has feelings for you." With one last pathetic shake of her head, Anne turned and left. Her sister was obviously hurting, and Louisa felt bad about it, but she wished Anne would stop trying to drag Louisa down with her. Why couldn't Anne just be happy for her for once?

Maybe she was jealous. Maybe Anne wanted Garrett for herself. Or maybe, like Louisa, she wanted someone to love her, to see her for who she really was. Even though Anne could be a real pain in the neck sometimes, deep down there was a sweetness about her, a tender side, and she was loyal to the death to the ones that she loved.

"You'll meet someone, too," Louisa whispered to the empty doorway, knowing with all her heart that it was true. Even though Anne was a little pessimistic and occasionally cranky, there was a man out there who would appreciate all her gifts and overlook her faults. He would love her for who she was, just the way Garrett would love Louisa.

Worried for her sister, she started out the door, intending to collect her Shih Tzu, Muffin—who had spent the afternoon with his groomer and behaviorist—and tell him all about her day, but she ran into Chris in the foyer.

"Poker game over already?" she asked. Typically they played well past eleven. Louisa didn't play cards, unless you counted War and Solitaire, but occasionally she liked to sit and watch them.

"Melissa was tired and Liv wanted to get back to the lab. Some new research project she's working on. I assume your evening was a success."

She smiled and nodded.

"Have you got a minute?"

"Actually, I was just on my way to get Muffin."

His expression darkened. "I suppose you heard what

your little mutt did to the pillows on the library sofa. There was stuffing everywhere."

She cringed. "Yes. Sorry."

"The day before that it was Aaron's shoes."

"I know. I offered to replace them."

"He's a menace."

"He just wants attention."

"What he's going to get is a nice doghouse in the gardens."

Even if she thought Chris was serious, that wouldn't work either because every time Muffin was let outside unsupervised he made a run for it.

"I'll keep a closer eye on him," she promised. "What did you want to talk about?"

"Let's go in the study."

She couldn't tell if this would be a good talk, or a bad talk. But she had the sneaking suspicion that it had something to do with Garrett.

Louisa sat on the sofa while Chris fixed himself a drink. In preparation for his role as future King, Chris had always been the most responsible and aggressive sibling. He honored the responsibility, oftentimes to his own personal detriment. Still it surprised and impressed Louisa, since having to take their father's place while he was ill, how effortlessly Chris had slipped into his place and taken over his responsibilities. She had no doubt that if, God forbid, their father didn't recover, Chris would make a fine king.

But she had every confidence that their father would make a full recovery. He simply *had* to.

"I want you to know," Chris said, his back to her, "I didn't appreciate you waiting until this morning to announce that you had invited Garrett to dinner."

So he'd asked her here to scold her. Wonderful. "Can you really blame me? Had I said anything earlier I never would have heard the end of it."

He turned to her, took a swallow of his drink, then said, "You could have been putting the family in danger."

She rolled her eyes. "You say that like you haven't known Garrett for years. If he was dangerous, I'm sure we'd have heard about it a long time ago."

"You still have to follow the rules. We've all had to make sacrifices, Louisa."

As if she didn't know that. If they didn't treat her like a child, she would have been more forthcoming. This was more her siblings' fault than hers. They drove her to it. Sometimes she just got tired of being the obedient princess.

"I'm assuming that he must have checked out," she guessed, "or he never would have made it through the front gate."

"Yes, he did."

"I knew he would, and I didn't need a team of security operatives to tell me."

He shook his head, as though she was a hopeless cause. He crossed the room and sat on the sofa beside her. "I had a talk with Father about this earlier today, regarding his wishes concerning the matter."

Louisa held her breath. If the King disapproved of a man she wanted to date, she would be forbidden. Those were the rules. "And?"

"He told me to use my discretion."

Louisa wasn't sure if that was a good or a bad thing. At least she knew their father would be fair. Would Chris forbid her to see Garrett to teach her a lesson?

This was probably something she should have considered when she waited until the last second before telling Chris about Garrett's visit.

"And what did you decide?" she asked, flashing him the most wide-eyed and hopeful look she could manage.

He regarded her sternly for a moment, then a grin tipped up the corner of his mouth. "It's clear that you have feelings for the man. Of course you can see him."

She let out an excited squeal and threw her arms around Chris, hugging him so hard that his drink nearly sloshed onto the sofa. "Thank you! Thank you!"

"You're welcome," he said with a chuckle. *"However..."*

Oh boy, here came the conditions. She sat back and braced herself.

"No more stunts like you pulled this morning."

She shook her head. "Never. I promise. I swear, it won't happen again."

"In addition, you will not leave the premises without a minimum of two bodyguards, and I need at least two days' advance notice before you visit any sort of public place or attend a function. No exceptions, or I will not hesitate to place you on indefinite house arrest."

Inconvenient, but definitely doable. "No problem."

"And please, let's try not to give the press anything to salivate over. With Father's health, the last thing the family needs is more gossip and rumors."

She refrained from rolling her eyes. Now he was being silly. "Honestly, Chris, have I *ever* been one to create a scandal?"

"It's not necessarily you I'm concerned about."

"You don't have to worry about Garrett, either. He's

a complete gentleman. So much so that when it came to kissing, I had to make the first move."

Chris cringed. "I really didn't need to know that. I'm counting on you to be…diplomatic."

Diplomatic? He made it sound as though she and Garrett were forming a business partnership. Besides, she knew for a fact that Chris hadn't been very "diplomatic" when he was first seeing Melissa. They couldn't seem to keep their hands off each other.

What he was really saying was that he expected her to live up to her reputation as the innocent and pure princess. Eventually her family was going to have to accept that she was a woman, not a child.

If only he knew what went on in her head, how curious she was about sex and eager to experiment. Most modern women didn't make it to twenty-seven with their virginity intact. He would probably drop in a dead faint if he knew about all of the reading she had done online about sex. When it came to intimacy, boy, was she ready. It was all she'd been able to think about since she had danced with Garrett on Saturday night.

"You don't have to worry about me or Garrett," she assured him and left it at that, and Chris looked relieved to have the subject closed.

"I want you to know that I like Garrett," he added.

"But…?"

"No buts. I think you and he would be a good match."

She eyed him skeptically. "Even though he isn't royal?"

"Liv isn't a royal," he reminded her.

True. Liv was an orphan from the States who didn't even know who her parents were, but there was always that double standard. A prince could get away with marrying a commoner. A princess on the other hand was held to a higher standard. She imagined that Garrett's money was probably his only saving grace. She would never be allowed to date a man of modest means.

"Given his background," Chris continued, "Garrett would be the perfect choice to take over Aaron's position now that he's going back to school. If you marry him, that is."

Oh, she would. The fact that he was already making plans to include Garrett in the family business was more than she could have hoped for. "I think that's a wonderful idea!"

"However," he added sternly, "I don't want you to think this means you should rush into anything."

How could she rush fate? Either it was or it wasn't meant to be. Time was irrelevant. Besides, Chris was one to talk. He'd asked Melissa to marry him after only two weeks. Of course, at the time, he'd expected nothing more than an arranged, loveless marriage. Boy, did he get more than he'd bargained for. But destiny was like that. And there was no doubt that he and Melissa were meant for one another.

Just like Louisa and Garrett.

She pictured them a year from now, married and blissfully happy, hopefully with their first baby on the way. Or maybe even born already. She would very much like to conceive on her honeymoon. What could be a more special way to celebrate the union of their souls than to create a new life? Some women dreamed of a career, and others liked to travel. Some spent their lives donating their time to charitable causes. All Louisa had ever wanted was to be a wife and mother. Archaic as some believed it to be, it was her ultimate dream. A man to cherish her, children to depend on her. Who could ask for more?

"By the way," Chris said. "Melissa and I are planning to go sailing Sunday."

"Is she allowed to do that so close to her due date?"

"As long as she takes it easy and stays off her feet. We figure we should get in as much time on the water before the babies come. You're welcome to join us. Garrett, too, if you'd like to invite him."

Her parents were leaving for England on Sunday morning for testing on her father's heart pump, and Anne was going with them. If Chris and Melissa were going to be gone, too, that would mean that she and Garrett could have some time alone, without her entire family watching over their shoulders. She wondered if there was any way she could get rid of Aaron and Liv, as well.

"Maybe next time," she told Chris. "I already have plans."

At least, she would have plans, just as soon as she called Garrett and invited him over.

<u>Five</u>

Garrett had just walked in the door of his town house when his cell phone rang. He looked at the display and saw that it was Louisa's personal line. When they had exchanged numbers earlier, he hadn't expected a call quite this soon. In fact, he'd just assumed he would be the one calling her.

It shouldn't have surprised him that she wouldn't let him make the next move. This so-called shy and innocent Princess seemed to have everyone snowed, because as far as he could tell, she didn't have a shy bone in her body. As for innocence, she certainly didn't act like an inexperienced virgin.

When he answered, she asked, "I'm not bothering you, am I?"

"Of course not." He dropped his keys and wallet on the kitchen counter then shrugged out of his jacket and draped it over the back of a chair. "I just walked in the door."

"I wanted to tell you again what a wonderful time I had this evening."

"I did, too." Things were progressing even more quickly than he'd hoped.

"I was wondering what you're doing Sunday afternoon. I thought you might like to come over."

He chuckled. "I suppose it's too much to expect that I might get to ask *you* on a date."

"Am I being too forward?" she asked, sounding worried.

"No, not at all. I like a woman who knows what she wants."

"I just wanted to catch you before you made other plans."

"If I'd made other plans, I would cancel them. And in answer to your question, I would very much like to come over. If it's all right with your family, that is."

"Of course it is. They love you."

That must have meant he'd passed the initiation. Not that he ever doubted he would. It was just nice to know that he'd scaled the first major obstacle.

"I thought maybe we could have a picnic," Louisa suggested. "Out on the bluff, overlooking the ocean."

"Just the two of us?"

"My parents and Anne will be leaving for England, and Chris and Melissa are going sailing. Liv will probably be tied up in the lab and lately Aaron has been down there assisting her. And as long as I stay on the grounds I don't need security at my heels, so we'll be alone."

He didn't miss the suggestive lilt in her tone, and

wondered what she expected they might be doing, other than picnicking that is.

"Muffin will be there, too, of course," she added.

"Muffin?"

"My dog. You would have met him today, but he was with the groomer and then his behaviorist. He's a Shih Tzu."

So, Muffin was one of those small yappy dogs that Garrett found overwhelmingly annoying. He preferred real dogs, like the shepherds and border collies they kept on the farm. Intelligent dogs with a brain larger than a walnut.

"He can be a bit belligerent at times," Louisa said, "but he's very sweet. I know you'll love him."

"I'm sure I will," he lied, and reminded himself again that this relationship would require making adjustments. It was just one more issue he could address after they were married.

The front bell rang and Garrett frowned. He wasn't expecting anyone. Who would make a social call this late?

"Was that your door?" Louisa asked.

"Yes, but I'm not expecting anyone."

"Could it be a lady friend perhaps?" Her tone was light, but he could hear an undercurrent of concern.

"The only woman in my life is you, Your Highness," he assured her, and could feel her smile into the phone.

The bell rang again. Whoever it was, they were bloody well impatient.

"I won't keep you," she said.

"What time would you like me there Sunday?"

"Let's say 11:00 a.m. We can make a day of it."

"Sounds perfect," he said, even though he'd never really been the picnicking type. He would much rather take her out to eat—preferably at the finest restaurant in town—but the heightened security was going to make dating a challenge.

They said their goodbyes and by the time Garrett made it to the door, the bell rang a third time. "I'm coming," he grumbled under his breath. He pulled the door open, repressing a groan when he saw who was standing there.

"What, you're not happy to see your baby brother?"

Not at all, in fact, but he did his best not to look too exasperated. "Last I heard you were working a cattle ranch in Scotland."

Ian shrugged and said, "Got bored. Besides, I have something big in the works. A brilliant plan."

In other words, he was let go and had formulated some new get-rich-quick scheme. One that, like all his other brilliant plans, would undoubtedly crash and burn.

"Aren't you going to invite me in?" Ian asked with forced cheer, but the rumpled clothes, long hair and the week's worth of beard stubble said this was anything but a friendly social call.

Letting Ian in was tantamount to inviting a vampire into the house. He had a gift for bleeding dry his host both emotionally and financially and an annoying habit of staying far past his welcome.

It was hard to believe that he was once the sweet little boy Garrett used to sit on his knee and read to, then tuck into bed at night. For the first eight years of Ian's life, he was Garrett's shadow.

"Mum and Dad turn you away?" Garrett asked, and

he could see by Ian's expression that they had. Not that Garrett blamed them.

The cheery facade fell and Ian faced him with pleading eyes, looking tired and defeated. "Please, Garrett. I spent my last dime on a boat to the island and I haven't had a proper meal in days."

Or a shower, guessing by the stench, and it was more likely that he'd conned his way to the island than paid a penny for passage. But he looked so damned pathetic standing there. Despite everything, Ian was still his brother. His family. The only family who would bother to give him the time of day.

Knowing he would probably regret it later, Garrett moved aside so his brother could step into the foyer. The cool evening air that followed him inside sent a chill down Garrett's back and when Ian dropped his duffel on the floor, a plume of dust left a dirty ring on the Italian ceramic tile. He would consider it a bad omen if he believed in that sort of thing.

"Spacious," Ian said, gazing around the foyer and up the wide staircase to the second floor. "You've done well for yourself."

"Don't touch anything." Things had a mysterious habit of finding their way into Ian's pockets and disappearing forever. "And take off your boots. I don't want you trailing mud on my floors."

"Could I trouble you for a shower?" Ian asked as he kicked off his boots, revealing socks so filthy and full of holes they barely covered his feet.

"You can use the one in the spare bedroom." It was the room that possessed the least valuable items. "Up the stairs, first door on the right. I'll fix something to eat."

Ian nodded, grabbed his duffel and headed up the

stairs. Garrett considered wiping up the dust on the floor, but there would probably be more where that came from, so he decided to take care of it in the morning after Ian was gone. He walked to the kitchen instead and put a kettle on for tea, then rummaged through the icebox to see what leftovers his housekeeper had stashed there. He found a glass dish with a generous portion of pot roast, baked red skin potatoes and buttered baby carrots from last night's dinner.

He reached for a plate then figured, why dirty another dish, and set the whole thing in the microwave.

While he waited for it to heat, he noticed his wallet lying on the counter and out of habit slipped it into his pants pocket. He wasn't worried about the cash so much as his credit and ATM cards. The last time Ian had stayed with their brother Victor, he'd run off with his Mastercard and charged several thousand pounds' worth of purchases before Vic even realized the card was missing. Electronic equipment mostly, which Garrett figured Ian had probably sold for cash.

Garrett wasn't taking any chances. After a shower and a meal and a good night's sleep, he would loan Ian a few hundred pounds—that he knew would never be repaid—and send him on his merry way. With any luck, he wouldn't darken Garrett's doorway again for a very long time.

Ian emerged a few minutes later, freshly shaven, his hair still damp, wearing rumpled but clean clothes. "Best shower I ever had," he told Garrett.

"I made you tea."

He saw the cup and scowled. "I don't suppose you have anything stronger."

Garrett shrugged and said, "Sorry." Unless he wanted

his liquor cabinet cleaned out, Garrett was keeping it securely locked for the duration of his brother's visit. Besides, Ian probably had a bottle or two stashed in his duffel. Given the choice between a meal and a bottle of cheap whiskey, the alcohol always won.

"Well, then, tea it is," Ian conceded, as though he had a choice. "You just get in from work?"

"Why do you ask?"

"Came by earlier, but you weren't here. I waited for you in the park across the road."

It was a wonder he wasn't arrested for loitering. The authorities in this neighborhood had no tolerance for riffraff. "I wasn't working."

"Got a lady friend then, do you? Anyone I know?"

Garrett nearly chuckled at the thought of Ian socializing with the royal family. "No one you know."

The microwave beeped and Garrett pulled out the dish.

Knowing Garrett couldn't cook worth a damn, Ian eyed the food suspiciously. "You made that?"

"Don't worry, my housekeeper prepared it."

"In that case, slide it this way," Ian said, rubbing his work-roughened hands together in anticipation. Garrett watched as he shoveled a forkful into his mouth, eating right there at the kitchen counter, standing up.

"Delicious," he mumbled through a mouthful of beef and potatoes. He followed it with a swallow of tea. He wolfed down the food with an embarrassing lack of regard for the most basic table manners. Their mum would have been horrified. They may have lived like paupers but his mum had always insisted they carry themselves with dignity.

"So," Garrett asked, "why did you get fired this time?"

"Who says I was fired?" Ian asked indignantly.

"Please don't insult my intelligence."

He relented and answered, "The owner of the ranch caught me in the hay barn with his youngest daughter."

"How young?"

"Seventeen."

Garrett was about to say that a twenty-eight-year-old man had no business chasing a girl more than ten years his junior, but that was almost exactly the age difference between himself and Louisa. But that was different. Louisa was an adult—even if her family didn't treat her like one. Not to mention that Garrett intended to marry her, while he was quite sure his brother was only using the young girl in question.

"Don't give me that look of disapproval," Ian countered. "It wasn't my fault. She seduced me."

Of course. Nothing was ever his fault. Someone else was always to blame for his irresponsibility. "Did you ever consider telling her no?"

"If you'd seen her, you wouldn't have told her no, either."

Unlike his brother, Garrett wasn't a slave to his hormones. He had principles. He didn't take advantage of women. Not sexually, anyway. Besides, he wasn't taking advantage of Louisa. If she married him, she would never be denied a thing she desired. With the exception of a few children, that is.

"What are you going to do now?" he asked Ian.

"Like I said, I have something fantastic in the works.

A sure thing. I just need a bit of capital to get it off the ground."

He didn't say it, but Garrett knew exactly what he was thinking and saved him the trouble of having to ask. "Don't look at me. I've thrown away enough money on your so-called sure things."

Ian shrugged. "Your loss."

Garrett doubted that.

Ian finished his dinner, stopping just shy of licking the dish clean. "Delicious. Best meal I've had in weeks."

"I assume you need a place to stay."

He leaned back against the countertop and folded his arms over his chest. "There's a very comfortable bench in the park I could sleep on."

"You're welcome to use the spare bedroom. For *one* night," he stressed. "And I expect everything to be as you found it when you go."

"I'll even make the bed."

"Well then, I'm off to bed," Garrett said.

"Already? I thought we might catch up for a while."

"I have an early breakfast meeting."

Ian looked appalled. "You're working on a Saturday?"

"Sometimes I work Sundays, as well." A concept Ian, who worked as little as possible, would never grasp. "Help yourself to whatever you find in the icebox, and I have satellite television if you want to watch it. I'll see you in the morning."

"See you in the morning," Ian parroted as Garrett walked from the room. He felt uncomfortable leaving his brother to his own devices, but short of staying awake all night, he didn't have much choice.

Consequently, Garrett didn't see Ian in the morning.

When he rolled out of bed at 6:00 a.m., Ian had already left. With half the contents of the liquor cabinet and Garrett's car.

The e-mail showed up in Louisa's personal in-box late Saturday afternoon. At first when she saw the blank subject line she assumed it was junk mail, then she noticed the return address—G.B. Man—and her heart nearly stopped.

That couldn't be a coincidence. It had to be him.

Not now, she thought to herself. Not when things were going so well. She took a deep breath, preparing herself for the worst, and reluctantly double clicked to open it. The body of the e-mail read simply, Did you miss me, Princess?

No gruesome nursery rhymes or threats of violence this time, still a cold chill slithered up her spine. This was going to put everyone into a panic and security back on high alert. Which meant her chances of leaving the castle and going on a normal date with Garrett were slim to none. Why did the Gingerbread Man have to choose now to start harassing them again?

She leaned over for the phone to ring security, when she noticed the time stamp on the e-mail and realized it had actually been sent yesterday morning. Louisa didn't check her in-box daily, but her brothers did. If they had gotten one, too, wouldn't she have heard about it by now?

Was it possible that the Gingerbread Man had sent a message to her alone? And if so, was it a coincidence that it started at the same time she began seeing Garrett? Was he trying to complicate things?

She sat back in her chair, wondering what she should

do. The e-mail hadn't been threatening at all. Just a reminder that he was still there, which they all had assumed anyway. If he had planned to actually harm a member of the family, wouldn't he have done it by now?

If she accidentally forgot to mention this to security, what difference would it really make?

She sat there with her finger hovering over the delete button, weighing her options. If it turned out her brothers and sister had gotten an e-mail, too, she could just tell them that she must have erased hers accidentally, assuming it was junk mail. She hated to lie, but this was her future on the line. Her relationship with Garrett might be destiny, but even destiny had its limits. Would Garrett want to court a woman who wasn't even allowed to leave the house, and by dating her very possibly make *himself* a target?

It would be best, for now, if no one else knew about this.

Before she could change her mind, she stabbed the delete key, promising herself that if he contacted her again, threatening or not, she would let the family know. Until then, it would be her secret.

Six

It was after noon when Garrett's meeting finally ended. He was in the company limo on his way to the club to play squash with Wes, when he received a call from the police informing him that his car had been in an accident. Apparently, in his haste to flee Garrett's town house, Ian had run off the road and into a tree.

"He was pretty banged up," the officer told him. "But he was conscious and alert when they put him in the ambulance."

Despite everything, Garrett was relieved Ian wasn't hurt too badly. If he'd died, Garrett would have been the one to break the news to his family. Since it was Garrett's car Ian had been driving, they would likely pin the blame on him. Not that he cared what they thought of him any longer. It was just a hassle he didn't need.

"Did he say how it happened?" Garrett asked.

"He claims he swerved to avoid hitting an animal in the road, a dog, and lost control."

Ian had always had a soft spot for animals. Dogs especially, so it was a plausible excuse.

Garrett dreaded the next question he had to ask. "Was alcohol involved?"

"We assumed so at first. There were a dozen or so broken bottles of liquor in the car. Expensive stuff, too."

Tell me about it, Garrett wanted to say.

"He denied being intoxicated, but we won't know for certain until we get the results of the blood test. He must have been going quite fast though. I'm sorry to say that the car is totaled."

It wouldn't be the first car Ian had demolished with his careless driving. Or the last. Besides, Garrett had never expected to get it back. He didn't have the heart to report it as stolen and Ian would have eventually sold it. At least now Garrett would get the insurance money, and Ian would have to face what he'd done while the wounds were still fresh.

He thanked the officer for the information and instructed his driver to take him to the hospital instead, then rang Wes to cancel. With any luck, this fiasco wouldn't find its way into the papers, or, if it did, he hoped no names were released. With the royal family keeping a close eye on him, the last thing he needed was a scandal. Not that he should be held accountable for his brother's actions, but in his experience royals had a… *unique* way of looking at things.

Garrett should have listened to his instincts and never let Ian in the house. Or maybe this time Ian would finally learn his lesson.

The limo dropped him at the front entrance of the hospital and Garrett stopped at the information desk to get his brother's room number. Ian's was on the third floor just past the nursing station, but when Garrett walked through the door, he was totally unprepared for what he saw. He'd expected Ian to have suffered a few bumps and bruises, maybe a laceration or two, but his baby brother looked as though he'd gone a dozen rounds with a prize fighter.

His face was swollen and bruised, his nose broken and both eyes blackened. His right wrist and hand were wrapped in gauze, and he'd suffered small nicks and cuts on both arms. From the broken bottles, Garrett figured. His left leg was in a cast from foot to midthigh and suspended in a sling.

Garrett shook his head and thought, *Ian, what have you done to yourself?*

Instead of seeing Ian the troublemaker lying there, under the bandages and bruises Garrett could only picture the little boy who used to come to him with skinned knees and splinters, and his anger swiftly fizzled away.

"Garrett Sutherland?" someone asked from behind him.

He turned to find a doctor standing just outside the room. "Yes."

"Dr. Sacsner," he said, shaking Garrett's hand. "I'm your brother's surgeon."

"Surgeon?"

"Orthopedics." He gestured out of the room. "Could we have a word?"

Garrett nodded and followed him into the hallway.

"Your brother is a lucky man," the doctor began to say.

"He doesn't look so lucky to me."

"I know it looks bad, but it could have been much worse. The fact that he suffered no internal injuries is nothing short of a miracle."

"What about his leg?"

The doctor frowned. "There he wasn't so lucky. His lower leg was crushed under the dash. The impact shattered the fibula and snapped his tibia in three places. The only thing holding it together are rods and pins."

"But he'll recover?"

"With time and physical therapy he should make a full recovery. The first six weeks will be the most difficult. It's imperative he stay off the leg as much as possible and keep it elevated."

"So he'll stay here?"

"For another day or two, then he'll be released."

Released? Where was he going to go?

He realized, by the doctor's expression, that Garrett was expected to take Ian home.

Bloody hell. He didn't have time for this now. Nor did he feel he owed his brother a thing after all the grief he'd caused. But who else did Ian have? Where else could he stay?

"I know it sounds like a daunting task," the doctor said. "But if money is no object, you can hire twenty-four-hour care if necessary." His pager beeped and he checked the display. "I'll be back to check on him later."

"Before you go, was it determined if alcohol was involved?"

"That was a concern at first, since he came in smelling

like a distillery. We were hesitant to give him anything for the pain, but he swore he wasn't drinking, and the tox screen came back clean. No drugs or alcohol in his system."

So he had just been driving too fast and lost control. If that wasn't Ian's life story. As a kid he was always pushing the limits and hurting himself. If there was a tree too high or dangerous to climb, Ian wasn't happy until he reached the highest branch. By the time he was eight, he'd suffered more broken bones and received more stitches than most people did in a lifetime.

Maybe this time he would learn his lesson.

"You didn't have to come here," he heard his brother say, his voice rusty from the anesthesia.

Garrett turned and walked to his bed. "Someone has to pay the bill."

Ian gazed up at him, bleary-eyed and fuzzy. "I guess 'I'm sorry' isn't going to cut it this time."

"It might if I thought you meant it." But Ian wasn't sorry for all the trouble he'd caused. Only that he'd been caught.

His eyes drifted shut, and Garrett thought that maybe he'd fallen asleep, then he opened them again and said, "I was going to bring it back."

"The car or the liquor?"

"Both."

Garrett wished he could believe that.

"I got a few miles from your house and I started to feel guilty."

That was even more unbelievable. "You don't do guilt."

"Apparently I do now. I thought if I got back fast

enough you would never know I'd left. Then that damned dog darted out in front of me." Ian studied him for several seconds. "You don't believe me."

"Is there a reason I should?"

He sighed. "Well, whether you believe me or not, I'm tired of living this way. I'm going to change this time. I swear I am."

Garrett might have believed his brother if he hadn't heard the same thing so many times before. "Let's just concentrate on getting you healthy. The doctor says you have to keep off the leg for six weeks. With my hectic schedule, I'll have to hire a nurse to stay with you."

"You don't have to do that."

And he didn't expect a penny of it back. "Where else would you go? You think Mum and Dad would let you stay with them?"

His expression said he knew the answer to that question was no. Even if their mother still had a soft spot for Ian, their father would put his foot down.

"I'll figure something out," Ian declared.

"You have a friend who will take you in?"

Ian was silent. They both knew that Ian had never made a friend he didn't eventually betray. Unfortunately, Garrett was all he had. "You're staying with me."

"I owe you too much already," Ian said, and Garrett wished the regret he heard in his brother's voice was genuine. He wasn't counting on it though.

"Face it, Ian, we're stuck with each other. If you really mean what you say about turning over a new leaf—"

"I do. I swear it."

"Then you can spend the next six weeks proving it to me."

* * *

Louisa woke early Sunday morning, planning her picnic with Garrett before she even got out of bed, until she heard the low rumble of thunder and the thrum of rain against her bedroom window.

Oh, damn!

Rubbing the sleep from her eyes, she climbed out of bed, rousing Muffin, who gave a grumble of irritation before settling back to sleep. She walked to the window and shoved the curtains aside. Dense gray clouds rolled in from the northwest, and a fierce wind pummeled the trees and whipped rain against the windows.

She sighed. It looked as though the weather front that was supposed to miss the island had changed course sometime during the night. It was only 7:00 a.m., but even if the rain stopped it would still be too wet for a picnic. She'd been so sure it would be a sunny day, she hadn't bothered with a plan B. Her options were limited considering she couldn't leave the castle with Garrett without giving Chris a two-day warning. And with the weather so dreary, she doubted that he and Melissa would be doing any sailing today.

So much for her and Garrett having some time to themselves. If they had to stay inside the castle, someone would be constantly looking over their shoulders, watching their every move.

She frowned. Being royalty, especially royalty under house arrest, could be terribly inconvenient.

But she refused to let this small setback dampen her spirits. She was sure if she put her mind to it, she could come up with something for them to do, some indoor activity they would both enjoy. Maybe a tour of the castle or a game of billiards. Or maybe they could just sit and talk.

On her way to the shower, Louisa passed her computer and was half tempted to log on, just to see if she had gotten another e-mail from their stalker. No one had said anything about getting the e-mail yesterday, so she could only assume his latest communication had been sent exclusively to her. She couldn't help wondering if her relationship with Garrett was the catalyst or if it was just a coincidence that he chose now to pick on her individually.

Maybe she should check, just in case. She took a step toward her computer, then stopped. What would be the point of checking? If he e-mailed her, he e-mailed her and nothing would change that, and the way she looked at it, what she didn't know wouldn't hurt her.

She gave her computer one last furtive glance and headed to the bathroom instead.

She showered using her favorite rose-scented body wash and took extra care fixing her hair. Instead of the conservative bun she typically wore, she used hot rollers then brushed her hair smooth, until it lay loose and silky down her back. She dressed in pale pink capris and a crème-colored cashmere sweater set, then slipped her feet into a pair of pink leather flats. She rounded out the look with mascara and pink, cherry-flavored lip gloss with a touch of glitter.

She stood back to examine her reflection, happy with what she saw, sure that Garrett would be pleased, too.

Anticipation adding an extra lift to her step, she headed downstairs to the dining room for a spot of tea, Muffin trailing behind her, but Geoffrey intercepted her at the foot of the stairs.

"Prince Christian asked that you call him as soon as possible."

She frowned. "Call him? Did they go sailing? The weather is horrible."

"No, Your Highness. He took Princess Melissa to the hospital early this morning."

Her heart skipped a beat. "What for?"

"He didn't say. He just asked that you call him as soon as you're up."

"Are Aaron and Liv up yet?"

"Not yet."

She was going to ask him to wake them, but there was no sense in starting a panic before she even knew what was wrong. It might be nothing.

"Could you see that Muffin is fed and let out?" she asked Geoffrey.

"Of course. Come along, Muffin."

Muffin just stood there looking back and forth between them.

"Breakfast," Geoffrey added, and Muffin scurried excitedly after him.

Forgetting about her tea, Louisa hurried back to her room and dialed her brother's cell phone. As soon as he answered she asked, "What's wrong? Is Melissa okay? Are the babies all right?"

Chris chuckled and said, "Relax, everyone is fine. Melissa started having contractions last night."

"Why didn't you wake me?"

"There was nothing you could have done and Melissa didn't want you to worry."

"Is she in labor? I thought it was too early."

"She was, but they gave her a drug to stop it. Unfortunately she's already dilated two centimeters, so she's on complete bed rest. They're keeping her in the hospital until she delivers."

"Oh, Chris, I'm so sorry. Is there anything I can do?"

"Actually, yes. Melissa made a list of things she needs. Makeup and toiletries and things like that. Could you gather everything and bring it to the hospital?"

"Of course." She grabbed a pad of paper and a pen and jotted down the list. "I'll be there as soon as I can."

"I want to stay here as often as possible, so I'd like you to meet with my assistant about taking my place at a few speeches and charity events."

For a second she was struck dumb. He never would have trusted her to a task like that before. She almost asked, what about Aaron or Anne, but caught herself at the last minute. She didn't want him to think she didn't want to do it.

"Of course I will," she told him instead. "Anything."

"Thanks, Louisa. I'll see you soon."

She hung up and was turning to leave her room when she remembered her date with Garrett and stopped dead in her tracks.

Bloody hell.

Well, as much as she wanted to see Garrett, family always came first. Especially now, when Chris seemed to be seeing her as a capable adult. She would just have to call him and reschedule. Maybe they could see each other later in the week.

She picked up the phone, mumbling to herself about bad timing, but as she put it to her ear there was no dial tone. She nearly jumped out of her skin when a deep male voice said, "Hello?"

"Garrett?"

"Well, that was strange," he said.

"What just happened?"

"I called your number, but before it could even ring, I heard your voice."

"Seriously? Because I just picked up the phone so I could call you!"

Garrett chuckled. "We must be on the same brain wave or something."

"I guess. Why were you calling?"

"Regrettably, something came up and I have to break our date for this afternoon."

Louisa laughed and said, "Seriously?"

Garrett paused for several seconds, then said, "Well, that wasn't exactly the reaction I'd been expecting."

"I'm laughing because I was calling you to say that *I* have to cancel our date."

"Hmm, that is pretty weird, isn't it?"

"I thought maybe we could get together later this week."

"We could do that. The first half of the week will be a little hectic for me, but maybe Thursday evening?"

That seemed so far off, but at least it would give her time to visit with Melissa while she adjusted to being confined to a hospital bed. "Just to warn you, if you want to take me off the palace grounds, Chris will need two days' warning to arrange for security."

"Well, then, I guess I'll call you Tuesday." There was a commotion in the background, and what sounded like a voice over a PA system, but she couldn't make out what they were saying. "I'm sorry, Louisa, but I have to go. I'll talk to you Tuesday."

Before she could say goodbye, he disconnected, and

she realized she hadn't even asked why he had to cancel today. Oh well, she was sure that it must have been very important. They could talk about it Tuesday.

She hated the thought of having to wait until Thursday to see Garrett again, but the anticipation would make their next date that much more special.

Seven

Sunday morning became a blur of doctors and nurses and representatives from the private home care facility that Garrett was hiring to look after his brother while his leg healed. And since Ian was being released tomorrow morning, there wasn't much time to get everything squared away.

Though Garrett wasn't too keen on the idea of his brother staying in his house for another six weeks or so, at least this time Ian would be physically incapable of running off with his belongings. The only time he was allowed out of bed was to bathe and use the loo, or he risked the bones shifting and healing incorrectly, leaving him with the threat of more surgeries and possible permanent disabilities. And while Ian could be irresponsible and self-absorbed, he wasn't stupid.

It was going on three when all the arrangements were completed and the appropriate paperwork signed. Garrett was walking down the hall to the elevator when someone called his name. He turned to see Louisa standing behind him, flanked by two very large and ominous looking bodyguards.

Oddly enough, his first instinct was to pull her close and kiss her, and he might have were it not for the risk of being tackled by her security detail.

"I thought that was you," she said, breaking into a wide smile. "What are you doing here? Did you come to see Melissa?"

"Melissa?" he asked.

She walked toward him, and with a subtle wave of her hand the guards fell back several steps. "Princess Melissa, my sister-in-law."

"No. Is she here?"

"In the family's private wing," she said, gesturing behind her. "She was brought in last night for early labor. That's why I had to postpone our date."

"I had no idea. I'm here visiting…an associate. He was in an accident yesterday."

"Oh, I'm so sorry. Is he okay?"

"He's banged up, but he'll recover."

"Is that why you had to break our date? To come here?"

He nodded. "Weird, huh?"

"Very weird. If we knew we were both coming here we could have carpooled," she joked.

He grinned. "Except I was already here when I called you."

"He must be a special friend for you to stay here all day with him."

"We've known each other most of our lives." He knew he should probably tell her the truth, but he just didn't feel like explaining. With any luck Ian would heal, then be out of Garrett's life forever, and the royal family would never be the wiser. "Is Melissa all right?"

"They managed to stop her labor, but she's on strict bed rest for at least four weeks, and they're keeping her in the hospital just to be safe."

"Please send her and Chris my best."

"She's having some tests right now, but I'm sure she would love a visit from you later. She's only been here a few hours and already she's crawling out of her skin."

Normally he wouldn't visit a stranger, but under the circumstances, it couldn't hurt. Besides, he'd liked Melissa from the moment he met her. She wasn't a typical royal. Of course neither was Liv, or Louisa for that matter. Maybe there was nothing unusual about any of them. Maybe it was his preconceived notion that was way off.

"I'd like that," he said. "As long as it's not an imposition."

"Of course not. Chris and Melissa really like you. In fact, Chris told me…" She paused and pressed her fingers to her lips.

"Chris told you what?"

Her cheeks flushed to match the pink of her pants. "Forget it."

He smiled. "You're blushing, Your Highness."

"I'm not sure if I should have said anything."

He folded his arms over his chest. She was usually so poised and self-confident. He liked that she had a vulnerable side. "Maybe you shouldn't have, but now you've piqued my curiosity. It wouldn't be fair to leave me hanging with no explanation, would it?"

"I suppose not." She glanced over at the busy nurses' station, then whispered, "Not here."

Whatever she had to say, it was apparently private in nature. All the more reason for him to know what was said. "Where?"

"I was on my way back to our private waiting room," she told him. "You could join me."

"I'd like that," he told her, realizing it was true, and not just for the information. Meeting like this in the hospital hallway could have been awkward, but instead he felt totally at ease with her. In fact, the moment he saw her standing there, some of the stress from the last few days seemed to melt away.

He held out his arm and she slipped hers through it. Thankfully the guards didn't knock him to the ground and cuff him. "Lead the way, Your Highness."

Louisa led Garrett into the royal family's private waiting room. She was relieved to find it empty. If this was the only time they could be alone, she could think of worse places.

"This is nice," Garrett said, gazing around. "More like a hotel suite than a hospital."

"It didn't used to be so modern, but the last few years, with my father's condition, we've spent a lot of time here so it was renovated."

"I expected Chris to be here."

"He's with Melissa. She's having a test to determine the development of the babies' lungs." She turned to set down her purse and felt Garrett's hands settle on her shoulders. A warm and delicious feeling poured through her like honey and the purse dropped with a clunk on the table.

"Does that mean we're alone?" he asked, and something in his tone made her heart skip a beat. Until now, she was the one to instigate the physical contact. It was exciting, and yes, maybe a little scary, that he had taken the upper hand.

"I guess we are."

His hands slipped off her shoulders and down her arms. His palms were smooth and felt hot to the touch. "Security won't barge in at any second?"

"Only if I call them."

"Are you going to call them?"

Now that they *finally* had some time alone? *Not bloody likely.* "I wasn't planning on it."

"Even if I do this?" He pulled her hair over one shoulder and brushed a kiss on the back of her neck. Goose bumps broke out across her skin, and her legs suddenly felt limp. Men had kissed her before, but it had been a long time since one made her tingle all over or feel the warm tug of arousal between her thighs and in her breasts.

He kissed her shoulder and she willed him to touch her, to cup her breasts in his palms, to slide his hand down, inside her panties. She almost moaned out loud imagining it, but she knew this wasn't the time or the place.

"I like your hair this way," he said, running his fingers through it. "You should wear it down all the time."

"Maybe I will."

"You were going to tell me what Chris said," he reminded her, his breath warm on her nape where he dropped soft kisses.

"I'd hoped you'd forgotten about that." She let her head fall to the side, giving him more area to explore, and he didn't disappoint. "Chris might be upset that I told you."

"We'll keep it between you and me."

"You promise?"

He turned her to face him and brushed his lips across hers. "Cross my heart and hope to die."

Even if she'd wanted to tell him no, there was no way she could. He could ask her the royal family's most intimate secrets right now and they would spill willingly from the lips he so skillfully nibbled. "I was talking to Chris the other day and he mentioned that if…well, if you and I were to get married, you would be a good choice to replace Aaron when he goes back to school."

He stopped kissing her. "He said that?"

"Just the other day."

"Well, I'm…I'm a bit speechless, actually. I'm flattered that he would even consider me."

"Nothing is set in stone, of course, which is why I never should have said anything in the first place. Me and my big mouth."

He smiled and made a growling sound deep in his throat. He cradled her face in his hand and brushed the pad of his thumb across her lower lip. "Hmm, I love your mouth."

She loved the way it felt when he touched it. Especially when he used his lips.

"Chris also insinuated that we shouldn't 'rush' things," she said.

"Are we rushing?"

She grinned up at him. "As far as I'm concerned, we're not moving fast enough. In fact, would you find it totally inappropriate to make out on the sofa in a hospital waiting room?"

"If it were only kissing, maybe not, but I'm having a tough time keeping my hands off of you."

She sighed and laid her head against his chest, heard the steady thump of his heart. "There has to be someplace we can go to be completely alone."

"I have a place in Cabo," he offered. "Maybe with enough advance warning, your family would let you go."

"I would *love* that! I'll talk to Chris about it."

"Unless security issues aren't his only concern."

She didn't have to ask what he meant. "I'm twenty-seven. My sex life is none of my family's business. And believe me when I say that they're in no position whatsoever to pass judgment. I hate that we have to even talk about this, that we can't just be a normal couple, let things happen naturally."

He led her to the sofa, pulling her close beside him as they sat. "All couples have issues, Louisa."

She drew her legs up over his thighs and curled against his chest. "Sometimes I wish I could lead a normal life. I'd like to shop in a store without a team of security parked outside, or eat dinner in a restaurant without a thorough background check of every employee." She looked up at him. "Have you ever considered what it would be like to be in a relationship with someone like me? The freedoms you would have to sacrifice? You'd be a fool not to run screaming in the opposite direction."

"Those things don't matter to me, Louisa." He cradled her chin in his hand and gazed into her eyes. They were so dark and compassionate and earnest it made her want to cry. "The way I feel about you, I'd be a fool not to stay."

He brushed his lips against hers, so tenderly. So sweet. But she didn't want tender and sweet. She was tired of that. She wanted fire and passion. She wanted to feel sexy and desired.

She slid her hands around Garrett's neck, pulled him down and kissed him. A kiss that was anything but tender. At first he resisted a little, until she drew herself up on her knees and straddled his lap.

"I can't seem to control myself when I'm with you," he mumbled against her lips.

"Good, because neither can I." She rocked her hips and rubbed against him. Garrett growled deep in his throat and tunneled his fingers through her hair, feeding off her mouth. She could feel his erection growing between them and she wanted so badly to touch him. She was so far gone, she didn't care that Chris could walk through the door at any second.

Which incidentally, he did.

Somewhere in the back of her hormone-drenched brain she heard the door open, then the exaggerated rumble of a throat clearing. She peeled herself away from Garrett and looked over to find Chris in the waiting room doorway, one brow lifted. She knew exactly what he was thinking. This was her idea of discretion?

She heard Garrett mumble a particularly colorful curse under his breath—one most men wouldn't dare speak in front of a princess—as he lifted her from his lap and dropped her onto the sofa beside him.

"Sorry to interrupt," Chris said, "but Melissa is back in her room and eager for visitors."

Louisa should have asked how Melissa was doing, or if the babies were okay, but to her surprise, and apparently her brother's surprise as well, the first thing out of her mouth was, "I'm going to Cabo with Garrett and you can't stop me."

Demanding she be allowed to leave the country with Garrett probably hadn't been the wisest course of action for Louisa to win a little freedom. Especially when Chris had just walked in on them making out like two lust-driven youths. Garrett was quite sure, considering her brother's look of exasperation, she wouldn't be leaving the country anytime soon. With Garrett or anyone else.

So much for convincing her family that he wasn't compromising her honor.

Garrett assumed Chris would be furious with him, but when he pulled the Prince aside later to apologize for his inappropriate behavior, Chris only laughed.

"I know you're smarter than that, Garrett. I don't believe for a second that my sister wasn't the aggressor. Just, if you could, try to keep her in check, at least when you're in public. I would appreciate it."

Garrett had been so stunned, he couldn't form a coherent reply, which seemed to amuse Chris even more.

"You think I don't know what my sister is like?"

"She can be…tenacious," Garrett said.

Chris chuckled. "That's putting it mildly. I've spent the better part of my life keeping her out of trouble. She whines incessantly that we shelter her, yet she refuses to exercise any common sense. If she wants something she goes after it, all pistons firing. Usually with no regard to the rules, or oftentimes her own safety. And if what she gets isn't what she wanted, watch out.

"Don't get me wrong, I love my sister to death. She has a heart of gold and you'll never meet a woman more loyal to her family and friends. I would lay down my life for her. I also believe that she'll make a fantastic wife and mother. But she is a handful. Let your guard down and she'll walk all over you."

In other words, her so-called reputation of being sweet and naive was *bollocks*. He'd basically figured that out already. He just hadn't realized the extent of her defiance. Some men might have considered that a negative quality, and maybe he should have, too, but the idea that she wasn't at all what he expected only intrigued him more.

The question was: what did Chris have to gain by his honesty? Was he trying to scare Garrett away? And why would he after he'd told Louisa that he was considering offering Aaron's position to Garrett?

"Why are you telling me this?" he asked Chris.

"I think you should know what you're getting yourself into. Louisa needs a man who's just as headstrong and determined as she is, and I see those qualities in you. She needs someone who can...rein her in."

He made it sound as though Louisa needed a babysitter more than a husband. Did the royal family cling to the archaic values that deemed women should be seen but not heard?

He wasn't sure if he should feel grateful for Chris's candid advice, or offended on Louisa's behalf. And since when did Garrett feel the need to defend her? When did he start caring about her feelings?

Probably right around the same time she smiled up at him and said she couldn't wait to see him naked.

"By the way," Chris said. "Send me a copy of your itinerary and I'll see what I can do. It will take at least two weeks to arrange."

It took a second for Garett to realize he was talking about the trip to Cabo. "I assumed that wasn't going to happen."

"If I tell her no, there's a good chance she'll go without permission. Besides, maybe some time away would do her good. With our father in fairly stable condition, I think we could all use a vacation."

Garrett, too, was looking forward to some time away. With his brother around, the less time he spent at home, the better as far as he was concerned. He and Ian had nothing left to say to one another, and all that talk about Ian changing his ways was rubbish. Ian would never change.

After a short visit with Melissa, who was indeed climbing the walls, Garrett said goodbye to Louisa, sealing their departure with another enthusiastic kiss. He made a short trip to the office to get a few documents that needed his attention. Then, because the cook had Sundays off, he picked up dinner on his way home.

Later, as he lounged in front of the television, mindlessly surfing the channels, he thought about calling Louisa to see if Melissa's tests came back favorable. Only, as usual, she called him first.

He picked up the phone after the first ring and said, "You probably won't believe this, but I was just about to call you."

"Were you really?" a sultry voice purred in his ear. "And here I thought you'd forgotten all about me."

The unfamiliar voice threw him for a moment, then he looked at the caller ID and realized it wasn't Louisa after all. It was Pamela, a woman he dated on occasion. Although to call what they did "dating" was a gross overstatement. They had sex. Unemotional, uncomplicated, no-strings-attached sex. Just the way he liked it.

"Pamela, sorry, I thought you were someone else," he said. "How have you been?"

Her voice dripped with the promise of something naughty. "Missing you terribly, love."

He used to find her sultry drawl warm and sexy. Now he recognized it for what it was: as insincere as her affection for him. She was using him, just as he had used her. Up until today that hadn't bothered him in the least, in fact he'd preferred it that way, but now it just seemed…sleazy.

"I've been busy," he said, but she totally missed what he'd hoped was a direct brush-off.

"Well, if you're not busy tonight, why don't I stop by for a while? We could get…reacquainted."

It wasn't the only time she'd offered herself up freely to him, but for the first time, he wasn't the least bit interested. Not that he had no appetite for female companionship, but the female he was interested in right now was Louisa.

"I'm afraid this isn't a good time," he told Pamela.

"How about tomorrow night instead?"

"That won't be a good time, either."

The sexy tone wavered, as though she was finally starting to catch on that something was up. "When *would* it be a good time?"

How about never? "The thing is, Pamela, I'm seeing someone."

"So?"

Admittedly, in the past, that wouldn't have stopped him. "What I mean is, I'm seeing someone...*special.*"

There was a pause, then a short burst of laughter. "Are you saying that you're in a serious relationship?"

"I am," he said, relieved that he didn't have to spell it out. Sometimes he could hardly believe it himself.

"Is she pregnant?"

"No, she's not pregnant."

"Blackmailing you?"

He laughed. "Is it so hard to believe I met a woman I want to date seriously?"

"I've known you almost ten years, Garrett, and in all that time not once did you ever have a serious relationship. You're far too selfish."

Pamela was right, but that selfish streak had led him to where he was now. He didn't miss the irony. Some might go so far as saying he was too selfish for his own good.

"Who's the lucky girl? Anyone I know?"

"No one you know," he assured her. Of course she knew *of* Louisa, but they had certainly never inhabited the same social circles.

"Well, I guess all I can say is good luck," Pamela said.

He said his goodbyes, hung up, then permanently deleted her number from his phone. He was about to set it down on the table beside him when it rang again.

This time it was Louisa, and he caught himself smiling. "I was just thinking about calling you," he said.

"Were you?" There was a distinct note of happiness in her voice.

"I wondered if you'd heard the results from Melissa's tests." As soon as the words left his mouth, he knew they were not entirely true. If he had called, it would have been just to talk to her. To hear her voice.

"How sweet of you," she responded, buying his fib without question. "She got the results just a bit ago and unfortunately the babies' lungs need at least a few more weeks to develop. They've started her on steroids to get things moving along. On the bright side, she hasn't had any more contractions."

"That's good news."

"Do you know why I called you?" she asked.

"Why?"

"I was lying in bed thinking about our kiss today and I just wanted to hear your voice."

Eight

Garrett found himself envying Louisa's unrelenting honesty. Why was he so incapable of expressing his feelings? Or maybe in her case, his discretion was the kindest thing he had to offer. Was it fair to lead her on when the emotions he was feeling now were driven by curiosity and fleeting at best?

He didn't think so.

"I'm starting to feel like I'll go crazy if we don't get some time alone soon," she said.

He could relate. If Chris hadn't stepped in the room when he did, things might have gotten out of hand. "I know what you mean."

"I think about it a lot," she admitted.

"Think about what?"

"Sex."

He sat up a little straighter in his chair. "You do?"

"I fantasize *all* the time."

"About what?"

"You. What it will be like when we're finally alone. How you'll touch me, and what it will feel like to touch you. Sometimes I get myself so worked up thinking about it that I have to…well, you know."

She couldn't possibly be saying what he thought she was saying. "You have to what?"

"*Touch* myself."

Bloody hell. He formed a mental picture of that and just about swallowed his tongue.

"I've been doing a lot of reading on the Internet, too," she said.

"What kind of reading?"

"Erotic short stories mostly. My favorites are the romantic ones, but there are a few with a bondage theme I thought were kind of fun."

Bloody hell. Now would be an excellent time to change the subject, but his brain just wasn't cooperating. Probably because all the blood in his body was pooling in the vicinity of his crotch. He was so hard he had to unfasten the button fly on his jeans.

"Nothing too extreme, of course. But I think I'd be willing to try silk scarves and feathers."

He resisted the visual representation, but it popped into his head anyway.

He was so stiff he was aching, and he was seriously considering asking what her feelings were on phone sex, but if he and Louisa were going to be intimate, he'd be damned if he was going to do it from across town.

"Are you trying to drive me insane?" he asked, and she laughed.

"Maybe. Is it working?"

"I'm in agony."

"You wouldn't believe all of the different things I could do to help you with that."

And, of course, a dozen or so instantly came to mind. "If you say another word, I swear to God I'm hanging up."

She laughed. "Okay, I promise I'll stop."

"All those rumors I've heard that you're inexperienced and pure—I'm not buying it."

"I hate to disappoint you, but the rumors are true."

"How is that even possible?"

"I was very sheltered. I wasn't even allowed to start dating until I was eighteen and when I did there was always a chaperone. I never had the chance to experiment, although not for lack of trying. Unfortunately, the more I tried, the tighter my family pulled back on the reins. It was as if everyone was determined to keep me unspoiled and pure. Eventually I got tired of fighting them and I just sort of, I don't know…lost interest, I guess."

"You seem interested now," he said.

"It was the Internet. I stumbled across a site full of stories and it opened up a whole new world to me. I finally started to realize what I've been missing all this time. It all just seemed so natural and…beautiful. I wanted to try everything. Well," she amended, "*almost* everything. When it comes to sex, people do some weird things."

"For the record, I'm not into weird."

"I'm glad," she said, sounding a little relieved.

"If you're so…interested, why don't you date more?"

"Because most men I meet are more interested in my wealth or my title than me."

How would she feel if she knew he was one of those men? That would remain his and Wes's secret.

"I find so many men, especially the ones close to my age, far too arrogant and entitled. So, here I am now, twenty-seven and still unspoiled, but dying to be corrupted. And don't ask me how, but when you took me in your arms on the dance floor, I just knew you were the one."

Though it made no sense at all, he felt honored that she had chosen him. "I can't say that I've ever corrupted anyone before, but I'd certainly be willing to give it a go. I'm free right now, in fact."

"Even with Chris and my parents gone, inviting you over at 11:30 p.m. might be pushing the envelope. But the time will come when we're completely alone, and I know it will be worth the wait. I just hope it's sooner rather than later."

"Me, too." What healthy heterosexual male didn't wish he had, at his disposal, a young, beautiful and sexy virgin willing to—in her own words—try practically everything? Men would pay exorbitant sums of money to trade places with him. And to think that he once believed he would have to take the sexual aspect of their courtship painfully slow. How completely wrong he'd been. This was working out far better than he ever could have imagined.

So why, somewhere deep down, did he feel so damned guilty?

The King had all the necessary adjustments performed on his heart pump Wednesday and the reinsertion after the capacity test went off without a hitch. Unfortunately, the news was not what they had hoped. Though some areas of the heart showed signs of healing, there had been little improvement in his overall heart function.

Everyone was disappointed, but Louisa refused to let the news get her down. As far as she was concerned, this was just a minor setback. His heart was just taking a little longer to heal, that's all.

Anne was still in England with their parents, so Louisa sat in a visitor's chair in Melissa's hospital room with Aaron, Liv, Chris, and of course Melissa, discussing how the setback would affect the family.

Chris sat on the edge of the bed with his wife. "Obviously I'll continue to perform Father's duties, and Aaron will cover my duties."

Liv leaned beside Aaron against the wall by the door. "But who will take over for Aaron when he starts school?" she asked, clearly concerned that his plans would be pushed aside yet another semester.

"I have a backup plan," Chris told her.

Aaron regarded him curiously. "Since when?"

"Recently," Chris said, glancing Louisa's way. "I'm considering offering a position to Garrett Sutherland."

Suddenly all eyes were on Louisa.

"What you mean is, if Louisa marries him," Melissa clarified.

Chris nodded. "Of course."

"He is more than qualified," Aaron confirmed.

"I agree," Melissa said. "But is it fair to put that kind of pressure on Louisa?"

"We're all under pressure," Chris told her. "Besides, she's always asking for more responsibility."

Louisa hated when they talked about her as though she wasn't sitting right there. Why did they insist on treating her like a child?

It was a moot point anyway. Their father was going to recover and resume his duties, then everything would go back to normal. These last couple years would be nothing more than a bad memory.

"What do *you* think, Louisa?" Liv asked.

Finally, she was part of the conversation. "I think you're blowing this way out of proportion. This is just a minor setback. Father will be fine."

She could tell by their expressions that they thought she was being naive, and she pitied them for their cynicism. This would be so much easier for all of them if they would just have faith.

No one scolded or tried to reason with her, and she was grateful for that, but she felt as though, if she didn't get out of there soon, she would lose her mind. Even though she wasn't supposed to see Garrett until tomorrow evening, that was one day too long as far as she was concerned.

She grabbed her purse and rose from her chair. "If the family discussion is over, I'm leaving."

"Where are you going?" Chris asked.

"Garrett is working from home today so I thought I would stop in and see him. If that's not a problem."

Chris and Aaron exchanged a look. Louisa honestly expected them to tell her no. In fact, she sort of hoped they would as she was itching for a fight. To her surprise though, Chris nodded and said, "Be sure to take a full detail with you. And you leave the vehicle only after the area has been secured."

"I know the rules," she snapped, and everyone looked surprised by her sharp tone. Did they think there was no limit to the flack she would take from them? That she was immune to their condescension?

"Remember that Anne is flying home and we're having dinner together here at the hospital," Chris told her, and there was an unspoken warning of *be there or else* in his tone. "Seven sharp."

If there was any way she could get out of it, she would, but for Melissa, who was desperate for company, Louisa couldn't say no. "I'll be here," she said and pulled the door open. Her bodyguards Gordon and Jack were waiting for her in the hall. She gestured to them and said, "We're leaving, gentlemen."

On the way to the car, Jack received a call on his cell. Chris, she was assuming, because when they got in the Bentley and she instructed Jack to take her to Garrett's town house he didn't bat an eyelash. It was a good thing she once again failed to mention the new e-mail she had gotten from the Gingerbread Man the day before. She would have mentioned it if there had been any direct threats or even an undertone of danger. All it had said was, Louisa and Garrett sitting in a tree K-I-S-S-I-N-G...

It was just his way of letting her know that he was keeping tabs on them. Par for the course.

When they got to Garrett's place, Louisa wasn't the least bit surprised to see that a team of security agents were already on the premises. Considering his net worth, she was a bit surprised he didn't live in a lavish home in a gated community. Not that his townhome wasn't very attractive, and very large, but he could afford much more. Although, she liked that he wasn't pretentious. Definitely not the kind of man interested in money and power.

It seemed to take forever before Gordon opened the car door and led her up the walk.

"You men will wait outside," she told him. Demanded

was more like it, even though she and Gordon both knew that he was obligated to do whatever Chris ordered. But he nodded and stepped to the side of the door where he had a clear view of the street. Louisa rang the bell, nearly buzzing with excitement at the idea of her and Garrett finally having some time to themselves.

It took him almost a full minute to answer the door, and when he did he was dressed more casually than she'd ever seen him, in lightweight jogging pants and a polo shirt with the emblem of the local yacht club embroidered over his left pec. The casual clothes for some reason seemed to accentuate his size. The thickness of his arms and the width of his shoulders. His lean waist and muscular thighs.

She expected a smile when he saw her standing there, maybe a hug and a kiss, but he just looked confused.

"Louisa? How did you…what are you doing here?"

It was true that Garrett hadn't technically invited her there, but she had been sure he wouldn't mind if she stopped by. How could he when they would get some much needed time alone? Wasn't that all they had been talking about? And why else would he mention, during their phone conversation Tuesday, that he would be working from home if he didn't want her to come over?

Now she wasn't so sure. Maybe the implied invitation hadn't been an invitation after all.

She pasted on a smile despite the sinking sensation in her belly. "I came to visit you."

"Chris let you?"

She nodded, keeping her smile bright. "I think he realized that if he forbid it, I might rebel." Garrett didn't say anything so she asked, "Aren't you going to invite me in?"

He looked behind him, into the town house, then back to her. "Um, sure, come on in."

He stepped aside to let her pass, but he was definitely edgy about something. He kept looking down a hallway that led to the rear of the unit. Behind him to the left was a staircase to the second floor.

She gazed around what was clearly a professionally decorated foyer and living room. It was undeniably male, but tastefully so. "This is nice."

He shrugged. "It suits my needs."

Why didn't he smile? Or take her into his arms and kiss her? Just a few nights ago he'd been dying to get his hands on her.

There was a brief, awkward silence, so she said brightly, "Aren't you going to offer me a tour?"

He shot another furtive glance behind him, and she began to wonder if he was with someone else. Maybe, despite his assurances that he was finished playing the field, he had another woman in his life. Her heart sank so hard and fast she could swear she felt it knocking around by her knees.

Please don't let him be like the others, she begged silently. He *had* to be the one. If not, her family would never let her live it down.

Garrett cleared his throat. "It's just that now isn't the best time."

Aware that her hands were shaking, she clasped them into fists, lifted her chin and asked him point blank, "Is there something you're not telling me?"

"Nothing that has anything to do with us. I promise. It's…complicated."

From down the hallway Louisa heard movement, then the timbre of a male voice called out, "Who is it, Garrett?"

It wasn't another woman, she thought with a relief that left her knees weak. Then it occurred to her, just because it was a man, it didn't mean Garrett wasn't... *involved* with him. Anne had dated a fellow for several months before she realized he was more interested in her bodyguard Gunter than her.

But Garrett was so masculine and virile.

Before she could work up the nerve to ask him, the owner of the voice appeared at the end of the hallway. His face was bruised and swollen and he leaned on a pair of crutches to take the weight off a leg that was encased in plaster from foot to midthigh. It was his friend from the hospital, she realized. The one who had been in the accident.

He walked toward them, the agony of each measured step clear on his poor battered face.

"Bloody hell, Ian!" Garrett barked in a tone Louisa had never heard him use. Like a father chastising a disobedient child. The way Chris had often spoken to her when she was younger. And sometimes still did. "The doctor said to stay off your feet as much as possible."

"Had to use the loo," the Ian person said with a wry smile, then he turned his attention to Louisa and opened his mouth to speak, but he must have recognized her because his jaw fell instead. He looked at Garrett and said, "Damn, that's the *Princess*."

Garrett cursed and shook his head, and when Ian just stood there gaping, he kicked him in his good leg and said, "Bow, you jackass."

"Sorry." He bowed his head, wearing a humble grin,

and said, "Must be all the pain medication they've pumped in me."

"Oh, it's all right," she assured him and offered a hand to shake. "Princess Louisa Josephine Elisabeth Alexander."

Balancing on one crutch, he took her hand, enfolding it in his rough, callused one and said, "I'm Ian. Ian Sutherland."

Nine

"Sutherland?" Louisa repeated, looking to Garrett, clearly confused. And why wouldn't she be when he'd told her this was an acquaintance who'd been in the accident. "You're related?"

Garrett cursed under his breath. Could this day possibly get any worse? He'd hoped to get Ian settled then leave him in the nurse's care and lock himself in his office for the rest of the day, but due to a scheduling snafu, the nurse wouldn't be coming until tomorrow morning.

And now, to top it all off, he had no choice but to tell Louisa the truth. "Ian is my brother."

"There's actually an uncanny family resemblance, when my face isn't all bruised and swollen," Ian told her. "Although I am the better looking one."

Louisa turned to Garrett, brow furrowed. "But you said—"

"I know. I lied."

This would normally be the time when Ian would jump in and say or do something to make Garrett look like even more of an ass, but instead he actually defended him. It was the least selfish thing Garrett had ever seen him do. "Compared to someone like me, Garrett here is a Boy Scout, Your Highness. If he did lie, I know he had a damned good reason."

She looked between Ian and Garrett as though she wasn't sure what to believe.

Though Ian would usually stick around for the fireworks, he yawned and said, "If you'll both excuse me, I'm feeling woozy from the pain medication. I think it's time for my afternoon nap. But I hope we'll get the chance to talk again, Your Highness."

"I'd like that," Louisa said with a smile, and as Ian limped back down the hall she turned to Garrett with a questioning look, as if to say, *Okay, what's the deal?*

"I know I owe you an explanation." He gestured to the staircase. "Let's go to my office, where we can talk in private."

She nodded and followed him up the stairs, but as they passed his bedroom, she stopped.

"This is your room?"

He nodded.

Without asking his permission, she stepped inside. She inhaled deeply and said, "Hmm, it smells like you."

He leaned in and sniffed, but to him it smelled the same way it always did. Just like the rest of the house.

He waited by the door for her to come out. Instead she dropped her purse on the floor, hoisted herself onto his bed and leaned back on her elbows, making herself comfortable. God, did she look sexy. She wore a sleeveless pink blouse and conservative white skirt, with her hair flowing loose and soft on her back. Maybe it was his imagination but it seemed the longer he knew her, the more attractive he found her.

She patted the mattress beside her, signaling him to sit down. Apparently they were having their talk right here.

He closed the door and crossed to the bed, taking a seat to her left. "Let me say first that I'm sorry I lied to you."

"When you first let me in and you looked so nervous, I thought maybe you were seeing another woman. Then I heard Ian's voice and for a second I thought maybe you were seeing a man."

The things that came out of her mouth never ceased to amaze him. "I told you before, Louisa, there's only you. And for the record, only *women*."

"Why didn't you tell me it was your brother in the accident?"

"Because I knew you would want to meet him."

"Is that such a bad thing?"

"Yes. Because he's a liar and a thief and I didn't want to expose you to someone like that. The only reason he came to see me is because my parents and my brothers have all written him off."

She frowned. "That's so sad."

"No, it isn't," he said, and told her some of the things Ian had done to the family, how he'd cheated and lied and stolen from them. And how Garrett was stuck with him now, until his leg healed. "He keeps telling me that he'll really change this time, but I've heard the story a hundred times before. People like that never change."

"But maybe this time he *really* means it."

"Do you know how he got into the accident? I told him I wouldn't give him money, so he stole my car instead."

"Are you sure he wasn't just borrowing it?"

"He admitted to stealing it, not to mention a dozen bottles of my best liquor. Then he tried to make me believe he'd had second thoughts and was bringing it back. But I know better. He left and had no intention of ever coming back."

"Yet you're letting him stay here," she said. "You must still care at least a little."

"I had no choice. He had nowhere else to go."

"If you really didn't care at all, that wouldn't have made a difference."

Though he hated to admit it, she had a point. But he didn't want her to be right. He wanted to hate Ian for all that he'd done. It was so much easier that way.

He groaned and flopped down on his back beside her.

"Stressed out?" she asked.

"Does it show?"

An impish smile curled her lips and he instantly knew she was up to no good. "You know what they say is supposed to be good for stress."

He had a few suggestions, but he was much more interested in her ideas. "Why don't you show me?"

She leaned over and brushed a soft, lingering kiss against his lips, then sat back and asked, "Better?"

Suppressing a smile, he shrugged and said, "A little, I guess."

Looking thoughtful, she said, "Hmm, maybe I'm just not trying hard enough."

She leaned over to give it another go, but he had a sudden revelation. "Hey, wait a minute."

She stopped abruptly and sat up. "What's wrong?"

"Something is missing."

She frowned. "What?"

He rose up on his elbows, looking around the room. "Security."

"Oh, they're here. They're outside, guarding the doors."

"Outside? As in, not inside?"

She looked at him funny. "Yes."

"And there's no chance of them possibly barging in and say, coming upstairs to this room?"

He could see by the slow smile creeping across her face that she knew where he was going with this. "Only if I ask them to. But what about your brother? Is there any reason he would come up here?"

"He's taking a nap. Besides, he can hardly walk, much less climb the stairs."

"You know what that means," she said.

They both smiled and said in unison, "We're finally alone."

Louisa was suddenly so excited her hands were trembling. "I have to be back to the hospital by seven for dinner."

He looked at his watch. "That gives us a little over two hours."

She thought of all the things they could do in two hours.

"Why don't you lie back against the pillows," Garrett said, and he had this look in his eyes, one that said, I'm going to eat you alive.

She realized that the dynamics had suddenly changed. A minute ago, when she was kissing Garrett, she had been the one in control. Now Garrett was clearly calling the shots, and though it scared her a little, it also thrilled her to the depths of her soul.

So why was she just sitting there wasting precious time?

Garrett regarded her curiously, "You're not getting cold feet, are you?"

She reached up and laid a hand on his cheek. "No! I want this, more than anything. It's all I've thought of for weeks. Maybe *too* much."

He leaned in and brushed a kiss against her lips and she could swear she felt it all the way down to her toes. "There's no such thing as too much."

"And that's the problem. Here we are alone, with no reason to stop if things start to go too far."

"How far is too far?"

"I know it's archaic and silly, but I want to be a virgin on my wedding night. I just think it will make it more special."

"It's not silly. It's an honorable decision, and knowing your wishes, I would never let things go too far."

His gaze was so earnest, she wanted to believe him, but who's to say he wouldn't get too carried away? "What if you can't stop?"

He grinned, his dimple winking at her. "Contrary to what you may have read, not all men are sex-starved fiends. You have my word that we won't go any further than we should."

She believed him, because she knew Garrett would never lie to her. At least, not about something so important. And when he had lied about Ian, he'd done it to protect her.

She sat up and scooted backward, laying her head on the pillow. Garrett lay down beside her and propped himself up on one elbow. He studied her face, softly tracing her features with his index finger. "Have I ever told you how beautiful you are?"

"Probably. But feel free to tell me again."

He kissed her instead. So tender and sweet—at first anyway. He kissed her lips and her chin and the side of her neck. He nibbled her earlobes and found a sensitive little spot behind her ear that made her shiver.

Her hesitance a memory now, she wrapped her arms around his neck, threaded her fingers through his hair, breathing in the scent of his skin and his hair. Feeding off his kisses.

Garrett cupped the side of her face, caressed her cheek with his thumb, but gradually his hand slipped lower, first down her throat and neck, then to her shoulder, but he stopped there.

A little voice inside of her was begging, *Keep going, please keep touching me.* Her breasts or even between her legs, anywhere that might relieve the ache building inside of her. It would be okay if he did, because he'd promised not to let this go too far, and she trusted him.

Maybe she was thinking loud enough for him to hear, because his hand started to move again, drifting slowly until it covered her breast. The ache between her thighs became a raging inferno, and her breasts felt swollen and tender. For a minute he just held his hand there, as though he worried she might be afraid—or he was trying to drive her mad. Louisa held her breath, anticipating his next move, and when he squeezed softly the sensation was so intense she gasped.

He stopped kissing her and gazed down with lust-filled eyes. "Too much?"

"No!" she said in a voice so husky with desire she barely recognized it as her own. "Not enough."

Wearing a sexy grin, he stroked one breast, then the other. When he took one nipple between his fingers and gently pinched, she whimpered. Men had touched her breasts before, but never had it felt this good. This... erotic.

Then he *stopped*. She opened her mouth to protest, but he started unbuttoning her blouse and the words died in her throat.

"I've been wondering something," he said, popping each button open with the flick of his skilled fingers. She watched as the last button gave way and he eased the sides back, exposing her pink lace bra. She wasn't particularly large, a modest B cup, but what she lacked in size, she made up for in quality.

"What were you wondering?" she asked.

"How inexperienced are you? I mean, you must have some experience."

"Some heavy petting, but always on top of the clothes. And kissing, of course."

"What kind of kissing?" he asked.

What kind? How many kinds were there?

Confused, she said, "Just regular kissing, I guess."

He flashed her an impish grin and she knew instantly that he was up to something.

"Anyone ever kiss you like this?" He dipped his head, brushing his lips on her breast at the very edge of the lace cup and Louisa could barely suppress the moan building in her throat. He kissed one, then the other, then he lifted his head to look at her.

"No," she answered in an unsteady voice. "Never like that."

"How about like this?" Using his tongue, he drew a damp path down the swell of one breast then up its mate. Then he looked at her and grinned.

Technically that wasn't a kiss, but this was no time to be splitting hairs. Kiss or not, she was so turned on she felt like crawling out of her own skin. "I'm going to have to say no. In fact, pretty much anything you do at this point will be new territory for me." And she could hardly wait to see where and how he touched her next. Fortunately she didn't have to wait long.

Garrett nudged the cup of her bra aside, and for a second all he did was look at her. Her nipple was small and pink and pulled tight with arousal.

"You have the most beautiful breasts I've ever seen," he said. She knew she should be polite and thank him, but he leaned forward and touched the very tip with his tongue and her brain went into shutdown mode. She didn't think anything could feel more erotic...until he drew her nipple into his mouth and sucked. Hard. She threw her head back and moaned, arching closer to his mouth.

He leaned back to look at his handiwork. Her nipple was damp and tinted deep red from the suction. She expected him to do the same to the other breast, but instead he gazed down at her, his expression serious, and said, "We should probably stop for now."

Wait, what? Was he serious? *"Stop?"*

"So things don't go too far."

She must have looked absolutely crestfallen, because he laughed and said, "Louisa, I'm teasing."

"Bloody hell, don't joke about a thing like that!" she scolded, expelling a relieved breath.

"We are running a little short on time."

She looked at his watch and couldn't believe how much time had passed already. And all they had done was kiss and touch. But she wanted more, and she wanted it now. If she was a little late for dinner, so be it. "Then let's not waste any more time."

She tugged on the hem of his shirt, and he helped her pull it over his head. His body was the most amazing she had ever seen and not just because his chest was wide and muscular, his abdomen hard and defined. She loved it because it belonged to him. She raised her hands and laid them on his chest, surprised by how hot his skin felt. Without his shirt to cover it, she could see his erection clearly against the loose jogging pants. So clearly that she realized he must not be wearing briefs or even boxers.

Garrett frowned and pressed one of his hands over hers. "You're shaking. Are you afraid?"

She shook her head. "Not at all. Just excited."

And fed up with going so slow.

She pushed Garrett onto his back, then sat up and straddled him, her skirt riding up all the way to the tops of her thighs. She shrugged out of her shirt then reached behind her and unclasped her bra, feeling an almost excruciating need to press her body to his, to rub her breasts against his chest. Garrett must have read her mind, because he seemed to know exactly what to do. As soon as her bra was off, he pulled her down to him, wrapping his arms around her. Their lips met in what was more of a mutual devouring than an actual kiss. They fed off one another, and if she could have eaten him alive, she would have.

Garrett's hands seemed to be everywhere at once. Up and down her back and arms, kneading her breasts, tangling in her hair. But when he reached under her skirt and cupped her behind in his big, warm hands, the ache between her legs became unbearable.

He rolled her onto her back, and it felt so good, the weight of his body on hers, lying chest to chest, stomach to stomach. She wrapped her legs around his waist, unaware until that very second that his erection had become pinned between them, centered perfectly in line with the crotch of her panties.

Louisa gasped with surprise and Garrett groaned, then they both went still, Garrett wearing an expression that suggested this time, they may have gone too far.

Technically this was her fault. Had she been more experienced, she would have anticipated this, and she knew they were tempting fate lying like this, with barely more than a thin layer of nylon and a swatch of lace to prevent this from going any further.

But it felt *so* good.

For several seconds they just stared at one another, as if neither was sure what to do next. She didn't relax her vise grip on his waist, and he didn't try to pull loose.

Then it happened. With his eyes locked on hers, Garrett rocked back then inched slowly forward, stroking her with the entire length of his erection. Louisa felt it like an electric charge that started between her thighs and raced outward. She shuddered involuntarily and all the fine hairs on her body shivered to life.

He did it again, but this time she arched up to meet

him and every inch of her skin, every cell in her body overflowed with pleasure, even though they still had their clothes on.

Garrett rocked into her, over and over, with the same slow, measured thrusts and her body moved naturally with him. She kissed his lips and his throat, bit his earlobes and raked her nails across his back and shoulders. She wanted to eat him up, brand him with her teeth and her nails. Not the way a proper princess should behave. But she didn't care. She felt naughty and sexy and half out of her mind with lust, his every thrust driving her closer and closer to ecstasy.

So close.

She looked up at Garrett. His eyes were closed, his breath ragged and sweat beaded his forehead. For some reason she'd thought he was doing this just to make her feel good, but in that instant she realized that he was going to climax, and that was all it took to drive her past the point of no return. Everything locked and a shudder that started in her center rippled out to encompass her entire being. She would have moaned but she couldn't breathe, couldn't even think past the numbing pleasure.

Feeling her climax must have done Garrett in. He groaned from deep within his chest then went rigid, hissing out a breath as he gave one final thrust then dropped beside her.

Ten

Louisa lay beside Garrett in his bed, limp and trying to catch her breath, and suddenly, for no reason, Garrett started to laugh. A deep throaty laugh, as though he found something about the situation profoundly amusing.

"What's so funny?" she asked.

He gazed up at the ceiling, shaking his head. "I can't believe we just did that."

She frowned. "Was it…bad?"

He rolled onto his side, rising up on one elbow to look at her. "No, not at all. It was…fantastic."

She was confused. "So why are you laughing?"

"Because the last time I did it that way I was fifteen. It's a bit like wet dreams. After a certain age, you just don't have them."

She nodded thoughtfully. "I guess that makes sense."

"What do you mean?"

"Well, despite all the stories I've read, I've never seen any mention of what we just did."

He grinned. "You would if they were written by adolescent boys."

"So what we did was…unusual?"

"Very. It usually takes actual intercourse for me to climax."

"Why is that, do you think?"

He shrugged. "I guess, once you start having sex, the novelty gradually wears off. But you turn me on so much, it's like being a kid again. Starting from the beginning."

That might have been one of the sweetest things a man had ever said to her. She grinned and said, "Think we could do it again?"

"Have you looked at the time?"

She read the display on his watch. Damn! It was already half past six. But if she hurried she could make it on time for dinner. "I'm sorry. I do have to go."

"I understand."

He looked so sexy lying there with no shirt on, wearing that adorable smile. She didn't want to leave. She wanted to curl into his chest and cuddle with him. She wanted to fall asleep in his bed and wake in his arms, but she knew that her family was expecting her. And if she didn't show, those guards who were waiting patiently outside might just break down the door to fetch her.

She rolled out of bed and grabbed her clothes.

Garrett lay there and watched her dress. "I have a grueling day at the office tomorrow, but maybe I could see you in the evening."

"Oh, I can't. I forgot to tell you, I'm filling in for

Chris at some executive dinner. Now that he's finally taking me seriously, I couldn't refuse. What about the night after that?"

"Friday? I have a dinner meeting."

"Do you have work to do Saturday?"

"If I do, it will have to wait. What would you like to do?"

Did he even have to ask?

Well, for propriety's sake she could at least *pretend* they weren't getting together just to ravish each other. "It might be difficult going out on an actual date," she reminded him. "With all the security issues."

"True," he agreed thoughtfully. "I suppose we could just stay indoors."

"I'm sure we could figure out *something* to keep us occupied."

He smiled that sexy smile and asked, with a voice full of sexual innuendo, "Your place or mine?"

They decided to meet at his place, since here they would have the least interruption, then Garrett walked Louisa to the door. She called her bodyguard to let him know she was ready, and through the front window Garrett could see that there was a slew of vehicles parked in the street in front of his town house.

"The media circus has begun," he told her.

She peered around him to see. "It sort of comes with the territory. But you get used to it. Once they have their photos and press releases, the hype will die down."

He hoped so. He preferred to keep his life low profile—one more thing he would sacrifice as Louisa's husband. Though he had a feeling, for a while at least, she would make up for it in *other* ways. And right now she looked so damned adorable, all rumpled and sexy, he wanted to drag her back upstairs.

There was a knock on the door and Garrett opened it to find two hulking bodyguards on his porch, the same ones from the hospital. Garrett was a big man, but these guys were giants, and he had little doubt Louisa would be quite safe in their care.

"We're ready, Your Highness," the one on the left said.

Louisa turned to Garrett, rose up on her toes and pressed a kiss to his lips, then she smiled and said, "See you Saturday."

As soon as her foot hit the step, he heard the dull roar of camera shutters firing away and reporters shouting questions from the street. Even knowing he would be tomorrow's fodder for the tabloids, he stood there and watched as she was helped in the car. She waved as the car pulled away and he waved back, watching until they rounded the corner at the end of the block. Then he heard from behind him, "My big brother, shagging a princess."

He closed the door and turned to find Ian standing a few feet away, at the end of the hallway.

"Who I 'shag' is none of your concern. And for the record, I'm not."

"Maybe, but you will be, because you always get what you want." Ian shook his head and laughed. "Leave it to Garrett the overachiever to set his sights on the royal family."

Garrett glared at him and walked past Ian to the kitchen to get himself a beer. If Ian hadn't cleaned him out already, that is.

Ian followed him.

Surprisingly, there was the same number of bottles as the night before. Garrett took one out and twisted off the cap.

"Aren't you going to offer me some?" Ian asked.

"Pain pills and alcohol. Smashing combination." He closed the refrigerator.

Ian leaned back against the counter and propped his crutches in the corner. "I knew you were a power hound, but I never imagined you had the stones to bag a princess. What do you think Mum and Dad would say?"

"Since they're not talking to me, I don't imagine they would say much of anything."

"I thought families were supposed to have only one black sheep," Ian said with a wry smile, but Garrett could swear he saw regret lurking behind his eyes.

Was it possible that he had a conscience after all? That he really did want to change?

Garrett washed the possibility away with a swallow of ale. If he let himself get his hopes up, he would only be disappointed later.

"He's jealous, you know," Ian said.

"Who?"

"Our father."

Garrett frowned. "Jealous of whom?"

"*You.*"

He had no idea what Ian was talking about. His father had made it very clear that he wanted nothing to do with Garrett or his money. "That's ridiculous."

"It's true. He was never what you would call a pleasant man, we both have the scars to prove that, but after you left for university things were bad."

Garrett automatically reached up to touch the small scar at the corner of his mouth. From a crack in the jaw he'd received for staying late at school to finish a project when he should have been home doing his chores. "How bad?"

"His temper became even more volatile. I had never seen him so angry. He and Mum were fighting all the time. But you know Mum, she would take it all. I was just a kid, but even I knew that wasn't right. I asked her one day why he hated us so much."

Garrett couldn't help but ask, "What did she say?"

"That he was an unhappy man. That he had dreams of going to university and doing more with his life, but being the oldest, it was his responsibility to take over the farm when his father retired. And he did it, because that was what was expected of him. He married and became a farmer, just like he was supposed to. He settled. Then you came along, knowing exactly what you wanted and not letting a single thing get in your way. He envied you, Garrett, maybe even hated you for it, because that's the kind of man he was. And he convinced everyone else that what you'd done was some sort of slight against the family."

And here Garrett had always believed his father had been content as a farmer, that he was happy with the simple life he'd chosen. "He never once said a word about wanting anything different."

Ian shrugged. "It wasn't his way."

"Even if I knew, it wouldn't have changed anything. I still would have left."

"I'm not blaming you, Garrett. I just thought you should know why he's such a bastard. I mean, at least I *deserve* the family's hatred. You haven't done anything wrong."

"A father should want better for his sons. He should

want them to strive for more. Instead he was always trying to hold me back."

"That's his problem, not yours."

So why did Garrett still feel like it was his fault? Like he'd done something wrong? Parents were supposed to love their kids unconditionally. Push them to succeed. And it wasn't just his father at fault. His mum bore just as much blame. She should have defended Garrett, should have been his advocate, not her husband's enabler.

Like Ian said, it wasn't Garrett's fault. But he couldn't decide if this new information was a relief or only made him feel worse.

How many times had he told himself that he'd stopped caring? That nothing they could say or do could hurt him, even if that meant them not saying or doing anything at all? Somewhere deep down, did he still care?

He took a long swallow, draining the bottle, then said, "Shouldn't you be lying down resting or something?"

"I'm bored," Ian said. "She's really nice by the way."

"Who?"

"*Who?*" Ian laughed. "The *Princess*. Your girlfriend. The one you aren't shagging. Who did you think I meant?"

His brother had just informed him that everything he knew about his life was untrue, so it was natural for Garrett to be a bit confused. "Yes, she is."

"I'll bet she's a handful though."

He narrowed his eyes at his brother. "Why would you say that?"

"Mischief recognizes mischief. And honestly, I think that's exactly the kind of woman you need. One who won't give you the chance to be bored."

It surprised Garrett how well Ian knew him. Ian had been so young when Garrett left. So carefree. Maybe there was more going on in his head than people realized.

Garrett had left his phone on the counter and it began to ring. Before he could reach for it, Ian grabbed it. Rather than hand it to Garrett, he answered himself. He greeted the caller just the way Garrett would, then for several seconds just listened. At first Garrett thought it might be some sort of automated call, then Ian said, "Sorry, I think it's Garrett you want to speak to." With another wry smile he handed the phone to Garrett. "It's a fellow named Wes. He called to say that he saw you on the news just now and it looks as though the situation with the Princess is going just as planned."

Bloody hell. Ian knew. Not specifically what, but he knew Garrett was up to something. And he wouldn't hesitate to hold it against him.

Garrett took the phone. "Wes?"

"Christ, Garrett, was that Ian? He sounds just like you."

"Yes, it was."

"I'm sorry. If I had known…"

"Don't worry about it."

"I called to tell you that I just saw footage on the telly of her leaving your place."

That was quick. "It was something of a media frenzy outside."

"Well, you certainly gave them fodder to chew on."

Garrett frowned. "What do you mean?"

Wes told him about the footage he'd seen and Garrett groaned. Suddenly what Ian did or didn't know was inconsequential.

"I take it that wasn't deliberate," Wes said.

No, and he had the feeling he would be hearing from Chris regarding the matter, if the family hadn't banished him from the castle, from Louisa's life, already.

"I'm here!" Louisa called cheerily as she breezed into Melissa's hospital room at seven on the nose…and was met by total silence.

Melissa reclined in bed and Chris stood beside her, arms crossed over his chest. Aaron and Liv sat in chairs across the room by the window, and Anne was seated across from them. And they all just stared at her.

Did they know what she'd been up to?

Of course not. She had looked a bit rumpled when she left Garrett's town house but she'd fixed her makeup and hair in the car. "What? Why are you looking at me like that?"

"We saw you on the telly," Anne remarked with a smirk.

Was *that* all? They were always on television for some reason or another. It's not as though her relationship with Garrett was some kind of secret.

She shrugged and asked, "So?"

Everyone exchanged a look, then Melissa said, "You looked a little…disheveled."

Yes, she probably should have fixed up herself before she left, but it wasn't that big of a deal. "So my hair wasn't perfect. Is it really the end of the world?"

"Well," Liv began, looking pained. "There was your shirt, too."

"What about it?" she asked, and Liv gestured for her to see for herself.

Louisa looked down and her heart sank. She must

have been in quite a rush when she dressed because she'd fastened the buttons on her blouse cockeyed.

"Oops." She turned away and swiftly fixed it.

"I guess this means you blew that vow to be a virgin on your wedding night," Anne snipped, and Louisa spun to face her. That was supposed to be private, a secret shared between sisters.

"What's your problem?" Louisa said, so tired of Anne dumping on her that she wanted to scream.

Anne just sneered. "Should we expect a shotgun wedding, or were you smart enough to use a condom?"

"Anne!" Chris cut in sharply.

"I wish you would do something to kill the bug that has crawled up your you-know-where, so I could have my sister back," Louisa retorted. "And not that it's yours or anyone else's business, but I am still pure as the driven snow." More or less.

"That may be true," Aaron said, "but it looked as though you'd spent the afternoon shagging."

She could understand why people might get that impression, and why Chris looked so disappointed in her. "It was an accident," she told him.

"Yes, well, it's not the kind of thing that someone would do on purpose. All that tells me is that you were being careless."

"I was in a hurry. I was running late and wanted to get here on time. If I had taken the time to fix myself up, I would have been late and you would have chastised me for that." No matter what she did, she couldn't win.

"Then you should have taken that into consideration and stopped whatever it was you were doing earlier to give yourself extra time. With everything else we have to worry about, this is the last thing the family needs, Louisa. It reflects badly on me."

Him? "How did this become about *you?*"

"Because it is my responsibility to hold this family together in our father's absence. How do you think he and Mother will feel when they see this on the news? Who do you think they'll blame?"

She hadn't thought about it like that. She bit her lip and lowered her eyes, suddenly filled with shame. "I'm sorry."

Sometimes she forgot how much pressure Chris must be under. First taking over their father's duties, and now having Melissa in the hospital and his children's health at risk. He was right. She was being irresponsible and selfish.

"I'm sending Anne to speak for me tomorrow," he told her, twisting the knife in a little deeper. Prince Chris giveth, then he taketh away.

She nodded, unable to meet his eyes. "I understand."

Not only had she let him and the rest of the family down, but the way Anne had been acting lately, she would take satisfaction rubbing this in Louisa's face.

"You *will* be more careful next time," he said, and she went limp with relief. At least he wasn't going to put her on house arrest, or insist she stop seeing Garrett. He was giving her another chance.

"I will," she told him. "I promise."

Her cell phone started to ring and she practically dove into her purse to grab it. It was Garrett's number. "I need to get this," she told Chris.

He nodded, signaling what she hoped was the end of

the tongue-lashing. At least for now, but God forbid she screw up again. Chris wouldn't be so lenient. He might do something drastic, like lock her in a tower and never let her out.

Eleven

Louisa escaped into the waiting room and answered her phone. "Hi."

"Did I get you at a bad time?" Garrett asked.

"No, your timing was perfect. Chris just finished chastising me to within an inch of my life," she said, and could swear she felt him cringe.

"I take it they saw the news clip."

"Yeah. Did you?"

"Yeah. A friend called to tell me so I put the television on. It's been on practically every channel, so it was hard to miss."

She tensed up. "Aaron said I looked like I spent the afternoon shagging."

"Yeah, you did. I'm sorry."

"Why are you apologizing?"

"Because I never should have let you leave my house. As you were getting ready to walk out the door I was thinking to myself how mussed you looked, but I just thought it was sexy as hell. It never occurred to me that the press would notice, too."

"What about my blouse?"

"That I honestly didn't notice or I would have told you." He paused then asked, "Chris was angry?"

"It was more of an I'm-not-angry-I'm-disappointed speech. And to be honest, anger would have been a lot easier to stomach. I feel terrible. I promised him that next time I would be more careful."

"Does that mean we're still on for Saturday?"

"Definitely. Although there was a point when I worried he might stick me on permanent house arrest. And coincidentally, I'm also free Thursday, as well. Chris asked Anne to sit in for him instead. I guess he doesn't trust me."

"Well, I made plans with my friend Wes to golf that evening, but I could cancel."

She shelved her disappointment. "No, don't do that. I don't want to be *that girl*."

"What girl?"

"The one who makes her boyfriend drop all of his friends and monopolizes his every waking moment. Go golfing and have fun. I'll see you Saturday."

The hospital room door opened and Anne stepped through. She shot a quick, nervous glance at Louisa then walked to the ladies' room. What was her deal?

"Are you sure? Because I know he would understand."

"I'm sure. I have plenty to keep me busy." She loved the idea that he wanted to be with her, but she needed to let him have some normalcy before things got too serious between them, because eventually he was bound to become a target for the Gingerbread Man and security would become an issue for him, as well. He should enjoy his freedom while he still could. "Maybe you could call me before you go to bed," she suggested.

"Eleven too late?"

"I'll keep the phone beside me just in case I drift off." Maybe they could even give that phone sex thing a try. She was about to mention it when she heard what sounded like retching from the ladies' room. Was Anne sick?

"Garrett, I have to let you go," she said. "I'll talk to you tomorrow."

They said their goodbyes and she walked over to the door to listen. It was quiet for a minute, then she heard the unmistakable sound echoing off the tile walls. She knocked on the door. "Anne, are you okay?"

"I'm fine," she called back, but immediately the vomiting started again. It sounded violent and painful, and Louisa started to actually worry something was seriously wrong.

"Do you need anything?" she asked.

"No. Go away."

She sighed. She was trying to help and Anne was still copping an attitude. "Would you stop being such a bitch and let me in? For reasons I cannot begin to comprehend, I'm worried about you!"

A few seconds passed and she heard the toilet flush, then the lock on the door snapped and Anne yelled, "You can come in."

She opened the door, taken aback by what she found. Anne was sitting on the floor near the commode, her cheek resting against the tile wall. A sheen of sweat dampened her face, and aside from two bright red patches on her cheeks, all the color had leeched from her skin.

Alarmed, Louisa stepped inside and shut the door. "What's wrong? Are you sick?"

She shook her head. "I'm fine."

"You are *not* fine." She reached down to feel her forehead, but Anne batted her hand away.

"I don't have a fever."

"If you're sick, you shouldn't be anywhere near Melissa."

"I told you I'm not sick."

Then what other explanation—

"Oh my God, are you bulimic?"

Anne laughed weakly. "Louisa, bulimics vomit *after* they eat. Not before."

"If you're not sick and you're not bulimic, what's going on? Healthy people don't throw up like that."

"Some healthy *women* do," Anne said.

It took a minute, but the meaning of her words finally sank in and Louisa gasped. "Oh my God," she hissed in a loud whisper. "Are you *pregnant?*"

"You can't tell *anyone*," Anne said.

"Oh my God," she said again, hardly able to believe it.

"Imagine how I felt when I took the pregnancy tests," Anne joked weakly.

"You took more than one?"

"I took five. I wanted to be sure."

That would definitely do it. "How far along are you?

"Just a few weeks."

"How did this happen?"

Anne raised a brow at her.

Louisa rolled her eyes. "Of course I know *how,* but when, and with whom? I didn't even know you were seeing anyone."

"I'm not. And the father is out of the picture. He doesn't want the baby or me."

"Are you sure?"

"*Very* sure."

"Oh, Anne, I'm so sorry." She sat down on the floor beside her sister and took her hand. She half expected her to pull away, but she didn't. At least this explained why Anne had been so cranky lately. Her hormones must have been raging, and to top it off, having the father reject her and the baby? She must have been devastated.

"Who is it, Anne?"

"It's not important."

"Yes, it is. Someone needs to make him own up to his responsibility."

"I'm not even sure what *I'm* going to do yet."

Louisa's heart skipped. "You don't mean…?"

"What I mean is, I haven't decided if I'm going to keep it, or give it up for adoption. If I choose adoption, I figure I can hold out until it's impossible to hide, then take an extended vacation. No one will have to know a thing."

That would be tough enough for an average woman to pull off, but a princess? Someone was bound to figure it out. "You don't want to have children?"

"Not like this. Besides, look how everyone reacted to you leaving your boyfriend's house looking a little untidy. Can you imagine how they would take the news of me having a child out of wedlock? I'm not sure Daddy could take the stress of a huge scandal right now."

She hadn't heard Anne call him "Daddy" in years. "He'll be okay."

Anne shook her head, looking troubled. "He doesn't look good, Louisa. He's lost so much weight and he has so little energy now. You should have seen the look on his face when the doctor said there was so little improvement. He was devastated. And Mum is a total wreck. I think she sees the same thing I do."

"What's that?"

"I think he's giving up."

Louisa shook her head. "He would never do that. He's strong."

"He's been so sick and in and out of hospitals for so long. I think he's just tired."

"I can't accept that."

"I know you love him. We all do, and I think right now he's holding on for us. But there is going to come a time when we have to let go. We have to let him know that it's okay to stop fighting."

She knew she was being selfish, but she didn't *want* him to stop fighting. He was going to walk her down the aisle at her wedding and be there to play with her children. She simply could not imagine her life without him in it. "How do you know he's ready to quit? Did he tell you?"

"He didn't have to. I just knew. I think you will, too. When you're ready."

She didn't know if she would *ever* be ready for that.

There was a soft rap at the door, startling them both.

"Come in," Anne called.

The door opened a crack and Liv stuck her head in, she looked around, then her gaze dropped and she frowned. "Oh, there you are. We thought maybe you'd left. Why are you sitting on the floor?"

"Hot flashes," Anne said. "Damned PMS. I thought it would be cooler down here."

It was the dumbest excuse Louisa had ever heard, but Liv didn't question it.

"Oh. Well, dinner is getting cold."

Louisa smiled. "Thanks, we'll be right in."

Liv shot them one last odd look that suggested her sisters-in-law were both a few beakers short of a complete lab, then disappeared. It probably did look odd, the two of them alone in the bathroom sitting on the floor and holding hands no less.

"I really like her," Anne said, "but she's way too uptight. Maybe she just needs a good shag."

"That's definitely not the problem," Louisa said, and to Anne's how-do-*you*-know look, she added, "My room is right down the hall, and suffice it to say they aren't exactly quiet. And for the record, I really didn't sleep with Garrett. I want to though. I'm not sure I can wait until my wedding night."

"I'm sorry for what I said, Louisa. About your virginity. That was rotten of me. And I'm sorry I've been such a bitch lately."

"Under the circumstances I guess I can cut you some slack." She looked at Anne and smiled. "I'm just glad to have my sister back."

Anne gave her hand a squeeze. "I think I'm just jealous that you found someone you care about. I should be happy for you, not trying to drag you down."

"You don't still think he's using me?"

She shrugged. "What the hell do I know? If I was so

damned smart I wouldn't have gotten myself into this mess."

"It'll be okay, Annie," she assured her, using the nickname from their childhood. Anne was Annie, and Louisa was Lulu. She wondered when they had stopped that, when they felt they were too mature or too refined for silly names. They used to be silly a lot back then, and Louisa missed that. Sometimes she wished they could go back to those days when things were so simple and uncomplicated.

Or maybe it was all relative. Problems that seemed enormous back then were, in retrospect, not such a big deal now.

"You ready?" Anne asked.

She nodded and asked, "You?"

Balancing on the wall, she pushed herself to her feet. "May as well get this over with."

Louisa followed her out, thinking that maybe the trick was going back over all the experiences she'd had up until this point—the good times and bad times, the hurts and the happiness—and starting fresh.

Of course, going back would mean leaving Garrett forever, and that wasn't something she would ever do.

The headline of the morning paper was brutal. Clever, but brutal.

"Has Snow White Drifted?"

The photo beneath it was even worse. It was a shot of her being ushered to the car, her hair messy, her makeup all but gone. And of course there was the sloppily buttoned shirt, which the paper had conveniently circled for their readers' viewing ease. Under that was a smaller photo of Garrett standing at his front doorway in bare feet, his hair a mess and his clothes wrinkled.

"We *do* look like we've been shagging," she told Garrett.

"It's not *that* bad. For all the press knows, we could have been out for a run."

She tossed the paper off the bed and switched the phone to her other ear. "Yes, I often run in a skirt and sandals."

"My point is, no one can know for sure *what* we were doing. Besides us, of course. Now if we'd made a sex tape that was leaked to the press…"

"Bite your tongue," she said and he laughed.

"Don't worry. It'll blow over."

She wondered how his family was reacting to the press. But he'd already told her that he no longer spoke to them.

"When was the last time you talked to your father?" she asked.

Her question seemed to surprise him. "Where did that come from?"

"I've been thinking about family a lot lately. I was just curious."

"I haven't spoken to him since the day I purchased his land."

"You bought his farm?"

"It was the first piece of property I ever owned. They were in trouble. They had a bad crop, and with their debt, he wasn't able to pay his taxes. The land was about to be seized and put up for auction. I bought it, thinking that I would present it to him as a gift. He and my mum could live there until the day he died and never have to worry about money again."

"He must have been so grateful."

"He tore the deed in half and threw it back in my face. He told me that I was no longer his son."

Louisa gasped. "He didn't!"

"He said he didn't want my charity."

The idea that he would do that to his son made Louisa's heart ache. And all Garrett had done was try to help. "You must have felt horrible."

"My father was always a proud man, but I admit I never expected that reaction. I thought he would finally see that my choice to go to college had paid off. That I'd made the right decision. He always told me that the land would someday be mine. I guess that only applied if I became a farmer like him. Instead he preferred that it be purchased off the auction block by some stranger rather than by his own flesh and blood."

Tears shimmered in her eyes. "I can't imagine how much that must have hurt you."

"It was a feeling of resignation more than anything. And maybe in a way a relief. He had drawn his line in the sand. I could finally stop trying to please him."

"You at least tried to talk to him, didn't you?"

"There wasn't much point. He made his feelings clear."

"But…he's your father. I'm sure he still loves you."

"Well, it's too late now."

"It's never too late, Garrett. If you don't at least try to heal the rift between you and he dies, it will haunt you for the rest of your life."

"Why this sudden interest in my family?"

"Anne told me something about our father the other day, and…" Tears welled up in her eyes again and she swallowed back a sob.

"Is something wrong?" he asked.

"It's not looking good." She told Garrett what Anne had said, and it took every ounce of energy she had not to fall apart.

Garrett figured he would be relishing the news of the King's permanent vacation from the throne. Because even if he didn't die, it sounded as though he would never be healthy enough to rule again. Which meant that Garrett was a shoo-in for that position Louisa had mentioned. At the very least, Garrett should have been relieved that finally all of his hard work was going to reap benefits.

Instead he felt like a piece of garbage.

He used to see the royal family as nothing more than an obstacle. A united front made up of faceless individuals he was determined to conquer. That attitude had suited him just fine—until he'd gotten to know them. Now everything had changed, and the idea that he could have been so greedy and shallow, so manipulative, disturbed him deeper than he could have imagined. He used to be a good person. He used to have principles, used to care about people.

He was revolted by the man he had become.

But he couldn't deny that he was really starting to care about Louisa. When she told him about the situation with her father, her voice so full of grief and fear, Garrett would have moved heaven and earth to take away her pain. To make it better. And quite frankly, it scared the hell out of him.

He didn't have time for attachments like that, time to worry himself with other people's baggage. He preferred to keep his life simple and uncomplicated.

And by choosing Louisa, that was what he believed he was getting. A sweet, demure, shell of a woman who would be easily manipulated and more or less trained to be exactly the kind of wife he wanted. The less seen and heard, the better.

Instead he got a feisty, passionate and independent woman. One who was about as likely to follow his "rules" as he was to don a tutu and become a ballerina.

Maybe she was his punishment for all his selfishness, his ruthless attitude. The thing is, she didn't *feel* like a punishment. Was it possible that she might actually be a blessing in disguise?

Twelve

Louisa lay in bed most of the night, tossing and turning, her mind working a million miles an hour. The idea of losing their father, and the possibility of Anne giving up her baby, was almost too much for her to bear. There was nothing much she could do for her father but be there to support him. And she could only do the same for Anne.

Early the following morning, she went to Anne's room to check on her. Louisa knocked, and when Anne answered she looked like death warmed over.

"Feeling sick?"

"Does it show?" Anne asked wryly, letting her in, then she crawled back into bed and burrowed under the covers.

"Is there anything I can do?"

She shook her head. "What's up?"

"I was wondering if you had decided what to do."

"About the baby, you mean?"

Louisa nodded and sat on the edge of the bed.

"Not definitively, but I'm leaning toward adoption. I'm just…I'm not ready to do this. Not this way. Besides, I would be a terrible single mother. I'm pessimistic and difficult. The baby would be much better off with someone else. Someone more…maternal. I'm just not cut out to be a mother."

"Of course you are! You would be a wonderful mother."

Anne shook her head. "Not now. Not like this."

Louisa wished there was something she could say to change her mind, but who was she to tell her sister how to live?

"What happened to this family, Anne? How did everything get all screwed up and turned around?"

"It just…happens. Things can't stay the same forever."

But she wanted them to. She wanted everything to go back to the way it used to be, when they were all healthy and happy and safe. Now it was just so…confusing. It seemed that the only really good thing in her life right now was Garrett. He made her happy. But it was a sort of happy she had never experienced before. Not with a man, anyway. When she was with him, she felt excited and hopeful and content all at once.

"Just for the record," Anne said, "I actually think you and Garrett will be really happy together."

"I think…I think I love him."

Anne regarded her curiously. "You sound surprised. From the second you met him, you've been so sure he was the one."

"I know, but that was different."

"Different how?"

"Let's face it, I've said I 'loved' at least a dozen other men before him. And yes, when I met Garrett I was convinced it was love at first sight. He was so dark and mysterious and sexy. But now that I've gotten to know him, the *real* him, I realize how immature and shallow those feelings really were. He's so much more than what I expected. And what I feel for him now is so much bigger than anything I've felt before. Complex and confusing and…wonderful."

"That's a good thing, right?"

"I hope so. A week ago I was absolutely certain that we were perfect for each other, that it was destiny. But what if I was wrong? What if I fell in love with him, but he doesn't love me back?"

"And what if he does?"

That would be wonderful, of course. "You know, the great thing about being naive is that you don't think about stuff like this. It's so much easier existing in a bubble, convinced life is wonderful and everything will work out."

"Yeah, but you can't live like that forever. Eventually the bubble will burst."

Maybe that was what had happened to her. Maybe her bubble had finally burst, because for the first time in her life she didn't have all the answers. She didn't believe that everything would be okay.

"By the way, as soon as I can manage to crawl out of bed, I'm telling Chris that I can't fill in for him anymore. Last night was miserable. Not only did I feel as though any second I would toss all over the podium, but when it comes to public speaking, you're just better than me.

You're in your element when you're interacting with people, and let's face it, I'm not."

"What if he says no?"

"I won't give him a choice. It's you or Aaron, and we both know Aaron won't want to do it."

After so many years of wanting her family to take her more seriously, to give her more responsibility, suddenly she was afraid. What if she wasn't good enough? What if she made another mistake?

She'd spent so much time whining and complaining and never had the slightest clue how easy she had it.

Technically she had been an adult for nine years, but until recently, she hadn't really grown up. She felt as though now it was finally time. But to grow up she would have to face one of her biggest fears. The one thing she'd been stalwartly avoiding.

"I have to go call Garrett," she told Anne.

"Is everything okay? You look...I don't know, like you're up to something." She frowned suddenly then asked, "You're not going to do something drastic are you?"

Drastic for Louisa maybe. "Everything is fine," she promised. Or at least, as close to fine as it could be under the circumstances.

Louisa dialed Garrett's home number, but he didn't answer.

She was about to try his cell when Geoffrey knocked on her door. "You have a visitor, Your Highness."

A visitor? This early? Then she realized it could be only one person. She raced to the door and flung it open. Garrett stood on the other side. He was dressed for work, a shy grin on his face. He looked delicious.

"Surprise," he said.

"Thank you, Geoffrey," Louisa said, grabbing Garrett's hand and tugging him into her room. The instant the door was closed she was in his arms. She must have looked a fright, still in her pajamas with her hair mussed, but she was so happy to see him she didn't care.

"I know it's early. I hope I didn't wake you."

"No, I've been up awhile." She pressed her cheek to his suit jacket, breathed in the scent of his aftershave. "And even if I had been asleep, I couldn't think of a better way to wake up."

He kissed the top of her head. "I've missed you, Princess."

Her heart overflowed with happiness. "I've missed you, too. But how did you get Geoffrey to bring you up here?"

"I lied and said you were expecting me. I know I'll see you tonight, but I didn't want to wait that long."

She really didn't want to do this, but she had to. "I was wondering if you would be upset if I cancelled our date."

"I guess that would depend on why you want to cancel it."

"I keep thinking about what Anne said, about our father. If she's right, I may not have a lot of time left with him. Not only that, but I think I need to see him for myself, but he's going to be in England for at least another week. Maybe longer. I'm thinking I should go stay with him. Just a few days."

"I think that's a good idea," he said.

She looked up at him. "You do?"

He touched her cheek. "Louisa, he's your father. Of course he should come first."

"I would leave this afternoon and fly back either Wednesday or Thursday."

"Take all the time you need. I'll still be here when you get back."

"You promise?"

He smiled. "I promise."

"Have I told you how wonderful you are?"

"Yeah, but you can tell me again." There was a smile in his voice, and it made her smile, too. "I suppose this means our trip to Cabo will have to wait awhile?"

"Are you angry?"

"Of course not."

She got up on her toes to press a kiss to his lips. "You're wonderful, and I'm going to miss you."

"You won't be on a different planet. We can still talk on the phone."

"I'd like that. In fact, if it's as bad as Anne has led me to believe, I might just need someone to talk to."

"In that case, I promise I'll call you every night."

"I'm terrified of what I'm going to find when I get there."

"Whatever it is, you'll deal with it. You're stronger than you give yourself credit for, you know."

She hoped so. "It would be so much harder going through this alone. I'm glad I met you, Garrett."

"You wouldn't be alone. You have your family."

"Yes, but they don't see me the way you do. They don't really listen to me, or take me seriously. But I know that you really care how I feel. I don't know what I would do without you."

"You never have to worry about that," he said.

She wondered if that was his way of saying that he wanted to marry her without actually saying it. But the truth was, right now she didn't care what it meant. She was just thankful to have him.

"How much time have you got?" she asked him.

He glanced at his watch. "A few minutes. Why?"

She slid her hands under his jacket and up his chest. "Well, since we won't see each other for several days, I thought we could spend some quality time together."

He grinned. "Oh, did you?"

"But if you only have a few minutes…"

He looped his arms around her and walked her backward toward the bed. "I'll make time," he growled, his eyes dark with desire.

Though he did eventually make it to work, he was very late.

Garrett did call her, just as he'd promised, and thank goodness she had him to talk to. Because things weren't as bad as Anne described. They were worse.

In the week he had been gone, it seemed as if her father had aged a decade. He was thin and sallow, as though the life had been sucked out of him, and when she embraced him, he felt frail. Gone was the strong and vibrant king. The leader. And in that instant she knew, without a shadow of a doubt, that he would never be coming back. Anne had been right. He'd lost his will to fight. His desire to live. It was a matter of time now.

Oddly enough, the person she felt more sorry for was her mother. She looked utterly exhausted and so brittle that with the slightest agitation, she could easily shatter.

"So, tell me about this new man of yours," her father

said, trying to sound jovial, but his voice was thready and weak.

"He's wonderful. He's handsome and smart and fun."

"Sounds like me," he said with a wink. "I'm anxious to meet him. I've heard good things from your brother."

It was odd, because this courtship hadn't been at all what she had imagined. She had expected it to be like a dream, like a fairy tale come true. Garrett would ride in like a knight in shining armor and whisk her away to a fantasy land. He would wine and dine her and take her on exotic trips. But thanks to security, they hadn't even had an actual date! And he hadn't showered her with lavish gifts and attention, like other men. He hadn't treated her like royalty at all. He'd treated her like…a person. And the strange thing was, she liked it. By acting the opposite of what she had expected, he'd won her heart.

"I know I've said this before about other men, but I really think he's the one. I…I like the way I feel when I'm with him. I like who I am."

"And who is that?" her mother asked.

"*Me*. And he seems to appreciate me for who I am."

"Are you saying I might finally get to walk one of my daughters down the aisle?" her father asked.

"It looks that way," she said, and oh, how she hoped he could. But if he couldn't be there physically, she knew he would be there in spirit. In her heart. "He hasn't actually asked yet, but I have this feeling it might be soon."

"You'll let us know the minute he does?" her mother prompted.

"I promise."

They chatted for a while, her parents carrying on as if everything was fine. They asked how Melissa was feeling, and how Chris was adjusting to having her away from home. They asked about Liv's research and if Aaron was still assisting her in the lab. They even asked about Muffin, who Louisa had left in the care of Elise, one of the maids. She had small children who loved to play with and pamper him, and an elderly mother who adored him. Of course Muffin, being a total attention hound, was in his glory. He needed someone who had more time to devote to him. Louisa confessed to her parents that as much as she loved him, in light of everything that was happening lately, she might let Elise keep him permanently.

After a while her father drifted off to sleep and her mother motioned her out into the private waiting room next door. As soon as they were there, she pulled her mother into her arms and gave her a big hug.

"What's this for?" she asked.

"Because you look like you need it."

"Oh, I'm fine," she said, waving Louisa's concerns away with the flip of her wrist. "I'm just a little tired. And homesick."

"And worried about Father?"

"Nothing to worry about," she said brightly, but Louisa could hear the undertone of strain in her voice, like guitar strings stretched too taut. "His cardiologist was in yesterday and he's still confident the heart pump will do its job and your father will be back on his feet in no time. We just have to be patient."

A week ago Louisa probably would have believed her, despite all the evidence to the contrary. She would have believed it because it was what she wanted to hear. Now the blinders were off and she was ready to view the world from all sides.

"That's a nice fantasy," Louisa told her. "Now, why don't you tell me what he really said."

She gave her mother credit. She managed to hold it together for a good ten seconds, but then everything in her seemed to let go and she crumbled before Louisa's eyes. In the past that might have scared Louisa to death, but now she just took her mother into her arms and held her while she sobbed her heart out. She stroked her hair and rubbed her back, the way her mother had for Louisa when she was little. When the downpour finally ceased, Louisa handed her a tissue, and as she dabbed her eyes, it seemed as though some of the stress she'd been carrying around had lifted.

"I'm sorry I fell apart like that," she said. "I must look a fright."

"We all need a good cry every now and then. And you look beautiful, as always."

"It's just been a long few weeks. A long few *years,* actually."

"It's not working, is it?" Louisa said. "The pump."

Her mother shook her head. "There should have been a much more drastic improvement since the last time they checked. They could leave him on it, but the longer he stays on, the odds of infection increase. In his weakened state it could be fatal."

"And without the pump?"

"He could live as long as a few years."

But they both knew he probably wouldn't. He didn't have the strength left. Or the will.

"What are the chances he would have another heart attack?" Louisa asked.

"Very likely."

"And the odds he would survive?"

"Slim to none. There's just too much damage already."

"How did he take the news?"

"You know, I think in a way he was…relieved. He's fought so hard. Maybe he feels he finally has an excuse to surrender without letting us down."

"He could never let me down," Louisa told her. Maybe it was partially due to the seed that Anne had planted in her brain, but after seeing his condition and talking with him, she honestly believed that he was ready to let go. It was his time.

The pain she felt when she thought of losing him was indescribable. Like a thousand arrows straight through the heart, yet knowing that he had made peace with the idea of dying was a deep comfort.

She was surprisingly calm when she talked to Garrett that night and explained the situation. Not that she wasn't sad or upset, but crying wouldn't help anyone at this point.

"If you need me, I can be on the next flight to London," Garrett told her more than once. "Just say the word and I'll be there."

It was so tempting to say yes, but she needed to do this alone. To know that she *could*. Because if she could handle this, she figured she could handle just about anything.

After they hung up, she booted up her laptop to research any information she could find about her father's condition. What they could expect to happen near the end. Waiting for her in her mailbox was another message from her pal the Gingerbread Man. It read, Send the old man my regards.

Thirteen

A well of emotions crashed down on Louisa like a tidal wave and she was suddenly so filled with rage, her first instinct was to lob her computer out the window and watch it smash onto the London streets below. She couldn't recall a time in her life when she had ever felt so angry at another human being.

So he knew where she was, *big bloody deal.* These childish little games he was playing were just plain ridiculous. He needed to grow a pair and confront her face-to-face.

Though they had been strictly forbidden from answering his e-mails for fear that it would provoke him, she'd had enough. Maybe they *should* provoke him, draw him out into the open where he could be identified and captured.

She wrote back, You're a coward.

She clicked the send button and it felt good. It gave her a sense of power.

Barely a minute later another e-mail appeared from him. It said, Careful, Lulu. Or Daddy won't be the only one to shuffle loose the mortal coil.

Seeing him use her nickname and what was a very direct threat gave her such a serious case of the creeps that she slammed the computer shut. Maybe replying to him hadn't been such a good idea after all. What if he did lash out? What if someone was hurt? Then it would be completely her fault.

Damn! If only she would think before she acted. She had to stop being so selfish. So quick to fly off the handle.

At the risk of further restricting her already limited freedom, she opened her computer back up and forwarded the e-mail to the head of security at the palace, then she called Chris to give him a heads-up.

"He's a persistent son of a bitch," Chris noted. "How many e-mails is it now, Louisa? Four or five in the past two weeks?"

"But…how did you—"

"I had the feeling you might be less than honest, so I've been monitoring your e-mail."

"My *private* e-mail?"

"Don't worry, security is under strict orders to read only the messages that come from him."

She wanted to scream at him, tell him that he had no right to violate her privacy, but how could she be angry when he was right? She *had* lied to him. And by doing so, she could have been putting everyone in danger. "I can't seem to stop letting you down, can I?" she lamented.

"I noticed that, too."

"I've been so selfish."

"Yes, you have. Although it probably hasn't helped that we've spent the last twenty-seven years sheltering and spoiling you."

"I don't want to be that person anymore, Chris. I'm tired of her. I want to grow up. I want to be responsible."

"I think we would all appreciate that."

She thought about what she had just done and frowned. "However…there is one last really stupid and irresponsible thing I have to confess to first."

"Oh God, what did you do?"

She told him about the e-mail that she sent to the Gingerbread Man.

"That *was* stupid. You know what they said about provoking him. What's the point of keeping all of this security around if we don't bother to listen?"

"Maybe this time they're wrong. What if we *should* be antagonizing him? Maybe we should draw him out so they can catch him."

"You know that's too dangerous."

"I'm beginning to wonder if it might be worth the risk. I mean, how much longer can we live like this, Chris? Constantly on high alert? Somebody has to *do* something."

"We're *all* frustrated, Louisa, but finding him isn't worth risking anyone's safety. You just have to be patient."

But she was tired of being patient. Sweet, patient, obedient—for the most part anyway—Princess Louisa. She was sick to death of her.

All the time they wasted worrying about their stalker

and what he *might* do was time they should spend living life to the fullest.

And from now on, living her life was exactly what she intended to do.

Garrett was bloody exhausted by the time he trudged up the steps and opened his front door Tuesday night. It had been another long, grueling day and all he wanted to do now was change out of his suit, collapse into bed and call Louisa. Hearing her voice had become the highlight of his day. But he looked forward to tomorrow evening, when she would finally return home. That phrase about absence making the heart grow fonder seemed to have some truth to it.

He let himself inside, dropped his briefcase at the foot of the stairs and headed to the kitchen for a drink. From the hallway he could see the light was on, and since the nurse had left more than an hour ago, that meant Ian was still up.

As odd as it was, Garrett had grown a bit fond of not coming home to an empty house. He didn't resent Ian's presence nearly as much as he thought he would. He no longer had the feeling that any second the other shoe was going to fall, or that he would arrive home from work and his house would be cleaned out. In fact, there were times when he actually enjoyed Ian's company.

But tonight, as he stepped into the kitchen, Ian wasn't alone.

"Louisa?"

Grinning brightly, she sat across from Ian at the kitchen table, a half-finished bottle of beer in front of her on the table. "Surprised to see me?"

Without even thinking about what he was doing, he

rounded the table and scooped up Louisa from her chair. She threw her arms around his neck and hugged him, and the stress of the entire day seemed to evaporate into thin air. He set her down and breathed in the scent of her hair and her skin, relished the feel of her body pressed against him. If Ian hadn't been sitting right there, he and Louisa would have been doing a lot more than just embracing.

Louisa on the other hand didn't seem to care that his brother was in the room. She rose up on her toes and pressed her lips to his. It wasn't a passionate kiss, but it wasn't exactly chaste, either. He considered her more of a champagne and caviar kind of woman, but he had to admit that the flavor of the ale on her lips was a major turn-on.

"I thought you weren't coming home until tomorrow," he said.

She grinned up at him. "I missed you. And I thought it would be fun to surprise you. I even made my security detail hide so you wouldn't see them."

They were apparently good at it, because he hadn't had a clue that they were there. "I'm definitely surprised. Have you been here long?"

"Only an hour or so."

"If I had known I would have left work earlier."

"That's okay." She looked over at Ian and smiled. "Your brother and I have been having a very nice chat."

Garrett regarded him curiously. "Oh, have you?"

Ian grinned. "Don't worry, I didn't tell her anything *too* embarrassing."

Or anything having to do with Garrett's ulterior

motives, he hoped. Of course, if he had, Garrett doubted Louisa would be so happy to see him.

Is this the way it would be from now on? Garrett always paranoid that something might slip and she would learn the truth? *And how would she take it?* he wondered. As far as he was concerned, the only thing that mattered was the way he felt about her right here. Right now.

"How long can you stay?"

"I told Chris that I wouldn't be home tonight." She gestured down the hall and said, "Can we talk upstairs?" Her expression gave him the feeling something might be wrong. Maybe Ian had said something.

"Of course."

He shot Ian a questioning look. Ian shrugged, as if to say, *Don't ask me.*

Louisa smiled at Ian. "It was really nice talking with you, Ian."

"You, too," Ian said.

"I know everything will work out."

Ian smiled and nodded.

Garrett wondered what that was about, but he was more concerned with what was on Louisa's mind. There was something about her tonight. Something... different.

Maybe it was her clothes. Clothes that for her, he suddenly noticed as she preceded him up the stairs, could almost be considered racy. She wore a sleeveless, fitted top made from a gauzy, pale pink fabric that was so sheer, he could see the faintest outline of her bra underneath. She also wore a fitted skirt in a deep fuchsia that ended at least six inches above her knee, and a pair of strappy white sandals with a modest heel.

What had happened in London?

"How is your father?" he asked when they reached the top of the stairs.

"He's very…peaceful."

"That's good, right?"

She nodded and followed him into his bedroom. He closed and locked the door, then turned to ask what she wanted to talk about, but before he could she was back in his arms, hugging herself close to him. Because she seemed to need it, he hugged her back.

"I missed you so much," she said. She nuzzled her face against his shirt, her hair catching in the stubble on his chin.

"I missed you, too."

"I did a lot of thinking while I was gone, about us and our future. I used to be so sure about everything, but now everything has changed. I've changed."

"I felt it. The second I saw you I knew something was different."

"I think I grew up."

"When you say everything has changed, do you mean us?"

"I know I said I want to wait until I'm married to make love, but now I'm thinking, maybe I shouldn't."

Making love to Louisa was pretty much all he'd been able to think of lately, but pushing her into something she wasn't ready for would be a mistake. "I thought waiting was important to you."

"It was. It *is*. But what if I was waiting for the wrong thing? What if it's not about the marriage vows?"

"What *is* it about?"

"The way I feel about you. Right now. I'm pretty sure

I love you, Garrett. In fact, I *know* I do. And I want you to be the first."

"I just don't want you to do something you'll regret later." Maybe, in a way, he didn't feel worthy. He didn't deserve something so special.

"Garrett, if we never made love, then something happened and things didn't work out, I would regret it the rest of my life."

"What makes you think it won't work out?"

"The way things have been going in my life lately, I'd be wise not to take anything for granted."

"I want to," he said. "You have no idea how much I want to. But it feels like we're just jumping into this."

"On the contrary, it's all I've been thinking about. This is not a hasty decision on my part."

"Well, maybe *I* need more time."

A quirky grin curled her lips.

"What?" he asked.

"It's just funny. I'm the virgin, and *you* need time. Most men would jump at the chance to defile me."

She was right. And a couple weeks ago, he might have been one of them. But he wasn't that man anymore. And he had her to thank for that. Being with her had forced him to take a good hard look at his life.

He shrugged and remarked, "I guess I'm just not most men."

"And that," she said, reaching up to stroke his cheek, "is why I want to make love to *you*."

"How about a compromise? Right now we don't say yes or no. We just let things progress naturally, and if it happens, it happens."

"I would be willing to compromise," she said. "If it happens, it happens."

Something in her expression, in the impish smile she was wearing, led him to believe it would be happening sooner rather than later.

"Until then there are other things we could do," she continued as she shoved his suit jacket off his shoulders and let it drop to the floor.

"What things?"

"Kissing." She tugged his tie loose and pulled it from around his neck. "And touching."

She unfastened the buttons on his shirt and it hit the floor in seconds flat.

"Are you in some kind of hurry?" he asked.

"I've just been dying to get my hands on you," she admitted. "And this time I want to touch *everything.*"

She wasn't going to get an argument from him. He just hoped she understood that she would have to play fair. A tit for a tat—pardon the expression. Or more appropriately, you can touch mine if I can touch yours.

She jerked the hem of his undershirt from the waist of his slacks and he helped her pull it over his head. She looked at his bare chest as though she had been fasting and he was her first meal in months.

"I love your chest," she said, laying her hands on him. "I love all of you, but I think this is my favorite."

She leaned forward and kissed one nipple, then the other, then she licked him. It was hot as hell, but what really turned him on was the look of pure ecstasy on her face as she did it. She looked halfway there already and he hadn't even touched her yet.

She slid her hands down his chest and across his stomach to the waist of his slacks. She undid the button, pulled the zipper down, then hooked her thumbs under the waistband and eased them down, leaving only his boxers resting low on his hips. He was so hard it seemed they barely contained him.

He waited for her to take those off, too, but instead she said, "Why don't you lie down?"

He climbed into bed and reclined with his head against the pillows. He expected her to climb in with him, but instead she pulled her shirt over her head, then reached behind her and unhooked her bra. As soon as that hit the floor, she tugged the skirt, which must have been made of some sort of stretchy material, down her hips and let it drop to the floor. When the score was even, both of them in only their underwear, she climbed on the bed and knelt beside him.

Suddenly Louisa wasn't admiring his chest anymore. Her eyes were glued to his crotch.

"It looks...*big*," she said.

"Why don't you touch me and find out for yourself?"

Looking excited and nervous all at once, she reached over and laid her hand on him. After a second or two she slid her hand back and forth, up and down the entire length of him. He couldn't begin to count how many women had touched him like this, but he couldn't recall it ever feeling this fantastic. He usually preferred a woman who knew her way around a man's body. At least, he used to. But watching Louisa touch him, knowing she had never touched a man this way before, was one of the hottest things he had ever seen.

"Feels pretty big to me," she confirmed, her eyes, and her hand, never straying from his hard-on. "But just to be sure that I'm making an accurate estimation, maybe I should take off your boxers."

"You're probably right," he agreed.

Looking as though she were about to unwrap a Christmas gift, she took hold of the waistband of his boxers and eased them down. He lifted his hips to help and when she got them to his feet, he kicked them away.

She made a soft sighing sound, as though she liked what she was seeing. For several seconds she just looked, then reached out and tentatively touched him.

"It's not going to bite," he said.

With a wry smile she repeated the question he'd asked only a few minutes ago. "Are you in some kind of hurry?"

Yes and no.

She wrapped her hand around him and squeezed, and Garrett inhaled sharply. Then she started stroking him and he was in ecstasy.

"Is this right?" she asked.

He groaned his approval and his eyes drifted shut.

"I think I was wrong. This is my favorite part of your body."

In that case, he could think of several ways she could show her appreciation, the majority using her mouth. But he knew that would be pushing too far, too fast. It could be weeks, or even months before she was ready for that, or maybe never. Some women just didn't get off on that sort of thing.

No sooner had the thought formed when Louisa leaned over, the ends of her hair tickling his stomach. He thought, *No way, not even possible.* He felt her breath, warm and moist. Then, starting at the base of his erection, with the flat of her tongue, she licked him, moving slowly upward, and when she reached the tip, the sensation was so intense he jerked.

Louisa lifted her head and shot him a curious look.

In a gravelly voice he said, "Sorry. I just wasn't expecting that."

"Should I stop?"

"No!" he said, a bit too forcefully, then added in a much calmer tone, "Not if you don't want to."

She answered him by doing it again, only this time when she reached the tip, she took him into her mouth. Garrett groaned and tangled his fingers through her hair.

Granted, it took a few tries to get the angle and the rhythm right and she got him with her teeth a couple times, but that didn't seem to matter because within minutes he was barely hanging on.

"If you don't stop, you're going to get more than you bargained for," he warned her, and either she didn't know what he meant, or she didn't care, because instead of stopping, she took him deeper in her mouth.

So damned deep that he instantly lost it.

If there was a world record for the fastest, most intense orgasm, Garrett was pretty sure he'd just broken it. When he opened his eyes, Louisa was still on her knees beside him, grinning.

"I've read that there are women who don't like doing that, but I can't imagine why. I thought it was awesome."

He closed his eyes and said a silent prayer of thanks.

"I'm sorry if I was a little awkward," she said.

He couldn't believe she was *apologizing*. Watching Louisa take him in her mouth, knowing he was the first, just might have been the single most erotic experience of his adult life. Although he was sure that eventually she would manage to top that, too.

"I guess there are some things you just can't learn from a book," she said thoughtfully. "Although I'm sure with practice I'll get better."

He honestly didn't think it could get much better, but he wasn't going to argue. "Feel free to practice on me as often as you like."

"Like right now?" she said, an eager gleam in her eyes. He realized she was serious. She would do it again. Right here, right now. As tempted as he was to say yes, he could never be that selfish.

The only thing he wanted right now was to make *her* feel good.

Fourteen

"Let's try something different instead," Garrett told Louisa, and she was disappointed—right up until the instant he put his hand on her knee then slid it up her inner thigh.

"Why don't we switch places," he suggested, so she took his spot against the pillow and he knelt beside her.

He stroked her thighs, starting low, then moving higher each time, until he was barely grazing the edge of her panties with each pass.

"Has anyone ever touched you like this before?" he asked.

"Does it count if I had clothes on?"

"Nope."

"Then I guess not."

"Then I guess no one ever did this, either." He brushed his fingers against the crotch of her panties and it felt so good Louisa moaned and spread her thighs farther apart. She didn't have to feel it to know that she was so wet, she'd soaked right through the lace.

He slipped his fingers under the edge of her panties and Louisa shuddered. He looked up at her and asked, "You shave?"

"Wax, actually."

"Everything?"

She nodded. "I read that some men like that."

He grinned. "I think I'm going to need a better look before I form a definitive conclusion."

So they were going to play *this* game again. "Do what you must."

Still grinning he hooked his fingers under the edge and slowly pulled the panties down and off her feet, then he tossed them over his shoulder and across the room. Was he worried she might try to put them back on? He knelt between her legs, spreading her thighs apart—*far apart*—then he just looked at her, and as he did, he started getting hard again. It excited and thrilled her to know that he was turned on simply by looking at her.

"Well?" she asked.

He shrugged apologetically. "Still not sure."

His erection said otherwise, but okay, she would play along.

"It might help if you touched me," she said, keeping with the script.

His smile turned feral and there was something wicked behind his eyes. "You're right," he conceded. "That would probably work." He scooted closer, then, instead of using his hands, he leaned forward and brushed his lips against her bare mound. It was so not what she expected, so exciting, Louisa gasped and fisted the sheet.

He had strayed from the script by totally reworking the touching scene.

Garrett looked up at her, wearing a mischievous grin.

"You cheated."

"Just keeping things exciting. Did you want me to stop?"

She glared at him.

He shrugged and said, "Just asking."

He leaned forward and kissed her again, then he licked her and she nearly vaulted off the bed.

He shot her another look and opened his mouth to speak and she said, "Ask me if I want to stop and I'll *hurt* you."

She could tell by his grin that she was right, and this time when he lowered his head, she tangled her fingers through his hair, just in case he got the idea that he would stop again.

But this time he didn't stop. He kissed and nibbled, teased her with his tongue, everywhere but the one place that needed to be kissed and nibbled and teased the most. He drove her to the point of mindless frustration, every muscle coiled so blasted tight she felt like a spring ready to snap.

She shifted her hips, trying to align his mouth just right, but went left when he would go right, and he ended up on the complete opposite side from where he was supposed to be. He got fed up with all of her wiggling and used his weight to pin her against the mattress. She realized the only way to get her point across was to just come right out and tell him.

She opened her mouth to give him a gentle pointer, when suddenly he found her center, and the word she'd been forming came out like a garbled moan. He took her into his mouth and the spring gave its final stretch then snapped like a dry twig, then it sparked and ignited, and burst into flames.

Louisa was still gasping for breath when Garrett flopped down next to her on his side and said, "I'm sorry if I was a little awkward."

She laughed weakly and gave him a playful shove. "You're making fun of me."

He smiled and pushed back a lock of hair that had fallen across her cheek. "Yep."

"What you really need is a geography lesson."

He frowned. "Geography of what?"

"The female anatomy."

He looked confused, then he realized what she meant and laughed. "Is that what all that squirming was for?"

"I was trying to help. You kept missing the target. Though for the life of me, I don't know how. It's right there in the middle."

"Did it ever occur to you that I might have been missing it for a reason?"

"To do what? *Torture* me?"

His grin said that was exactly what he was doing. "You can't tell me you didn't enjoy it."

She could, but it would be a lie.

"I guess I see your point." She rolled close and snuggled up against him, laying her head on his chest, touching him. She just couldn't seem to get close enough, get enough of her hands on his skin. It just felt so...good. But she still wanted more.

She used to hear girls talk about saving themselves

for marriage, and a month or two later admit that they'd given in and slept with their boyfriend. She never got why they didn't just wait. But now, for the first time in her life, she understood. All the kissing and touching and orgasms in the world wouldn't satiate this yearning to be closer to him. To be connected in a way she never had been before.

"I can hardly believe that I'm twenty-seven and I've never been in bed with a naked man before," she said.

"Well, technically, neither have I. But you don't hear me bragging about it."

She laughed and tickled his ribs, making him squirm.

He batted her hand away. "Don't do that."

"Why, are you ticklish?"

He frowned. "I refuse to answer that on the grounds that it might incriminate me."

She waited a minute or two, then did a sneak attack on his belly and he nearly jumped out of his skin. There was nothing more adorable than a big, tough man who was ticklish.

His tone stern, he said, "*Don't,* Louisa."

Two minutes ago didn't he admit to deliberately torturing her? And he thought she would cut him any slack?

She dove for his armpit, but he was too quick. He captured her wrists and rolled her onto her back, pinning her to the mattress with the weight of his body, and just like that, they were back in the position they had been in the other day, his erection cradled between her legs, only this time there were no clothes to get in the way. This time it was just skin against skin.

Just like before they both went completely still and Garrett got that *what-have-I-done* look.

"If it happens, it happens," she reminded him, but they both seemed to realize that, ready or not, it was happening.

In an odd way, she sort of felt as if she was the veteran and he was the virgin, which certainly put an interesting spin on things.

She pulled free of his grasp, wrapped her arms around his neck and kissed him. For a while that was all they did…kissed and touched, and it was really…*sweet*. But she didn't want sweet. She wanted sexy and crazy and out of control. Grinding and thrusting and writhing in ecstasy. She was *aching* for it. But every time she tried to move things along, he shut her down. If she tried to touch his erection, he would intercept her hand and put it on his chest instead. If she tried to kiss his throat or nibble his ear, he would duck out of the way. It was almost as if, the instant he realized where this was going, he'd switched off emotionally. Now she was feeling more frustrated than aroused.

She slipped her hand down from his shoulder, and when she hit the fleshy part just below his underarm, she gave it a good, hard pinch.

"Ow!" He jerked his arm away and looked at the red mark she'd created. "What was that for?"

"I thought you might enjoy actually feeling something."

His expression softened. "Louisa, what are you talking about? Of course I feel something."

She shrugged. "I couldn't tell."

"I'm just taking it slow."

"I noticed." At the rate he was going, she would be

eighty before they finally made love. "I have an idea. Let's pretend I'm not a virgin. Make love to me like you would if this wasn't my first time."

"But it is, and I don't want to hurt you."

"Maybe I want you to hurt me. I'd rather feel pain than feel *nothing!*"

Anger sparked in his eyes and she thought, *good, at least he's feeling something*. Now that she had her foot in the door, rather than back down, she stoked the fire.

"Do you even want this, Garrett?"

"You know that I do," he growled.

"Then bloody well act like it or stop wasting my time!"

Garrett stared down at Louisa, his temper blazing, unable to believe what he'd just heard her say. What had happened to his sweet, innocent princess?

Good riddance to her, he thought. He liked this Louisa better anyway. She had spunk and passion. This Louisa, the one who was now unflinchingly meeting his eye, unwilling to back down until he realized what an ass he was being, would never bore him.

She was right, he was trying like hell not to feel this, because he knew deep down that once he made love to her, once he accepted the gift that she offered with no question or reserve, every one of his defenses would crumble. He might be taking her virginity, but in exchange she would be taking from him something even more remarkable. The love in a heart he believed he had locked away for good.

If passion was what she wanted, that's what he would give her.

He wrapped a hand under the back of her neck,

lifted her head right off the pillow and crushed his lips to hers. If he startled her, she didn't let it show. She moaned against his lips and wrapped herself around him, pressing her body to his.

Everything they had done up to now, all the kissing and touching, had been child's play. Right here, right now, this was the real thing. He held nothing back, and neither did she. Her ability to give herself so freely, with no shame or hesitation, never ceased to amaze him.

Her body language said she was more than ready, and he could only endure so much of her writhing around underneath him. He was considering warning her first, so she could prepare herself before he took the plunge, but he never got the chance. He rocked against her and as he did, she arched up, by some fluke of nature creating the perfect angle, and the next thing he knew, he was inside her.

Louisa's eyes went wide and she gasped softly, her mouth forming a perfect *O,* and he imagined he was wearing a similar expression.

"Did you mean to do that?" she asked.

He shook his head. "It just…happened."

Was it fate? She had talked about that often during their phone conversations while she was in London, how she used to believe in it, but now she wasn't so sure. He never believed in things like fate and Karma, but the ease of their bodies coming together in what seemed to be perfect sync, could that really be an accident? *Everything* about their relationship seemed somehow… predisposed.

"You're all the way in, right?" Louisa asked.

"As far as I can go." And she was tight. Tight and wet and warm. And wonderful.

She blinked, looking adorably confused, and asked, "When is it going to hurt?"

"Actually, if it was going to, I think it would have already." *Now can we please get on with it?*

"But it's *supposed* to," she insisted.

Well, that had to be a first, a virgin who *wanted* sex to hurt.

"I don't know what to tell you," he said.

She opened her mouth to say something, and before she got a word out, he covered her lips with his and kissed her. Not so easy for her to talk with his tongue in her mouth.

He started to move inside her, slow and easy, savoring the sensation of slippery walls hugging him so tightly, knowing that at this rate he would be lucky to last five minutes.

Louisa sighed against his lips, tunneled her fingers through his hair, looking as though she was in pure ecstasy. It took all of his concentration, and a little extra he didn't even know he had, to keep up the slow, steady pace.

Louisa pushed at his chest, saying, "I want to see."

He leaned back and braced himself up on his arms, increasing the friction and giving all new meaning to the word *torture*. He could barely watch as Louisa rose up on her elbows, spreading her legs wide so to gaze at the place where their bodies were joined.

"That's us," she whispered, her face flushed, her eyes glazed and full of wonder. "You're inside me, Garrett."

If she was going to give him a play-by-play, he wouldn't last five seconds. He was barely hanging on as it was, then Louisa's head rolled back and her body began to tremble with release, clamping down around him, squeezing and contracting until he lost it, too, riding out the crest of the wave with her.

Louisa was no longer a virgin.

She always thought that afterward she would feel different somehow, that anyone who looked at her would just *know*. But as she and Garrett lay wrapped around each other, arms and legs entwined, she didn't really feel any different. There was something else she didn't feel, either. Regret.

Wait a minute…had they…?

"Garrett?"

"Hmm," he mumbled sleepily.

"Did we…*forget* something?" she asked. "When we made love?"

"If we did, it's going to have to wait, because I need to sleep for a while."

"Garrett, did we use birth control?"

He was quiet for a minute, like he was scanning the memory banks, then he mumbled a curse.

She cringed. "Should I take that as a no?"

"Maybe I was thinking you had it covered, or maybe I just *wasn't* thinking. I don't know."

"My period is due any second, so odds are that I'm not fertile, but there's no guarantee."

He nodded and yawned. "Okay."

She untangled herself from him and sat up. "You're not worried?"

He pried one eye open and peered up at her. "Didn't you just tell me not to be?"

"I also said there's no guarantee."

He shrugged. "So we'll wait and see."

"That's it?"

"I don't see what you're so worried about," he grumbled. "Aren't you the one who said you want sixteen kids?"

"I didn't say sixteen, I said *six*. And yes, of course I want kids. But I also don't want to get you stuck in a situation you don't want to be in."

"You won't."

"How can you know that?"

"Because I know."

"But *how?*"

Garrett pushed himself up on his elbows and rubbed his eyes with his thumb and forefinger. "Okay, I was going to wait and do this right, with a nice candlelit dinner and maybe some soft music playing. But if it'll ease your mind, and you don't mind that I haven't gotten the ring yet, or the fact that I'm too bloody tired to get on one knee, I could ask you to marry me right now."

She bit her lip, to hold back the huge smile that was just dying to get out. He wanted to *marry* her.

"No, that's okay," she said. "I can wait."

"Does that mean I can sleep now?"

"Of course."

He collapsed back down and closed his eyes. Unfortunately, she wasn't the least bit tired. She had just lost her virginity and Garrett had more or less proposed to her. How could she even think of sleeping? Not to mention that there was the slightest possibility that she could be *pregnant!* If she was, her baby would be close in age to the triplets. Who could be born very soon.

"Garrett?" she said softly.

He groaned.

"Sorry. I just wondered if you would mind me using your computer. I wanted to look online for some gifts for the babies, since getting out to shop these days is complicated, to say the least."

He nodded and grumbled something incoherent.

"Thanks!" She pressed a kiss to his cheek and rolled out of bed. Since she didn't feel like getting dressed, she found a robe hanging on the back of his closet door and slipped it on. She thought about going downstairs and making herself a cup of tea, but Ian was camped out on the family-room couch and she didn't want to disturb him.

Garrett's office was across the hall at the opposite end, and typically male. Lots of glass and steel and hundreds of books. She'd never realized what an avid reader he must be. But she had pulled a few strings and discovered that he had graduated at the top of his class at both primary school and university. She hoped their children would inherit his intelligence. Not that she was a dummy. Louisa had done all right in school. Her problem was that she just didn't care.

Louisa doesn't work to her potential became her slogan for the better part of her childhood.

She made herself comfortable in Garrett's chair and when she touched the mouse, the computer screen flashed to life. His e-mail program was open and she was about to click it closed when she saw a list of e-mails with the subject: Princess Louisa. They had been sent back and forth between Garrett and someone named Weston. She noticed the oldest one dated back to the weekend of the charity ball. Had it really been less than three weeks ago? It felt as though she had known him forever.

Garrett probably wrote about meeting her, and how

magical it had been. Not that he would have used the term *magical,* but something equivalent in guy speak.

Louisa knew firsthand what it was like to have someone shuffling through her personal messages, and realized how wrong it would be to invade his privacy, but she was *dying* to know what he'd said about her.

Maybe if she just took a quick peek. Just the first one, and that was it.

She clicked it open, and as she expected, it was about her. But the more she read, she realized it had nothing to do with meeting her at the ball, and the things he'd written were never meant for her eyes. And as she clicked open one message after the other, it only got worse. She felt sick to her stomach and sick in her heart, and she finally had to face the realization that her family had been right about her all along. It was as though destiny had painted a target on her back that announced: *Use me! I'm dense and naive!*

A lot of men had taken aim and missed, but Garrett, the man she thought she would spend the rest of her life with, had hit the target dead on. He had her totally duped. And if she'd only been paying attention, if she'd bothered to look hard enough, maybe she would have noticed the arrow planted in her back.

Fifteen

Garrett jerked out of a sound sleep and bolted up in bed. He reached over to feel for Louisa, but the sheets were cold.

He'd been dreaming about his computer, about Louisa asking to use it. Or had that really happened?

They had talked about birth control, then he'd started dozing....

Yes. She'd asked to use it to shop for baby things.

Then he realized why he'd been jolted awake. He had closed his e-mail program, hadn't he?

He flung back the covers and groped around the floor for his slacks. If not, would she have noticed the e-mails with her name in the subject? And if she noticed them, would she have read them?

He yanked his pants on and was out the bedroom door before he even got them fastened. He half ran down the hall to his office and burst through the door, but he knew the second he saw her sitting there, her face ashen, that not only had she seen the e-mails, she'd read them, too.

Bloody goddamn hell.

Why hadn't he just erased them? Why leave evidence? Unless he actually wanted to get caught. Was living with the guilt of the way he had planned to use her too much to bear? And it was all there, every gruesome detail.

For what felt like an eternity he just stood there, at a loss for what to say. At a time like this, *I'm sorry* didn't even begin to cover it.

Finally she looked up at him and said in a very calm voice, "Everything my family has said, about me being too trusting and naive, I guess they were right."

"Louisa—"

"You and this Weston fellow must have had a good laugh at my expense. I mean, I fell for it, hook, line and sinker, didn't I? You had me totally duped."

"If you would just let me explain—"

"Explain what?" She gestured to the screen. "It's all right here. I've read each one at least a dozen times, so I'll never forget how stupid I've been."

The idea that she could believe he was that man, the one who had been so selfishly obsessed, made him sick. Why didn't she scream at him and call him names? Instead she sounded so...disappointed.

Anger he could handle, but this? This was...*awful*. It was heart wrenching and painful. It wasn't the first time he'd let someone down, but Louisa didn't deserve this.

"That's not me," he said. "Not anymore. I don't even recognize that man."

"People don't change, isn't that what you told me? You can't have it both ways."

She was using his own words against him. And could he blame her? He'd painted himself into this corner.

"I was an ass, I admit it. I was greedy and selfish, and yes, I used you, and I will never be able to adequately express how sorry I am for that. But then everything… changed. The money and the power, none of that matters to me now. *You* are the only thing that matters."

"I don't believe you. This is all just a game to you. I think you're just sorry that you lost, and you would do or say anything to get what you want." She shrugged and said, "What the hell, I should be thanking you. You've given me a gift, Garrett. You've finally made me see things clearly. See people for who they are. My family spent all those years sheltering me, but you gave me what I really needed. You've taught me how not to trust."

Her honesty, her ability to trust people enough to always say exactly what was on her mind, was what made her special and different from everyone else. And what she was telling him now was that he had killed that. He'd made her less than whole.

The idea that he had done that to her was almost too much to comprehend. No man should have that kind of power over another human being. Especially a man like him. And he would do anything, *anything* it took to turn the clock back, but there was no way to fix this. No way to repair the damage he'd done.

"I should go now," she said rising to her feet, wearing his robe. She walked past him to the door, but stopped halfway through and looked back. "Just so you know,

I don't regret that we made love. It doesn't make sense, but despite everything, I'm still glad it was you."

If she would hit him or cry or show some sort of emotion, he wouldn't feel so rotten. He would at least know that she cared. And as long as she cared there was still a chance. But her eyes looked…dead. The spark was gone.

He stood there listening as she dressed and gathered her things from his room and walked down the stairs. He heard the front door open, and hushed conversation between Louisa and her bodyguards. Then, when he heard it close, he had to fight to keep from going after her.

He wanted to beg her to stay. He wanted to tell her that without her in it, his life meant nothing.

But maybe without him around to poison her soul she would recover. Maybe someday she would be herself again.

It was no longer about what he wanted or needed. This was about Louisa. And the kindest thing he could do for her now was let her go.

On autopilot, Garrett walked down to the kitchen and made himself a cup of tea, then sat at the table, cupping the steaming mug in his hands, trying to chase away the chill that had settled in his bones.

He was still sitting there when Ian hobbled in, hours after the tea had gone cold.

Ian saw Garrett's wrinkled pants and robe, and with one brow lifted said, "Must have been some night. You're usually off to the gym by now."

"What time is it?" Garrett asked, but his voice was so rusty he had to clear his throat.

"After eight. Louisa still sleeping?"

"She left last night."

Ian limped to the stove and put the kettle on. "Sorry to hear that. She mentioned something about making crepes for breakfast. Maybe another time."

"There won't be another time."

Ian turned to him, frowning. "What do you mean?"

"I messed up. I lost her."

Ian turned the kettle off and crossed the kitchen, easing into the chair across from Garrett. "Give her a day or two to cool down. It's probably not as bad as it seems."

If only it were that simple. "No, it's pretty bad."

"Something to do with that plan your mate Wes mentioned?"

Since Garrett no longer had to worry about the truth getting out, he told Ian the entire grisly tale, right up to the confrontation in his office.

Ian winced. "Ah, you gotta hate it when they lay on the guilt. Women do love their drama."

"Louisa doesn't have a manipulative bone in her body."

"Don't misunderstand. I'm not suggesting she's doing it on purpose. Women just open their mouths and out it comes. They don't even realize it's happening."

"You didn't see her face. Her eyes. I think she honestly has no feelings left for me whatsoever."

"Take it from someone who's been in his share of relationships—she does. Besides, I've seen the way she looks at you. That woman loves you."

"Even if she does, I don't think I deserve her. Even if I could get her back, which seems bloody unlikely at this point, I'd always worry that I might screw up and disappoint her again."

"And you will. But so will she."

Somehow he couldn't imagine Louisa ever making a mistake. Other than trusting him.

"You love her, don't you?" Ian asked, and Garrett nodded. "Did you tell her?"

"I couldn't."

"Why the hell not?"

"Because she wouldn't have believed me. She would have thought I was saying it to try to win her back."

Ian nodded grimly. "Good point. It's confusing as hell, isn't it? Being in love. It's like you lose a part of yourself, but at the same time, you gain so much back."

"You sound as though you're speaking from experience."

Ian rubbed his palms together, his brow wrinkled. "I guess now is as good a time as any to tell you."

"Tell me what?"

"Though I appreciate all you've done for me, I'm going to be leaving soon."

"Where are you going?"

"Remember the girl I told you about? Maggie?"

"The farmer's daughter?" Garrett asked, and Ian nodded.

"Well, her father has offered to make me a partner in his cattle business. I've just been waiting for my leg to stabilize enough to travel."

"Why would he do that?"

"Because I'm going to be the father of his grand-child."

Garrett's jaw fell. He tried to come up with an appropriate response, but he was too flabbergasted to speak.

"Hard to believe, I know. *Me,* someone's papa."

"How long have you known?"

"A while. We found out a few weeks before her father chased me off. Maggie and I have been communicating behind her father's back ever since I left. We've been planning to run away together, but we needed money. That's why I took your car. I was going to sell it. But as I was driving away, I felt so damned guilty. Which of course was an odd sensation for me, seeing as how I never feel guilty. I really was bringing it back. I was going to tell you the truth and ask for your help. I was going to beg you for a job and maybe a small parcel of land to get started. A loan I could pay back over time."

"So why didn't you tell me the truth?"

"After the accident, I knew you would never believe me. I knew I would have to prove myself to you. As soon as I was able to work, I was going to get Maggie and bring her back here, but her parents found out she was pregnant and now they want me to come live with them instead." He leaned forward. "I know changing won't be easy, but I'm determined to try. I want to do right by my child. I won't make the mistakes our father made."

Garrett clasped his brother's hand. "Then you'll be a damned fine father. And a good man."

Ian gave his hand a squeeze then quickly turned away, but not before Garrett saw what looked like a tear spill from his eye. Ian got up from his chair and hobbled over to the stove to put on the kettle. "Might as well get comfortable. We have work to do."

"What kind of work?"

Ian turned to him and grinned. "We're going to figure out a way to get your princess back."

Louisa wanted to cry, but the tears wouldn't come. She wanted to scream and throw things, but she couldn't work up the will to feel angry. She wanted to hate Garrett for being so cold and calculating, for lying to her, but she couldn't make herself hate him.

The only emotion she had been able to feel was disgust. Disgust in herself, for letting this happen. For being so unsuspecting and so blind.

She'd come home from Garrett's in a daze and had gone straight to her room. She stood there for several minutes, looking around, really seeing it. The frilly pink curtains and canopy bed, the doll collection lining the wall. She was twenty-seven years old and she was living in a little girl's room.

Disgusted with herself, she shoved it all into trash bags. First thing the next morning, she picked up the phone and called a decorator. She didn't tell anyone or ask anyone's permission. She just did it, and surprisingly, no one seemed to care.

"You can't stay like this," Anne told her a few days later. She was the only one Louisa had confided in. She just couldn't bear facing the rest of them yet, knowing how disappointed they would be in her and how all this time they had been right.

"Stay like what?" she asked Anne.

"So unhappy. Without you to cheer me up and your

glass-half-full mentality, I could very possibly sink into a bottomless pit of negativity."

Louisa didn't want the responsibility any longer. She was sick of trying to convince herself and everyone else that everything was roses and sunshine. She wanted to start living in the real world. She even wondered, since she had never actually experienced real, soul-deep grief before, if this funk she had slipped into, this abyss of nothingness, was just her peculiar way of coping. She'd even stopped caring about the Gingerbread Man, who it would seem had slipped under the radar.

Five days after she and Garrett had split up, Louisa was in a meeting with her decorator finalizing the plans for her new room when Chris popped his head in. He was usually at the hospital with Melissa, so it was a pleasant surprise to see him. "Is this a bad time?"

"Not at all—we're just finishing up."

"In that case, why don't you come to the study? There's someone I want you to meet."

"Who?"

"A friend."

Curious as to who this mystery friend could be, she said goodbye to the decorator and followed Chris down the hall to the study. She followed him in, and when she saw the man standing by the window, dressed in jeans, a polo shirt and Docksiders, she froze.

"Louisa, this is a good friend of mine, Garrett Sutherland, and Garrett, meet my sister Princess Louisa."

Garrett walked slowly toward her, one hand tucked into his pants pockets, the other holding a thick legal-size manila envelope, and for the first time in days she finally felt something.

Confusion.

It must have shown on her face, because Garrett said, "I thought we should be reintroduced, since the man you met the first time, at the ball, wasn't really me."

Louisa looked at Chris, who didn't seem to find it the least bit unusual that he was reintroducing her to the man who, as far as he knew, she was planning to marry.

"He knows everything," Garrett explained. "I figured it would be best to come clean with everyone."

"Well, I've done my part," Chris told Garrett. "I'll leave you to it."

The idea of being alone with Garrett made Louisa's heart jump into her throat. "Leave you to what?"

"Win you back," Garrett declared, looking so confident it was unsettling. That night when he'd found her reading the e-mails, he had looked so beside himself, so at a loss for what to do or say, it had been empowering. It had given her the strength to do what she had to. She wasn't feeling quite so confident now.

"You can't have me," she told him.

"If you're so sure about that, then what's the harm in hearing me out?" He paused then added, "Unless you're afraid."

She wasn't afraid—she was *terrified*. But she couldn't let it show, because men like him fed off fear. "Fine," she said, walking to the sofa, remembering halfway there that it was where they had sat together his first time here, so she changed course for the chair instead. She sat primly on the edge, arms folded over her chest. "Say what you have to say. Even though it will be a waste of time."

"First," he began, taking a seat on the sofa and setting the envelope beside him, "I want to thank you."

Thank her? "For what?"

"For reading those e-mails. You needed to know the truth, and God knows I never would have had the guts to tell you myself. The fear of you someday finding out and of what it would do to us would have haunted me for the rest of my life."

She didn't know what to say to that, but he didn't seem to expect her to say anything.

"Second, for the record, as far as lies go, I only lied to you twice. And before you go saying that a lie by omission is still a lie," he continued, which was exactly what she'd been about to do, "you have to admit that it's at the very least a slippery slope, because *no one* says everything they're thinking one hundred percent of the time. And while I may not have always been forthcoming about my intentions, I was always honest. Except those two times."

"One was about your brother, right?"

"Right."

"So what was the other one?"

"No man, especially one with my past dating habits, forgets to use a condom."

Her jaw dropped. "You did that on *purpose?* Why? So I would *have* to marry you? And isn't it typically the woman who traps the man?"

He grinned, his dimple winking at her, and her knees went soft. "It had nothing to do with trapping you. It was more of a base instinct thing. My way of branding you or possessing you or something."

She frowned. "I'm pretty sure the last man to act on that particular instinct wore animal skins and carried a club."

"Nope. Men still do it. And if they don't, they want to. It's nature."

She didn't know if she was buying that.

"And, quite frankly, it feels better," he admitted, and she thought that sounded like a much more plausible excuse.

"But back to my original point. I lied twice. That's it."

Okay, fine, so he wasn't a liar. That didn't mean he wasn't a lot of other awful things that she wanted nothing to do with.

"Okay, third," he said, "for all the times in my life that I told myself I didn't give a damn what my father thought of me, I was still trying to impress him. To show him that he was wrong about me. And unfortunately, that desire manifested itself in an overdeveloped sense of greed and entitlement. Coincidentally, all the things you claimed to hate in men. I guess I was just good at hiding it."

"So, Daddy made you do it?" she snapped, and instantly felt guilty for the heartless comment. She was just no good at being snarky.

But Garrett didn't look wounded. "Don't misunderstand. It's not an excuse. What I did was wrong and inexcusable. It's only an explanation of why I acted that way."

"Do you still care?"

"What my father thinks?" He regarded her curiously, as though he'd never really considered it before. "I suppose I'll always care somewhere deep down, or at the very least, wish things were different. The difference is, now I know that the things my father said and did were his problem. They had nothing to do with me."

So, unresolved past family issues were always a nuisance, and she was glad that he'd finally made peace with it, but it had nothing to do with her. And it certainly didn't mean she could trust him.

"Okay, fourth, and this one is important so you need to really pay attention. You are *not* stupid or naive. In fact, you're one of the smartest, most resourceful people I know." He leaned forward, meeting her eye. "When I met you, Louisa, I was in a dark place. I had sunk about as low as I could go, but despite that, you saw the good in me. The *real* me that was trapped underneath all the lies. By putting your trust in me, you drew me back out into the light. You *saved* me. You also made me realize what's important." He picked up the envelope. "And it isn't this."

He held it out to her, and only when she took it did she realize her hands were trembling. Her heart was pounding, too. So hard it felt as if it might beat right through her chest.

"What's in here?" she asked.

"The deed to every parcel of land I own on both Thomas and Morgan Isle. Everything I own. Except my father's land. That one I want to keep."

He was going to sell his land?

"Of course, the names will have to be legally transferred," he explained. "But as far as I'm concerned, they're yours now."

"*Mine?* You're *giving* it to me?"

"Consider it an early wedding gift."

"But what if I won't marry you?"

He shrugged. "Then just consider it a gift."

"But…Garrett, this is your livelihood. Everything you've worked so hard for. You can't just give it away."

"I just did."

"But—"

"Louisa, I would rather be penniless than *ever* be that man again."

"But…what will you do?"

He shrugged. "Who knows, maybe I'll try farming."

God, he was serious. He was going to give up everything for her. But not just for her, for himself. *Everything.*

This was crazy.

No, this was Garrett. The real Garrett. The one she had fallen in love with. And *still* loved.

"Well," he said, rising from the couch, "that was pretty much all I came here to say. I won't take up any more of your time."

He made a move toward the door, and Louisa launched herself at him. She didn't even know she was going to do it until she was on her feet. But she knew, deep down to the depths of her soul, that she couldn't let him go. Not ever. And when his arms went around her and he held her close, all the emotions she thought might have shut down forever came rushing back at the same time.

It was a little overwhelming, and even a little scary, but it was wonderful.

Garrett buried his face in her hair, nuzzled her neck. "I love you so much, Louisa."

"I love you, too."

"As long as we both shall live?"

She squeezed him tighter. "Definitely. Even longer."

"I have a ring in my pocket with your name on it, and if you would let go for a second, I'll even get down on one knee."

Instead of letting go, she held him tighter. "The ring can wait. This can't."

For a long time they just held each other, and Louisa thought about marriage and babies and loving only him for the rest of her life, and she started having another feeling, one she was sure both she and Garrett would be feeling a lot from now on.

Happy.

* * * * *

THE TYCOON'S ULTIMATE CONQUEST

CATHY WILLIAMS

CHAPTER ONE

'THERE'S A PROBLEM,' the middle-aged man sitting in the chair in front of Arturo da Costa stated without preamble.

Art sat back, linked his fingers on his stomach and looked at Harold Simpson, a man who was normally calm, measured and so good at his job that Art couldn't think of a time when *anything* had been a problem for him. He ran the vast legal department of Art's sprawling empire with impeccable efficiency.

So at the word *problem* Art frowned, already mentally rescheduling the meeting he was due to attend in half an hour as he anticipated a conversation he wasn't going to enjoy, about a situation he would not have foreseen and which would be tricky to resolve.

'Talk to me,' he said, his deep voice sharp, knowing Harold was a rare breed of man who wasn't intimidated by his clever and unashamedly arrogant and unpredictable boss.

'It's the development in Gloucester.'

'Why is there a problem? I've got all the necessary planning permission. Money's changed hands. Signatures have been put on dotted lines.'

'If only it were that simple.'

'I don't see what could possibly be complex about this, Harold.'

'I suppose *complex* wouldn't quite be the right word, Art. *Annoying* might be the description that better fits the bill.'

'Not following you.' Art leaned forward, frowning. 'Don't I pay you to take care of annoying problems?'

Harold deflected the direct hit with a reprimanding look and Art grinned.

'You've never come to me with an annoying problem before,' he drawled. 'Perhaps I was rash in assuming that you dealt with them before they could hit my desk.'

'It's a sit-in.'

'Come again?'

Instead of answering, Harold opened up his laptop and swivelled it so that it was facing his boss, then leaned away as if waiting for the reaction he was expecting, a reaction which would have sent strong men diving for cover.

Fury.

Art looked at the newspaper article staring him in the face. It was from a local paper, circulation circa next to nothing, read by no one who mattered and covering an area where sheep probably outnumbered humans, but he could immediately see the repercussions of what he was reading.

His mouth tightened and he reread the article, taking his time. Then he looked at the grainy black-and-white picture accompanying the article. A sit-in. Protestors. Placards. Lots of moral high ground about the wicked, cruel developers who planned to rape and pillage the countryside. *Him*, in other words.

'Has this only now come to your attention?' He sat back and stared off into the distance with a thoughtful frown, his sharp mind already seeking ways of diverting the headache staring him in the face and coming up with roadblocks.

'It's been simmering,' Harold said as he shut the lid of his computer, 'but I thought I could contain the situation. Unfortunately, the lawyer working on behalf of the protesters has got the bit between her teeth, so to speak, and is determined to put as many obstacles in the way of your development as she can. Trouble is, in a small community like that, even if she loses the case and of course she will because, as you say, all the crosses have been made in the right boxes, the fallout could still be…unfortunate.'

'I admire your use of understatement, Harold.'

'She can rally the community behind her and the luxury development that should, in normal circumstances, sell in a heartbeat with the new train link due to open a handful of miles away, could find itself sticking on the open market. She's anti building on green fields and she's going to fight her corner, win or lose and come what may. Expensive people moving into expensive houses like to fancy themselves as mucking in with the locals and eventually becoming pillars of the community. They wouldn't like the prospect of the locals going quiet every time they walk into the village pub and pelting eggs against their walls in the dead of night.'

'I had no idea you had such impressive flights of fancy, Harold.' Art was amused but there was enough truth in what his lawyer had said to make him think. 'When you say *she*...?'

'Rose Tremain.'

'Miss... Mrs...or Ms?'

'Very definitely *Ms*.'

'I'm getting the picture loud and clear. And on the subject of pictures, do you have one of her? Is she floating around somewhere on the World Wide Web?'

'She disapproves of social media insofar as it personally pertains to *her*,' Harold said with a trace of admiration in his voice that made Art's eyebrows shoot up. 'No social media accounts...nothing of the sort. I know because I got one of my people to try to find out how we could follow her, try to get a broader picture of her, but no luck. There's the bones of past cases but no personal information to speak of at all. It would appear that she's old-fashioned like that.'

'There's another word for it,' Art drawled drily.

'I've only had dealings with her over the phone so far, and of course by email. I could give you my personal impressions...'

'I'm all ears.'

'Can't be bought off,' Harold said bluntly, instantly killing Art's first line of attack.

'Everyone has a price,' he murmured without skipping a beat. 'Have you any pictures of her at all?'

'Just something in one of the articles printed last week about the development.'

'Let's have a look.' Art waited, thinking, as Harold

expertly paged through documents in his pile of folders before eventually showing him an unsatisfactory picture of the woman in question.

Art stared. She *looked* like a *Ms*. The sort of feminist hippy whose mission might be to save the world from itself. The newspaper article showed him a picture of the sit-in, protesters on his land with placards and enough paraphernalia to convince him that they weren't going anywhere any time soon. All that was missing was a post office and a corner shop, but then summer was the perfect time for an impromptu camping expedition. He doubted they would have been quite as determined if those fields had been knee-deep in snow and the branches of the trees bending at ninety-degree angles in high winds.

Whatever the dark-haired harridan had said to them to stoke up public outrage at his development, she had succeeded because the untidy lot in the picture looked as self-righteous as she did.

The picture he was now staring at, of *Ms Rose Tremain*, showed a woman jabbing her finger at someone out of sight, some poor sod unfortunate enough to be asking her to answer a few questions she didn't like. Her unruly hair was scraped back into *something*, leaving flyaway strands around her face. Her clothes beggared belief. Art was accustomed to dating women who graced catwalks, women who were best friends with cutting-edge designers and spent whatever time they had away from their modelling jobs in exclusive salons beautifying themselves.

He squinted at the picture in front of him and tried to

get his head around the image of someone who looked as though she had bulk-bought her outfit from a charity shop and hadn't been near a hairdresser in decades.

No. Money wasn't going to get her off his back. One look at that jabbing finger and fierce scowl was enough to convince him of the rashness of going down that road.

But there were many ways to skin a cat…

'So, she can't be bought,' Art murmured, half to himself. 'Well, I will have to find another way to convince her to drop her case against me and get those protestors off my land. Every day lost is costing me money.' With his dark eyes still on the picture in front of him, Art connected to his PA and told her to reschedule his calendar for the next fortnight.

'What are you going to do?' Harold asked, sounding alarmed, as if he couldn't make sense of his workaholic boss taking two weeks off.

'I'm going to take a little holiday,' Art said with a slow smile of intent. 'A busman's holiday. You will be the only one privy to this information, so keep it to yourself, Harold. If *Ms Tremain* can't be persuaded to my way of thinking by a generous contribution to whatever hare-brained "Save the Whale" cause she espouses, then I'm going to have to find another way to persuade her.'

'How? If we're talking about anything illegal here, Art…'

'Oh, please.' Art burst out laughing. 'Illegal?'

'Maybe I don't mean *illegal*. Maybe a better word might be *unethical*.'

'Well, now, my friend. That depends entirely on your definition of unethical…'

* * *

'Someone here to see you, Rose.'

Rose looked up at the spiky-haired young girl standing by the door of the office she shared with her co-worker, Phil. It was little more than a large room on the ground floor of the Victorian house which was also her home but it was an arrangement that worked. The rent she got from Phil and from the occupants of the other two converted rooms—who were variously the local gardening club twice a week, the local bridge group once a week and the local children's playgroup twice a week—covered the extensive running costs of the house she had inherited when her mother had died five years previously. Well, alongside the sizeable loan she had had to take out in order to effect urgent repairs on the place.

She occasionally thought that it would have been nice if she could have separated her work life from her home life but, on the other hand, who could complain about a job where there was no commute involved?

'Who is it, Angie?' Bad time. Middle of the afternoon and she still had a bucketload of work to do. Three cases had cropped up at precisely the same time and each one of them involved complex issues with employment law, in which she specialised, and demanded a lot of attention.

'Someone about the land.'

'Ah. The land.' Rose sat back, stretched and then stood up, only realising how much she'd cramped up when she heard a wayward joint creak.

The land.

No one called it anything else.

Between Phil's property law side of the business and her labour law, *the land* had become the middle ground which occupied them both, far more than either had expected when the business of some faceless tycoon buying up their green fields to build yet another housing estate had reared its ugly head.

Phil was a relative newcomer to the area, but she had lived in the village her whole life and she had adopted the cause of the protestors with gusto.

Indeed, she had even allowed them to use her sprawling kitchen as their headquarters.

She was unashamedly partisan and was proud of her stance. There was nothing that stuck in her throat more than big businesses and billionaire businessmen thinking that they could do as they pleased and steamroll over the little people so that they could make yet more money for themselves.

'Want me to handle it?' Phil asked, looking up from his desk, which was as chaotic as hers.

'No.' Rose smiled at him. She could never have hoped for a more reliable business partner than Phil. Thirty-three years old, he had the appearance of a slightly startled owl, with his wire-rimmed specs and his round face, but he was as sharp as a tack and won a breathtaking amount of business for them. 'If they've actually got around to sending one of their senior lawyers then I'm ready for them. It's insulting that so far they've only seen fit to send junior staff. Shows how confident they are of being able to trample us into the ground.'

'I like your faith in our ability to bring a massive corporation to its knees,' Phil said with a wry grin. 'DC Logistics pretty much owns the world.'

'Which,' Rose countered without skipping a beat, 'doesn't mean that they can add this little slice of land to the tally.'

She tucked strands of her unruly hair into the sort of bun she optimistically started each and every day with, only to give up because her hair had a will of its own.

She glanced at the sliver of mirror in between the bookshelves groaning under the weight of legal tomes and absently took in the reflection that stared back at her every morning when she woke up.

No one had ever accused her of being pretty. Rose had long accepted that she just wasn't, that she just didn't fit the mould of *pretty*. She had a strong, intelligent face with a firm jaw and a nose that bordered on sharp. Her large eyes were clear and brown and her best feature as far as she was concerned.

Everything else…well, everything else worked. She was a little too tall, a little too gangly and not nearly busty enough, but you couldn't concern yourself with stuff like that and she didn't. Pretty much.

'Right! Let's go see what they've thrown at us this time!' She winked at Phil and made approving noises when Angie said that she'd stuck their visitor in the kitchen—it would do whoever it was good to see the evidence of their commitment to the cause—and headed out of the office.

She didn't know what to expect.

Overweight, overfed, overpaid and over-confident. Someone at the height of his career, with all the trappings that an expensive top job afforded. Angie had given nothing away and wouldn't have. She was gay and paid not a scrap of attention to what members of the opposite sex looked like.

Rose was only twenty-eight herself but the young people who had been sent to argue the case had seemed so much younger than her.

She pushed open the kitchen door and then stood for a few moments in the doorway.

The man was standing with his back to her, staring out at the garden, which flowed seamlessly into open land, the only boundary between private and public being a strip of trees and a dishevelled hedge of sorts.

He was tall. Very tall. She was five eleven and she guessed that he would be somewhere in the region of six three.

And, from what she was seeing, he was well built. Muscular. Broad shoulders tapering to a narrow waist and legs that moulded perfectly to the faded jeans he was wearing.

What sort of lawyer was *this*?

Confused, Rose cleared her throat to give notice of her presence and the man turned around slowly.

'My secretary didn't tell me your name, Mr...'

'Frank.' The stranger took his time as he walked towards her, which annoyed Rose because this was her house and her kitchen and yet the man seemed to dominate the space and own it in a way she didn't care for.

'Well, Mr Frank. You're here about the land, I gather. If your company thinks that this ploy is going to work, then I hate to disappoint you but it won't.'

Alarmed because he had somehow managed to close the distance between them and was standing just a little too close for comfort, Rose sidestepped him to the kettle, only offering him something to drink seemingly as an afterthought.

'You can sit,' she said crisply. 'Just shove some of the papers out of the way.'

'What ploy?'

Rose watched as he looked at the placards in the making on the kitchen table, head politely inclined. After some consideration, he held up one and examined it in reflective silence before returning it to its original position on the table.

'What ploy?' he repeated.

'The lawyer-in-jeans ploy,' Rose said succinctly. She shot him a look of pure disdain, but only just managed to pull it off because the man was just so...so...crazily good-looking that her nervous system felt as though it had been put through a spin cycle and was all over the place.

He'd sat down but not in a lawyer-like manner, which was also annoying. He'd angled the pine chair, one of ten around the long rectangular table, and was sprawled in it, his long legs stretched right out in front of him, one ankle over the other. He looked effortlessly elegant and incredibly *cool* in his weathered jeans and faded polo shirt. Everything clung in a way that made her think that the entire outfit had been especially designed with him in mind.

She pushed the coffee over to him. He looked just the kind of guy to take his coffee black, no sugar.

'Does your company think that they can send some-one who's dressed down for the day in the hope that we might just soften our stance? Maybe be deluded into thinking that he's not the stuffed shirt lawyer that he actually is?' She narrowed her eyes and tried and failed to imagine him as a stuffed shirt lawyer.

'Ah…' Mr Frank murmured. '*That* ploy.'

'Yes. *That* ploy. Well, it won't work. My team and I are committed to the cause and you can tell your em-ployers that we intend to fight this abhorrent and unnec-essary development with every ounce of breath in us.'

'You overestimate my qualifications,' Mr Frank said smoothly, sipping the coffee. 'Excellent coffee, by the way. I'm no lawyer. But were I to be one, then I would try very hard not to be a stuffed shirt one.'

'Not a lawyer? Then who the heck are you? Angie said that you were here about the land.'

'Angie being the girl with the spiky hair and the nose ring?'

'That's correct. She also happens to be an extremely efficient secretary and a whizz at IT.'

'Well, she was certainly right in one respect. I *am* here about the land. Here to join the noble cause.'

Art's plan had been simple. It had come to him in a blinding flash shortly after Harold had informed him that money wasn't going to make the problem of squat-ters on his land go away.

If you can't lick 'em, join 'em.

Naturally he'd known what to expect but somehow,

in the flesh, the woman staring at him through narrowed eyes wasn't *quite* the hippy he had originally imagined.

He couldn't put his finger on what was different and then, in the space of a handful of seconds, decided that it was a case of imagination playing tricks because she was certainly dressed in just the sort of attire he'd expected. Some sort of loose trousers in an assortment of clashing colours. Practical, given the hot weather, but, in all other respects, frankly appalling. A shapeless green vest-like top and a pair of sandals that, like the trousers, were practical but ticked absolutely no other boxes as far as he was concerned.

Her hair seemed to be staging a full-scale revolt against its half-hearted restraints. It was very curly and strands of it waved around her cheeks.

But the woman emanated *presence* and that was something he couldn't deny.

She wasn't beautiful, not in the conventional sense of the word, but she was incredibly arresting and for a few seconds Art found himself in the novel situation of temporarily forgetting why he was sitting here in a kitchen that looked as though a bomb had recently been detonated in it.

And then it all came back. He would join the band of merry protestors. He would get to know the woman. He would convince her from the position of insider that she was fighting a losing battle.

He would bring her round to his way of thinking, which was simply a matter of bringing her round to common sense, because she was never going to win this war.

But strong-arm tactics weren't going to work because, as Harold had made perfectly clear, storming in and bludgeoning the opposition would be catastrophic in a community as tightly knit as this one clearly was.

He was simply going to persuade her into seeing his point of view and the best and only way he could do that would be from the inside, from the position of one of them. From the advantageous position of trust.

Art didn't need opposition. He needed to butter up the unruly mob because he had long-term plans for the land—plans that included sheltered accommodation for his autistic stepbrother, to whom he was deeply attached.

He hadn't gone straight to the site though, choosing instead to make himself known to the woman standing firmly between him and his plans. He was good with women. Women liked him. Quite a few positively adored him. And there weren't many who didn't fall for his charm. Art wasn't vain but he was realistic, so why not use that charm to work its magic on this recalcitrant woman?

If that failed to do the trick then of course he would have to go back to the drawing board, but it was worth a shot.

To this end, he had taken his unprecedented leave of absence. A few days to sort out urgent business that wouldn't happily sit on the back burner and now here he was.

He was sporting the beginnings of a beard, was letting his hair grow, and the sharp handmade suits had ceded to the faded jeans and a black polo shirt.

'Really?' Rose said with a certain amount of cynicism.

'Indeed. Why the suspicion?'

'Because you don't exactly fit the role of the protestors we have here.'

'Don't I? How so?'

'Basically, I have no idea who you are. I don't recognise you.'

'And you know everyone who's protesting?'

'Everyone and, in most cases, their extended families, as well. You're not from around here, are you?'

'Not quite,' Art murmured vaguely, unprepared for such a direct line of attack before he'd even started writing incendiary messages on a placard.

'Well, where *are* you from? Exactly?'

Art shrugged and shifted in his chair. He was beginning to understand why the deputies sent to do this job had failed. Right now, Rose was staring at him as though he was something suspect and possibly contagious that had somehow managed to infiltrate her space.

'Can anyone say *exactly* where they're from?' he threw the question back at her, which only made her look at him with even more suspicion.

'Yes. Everyone on the site, for a start. As for me, I'm from here and always have been, aside from a brief spell at university.'

'I largely live in London.' Which was technically accurate. He *did* largely live in London. In his penthouse in Belgravia. He was also to be found in five-star hotels around the world, several of which he owned, or in one of the many houses he owned, although those occasions were slightly rarer. Who had time to wind down in a villa by the sea?

Strangely, that non-answer seemed to satisfy her because she stopped looking as though she had her finger on the buzzer to call for instant backup. 'So what are you doing here?' she asked with curiosity. 'I mean, why this cause? If you're not from around here, then what does it matter to you whether the land is destroyed or not?'

'*Destroy* is a big word.' Art was outraged but he held onto his temper and looked at her with an expression of bland innocence.

Definitely arresting, he thought. Exotic eyes. Feline. And a sensuous mouth. Wide and expressive. And an air of sharp intelligence which, it had to be said, wasn't one of the foremost qualities he ever sought in a woman, but it certainly worked in this instance because he was finding it hard to keep his eyes off her.

Rose fidgeted. To her horror, she felt the slow crawl of colour stain her cheeks. The man was gazing at her with hooded eyes and that look was doing all sorts of unexpected things to her body.

'It's *exactly* the right word,' she snapped, more sharply than she had intended, a reaction to those dark, sexy eyes.

Never had she felt more self-conscious, more aware of her shortcomings. The comfortable and practical culottes, which were the mainstay of her wardrobe on hot summer days, were suddenly as flattering as a pair of curtains and the loose-fitting vest as attractive as a bin liner.

She reminded herself that she wasn't the star attraction in a fashion parade. Clothes did not the man, or woman, make!

But for the first time in living memory she had the crazy urge to be something other than the determined career lawyer who worked hard on behalf of the underdog. She had the crazy urge to be sexy and compelling and wanted for her body instead of her brain.

'Too many developers over the years have whittled away at the open land around here.' She refocused and brought her runaway mind back on track. 'They've come along and turned the fields, which have been enjoyed for centuries by ramblers and nature lovers, into first a stupid shopping mall and then into office blocks.'

Rose half expected him to jump in here and heatedly side with her but he remained silent and she wondered what was going through that impossibly good-looking head of his.

'And this lot?'

'DC Logistics?' She loosed a sarcastic laugh under her breath. 'The worst of the lot. Certainly the biggest! They want to construct a housing development. But then I don't suppose I'm telling you anything you don't already know. Which brings me back to my question— why the interest in joining our protest?'

'Sometimes—' Art played with the truth like a piece of moulding clay '—big, powerful developers need to understand the importance of working in harmony with nature or else leaving things as they stand and, as you say, DC Logistics is the mother of all big companies.'

He succeeded in not sounding proud of this fact. When he thought of the work that had gone into turning the dregs of what had been left of his father's companies, after five ex-wives had picked them over in outrageous alimony settlements, into the success story of today he was pretty proud of his achievements.

Art had lived through the nightmare of his father's mistakes, the marriages that had fallen apart within seconds of the ink on the marriage certificates being dry. He'd gritted his teeth, helpless, as each ex-wife had drained the coffers and then, after his father had died several years previously, he'd returned to try to save what little remained of the thriving empire Emilio da Costa had carefully built up over time.

Art had been a young man at the time, barely out of university but already determined to take what was left and build it again into the thriving concern it had once been when his mother—Emilio da Costa's first wife and only love—had been alive.

Art might have learned from the chaos of his father's life and the greed of the women he had foolishly married that love was for the birds, but he had also learned the value of compassion in his unexpected affection for his stepbrother, José—not flesh and blood, no, but his brother in every sense of the word, who had been robustly ignored by his avaricious mother. The land was integral to his plan to make a home for José—the reason for Art needing to shut this protest down as quickly and as quietly as possible.

'Yes, it is,' Rose concurred. 'So you're idealistic,' she carried on in an approving tone.

The last time Art had been idealistic had been when he'd believed in Santa Claus and the Tooth Fairy. Witnessing the self-serving venom camouflaged as *true love* that had littered his father's life right up until his death had taken whatever ideals he might have had and entombed them in a place more secure than a bank vault.

'Well, you're in the right place.' Rose gestured to the paraphernalia in the kitchen. 'Obviously I don't devote all of my time to this cause. I couldn't possibly, but I do try to touch base with the people out there on a daily basis.'

'What's your main line of work?'

'Employment law.' Rose smiled and, just like that, Art felt the breath knocked out of his body.

The woman was more than arresting. When she smiled she was...*bloody stunning.* He felt the familiar kick of his libido, but stronger and more urgent than ever. Two months without a woman, he thought, would do that to a red-blooded man with a healthy sex drive. Because this outspoken feminist was certainly, on no level, what he looked for in a woman. He didn't do argumentative and he definitely didn't do the *let's-hold-hands-and-save-the-world* type. He did blondes. Big blonde hair, big blue eyes and personalities that soothed rather than challenged.

Rose Tremain was about as soothing as a pit bull.

And yet... His eyes lingered and his inconvenient erection refused to go away. The blood surging in his veins was hot with a type of dark excitement he hadn't felt in a very long time. If ever.

'Come again?' He realised that she had said something.

'Your line of work? What is it?'

'I dabble.'

'Dabble in what?'

'How much time have you got to spare? Could take a while.'

'Could take a while covering your many talents? Well, you're far from modest, aren't you?' She raised her eyebrows, amused and mocking, and Art smiled back slowly—deliberately slowly.

'I've never been a believer in false modesty. Sign of a hypocritical mind. I prefer to recognise my talents as well as my...er...shortcomings.'

'Well, whatever you do is your business—' she shrugged and stood up '—but if you're good at everything, which seems to be what you're implying, then you're going to be very useful to us.'

'How so?' Art followed suit and stood up, towering over her even though she was tall. 'Useful in what respect?'

'Odd jobs. Nothing major so no need to sound alarmed.' She looked around the kitchen. 'Everyone lends a helping hand when they're here. It's not just a case of people painting slogans on bits of cardboard with felt tip pens. Yes, we're all protesting for the same reason, but this is a small, close community. The guys who come here do all sorts of jobs around the house. They know I'm representing them for free and they're all keen to repay the favour by doing practical things in return. There are a couple of plumbers behind us and an electrician, and without them I have no idea how much money I would have had to spend to get some vital jobs on the house done.'

'So this is your house?' Art thought that it was a bit hypocritical, clamouring about rich businessmen who wanted to destroy the precious space around her so that they could line their evil pockets when she, judging from the size of the house, was no pauper.

Accustomed to storing up information that might prove useful down the line, he sensed that that was a conversation he would have in due course.

'It is, not that that's relevant,' Rose said coolly. 'What *is* relevant is that most of the town is behind us, aside from the local council, who have seen fit to grant planning permission. I've managed to really rally a great deal of people to support our cause and they've all been brilliant. So if you're a jack-of-all-trades then I'm sure I'll be able to find loads of practical ways you can help, aside from joining the sit-in, of course. Now, shall I take you to the scene of the crime…?'

CHAPTER TWO

'YOU HAVE A nice house,' Art commented neutrally as they exited the cluttered kitchen, out into the main body of the house which was equally cluttered. 'Big. You rent out rooms, I take it?' He detoured to push open the door to one of the huge ground-floor rooms and was confronted with an elderly man holding court with an image of a bunch of flowers behind him on the wall. The image was faded and unsteady because the projector was probably a relic from the last century. Everyone turned to stare at Art and he saluted briskly before gently shutting the door.

'If it's all the same to you, Mr Frank, I'll ask the questions. And please refrain from exploring the house because, yes, other organisations do avail themselves of some of the rooms and I very much doubt they want you poking your head in to say hello. Unless, of course, you have something to impart on the subject of orchid-growing or maybe some pearls of wisdom you could share with one of our Citizens Advice Bureau volunteers?'

'I've never been into gardening,' Art contributed truthfully. He slanted his eyes across to Rose, who was walking tall next to him, her strides easily matching his as they headed to the front door. The walls of the house were awash with rousing, morale-boosting posters. Voices could be heard behind closed doors.

'You're missing out. It's a very restful pastime.'

Art chuckled quietly. He didn't do *restful*.

'Wait a minute.' She looked at him directly, hands on her hips, her brown eyes narrowed and shrewdly assessing. 'There's one little thing I forgot to mention and I'd better be upfront before we go any further.'

'What's that?'

'I don't know who you are. You're not from around here and I'm going to make it clear to you from the start that we don't welcome rabble-rousers.'

Stunned, Art stared at her in complete silence.

He was Arturo da Costa. A man feared and respected in the international business community. A man who could have anything he wanted at the snap of an imperious finger. Grown men thought twice before they said anything they felt might be misconstrued as offensive. When he spoke, people inclined their heads and listened. When he entered a room, silence fell.

And here he was being accused of being a potential *rabble-rouser*!

'Rabble-rouser,' he framed in a slow, incredulous voice.

'It's been known.' She spun around on her heel, headed to the door and then out towards a battered navy blue Land Rover. 'Idlers who drift from one protest site to another, stirring up trouble for their own political motives.'

'Idlers…' Art played with the word on his tongue,

shocked and yet helpless to voice his outrage given he was supposed to be someone of no fixed address, there to support the noble cause.

'Granted, not all are idlers.' Rose swung herself into the driver's seat and slammed the door behind her, waiting for him to join her. She switched on the engine but then turned to him, one hand on the gearbox, the other on the steering wheel. 'But a lot of them are career protestors and I can tell you straight away that we don't welcome that lot. We're peaceful. We want our voices to be heard and the message we want to get across is not one that would benefit from thug tactics.'

'I have never been accused of being a rabble-rouser in my life before, far less a thug. Or an *idler*...'

'There's no need to look so shocked.' She smiled and pushed some of her curly hair away from her face. 'These things happen in the big, bad world.'

'Oh, I know all about what happens in the big, bad world,' Mr Frank murmured softly and the hairs on the back of her neck stood on end because his deep, velvety voice was as seductive as the darkest of chocolate.

In the sultry heat of the Land Rover, she could almost breathe him in and it was going to her head like incense.

'And before you launch into another outrageous accusation—' he laughed '—something along the lines that I don't know about the big, bad world because I'm a criminal, I'll tell you straight away that I have never, and will never, operate on the wrong side of the law.'

'I wasn't about to accuse you of being a criminal.' Rose blinked and cleared her throat. 'Although, of course,' she added grudgingly, 'I might have got round to that sooner or later. You can't be too careful. You should roll your window down. It'll be a furnace in here otherwise.'

'No air conditioning?'

'This relic barely goes,' she said affectionately before swinging around to expertly manoeuvre the courtyard which was strewn with cars, all parked, it would seem, with reckless abandon. 'If I tried to stick air conditioning in it would probably collapse from the shock of being dragged into the twentieth century.'

'You could always get a new car.'

'For someone who dabbles in a bit of this and that, you seem to think that money grows on trees,' she said tartly. 'If I ever win the lottery I might consider replacing my car but, until then, I work with the old girl and hope for the best.'

'Lawyers,' he said with a vague wave of his hand. 'Aren't you all made of money?'

Rose laughed and shot him a sideways look. He was slouched against the passenger door, his big body angled so that he could look at her, and she wondered how many women had had those sexy dark eyes focused on them, how many had lost their head drowning in the depths.

She fancied herself as anything but the romantic sort, but there was a little voice playing in her head, warning her that this was a man she should be careful of.

Rose nearly laughed because her last brush with romance had left a nasty taste in her mouth. Jack Shaw had been a fellow lawyer and she had met him on one of her cases, which had taken her to Surrey and the playground of the rich and famous. He had been fighting the corner for the little guy and she had really thought that they were on the same wavelength—and they should have been. He'd ticked all the right boxes! But for the second time in her adult life she had embarked on a relationship that had started off with promise only to end in disappointment. How was it possible for something that made sense to end up with two people not actually having anything left to say to one another after ten months?

Rose knew what worked and what didn't when it came to emotions. She had learned from bitter childhood experience what to avoid. She knew what was unsuitable. And yet her two suitable boyfriends, with their excellent socialist credentials, had crashed and burned.

At this rate, she was ready to give up the whole finding love game and sink her energies into worthwhile causes instead.

'Not all lawyers are rich,' she said without looking at him, busy focusing on the road, which was lined with dense hedges, winding and very narrow. 'I'm not.'

'Why is that?'

'Maybe I chose the wrong branch of law.' She shrugged. 'Employment law generally doesn't do it when it comes to earning vast sums of money. Not that I'm complaining. I get by nicely, especially when you think about all the perfectly smart people who can't find work.'

'There's always work available for perfectly smart people.'

'Is that your experience?' She flashed him a wry

sidelong glance before turning her attention back to the road. 'Are you one of those perfectly smart people who finds it so easy to get work that you're currently drifting out here to join a cause in which you have no personal interest?'

'You're still suspicious of my motives?'

'I'm reserving judgement. Although—' she sighed '—I can, of course, understand how easy it is to get involved if you're a nature-lover. Look around you at the open land. You can really breathe out here. The thought of it being handed over to a developer, so that houses can be put up and the trees chopped down, doesn't bear thinking about.'

Art looked around him. There certainly was a great deal of open land. It stretched all around them, relentless and monotonous, acres upon acres upon acres of never-ending sameness. He'd never been much of a country man. He liked the frenetic buzz of city life, the feeling of being surrounded by activity. He made some appreciative noises under his breath and narrowed his eyes against the glare as the perimeters of his land took shape.

'So you've lived here all your life,' Art murmured as she slowed right down to access the bumpy track that followed the outer reaches of his property. 'I'm taking it that some of the guys protesting are relatives? Brothers? Sisters? Cousins? Maybe your parents?'

'No,' Rose said shortly.

Art pricked up his ears, detecting something behind that abrupt response. It paid to know your quarry and

Harold had been spot on when he'd said that there was
next to no personal information circulating out there
about the prickly woman next to him. Amazing. Social
media was the staple diet of most people under the age
of thirty-five and yet this woman had obviously managed to turn her back firmly on the trend.

Since he was similarly private about his life, he had
to concede some reluctant admiration for her stance.

'No extended family?'

'Why the Spanish Inquisition?' She glanced across
at him. 'What about *you*? Brothers? Sisters? Cousins?
Will some of *your* extended family be showing up here
to support us?'

'You're very prickly.'

'I…don't mean to be, Mr Frank.'

'I think we should move onto a first name basis.
That okay with you? My name's Arturo. Arthur if you
prefer the English equivalent.' Which was as close to
the truth as it was possible to get, as was the surname,
which hadn't been plucked from thin air but which was,
in fact, his mother's maiden name.

'Rose.'

'And you were telling me that you weren't prickly…'

'I'm afraid the whole business of an extended family is
something of a sore point with me.' She half smiled because her history was no deep, dark secret, at least locally. If Arthur, or Arturo because he looked a lot more
like an exotic Arturo than a boring Arthur, ended up
here for the long haul, then sooner or later he would hear
the gossip. The truth was that her background had made

her what she was, for which she was very glad, but it wasn't exactly normal and for some reason explaining herself to this man felt...awkward and a little intimate.

Aside from that, what was with the questioning? Shouldn't he be asking questions about the land instead of about *her*?

On a number of levels he certainly didn't respond in the predicted manner and again Rose felt that shiver, the faintly thrilling feathery sensation of being in slightly unchartered territory.

'You asked about me,' he said smoothly, filling the silence which had descended between them, 'and extended family is a sore point for me, as well. I have none.'

'No?' They had arrived at the protest site but Rose found that she wanted to prolong the conversation.

'Do you feel sorry for me?' Arturo grinned and Rose blinked, disconcerted by the stupendous charm behind that crooked smile. She felt it again, a whoosh that swept through her, making her breath quicken and her stomach swoop.

'Should I? You don't strike me as the sort of guy someone should be feeling sorry for. How is it that you have no extended family?'

'First, I'll take it as a compliment that you think I'm the kind of dominant guy people should fear, respect and admire instead of pity...'

'Did I say that?' But her mouth twitched with amusement.

'And, second, I'll tell you if you tell me. We can hold hands and have a girly evening sharing confidences...join me for dinner later. I'd love to get to know you better.'

Hot, flustered and suddenly out of her depth, Rose gaped at him like a stranded fish, scarcely believing her ears. She reddened, lost for words.

'Is it a promising start that I'm taking your breath away?' Arturo drawled, his voice rich with amusement.

'No... I... You're asking me on *a date*?'

'You sound as though it's something that's never happened to you before.'

'I...no... I'm very sorry, Mr Frank, but I...no. I can't accept. But thank you very much. I'm flattered.'

'Arturo.' He frowned. 'Why not?'

'Because...' Rose smoothed her wayward hair with her hand and stared off into the distance, all the while acutely aware of his dark, sexy eyes on her profile, making a nonsense of her level head and feet-firmly-planted-on-the-ground approach to life. She was no frothy, giggly bit of fluff but he was making her feel a bit like that and anyone would think that she was a giddy virgin in the company of a prince!

'Because...?'

'Well, it's not appropriate.'

'Why not? I may be about to join your cause, but you're not my boss so no conflict of interest there.'

'I...' Rose licked her lips and eventually looked at him, leaning against the open window. 'I...'

'You're not married. You're not wearing a wedding ring.'

'Observant. That's hardly the point, though.'

'Boyfriend?'

'No...not that it's any of your business, Mr Frank.

Arthur. *Arturo*. Do you usually ask women you've only known for five seconds out on a date?'

'How else am I supposed to get to know them for longer than five seconds if I don't? So you're not married, no boyfriend…gay?'

'No!'

Arturo grinned and Rose was certain she was blushing furiously, her reddened cheeks thoroughly letting the side down. 'Then where's the problem?'

'You're very sure of yourself, aren't you?' Rose gathered herself and opened her door. It was very hot. A blazing summer afternoon, with the sun still high in the sky and the clouds little more than cotton wool puffs of white idly floating by. The land looked glorious and untouched. It was a short walk to get to the site where the protestors had set up camp. Yes, she could have driven there, but it was easier to park here and a nice day for walking. Except now she would be walking in a state of nervous tension.

'Is that a crime?' Arturo had followed her out and he looked at her, still grinning.

'I've never been attracted to men who are too sure of themselves.'

'Challenging observation…'

'That's not my intention! You're here to…support us! And I won't be going out with you because… I'm not interested in any sort of relationship at this point in time.'

'Who's talking about a relationship?'

'I don't do casual sex.' Rose was staggered that she was having this conversation, but she had yet to meet a man who was open about what he wanted and surely he couldn't want *her* because, rich or poor, he had the sort of charisma and good looks that would guarantee him a spot in any woman's little black book.

So why her?

But heck, was she flattered? It had been a while since her last disastrous relationship, a while since she had felt like a woman. And, if she was honest, even Jack, earnest and brimming over with admirable integrity, hadn't made her feel like this.

'I thought I just mentioned having dinner,' Arturo murmured, which made Rose feel her cheeks flush what was surely an even deeper shade of red.

'You're playing with me,' she said sharply. 'And I don't like it.'

Their eyes tangled but Rose refused to be the first to back down even though she wanted to.

Art was learning what it felt like to be politely but firmly pushed to the kerb.

'Tell me about the protest,' he encouraged, changing tack, matching her gait with his and releasing her from the stranglehold of her embarrassment as they continued to walk towards the distant horizon. 'How many people are there at the site?'

'Ever been on a protest before?'

'I can honestly say that I haven't.'

'Well, I'm glad that this is of sufficient interest to you to get you motivated into doing more than just sitting on the sidelines and sympathising. So many people have strong views about something and yet they never quite go the distance when it comes to doing something about those views.'

'What made you choose employment law over something better paid?'

'Because money isn't everything! And I'm taking it that you feel the same as I do.'

'Money *can* often be the root of all evil,' Art hedged. 'It's also pretty vital when it comes to putting food on our plates.'

'I like to think that in my job I'm helping other people put food on their plates.'

'And you've always worked for yourself or did you work for a bigger company after you graduated?'

'You ask a lot of questions, don't you?' But she seemed flattered by his interest.

'It's the only way to get to know someone.' Art had the grace to flush. He was here for a purpose though and with him the practical would always take precedence over any unruly conscience. Vast sums of money were at stake and he was only trying to make his point of view known to a group who probably thought that their opinion was the only valid one on the table.

A rich diversity of opinion was a bonus in life. By *subtly* introducing a different viewpoint to theirs, he would effectively be doing her and all of the protestors there a laudable favour.

'Nearly twenty-five,' Rose told him briskly, walking fast, each stride determined and sure-footed.

'Nearly twenty-five what?'

'You asked how many protestors there were on the site. Nearly twenty-five and growing by the day.'

'And what lovely days we've been having...'

'They'd be here come rain or shine,' Rose informed him tartly and he grinned at her.

'And quite right too. Nothing worse than a protestor who packs up his placards and heads for his car the minute the skies open.'

'I can't tell when you're joking,' Rose said, pausing to look at him.

'Oh, I'm very serious about being here indeed. Make no mistake about that,' Art said softly.

'And how long do you plan on staying?' She began walking again and he fell in beside her.

'I reckon at least a few days, maybe longer. Perhaps a week or two.'

'Getting first-hand experience of putting your money where your mouth is.' Rose smiled. 'I commend that. The camp's just up ahead. We've managed to get running water and electricity going. It's been a nightmare but where there's a will there's a way and, like I said, there are a lot of people with a lot of talent who have been keen to help us out.'

Art was looking at a collection of makeshift dwellings. Tents rubbed shoulders with slightly more solid constructions. There was an elaborate portable toilet. People were milling around. Children were playing. It was, he had to concede, a wonderful campsite, dissected by a clear, bubbling stream and surrounded by trees and flowers. It was, however, a campsite on *his* land.

Clearly much loved and admired, the second they were spotted, Rose was surrounded by people, young and old alike. She was part and parcel of the community and Art could see the warmth of the supporters surround her like a blanket, seemingly reaffirming her belief in what they were doing—saving the land for the locals. Several dragged her along to have a look at some new ideas for placards. One old guy involved her in an elaborate discussion about some legal technicality, which she handled with aplomb and a great show of interest, even though he could somehow tell that she was answering his questions automatically.

No one paid the slightest bit of attention to him.

He was introduced, of course, and he, likewise, was shown yet more placards to add to the already healthy supply in evidence.

'Very artistic,' he contributed to one of the middle-aged women who had carted him off to one side. 'I like the…er…'

'Drawings?' She delightedly pointed to the illustration of stick figures holding placards showing stick figures holding placards. 'I'm trying to convey the idea that all of this is a never-ending problem which will just keep recurring until everyone feels as passionately about the countryside as we do.'

'Very imaginative.'

'I guess you'll be helping? Rose says you're interested in what's taking place in this little pocket of the world.'

'Very interested,' Art said with heartfelt honesty, relieved to be dragged away before he could be quizzed further. The woman struck him as the sort who took no prisoners.

Overhead, the sun continued to beat down with ferocity. He felt hot and sweaty and in need of just a handful of those minor luxuries he took for granted. A nice cool shower, for one thing.

He'd brought the minimum of clothes, stuffed into a holdall which he'd left in the Land Rover. They nestled on top of his computer, because there was no way he intended to be completely out of reach. That would have been unthinkable.

'So,' Rose said brightly when she was back at his side, having done the rounds, including squatting on the ground to talk to some of the children, 'I notice that you didn't think to bring a tent.'

'Come again?'

'I'm getting ahead of myself.' She drew him to one side. 'You said that you planned on staying for a few days and you don't have a tent, but I think it might be possible for you to share one. I know Rob over there has a tent that's as big as a house and I'm sure he'd be delighted to share his space with a fellow protestor.'

Art tried not to recoil with horror. 'That,' he all but choked, 'won't do.'

'Why not?'

'Because I have some savings and I will dip into them to stay somewhere…er…locally…'

'But why? Honestly, the site is really very comfortable. Everyone enjoys staying there.'

'And I applaud them, but that's not for me.'

'It's stupid to use your savings to rent somewhere for a week. Or however long you plan on staying. Besides, in case you haven't noticed, this is an extremely touristy part of the country. Dead in winter but the hotels around here are expensive and almost all of them will be fully booked in summer.' She stood back and looked at him narrowly.

'I believe you when you say that you don't have criminal tendencies.' She folded her arms and inclined her head to one side.

'I'm breathing a sigh of relief as I stand here.'

'And I think it's ridiculous for you to waste your money trying to find somewhere around here to rent. You'll be broke by the end of a week. Trust me.' She said nothing for a few minutes, giving him ample time to try to figure out where this was heading.

But she didn't expand, instead choosing to begin walking back to the Land Rover, which was a long-winded exercise because she was stopped by someone every couple of steps. On the way she collected an offering of several files, which she promised to look at later.

'Nothing to do with the land,' she confided to Art when they were finally back in the muddy four-wheel drive and she was swinging away from the land, back out to the open road. 'George is having issues with one of his employees. Wants some advice. Normally it's the other way round for me, but I promised I'd have a look at the file.'

'Generous of you. I can see how popular you are with everyone there.'

Rose laughed, a musical sound of amusement that did the same thing to Art as her smile did, rousing him in ways that were unexpected and surprisingly intense.

He did know that there were pertinent questions he should be asking to further his understanding of how he could win this war without losing the battle but he couldn't seem to get his head in the right place to ask the right questions. Instead, he found himself staring at her from under his lashes, vaguely wondering what it was about her that was so compelling.

'Now that you've turned down my dinner invitation,' he drawled, 'perhaps you could drive me to the nearest, cheapest B&B. I'm touched at your concern for the level of my savings, but I'll manage.'

'There's no reason why you can't stay at my place.'

'Your place?'

Rose laughed, caught his eye sideways and forced a grin out of him. 'It's big and you can pay your way doing things around the house while you're there. Two of the rooms need painting, which is a job I never seem to get round to doing, and there's a stubborn leak in the tap. A constant drip, drip, drip.'

'You want me to fix leaks and paint your house?' DIY and Art had never crossed paths. Paint a room? Fix a leak? He couldn't have flung himself further out of his comfort zone if he'd tried.

'In return for free board and lodging. Oh, how good are you at cooking?'

'It's something I've always tried to avoid.'

'Do we have a deal?'

'Why do you live in such a big house if you can't afford to?'

'Long story.'

'I'm a very good listener. There's nothing I enjoy more than a long story. I guess we can get to that in due course because I would love to accept your generous offer.' He wondered what other skills she thought he possessed. There was a chance they would both end up in Casualty if he tried his hand at cooking, so he disabused her straight away on that count and she laughed and shrugged and laughed again and told him that it had been worth a shot.

'I can cook and when I put my mind to it I actually enjoy it, but I'm so busy all of the time that it always feels like a chore.'

'You might regret asking me to paint a room,' Art said seriously as she bumped along the narrow lanes, driving past clusters of picturesque houses with neat box hedges before the open fields swallowed them up again, only to disgorge them into yet another picturesque village. 'I'm very happy to try my hand at it, but one thing I do insist on doing is paying you for my accommodation.'

'Don't be stupid.'

'If you don't agree to this then you can dump me off right here and I'll sort myself out, whatever the cost.'

Rose clicked her tongue impatiently.

'You obviously need the money,' Art continued almost gently, as the outskirts of the village loomed into view. 'You rent rooms out and the place, from all accounts, is falling apart at the seams...'

'Very well.' She kept her eyes firmly focused on the road ahead. 'In which case, I'll accept your dinner invitation on the proviso that I cook dinner for you.'

'Deal,' Art drawled, relaxing back into the passenger seat. Could he have hoped for a better outcome than this? No.

He was looking forward to this evening. The thorny business of going undercover to talk some sense into his opposition wasn't going to be the annoying uphill trek he had originally foreseen after all…

In fact…hand on heart, Art could honestly say that he was looking forward to this little break in his routine.

CHAPTER THREE

BY THE TIME they were back at the house the clatter of people had been replaced by the peace of silence. The gardening club crew had departed, as had whoever else was renting one of the downstairs rooms. Phil popped out and Art watched as he and Rose huddled in a brief discussion.

While they talked in low voices, he took the opportunity to look around him.

It was a big house but crying out for attention. The paint was tired, the carpet on the stairs threadbare and the woodwork, in places, cracked or missing altogether.

He made himself at home peering into the now empty rooms and saw that they were sizeable and cluttered with hastily packed away bits and pieces.

It was impossible to get any real idea of what the house might once have looked like in grander times because every nook and cranny had been put to use. Work desks fitted into spaces where once sofas and chaises longues might have resided, and in the office where she worked books lined the walls from floor to ceiling.

'Finished looking around?'

Art turned to find that she had broken off from talking to Phil, who was heading out of the front door, briefcase in hand and a crumpled linen jacket shoved under his arm.

'Which of the rooms needs the paint job?' was his response.

'It's actually upstairs,' Rose said, steering him away from the hall and back towards the kitchen where, he noted, no one had seen fit to tidy the paraphernalia of protest. 'Now—' she stood, arms folded, head tilted to one side '—tell me what you thought of our little band of insurgents.'

'Well organised.' Art strolled towards one of the kitchen chairs and sat down. 'But I'm curious—how long do they intend to stay there and what is the end objective?'

'That's an odd question,' Rose mused thoughtfully. 'Does your contribution to the cause depend on an answer to that?'

'I have a strong streak of practicality.' Art wasn't lying when he said that. 'I'm interested in trying to find out if there's any real chance of you winning with your protests.'

Rose sighed. 'Perhaps not entirely,' she admitted, 'but I really hope we can make some kind of difference, perhaps get the company to rethink the scale of their project. They're eating up a lot of open land and there's no question that the end result will be a massive eyesore on the landscape.'

'Have you seen the plans?' Art asked curiously.

'Of course I have. It's all about houses for wealthy commuters.'

'The rail link, I suppose…'

'You're the only person who has actually taken time out to think this through,' Rose admitted. 'And you're not even from round here. I think everyone somehow hopes that this is a problem that will just go away if we can all just provide a united front. It's a relief to talk to someone who can see the pitfalls. Just strange that you should care so much, considering this has never been your home.'

'I have general concerns about the…er…country-side.' Art had the grace to flush. Yes, all was fair in love and war, and it wasn't as though this little decep-tion was actually harming anyone, but the prick of his conscience was an uneasy reminder that playing fast and loose with the truth was a lie by any other name.

'Does that extend to other concerns?' Rose asked with interest.

'What do you mean?'

'Problems on a larger scale. Climate change. Dam-age to the rainforests. Fracking and the impact on the green belt.'

Art was used to women who were either career-driven—those with whom he came into contact in the course of his working life—or else women he dated. On the one hand, he conversed with his counterparts with absolute detachment, regardless of whether he picked up any vibes from them, any undercurrent of sexual in-terest. And then, when it came to the women he dated… well, that was sex, relaxation and pleasure, and in-depth conversations were not the name of the game. Quite honestly, he thought that the majority of them would have been bored rigid were he ever to sit them down and initiate a conversation about world affairs. If there was a world out there of smart, sassy women who had what it took to turn him on, then he'd passed them by.

Until now…

Because, against all odds, he was finding that this outspoken woman was a turn-on and he didn't know why. She should have been tiresome, but instead she was weirdly compelling.

'Doesn't everyone think about the bigger picture?'

'I like that,' Rose murmured. 'I really get it that you think about the bigger picture. But you surely must have some form of employment that enables you to take off when you want to, be it here or somewhere else…' She turned away and began rustling for something to cook.

'Let me order something in.' Art was uncomfortable with this.

'Order something in?' She looked at him incredulously.

'There's no need for you to prepare anything for me.'

'We both have to eat and it won't be fancy. Trust me.'

'Are you usually this welcoming to people who walk off the street into your house?'

'You're a one-off.' She smiled a little shyly. Yes, she had lots of contact with the opposite sex. Yes, there was Phil and a wide assortment of men she met on a daily basis, either because they lived locally and she bumped into them or in the course of her work. But this was different. This was a reminder of what it felt like to be with a man and she was enjoying the sensation.

Of course, she sternly reminded herself, it wasn't as though he was anything more than a nice guy who happened to share the same outlook on life as she did.

A nice guy who just so happened to be drop-dead gorgeous...

'A *one-off*...?' He looked at her with assessing eyes and Rose burst out laughing. He sounded piqued, as though someone had stuck a pin in his ego. In a flash of wonderment because he was simply nothing like any man she had ever met before, she gathered that he was piqued because she wasn't bowled over by him. Or at least because that was the impression she had given. She had turned down his dinner date, had rejected his offer to pay rent and had set him a number of tasks to complete, which was probably a first for a guy like him. He might not have money but he had style and an underlying aggressive sexual magnetism that most women would find irresistible.

Their eyes tangled and Rose felt her nipples pinch in raw sexual awareness, and the suddenness of its potency made her breath catch in her throat.

'That's the problem with living in a small community.' Rose laughed breathlessly, deflecting a moment of madness which had smacked of her being lonely, which she most certainly was not. 'You tend to know everyone. A new face is a rare occurrence.'

'Surely not.'

'Maybe not at this time of year,' she admitted, 'when the place is swarming with tourists, but a new face here for something other than the nice scenery and the quaint village atmosphere…that's a bit more unusual.'

'Why do you stay?' Art asked with what sounded like genuine curiosity. 'And, if that's the case, then surely you must find it a little dull?'

'No, I don't. I'm not just a statistic here, one of a million lawyers sweating to get by. Here, I can actually make a difference. And I don't know why I'm telling you any of this.'

'Because I'm a new face and you don't get to have conversations with people you haven't known since you were a kid?'

Rose flushed and looked at him defiantly. 'Not all of us are born to wander, which reminds me—you never told me how it is that you can afford to take time out to be here. Yes, you've said you do a bit of this and a bit of that but you're obviously not a labourer.'

'What makes you say that?'

'Your hands, for a start. Not calloused enough.'

'I'm not sure that's a compliment,' Art drawled, glancing at his hands. The last time he'd done anything really manual had been as a teenager when he'd had a summer job working on a building site. He recalled that his father had been going through divorce number three right about then.

'Office jobs?'

'You ask a lot of questions.'

'No more than you,' Rose pointed out and Art grinned at her, dark eyes never leaving her face.

He hadn't thought through the details of why he was

here and it hadn't occurred to him that his presence would be met with suspicion. He was having to revise his easy assumption that he could just show up, mumble something vague and get by without any questions.

'I've been known to sit behind a desk now and again. I confess I'm interested in the details of a sit-in, in what motivates people to give up their home comforts for a cause.'

'You're not a reporter, are you?'

'Would you object if I told you that I was?'

'No. The more coverage the better...'

'Well, sorry to disappoint but,' Art drawled with complete honesty, 'I personally can't stand the breed. Nosy and intrusive.'

'But excellent when it comes to getting a message out there to the wider public.'

'They're a fickle lot,' Art countered. 'You think that they're on your side and you usually open yourself up to inevitable disappointment. If you're going to make me dinner and you won't allow me to buy anything in, then the least I can do is help.'

'Okay. You can chop vegetables and tell me why you're interested in what's happening here.' Rose rummaged in the fridge and extracted a random assortment of vegetables, fetched a couple of chopping boards and nodded to Art to take his place alongside her. 'Asking questions is what I do for a living.' She smiled, not looking at him. 'So you'll have to excuse me if I'm asking you a lot of them.'

Art was busy looking at the bundle of onions and tomatoes neatly piled in front of him. He held the knife and began fumbling his way to something that only laughably resembled food preparation. He only realised that she had stopped what she had been doing and was staring at him when she said with amusement, 'You haven't got a clue, have you?'

'These bloody things are making my eyes sting.'

'They have a nasty habit of doing that,' Rose agreed. 'And you're in for a rough ride if you intend to take a couple of hours dicing them. By the way, you need to dice them a whole lot smaller.'

'You're having fun, aren't you?'

'I'm thinking you look like a man who doesn't know his way round a kitchen very well.'

'Like I said, cooking has never appealed.'

'Not even when you're relaxing with someone and just having fun preparing a meal together?'

'I don't go there,' Art said flatly. He gave the onion a jaundiced look and decided to attack the tomatoes, which seemed a safer bet. 'I don't do domestic.'

'You don't *do* domestic? What does that mean?'

'It means that I don't share those cosy moments you've just described.'

'Why not?' she asked lightly.

'I don't do personal questions either.'

Looking into the ancient mirrored tiles that lined the counter, Art noted her pink cheeks. He met her eyes to find her staring at him, her pink cheeks going even pinker. She looked away hurriedly to continue slicing and dicing. Strands of her wildly curly hair fell around her face and she blew some of them out of her eyes, blatantly making sure *not* to look in those mirrored squares in case she caught his eye again.

'You don't do cosy and domestic,' Rose said slowly, swivelling to lean against the counter, arms folded, eyes narrowed, 'and you don't do personal questions. So, if I'm joining the dots correctly, you don't invite women to ask you why you're not prepared to play happy families with them.'

'Something like that.' Art shrugged. He was sharp enough to realise that there was no way he would ever get her onside if he came across as the sort of unliberated dinosaur she would clearly despise.

'No cooking together…no watching telly entwined on a sofa…'

'I definitely do the *entwined* bit,' Art joked. Rose failed to return his smile.

'You don't want to encourage any woman to think you're going to be in it for the long haul because you're a commitment-phobe.'

'I could lie and tell you that you're way off target there,' Art drawled, holding her stare, 'but I won't do you the disservice.'

'I like that,' Rose said slowly, not taking her eyes off him.

'Which bit?'

'The honesty bit. In my line of work, I see a lot of scumbags who are happy to lie through their teeth to get what they want. It's laudable that you're at least honest when it comes to saying what you think.'

'You're giving me more credit than I'm due.' Art stopped what he was doing and let his eyes rove over her. Her skin was satiny smooth and make-up-free. 'I like the way you look,' he murmured. 'I like the fact that you're completely natural. No warpaint. No pressing need to clone yourself on the lines of a certain doll. Really works.'

Rose glanced at him and looked away hurriedly. Those dark eyes, she thought, could open a lot of boxes and kick-start a whole host of chain reactions and she might not know how to deal with them.

Rose wasn't ready for a relationship with anyone and she certainly wasn't up for grabs when it came to any man who was a commitment-phobe. *Thanks, but no thanks.* Enjoying this man's company was a wonderful distraction but anything more than that was not going to be on the table.

She had to shake herself mentally and laugh inwardly at her fanciful thoughts; it wasn't as though she was in danger of any advances from this passing stranger, who had been nothing but open and polite with her!

And even if he *had* made any suggestive remarks then she would, of course, knock him back regardless of whether he was a drop of excitement in her otherwise pleasantly predictable life.

She was careful. When it came to men, she didn't dive head first into the water because you never knew what was lurking under the surface.

With the electrifying feel of those dark eyes broodingly watching her, Rose breathed in deep and remembered all the life lessons from her past. Remembered her mother, who had gone off the rails when Rose's father had died. She'd lost her love and she had worked her way through her grief with catastrophic consequences, flinging herself headlong into a series of doomed relationships. Rose had been a child at the time but she could remember the carousel of inappropriate men and the apprehension she had felt every time that doorbell had sounded.

Then Alison Tremain had fallen in love—head over heels in love—with a rich, louche member of the landed gentry who had promised her everything she'd been desperate to hear. God only knew what she'd been thinking. She'd been hired to clean the exquisite Cotswold cottage owned by his parents, where he and twelve other fast-living friends had been staying for a long weekend. Had her mother really thought that it was love? But he'd swept her off her feet and maybe, Rose had later thought, when she had looked back at events through adult eyes, his heart had been in the right place.

The two had hurtled towards one another for all the wrong reasons. Rose's mother because she'd wanted an anchor in her life. She'd been swimming against the tide and had been on the verge of drowning and he had given her something to hold onto and she hadn't looked further than the wild promises he'd made.

And he…he'd wanted to rebel against restrictive parents and Alison Tremain had been his passport to asserting authority over a life that had been dictated from birth. Their disapproval would underline his independence, would prove that he could choose someone outside the box and damn the consequences. Brimming over with left-wing principles, he would be able to ditch the upper-crust background into which he had been born.

It had been a recipe for disaster from the word *go* and, for Rose, the personal disaster had started when her mother had dumped her with their neighbour: *'Just for a bit...just until I'm sorted...and then I'll come to fetch you, that's a promise.'*

Everyone had rallied around as she had found herself suddenly displaced—the benefit of a small community—but there had been many times when she had entered a room unexpectedly to be greeted by hushed whispers and covert, pitying looks.

Rose knew that things could have been a lot worse. She could have ended up in care. As it was, she spent nearly two years with the neighbours, whose daughter went to the same school as her.

Her mother had written and Rose had waited patiently but by the time a much-chastened Alison returned to the village Rose had grown into a cautious young girl, conscious of the perils of letting her emotions rule her life.

She'd witnessed her mother going off the rails because of a broken heart and had lived through her disappearing and getting lost in a world, she later learned, of soft drugs and alcohol because Spencer Kurtis had been unable to cope with the daily demands of a life without money on tap. So much for his rebellion. He had eventually crawled back to the family pile and Alison Tremain had returned to village life, where it had taken her a further year to recover before she was properly back to the person she had once been.

Rose knew better than to ever allow her behaviour to be guided by emotion. Sensible choices resulted in a settled life. Her sensible choices when it came to men, all two of them, might not have worked out but that didn't mean that she was going to rethink her ground plan.

She also knew better than to trust any man with money and time had only served to consolidate that opinion.

Her mother had been strung along by a rich man and in the end he hadn't been able to tear himself away from his wealthy background. But, beyond the story of one insignificant person, Rose had seen how, time and again, the wealthy took what they wanted without any thought at all for the people they trampled over.

The community that had rallied around her was, over the years, being invaded because developers couldn't keep their hands away from the temptation to take what was there and turn it into money-making projects. Their little oasis in the Cotswolds was achingly pretty and was also close enough to Oxford to save it from being too unremittingly rural.

In a very real sense, Rose felt that she owed a duty to the small community that had embraced her when her mother had started acting erratically and that included saving it from the whims of rich developers.

She was, for the first time in her life, sorely tempted to explain all of this to the ridiculously good-looking guy who, she noted wryly, had completely abandoned all attempts at vegetable preparation and was now pushing himself away from the counter to hunt down whatever wine was in the fridge.

'I never know what's there,' Rose said, half turning. 'The fridge has ended up being fairly communal property. Once a week someone has a go at tossing out whatever has gone past its sell-by date and everyone more or less tries to replace what's been taken so that we never find ourselves short of essentials like milk.'

'Doesn't that bug you?'

'No. Why should it?'

'Maybe because this is your house and a man's house should be his castle? What's the point of a castle if you let down the ramparts every two seconds to welcome in invaders? Who go through your belongings like gannets? Is this wine common property? Who does it belong to?' He held up a cheap bottle of plonk, which was better than nothing.

'That's mine and on the subject of one's house being one's castle, I can't afford that luxury.' Rose wasn't looking at him as she delivered this observation. In the companionable peace of the kitchen it felt comfortable to chat and she realised that, yes, quite often she longed for the pleasure of having the house to herself. 'I'm just lucky that I have this place. It was given to my mum by…er…by a friend and when she died it was passed onto me…'

Arturo looked at her carefully, but his voice was casual enough when he next spoke.

'Generous gift,' he murmured. 'Boyfriend? Lover? That kind of friend?'

'Something like that.' Rose swivelled, took the wine from him and, having bunged all the vegetables and seasoning into a pan with some sauce, she edged towards the kitchen table, absently sweeping some of the papers away and stacking half-finished cardboard placards into a pile on the ground. 'You're doing it again.'

'Doing what?' Arturo sipped some wine and looked at her over the rim of the glass.

'Prying,' she said drily. 'Is that a habit of yours? No, don't answer that.' She raised her eyebrows and shot him a shrewd assessing look. 'You pry. I gathered that the second you started opening doors to rooms when you first arrived, wanting to find out what was going on where. Must be your nature.'

'Expertly summed up… I like to find things out. How else can anyone have an informed opinion unless they're in possession of all the facts?'

'You're very arrogant, aren't you?' But she laughed, seeing that as commendable in someone who felt passionate about what was happening in the world around him. Too many people were content to sit on the fence rather than take a stand. Digging deep and arriving at an informed opinion was what separated the doer from the thinker. 'I mean that if you don't encourage domesticity and you don't do much talking to women then it's unlikely you ask them many questions about what they think. So why,' she added, 'are you being so inquisitive with me?'

'Maybe because I've never met anyone like you before.'

'Is that a good thing?' Rose detected the breathless note in her voice with a shiver of alarm. She was mesmerised by the lazy smile that lightened the harsh beauty of his face.

'For me, it's…strangely exciting.'

Her eyelids fluttered and her breathing hitched and her whole body suddenly tingled as though she had been caressed.

Arturo looked at her with leisurely, assessing eyes. He was clearly used to having what he wanted when it came to women. She sensed it included immediate gratification.

'I… Look… I didn't ask you to stay here…because… because…' She cleared her throat and subsided into awkward silence.

'Of course not, but I'm not the only one feeling this thing, am I?'

'I don't know what you're talking about.'

'No? We'll run with that for the time being, shall we? Tell me about the house.'

Rose blinked. Somewhere along the line she'd stopped being the feisty lawyer with the social conscience and had morphed into…a gawky adolescent with a teenage crush on the cute new boy in class. The chemistry between them was overwhelming. It slammed into her like a fist and the fact that he felt it as well, felt *something* at any rate, only made the situation worse. She'd spent a lifetime protecting herself from her emotions getting the better of her, had approached men with wariness because she knew the sort of scars that could be inflicted when bad choices went horribly wrong. On no level could this man be described as anything but a bad choice. So why was she perspiring with nerves and frantically trying to shut down the slide show of what could happen if she gave in…?

'The house?' she parroted, a little dazed.

'You were telling me that you inherited the house... that your mother was given it...'

'Right.'

And how had that come about? she wondered. *When she was the last person who made a habit of blabbing about her personal life?*

Disoriented at the chaos of her thoughts, she set to finishing the meal—anything to tear her gaze away from his darkly compelling face—but her hand was shaking slightly as she began draining pasta and warming the sauce.

'My mother had a fling with a guy,' she said in a halting voice, breathing more evenly now that she wasn't gawping at him like a rabbit caught in the headlights.

'Happens...'

'Yes, it does.' She swung around to look him squarely in the eyes. 'Especially when you're in mourning for the man you thought you'd be sitting next to in your old age, watching telly and going misty-eyed over the great-grandchildren...'

'What do you mean?'

Rose sighed. 'Nothing.'

'Tell me more.' Art hadn't eaten home-cooked food in any kitchen with any woman for a very, very long time. He dug into the bowl of pasta with gusto, realising that he was a lot hungrier than he'd thought.

He was eating here, just a stranger passing through instead of a billionaire to be feared, feted and courted by everyone with whom he came into contact. This was what normality felt like. He could scarcely remember the feeling. He wondered whether this was why he was intensely curious about her because she, like this whole experience, represented something out of the ordinary. Or maybe, he decided, it just stemmed from the fact that no information he could glean from her would be put to waste, not when he had a job to do. This was all just part of the game and what else was life but an elaborate game? In which there would inevitably be winners and losers and when it came to winning Art was the leader of the pack.

Far more comfortable with that pragmatic explanation, Art shot her an encouraging look.

'It's no big deal.' Rose shrugged and twirled some spaghetti around her fork, not looking at him. 'My father died when I was quite young and for a while my mum went off the rails. Got involved with...well...it was—' she grimaced and blushed '—an interesting time all round. One of the guys she became involved with was a rich young minor aristocrat whose parents owned a massive property about ten miles away from here. It ended in tears but years later, out of the blue, she received this house in his will, much to everyone's surprise. He'd been handed swathes of properties on his twenty-fifth birthday and he left this house to Mum, never thinking he'd die in a motorbike accident when he was still quite young.'

'A tragedy with a fortunate outcome.' Art considered the parallels between their respective parents and felt a tug of admiration that she had clearly successfully navigated a troubled background. He had too, naturally, but he was as cold as ice and just as malleable. He had been an observant, together teenager and a controlled, utterly cool-headed adult. He'd also had the advantage of money, which had always been there whatever the efforts of his father's grasping ex-wives to deprive him of as much of it as they possibly could.

She, it would seem, was cut from the same cloth. When he thought of the sob stories some of his girl-friends had bored him with, he knew he'd somehow ended up summing up the fairer sex as hopeless when it came to dealing with anything that wasn't sunshine and roses.

'Guilty conscience,' Rose responded wryly. 'He really led my mother off the straight and narrow, and then dumped her for reasons that are just too long-winded to go into. Put it this way—' she neatly closed her knife and fork and propped her chin in the palm of her hand '—he introduced her to the wonderful world of drugs and drink and then ditched her because, in the end, he needed the family money a lot more than he needed her. He also loved the family money more than he could ever have loved *her*.'

'Charming,' Art murmured, his keen dark eyes pinned to the stubborn set of her wide mouth.

'Rich.'

'Come again?'

'He was rich so he figured he could do as he pleased and he did, not that it didn't work out just fine in the end. Mum…came home and picked up the pieces and she was a darn sight better off without that guy in her life.'

'Came home…? Picked up the pieces…?'

Rose flushed. 'She disappeared for a while,' she muttered, rising to clear the table.

'How long *a while*?'

'What does any of this have to do with the protest?'

'Like I told you, I'm a keen observer of human nature. I enjoy knowing what makes people tick…what makes them who they are.'

'I'm not a specimen on a petri dish,' she said with more of her usual spirit, and Art burst out laughing.

'You're not,' he concurred, 'which doesn't mean that I'm any the less curious. So talk to me. I don't do domestic and I don't do personal conversations but I'm sorely tempted to invite you to be the exception to my rule. My *one-off*, so to speak…'

CHAPTER FOUR

TELL ME MORE...

Art bided his time. Curiosity battled with common sense. For some reason, over the next three days he kept wanting to return to the story of her past. His appetite to hear more had been whetted and it was all he could do to stamp down the urge to corner her and pry.

But that wasn't going to do.

He hadn't pursued the subject three days previously when his curiosity had been piqued because he had known that playing the waiting game was going to be a better bet.

He'd already gleaned one very important piece of information. She needed money. And while she might carry the banner of *money can't buy you happiness* and *the good things in life are free*, Art knew that reality had very sharp teeth.

The house was falling down around her and whilst she did get some money from the tenants, enough to cover the essentials, from what she had told him in dribs and drabs she simply didn't earn enough to keep things going.

And houses in this part of the world weren't cheap. He knew because he'd strolled through the village, taking in all the great little details that made it such a perfect place for an upmarket housing development.

He wondered whether he could offer her something tantalising to call off the protest. He might have to dump the fellow protestor guise and reveal his true identity or he could simply contrive to act as a middleman to broker a deal. At any rate, he played with the idea of contributing something towards the community, something close to her heart that would make her think twice about continuing a line of action that was never going to pay dividends. Harold had been right when he'd painted his doomsday picture of a close-knit, hostile community determined to fend off the rich intruders with their giant four-wheel drive wagons and their sense of entitlement. They'd be wrong but since when did right and wrong enter into the picture when emotions were running high?

And Art needed peace. He needed the community onside. He needed to get past this first stage of development to reach the important second stage. When he thought of the benefits of the equestrian and craft centre he hoped to develop, for his stepbrother and the small intake of similar adults like his stepbrother, he knew just how vital it was for him to win this war with the backing of the people waving the placards. If he barrelled through their protest with marching boots they would turn on him and all his long-term plans would lie in ruins.

He'd met all the people who were protesting and the majority of them had kids who attended the local school.

He could appeal to them directly, imply that the heart-less developers might be forced to build a new school.

His role, he had made sure to establish, was a fluid one. He had gone from protestor in situ to keen ob-server of human nature and general do-gooder who cared about the environment. He'd been vague about his actual background but had somehow managed to imply that he was more than just a drifter out to attach himself to a worthwhile cause. He'd used his imagina-tion and he knew that a lot of the protestors were begin-ning to turn to him to answer some of their questions.

It irked him that even as he tried to find a solution to the situation and even as he mentally worked out the cost of digging into his pocket to effectively buy them off when there was, technically, no need for him to do so, he was still managing to feel bloody guilty at his charade.

He'd had no idea his conscience was so hyperactive and it got on his nerves.

Although…he had to admit a certain desire to im-press the woman he was sharing a house with—fistfuls of cash would mean she could do the improvements she needed. He was cynical enough to suspect that if suf-ficient hard cash was put on the table she would not be able to resist because she was human and humans were all, without exception, susceptible to the lure of money.

Trouble was, he had to content himself with the painting job she had delegated to him.

'You don't have to,' she had said two days previously, when she had led him to a part of the house that looked as though the cobwebs had set up camp the day after the final brick in the house had been laid. 'You pay rent and, believe me, that's sufficient help.'

But Art had felt obliged to make good on his vague assurances that he was capable of helping out.

Besides, painting the room was proving to be a valuable way of avoiding her because the more contact he had with her, the more interested he became in digging deeper, past the polite conversation they shared, usually in the company of a million other people. After that first night she had shared nothing more about herself. They had had no time alone together. Her house was apparently a magnet for every person in the village who had nothing better to do than drop by for a chat.

The night before, someone she had bumped into several weeks previously had shown up for an informal chat about a problem he was having with his new employer, who had taken over the company and was trying to get rid of all the old retainers by fair means or foul.

To Art's amazement, Rose had been happy to feed the guy and give him free advice. Little wonder she didn't have much money going spare when she failed to charge for most of her services.

Her absolute lack of interest in making money should have been anathema to him but the opposite appeared to be the case. The more she invited the world into her house, the more he wanted her to slam the front door so that he could have her all to himself.

Nothing to do with the reason he was here.

Just because…he wanted to have her all to himself.

He'd managed to find a couple of hours during which he'd touched base with several of his clients and answered a couple of urgent emails and then he'd done some painting.

Now, at a little after six-thirty, he stood back to inspect his efforts and was quietly pleased with what he had managed. The mucus shade of green was slowly being replaced by something off-white and bland. Big improvement.

Still in paint-spattered clothes, Art went downstairs, fully expecting to find a few more waifs and strays in the kitchen, but instead there was just Rose sitting at the kitchen table, poring over a file.

From the doorway, he stood and looked, giving in to the steady pulse of desire rippling through him like a forbidden drumbeat. She was frowning, her slender hands cupping her face as she peered down at the stack of papers in front of her. She reached to absently remove the clasp from her hair and he sucked in a sharp breath as it fell around her shoulders in a tumble of uncontrolled curls. Deep chestnut brown...shades of dark auburn...paler strands of toffee...a riot of vibrant colour that took his breath away.

For once she wasn't wearing something long and shapeless but instead a pair of faded blue jeans and an old grey cropped tee shirt and, from the way she was hunched over the table, he was afforded a tantalising glimpse of her cleavage.

She looked up, caught his eye and sat back.

She stretched and half yawned and the forbidden drumbeat surged into a tidal wave of primal desire.

No bra.

He could see the jut of her nipples against the soft

cotton and the caution he had been meticulously cultivating over the past few days disappeared in a puff of smoke.

His erection was as solid as a shaft of steel and he had to look away to gather himself for a few vital seconds or else risk losing the plot altogether.

'Took the afternoon off.' Rose smiled and stood up. 'Hence the casual gear. Drink? Tea? Coffee? Something stronger? I've actually gone out and bought some wine.'

'The rent I pay doesn't cover food. It's Friday. Allow me to take you out for a meal.'

Rose hesitated. She hadn't been out for a meal with a man for ages. She was twenty-eight years old and the thrills of her social life could be written on the back of a postage stamp.

'Restaurants will be packed out.' She laughed, anticipation bubbling up inside her. 'Tourists…'

'We can venture further afield. Name the place and I'll reserve a table.'

'Don't be silly. You don't have to…'

'You don't have to…?' Arturo shot her a wry look from under sooty lashes. 'Anyone who knows me at all would know that those four words would never apply to me because I make it my duty never to feel that I have to do anything I don't want to do. If I didn't want to take you out to dinner I would never have issued the invitation in the first place. Now, name the place.'

God, Rose thought, who would ever think that she would go for a guy who took charge? She was much more into the sensitive kind of guy who consulted and discussed. Arturo Frank couldn't have been less of a consulting and discussing man, and yet a pleasurable shiver rippled through her as she met his deep, dark eyes. 'Name the place? Now, let me think about that. How generous are you feeling tonight...?'

Rose shocked herself because she wasn't flirtatious by nature. Her mother had always been the flirt, which was probably why she had ended up where she had. That was a characteristic Rose had made sure to squash, not that there had ever been any evidence of it being there in the first place.

But she felt like a flirt as their eyes tangled and she half smiled with her head tilted pensively to one side.

'I'm just kidding.' She grinned and ran her fingers through her tangled hair. 'There are a couple of excellent pizza places in the next village along. I can call and reserve a table. So...in answer to your invitation, it's a yes.'

'I'm saying no to the cheap and cheerful pizza place,' Arturo delivered with a dismissive gesture, eyes still glued to her face.

'In that case...'

'Leave it with me. I'll sort it.'

'You will?'

'Expect something slightly more upmarket than a fast-food joint.'

'In which case, I'll naturally share the bill.'

'That won't be happening. When I ask a woman out, she doesn't go near her wallet.'

There she went, tingling all over again! Behaving like the frothy, frilly, girly girl she had never been. He was so macho, so alpha male, so incredibly intelligent, and yet he cared about all the things she cared about. She prided herself on being savvy but she could feel the ground slip beneath her feet and she liked the way it felt, enjoyed the heady sensation of falling.

She wasn't interested in any man who was just passing through, but a little voice asked inside her head… *What if she took a risk?* After all, where had being careful got her?

And an even more treacherous little voice whispered seductively, *What if he delays his plans to move on…? In the end all nomads found their resting ground, didn't they? And there were jobs aplenty for a guy as smart and proactive as he was…*

'Okay.'

'You look a little bemused. What kind of guys have you gone out with in the past? Did they take out their calculator at the end of the meal so that they could split the bill in half? Call me antiquated—' his voice lowered to a murmur '—but I enjoy being generous with the women I take out.'

So we're going on a date.

Excitement surged through Rose in a disturbing, all-consuming tidal wave.

Maybe—she brought herself back down to earth—it wasn't a date. As such. Maybe it was simply his way of saying thank you for renting a room in her house and having whatever food and drink he wanted at his disposal. He was paying her a lot more than she'd wanted but it was still a lot less than if he'd been staying in even the cheapest of the local hotels.

But the warmth of his gaze was still turning her head

to mush when, an hour later and with no idea where they would be going, she stood in front of her wardrobe surveying the uninspiring collection of comfortable clothes that comprised her going-out gear.

It bore witness to the alarming fact that when it came to going out she had become decidedly lazy over time. Easy evenings with friends, the occasional movie, casual suppers at the kitchen table, for which she could have shown up in her PJs and no one would really have cared one way or the other.

In fact, working largely from the house as she did, her work clothes were interchangeable with her casual wear. Everything blurred into loose-fitting and shapeless.

Practical, she reminded herself, hand brushing past the baggy culottes to linger on the one and only figure-hugging skirt she possessed. Her wardrobe was filled with practical clothes because she was, above all else, practical. Her mother had had the monopoly on impulsive behaviour. She, Rose, was practical.

Yet she didn't feel practical as she wriggled into the clinging jade-green skirt and the only slightly less clinging black top with the little pearl buttons down the front, the top four of which she undid. Then promptly did back up.

There was little she could do with her hair, but she liked the way it hung in a riot of curls over her shoulders, and when she plunged her feet into her one and only pair of high-heeled shoes…well, she would have dwarfed a lot of men but she wasn't going to dwarf the one who would be waiting for her downstairs.

In fact, she would be elevated to his level. Eye to eye…nose to nose…*mouth to mouth…*

Waiting for her in the kitchen with a glass of wine in his hand, Art was just off the phone from one of the finest restaurants in the area. He wasn't sure how he was going to explain away the extravagance but he was sick of mealtimes being pot luck, along the lines of a bring-and-buy sale in someone's backyard.

He was also sick of conversations with her being halted by someone popping their head around the door. She worked from her house and so seemed accessible to any and everyone. While he had been busy planting questions in the heads of all those protestors squatting on his land in the misguided belief that they were going to halt the march of progress, he hadn't actually got around to planting a single question in Rose's head because he never seemed to find the time to be alone with her for longer than five seconds.

He was also disgruntled and frustrated at the tantalising glimpses of her personal life which he had been unable to explore. He accepted that that was just thwarted curiosity but it was still frustrating. He existed on a diet of being able to get exactly what he wanted, and that included a woman's full and undivided attention.

She had told him something about herself and he had found himself wanting to hear more and had been unable to. When had that ever happened before? Given half a chance, there was no woman he could think of who wouldn't have clawed her way back to that interrupted personal conversation with the tenacity of a tigress.

But no. It was almost as though Rose had more pressing things to do than talk to him.

And yet…there was *something* between them. He felt it and so did she. It was just not big enough for her to actually put herself out to try to cultivate it and that irked him.

All in all, he was looking forward to this meal out more than he could remember looking forward to anything in a long time.

He swirled the wine in his glass, looked down at the golden liquid and then, when he looked up…

There she was.

Art straightened. His mouth fell open. Rooted to the spot, he could feel the throb of sexual awareness flower and bloom into something hot and urgent and pressing.

She was…bloody *stunning*.

That body, long-limbed and rangy under the challenging attire, was spectacular. Lean and toned and effortlessly graceful. She lacked the practised art of the catwalk model, the strutting posture and the moody expression, and she was all the sexier for that.

And she wasn't wearing a bra.

He did his utmost not to stare at the small, rounded pertness of her breasts and the indentation of pebbly nipples pushing against the fine cotton.

He could see Rose's whole body react to that leisurely appraisal and the horrified look on her face which accompanied her involuntary response. It galvanised her into speech and action at the same time, moving into the kitchen whilst simultaneously pinning a bright smile to her face as she quizzed him on where they were going.

Art snapped out of his trance.

'I'll just grab my bag.' She interrupted her nervous chatter to look around her.

'Why?'

'Car keys, for one thing!' she announced gaily.

The kitchen felt too small for both of them to be in it. He was wearing nothing more than a pair of dark trousers and a white shirt, staple components of any wardrobe, and yet he looked jaw-droppingly beautiful. He filled the contours of the shirt to perfection. She could see the ripple of muscle under the fabric and he had rolled the sleeves up so that her eyes were drawn to his forearms, liberally sprinkled with dark, silky hair. The minute her eyes went there they couldn't help but move further along to his long brown fingers and it was then a hop and a skip until she wondered what those fingers would feel like…on her and…*in her*.

'What? Sorry?'

Had he said something?

'I've ordered a taxi so there's no need for you to drive,' he delivered smoothly, allowing her no time to lodge a protest.

'You're so good at taking over,' Rose murmured, blushing and smiling.

'I can't help it,' Arturo said without apology. 'It's part of my personality.'

He lowered his eyes and offered his arm to her.

'It's been a while since…'

'Since?'

'Since I've been out for a meal.'

'You mean…on a date?'

'Is that what this is?' They were outside and he was opening the car door for her, waiting as she slid into the back seat before joining her. 'I thought…' she turned to him and breathed in the clean, woody smell of him, which made her want to pass out '…that this was just your way of thanking me for putting you up. Not—' she laughed '—that it's been any bother at all!'

'That as well…'

'You needn't have.'

'Again. Those annoying words. It's not a declaration of intent,' he interjected, then his voice lowered. 'It's a… I haven't told you, but you look…remarkable…'

'I know it's not a declaration of intent! You're just passing through and, besides, you're the guy who doesn't do domesticity, home cooking or women asking personal questions. And thank you for the compliment, by the way. I… I haven't worn this old outfit in a long time.'

Her breathing was jerky and she took refuge in gazing through the window at the familiar countryside. She had no idea where they were going, but it wasn't long before she found out because she recognised the impressive drive that led to one of the top hotels in the county, where a famous Michelin-starred chef produced food she could never have afforded in a million years.

She turned to him, her face a picture of bemusement and shock.

'I recently came into some money,' Arturo said smoothly, 'and I can't think of a better way of spending some of it than on bringing you here.'

'I'm not dressed for this place.'

'Do you care what other people think?' He swung out of the car and walked around to open her door.

'Who doesn't?'

'I don't.'

'Maybe it's a legacy from when my mum went away.' Rose was agog as they were shown into the splendid hotel and then escorted like royalty to the most impressive dining room she had ever been in. She was hardly aware of what she was saying. She was way too focused on trying to take in everything around her.

'You were saying…?' he said as soon as they were seated, a corner table with a bird's eye view of the richly ornate interior.

'I was saying that my eyes are popping out.' She swivelled to look at him and her breathing became shallow. What money, she wondered, had he come into? But then, hot on the heels of that thought, came another—her mother had been the recipient of an equally surprising inheritance. Stranger things happened in life. It certainly explained how he was footloose and fancy free…and able to indulge his interest in saving the countryside.

And if he was generous by nature, as he clearly was, then he would probably travel around until the cash ran out before returning to whatever job he had had before. That was a small detail he had never filled her in on.

He'd warned her off reading anything into this dinner invitation but he was crazy if he thought that she wasn't going to be impressed to death by his generosity and by the time and effort he'd put into sourcing this place for them. God only knew how he'd managed to wangle a table but she had seen, in his interactions with the people on the site, that he could charm the birds from the trees.

'And you were telling me why it is that you care about what people think…'

Rose looked at him. He'd shaved but still managed to look darkly dangerous. There was a stillness about him that made her nerves race and brought a fine prickle of perspiration to her skin. Something about the lazy intensity of his eyes when they focused on her.

'And how long did your mother go away for?'

'Two years,' Rose admitted, flattered at his interest.

'Two *years*?'

'I know in the big scheme of things it doesn't seem like a lifetime but, believe me, when you're a kid and you're waiting by the window it *feels* never-ending.'

'In the big scheme of things it bloody *is* never-ending, Rose, and to a kid… How old *were* you?'

'Eight.'

'Eight.' Art was shocked. His father had lost the plot for very similar reasons, which pretty much said everything there was to say on the subject of love, but abandonment had not been an issue. 'Where did you stay… at the age of eight…while your mother vanished on her soul-seeking mission?'

'You shouldn't be too hard on her. She was screwed up at the time. I stayed in the village, of course. Where else? I lived with the neighbours. I'm not sure whether they thought that they'd be hanging onto me for as long as they had to but they were wonderful. That said, I knew there was gossip and that hurt. I was saved from a much harsher fate when my mother started acting up because I happened to live where I did. In a small village that protected its own. I owe them.'

'You owe them…the entire village…a sizeable debt. So…' this half to himself '…*that's* why this fight is so personal to you.'

'Something like that. But you must be bored stiff listening to me rattle on.'

'The opposite.' Art forced himself to relax. All problems had solutions and he was solution-orientated. 'I've wandered through the village,' he said, adroitly changing the subject as he perused the menu without looking at her. 'I'm surprised you haven't thought to use a little bribery and blackmail with the developers who want the land you're occupying…'

'Sorry?' Rose's head shot up and she stared at him with a frown.

'You recall I asked Phil to have a look at the paperwork? Not because I'm any kind of expert, but I wanted to see for myself what the legal position was with the land. Some of the protesters out there have been asking questions…'

'You never mentioned that to me.'

'Should I have? Passing interest. Nothing more.' Art paused. 'The land is sold and there's nothing anyone can do about that.'

'You'd be surprised how public opinion can alter the outcome of something unpleasant.' Rose's lips firmed. She wasn't sure whether to fume at his intrusion or be pleased at his intelligent interest in the situation.

'People might be open to alternative lines of approach,' he implied, shutting his menu and sitting back.

'You're very optimistic if you think that a company the size of DC Logistics would be interested in anything other than steamrollering over us. We're fighting fire with fire and if we lose…then we can make sure that life isn't easy for them as they go ahead with their conscienceless development.'

'Or you could try another tack. Apparently the local school could do with a lot of refurbishment. The sports ground is in dire need of repair. One section of the building that was damaged by fire last year is still out of bounds. Frankly, that's a lawsuit waiting to happen. Ever thought that instead of threatening a company that has deeds to the land, you could always coerce them into doing their bit for the community?'

'You've certainly been digging deep.' Rose sat back and looked at Art. 'Have you been discussing this alternative with my protestors?'

'They're not *your* protestors,' he fielded coolly, meeting her gaze without blinking. 'If you have deeper, more personal reasons for your fight, then they don't necessarily share those reasons. They might be open to other ways of dealing with the situation.'

Wine was being brought to the table. He waited until the waiter had poured them both a glass then he raised his.

'But enough of this. We're not here to talk about the land, are we? That said…it's just something you might want to think about.'

CHAPTER FIVE

IT WAS THE best meal she had ever had in her life although, as she reluctantly left a morsel of the *crème brulée* in its dish because she physically couldn't manage another mouthful, Rose had to admit that it was much more than the quality of the food that had made the evening quite perfect.

It was the fact that she was here with Arturo.

They had not had an opportunity to talk, to really talk, since he had moved in and for four hours they more than made up for that. He was fascinating. He knew *so much.* He could converse with ease on any topic and he had a wonderful knack of drawing her out of herself, making her open up in a way that revealed to her just how private she had become over the years.

He could be self-deprecating one minute and, almost without pausing to draw breath, ruin the illusion by being astoundingly arrogant—but arrogant in a way that somehow didn't manage to get on her nerves. She couldn't understand how that was in any way, shape or form possible…but it clearly was.

And he'd made her think—about the protest and

other ways that might be found to bring about a positive outcome. He had touched only once more on the subject and the notion of inevitability had been aired—yes, it was inevitable that the land would be developed, but that suggestion he had planted in her head was beginning to look quite promising. She had certain trump cards and there was much that could be done to improve the village.

She was tipsy and happy as they stepped out into the velvety black night.

'I haven't had such a lovely time in ages,' she confided as a taxi pulled to a stop as soon as they were outside. She waited until he was in the back seat with her before turning to him. The darkness turned his face into a mosaic of hard shadows and angles and, just for a few seconds, she felt a tingle of apprehension that warred with the warm, melting feeling making her limbs heavy and pleasantly blurring her thoughts.

She was smiling—grinning like a Cheshire cat—but he was quite serious as he looked at her.

'You look as though you can't wait for the evening to end,' she said lightly, sobering up, smile wavering. 'Don't blame you. You must be accustomed to far more exciting company than me.'

Looking back at her, Art thought that she couldn't have been further from the truth. He hadn't sat and talked with any woman for that length of time for years. In the normal course of events, an expensive meal would have included some light conversation but the evening would have been overlaid with the assumption of sex and the conversation would have been geared towards that.

'What makes you say that?'

'Something about you,' Rose admitted truthfully. 'You're not like anyone I've ever met before and if I can see that, then so can everyone else. You strike me as the sort of guy who's never short of female company. Is that why you steer clear of involvement? Because you don't see the point of settling down when there are so many fish in the sea?'

'I steer clear of involvement because I watched my father ruined by too much of it.'

'Oh.' Rose paused. 'How so?' she asked seriously.

Art had surprised himself by that admission and now he wondered what to say. A series of divorces? A carousel of avaricious blonde bombshells who had been out to feather their own nests? A fortune depleted by the demands of alimony payments? Where to start?

Art had been defined by one disillusionment after another, from the isolation he had had to endure as a child when his father had retreated into himself after his wife's sudden death to the abruptness of having to deal with boarding school, and all played out to the steady drumbeat of his father's failed relationships and the consequent, expensive fallout.

He shifted, stared briefly out of the window then back at her. Her gaze was calm, interested but without fuss and fanfare—curious but not overly so.

'My father had a habit of repeating his mistakes,' Art told her heavily. 'He was always quick to get involved, only to regret his involvement but then, just when he'd managed to free himself from one woman, he would repeat the cycle all over again. Your mother had her way of coping with losing her husband...' His mouth twisted into a crooked smile. 'My father coped in a slightly different way.'

'But in a way that would have equally damaging consequences... We certainly didn't strike jackpot when it came to childhood experiences, did we?' She shot him a rueful smile and reached out, almost impulsively, to rest her hand on his.

The warmth of her hand zapped through him like a powerful electric charge, tightening his groin and sending a heavy, pounding ache between his thighs.

With relief, he recognised that the taxi was pulling up outside her house.

He was in urgent need of a cold shower. Maybe even a cold bath. Blocks of ice would have to play a part. Anything to cool the onset of his ardour.

'All experience,' he said neutrally, pushing open his door and glancing back at her over his shoulder in a gesture that implied an end to the conversation, 'is good experience, in my opinion. But I'm very glad you enjoyed the evening.'

He all but sprinted to the front door. She fumbled with the front door key and he relieved her of it, acutely aware of the brush of her skin against his.

'I don't usually drink as much as I did tonight,' Rose apologised with a little breathy laugh, stepping past him into the hall. 'I'm beginning to think that I should get out more, live a little...'

'All work and no play... You know the saying...'

* * *

For a few moments they both stood in the semi-darkened hallway, staring at one another in taut silence, and the breath caught in her throat because she could see the lick of desire in his eyes, a sexual speculation that set her ablaze with frantic desire because it mirrored her own.

'Right, well...' Rose was the first to break the lengthening silence. 'Thanks again for a brilliant evening...' She began turning away but then felt his hand circle her arm and she stilled, heart racing, pulse racing—*everything* racing.

'Rose...'

With one foot planted firmly in the comfort zone of common sense and the other dangling precariously and recklessly over the edge of a precipice, Rose looked at him, holding herself rigid with tension.

'It would be madness.' Arturo looked away, looked back to her, looked away again, restless and uncomfortable in his own skin and yet powerless to relieve either discomfort.

'What?' Rose whispered.

'You know what. This. Us. Taking this any further.'

For a few seconds she didn't say anything, then eventually she murmured, briefly breaking their electrifying eye contact, 'I agree.'

'You can't even begin to understand the complications...'

'Do I need to?'

'Explain.'

'We're not anticipating a relationship.' She tilted her

chin at a defiant angle. Sex for the sake of sex? She'd never contemplated that. The urgent demands of lust, the taste of a passion that was powerful enough to make a nonsense of her principles...well, those were things that had never blotted her horizon. 'We don't have to think about all the complications or all the reasons why it wouldn't make sense for us to...to...' She reddened and caught his eye.

'Make wild, passionate love until we just can't any longer?'

'You're just passing through...'

'Sure that doesn't bother you? Because I won't be staying. A week, tops, and I'll be gone and that'll be the last you'll ever see of me.'

'You wouldn't be curious to see where the protest you joined will end up?'

'I know where it'll end up.' He clearly didn't want to talk about that. He raised his arm to stroke her cheek with the back of his hand, a light, feathery touch that made her sigh and close her eyes.

'Let's go upstairs,' she breathed unevenly, her eyes fluttering open to gaze at his impossibly handsome face. She stepped back and took his hand. If this was wrong, then why did it feel so *right*? Before hitting the stairs, she kicked her shoes off and then padded up ahead of him, still holding his hand, glancing back over her shoulder twice, wishing that she knew what was going through his head.

She shyly pushed open her bedroom door and stepped in, ignoring the overhead light in favour of the lamp by her bed, which cast an immediate mellow glow through the room.

It was a large square room, with high ceilings and both picture rails and dado rails.

Arturo had not been in it before. He looked around briefly and then grinned. 'I didn't take you for having such a sense of drama…'

Rose laughed, walked towards him and linked her arms around his waist. 'I'm sensible when it comes to pretty much everything but—' she looked at the dreamy four-poster king-sized bed with floaty curtains and dark, soft-as-silk bed linen '—I used to dream of having a four-poster bed when I was a kid.'

'Was that when you were waiting for your mother to reappear?' Art murmured, burying his face into her hair and breathing in the sweet smell of the floral shampoo she used.

'How did you guess?'

'I'm tuned in like that.' A memory came from nowhere to knock him for six—a memory of his mother leaning over him, smiling, with a book in one hand. Had she just read him a story? Was she about to? She was dressed up, going out for the evening.

He clenched his jaw as the vivid image faded. 'Enough talk,' he growled, edging them both towards the bed. Rose giggled as her knees hit the mattress and she toppled backwards, taking him with her, although he niftily deflected the bulk of his weight from landing directly on her. But he remained where he was, flat on his back next to her.

'The canopy has stars,' he commented, amused, and he heard the grin in her voice when she replied.

'That's the hidden romantic in me.'

Art turned his head to look at her and she did likewise.

'You don't have to worry,' she said flatly, before he could jump in with another warning lecture on his nomadic tendencies—warning her off the temptation to look for more involvement than was on the table.

'Worry about what?'

'I may have the occasional romantic lapse, but I'm pretty level-headed when it comes to men, and latching onto a good-looking guy who has an aversion to putting down roots is the last sort of guy who would tick any boxes for me.'

'I tick at least *one* box,' Art murmured, smiling very slowly.

'Well, yes…you tick that one box.' Flustered, she held her breath as their eyes locked.

'Never knock the physical attraction box. It's the biggest one of all.'

'We'll have to agree to differ on that.'

'Think so?' Art grinned, settling on his side and manoeuvring her so that they were now facing one another, clothes still on and that very fact sending the temperature into the sizzling stratosphere. 'Oh, I wouldn't talk too fast if I were you…' He slipped his hand under her top and took his time getting to her breast, waiting until her breathing had become halting, her eyelids fluttering and her nostrils flaring. Then and only then did he touch her, cup her naked breast, feel the tight bud of her nipple. He'd spent the meal in a state of heightened awareness and the feel of her now was electrifying.

While he was busy telling her just how fast he could make her believe in the importance of sexual attraction because nothing was better than good sex, and he was very, *very* adept at giving very, *very* good sex, he was simultaneously on the verge of blowing it by getting turned on too quickly. In his book, speed and good sex rarely went together for a sensational experience.

He kept looking at her, holding her gaze, while he played with her nipple.

He wasn't going to go a step further until he got himself under control.

But, hell, those sexy eyes that were just on the right side of innocent, however sassy she was, were doing a million things to his body.

'You think you can convert me?' Rose breathed, squirming with want.

'No harm in trying.' Art let loose a low, sexy laugh. In one slick movement, he eased himself up to straddle her prone body, caging her in with his thighs. He hooked his fingers under the top and began slowly tugging it up.

'No bra,' he murmured. 'I like that.'

'I...' Rose gulped and wished that she hadn't switched any lights on at all, although would she have sacrificed the joy of looking at him to preserve her modesty? She felt faint as her top rode higher and then the whisper of cool air brought goosebumps to her naked skin. Automatically, she lifted her arms to cross them over her bare chest and, just as fast, Arturo gently pushed them aside and stifled a primal groan of pleasure as his eyes feasted on her.

'Beautiful,' he whispered, circling one straining bud with the tip of his finger.

Rose had never felt quite so exposed. She wasn't ashamed of her body. She simply recognised its limitations. Lights off worked when it came to dealing with those limitations and to have him looking at her like that…

She sneaked a glance at him and felt a surge of thrilling excitement because his eyes were dark with masculine appreciation.

'I'm not exactly the most voluptuous woman on the face of the earth,' Rose apologised, blushing. 'That's why I can go without a bra a lot of the time. Not much there to contain.' She laughed and watched his finger as it continued to circle her nipple, moving onto the other.

'You should never have hang-ups about your body,' Arturo said thickly. 'It's amazing. Your nipples are stunning…dark…*succulent*…'

'Arturo!'

He laughed and shot her a wicked look from under his lashes. 'Is that the sound of you begging me to continue telling you why you should be proud of your body?'

'No!' But she laughed, a little breathless laugh that was unsteady with anticipation.

'I'm going to have fun tasting them,' Arturo told her conversationally. 'Does it turn you on to imagine the feel of my mouth on your nipple?'

'Stop!'

'You're red as a beetroot.' Arturo grinned and gently tilted her averted face so that she was looking at him.

He vaulted off the bed, fumbled to make sure protection was handy and then he began getting undressed.

Rose stared.

She forgot all about her inhibitions because never had she seen anything so glorious in her life before.

He was all muscle and sinew, his broad shoulders tapering to a washboard-flat stomach. He ditched the shirt and raised his eyebrows with amusement at her rapt expression.

'You have no idea,' he murmured, taking a step towards her, at which she promptly hoisted herself onto her elbows, automatically leaning towards him, 'what that expression is doing to my libido.'

'Really?' Riveted, Rose continued to stare at him.

'Really,' Arturo said drily, 'but you'll see for yourself soon enough...' He burst out laughing when her eyes skittered away just as he began unbuttoning his trousers.

He seemed to revel in the intensity of her gaze.

The trousers were off.

The boxers followed suit.

Rose gulped. He was more than impressive. Big, thick, throbbing with *want*. Standing there, he was absolutely lacking in inhibition, carelessly indifferent to the perfection of his nakedness.

Rose sat up, then slid off the bed to stand in front of him. She was half naked and now all she wanted to do was yank down the skirt but, before she could, he stayed her fluttering hand and moved towards her, holding her just for a moment so that she could feel his hardness pressing against her belly.

'Allow me…' he murmured.

Arturo wasn't going to rush anything, even though his body must be clamouring for satisfaction.

He eased the skin-tight skirt off her to reveal plain cotton panties. For a few seconds, Arturo stilled.

He was kneeling and he drew back to look at her. Hands on her bare bottom, Arturo delicately teased the folds of her womanhood with a gentle touch, causing her to gasp and then exhale on a whimper.

When his tongue slid into the slippery crease she gasped again, this time on a guttural moan, and her fingers curled into his hair as she opened her legs wider to receive his attentions.

Rose was melting. Every bone in her body was turning to water as his tongue flicked over her, squirming deeper until he located the pulsing bud of her core.

The pleasure was intense, unbearable almost, nothing that she had ever felt before or could ever have imagined feeling. It was pure sensation and every thought, confused or otherwise, shot straight out of her head.

She realised that she was moving against his mouth in an unconscious rhythm.

She almost squeaked a protest when he drew back and stood up to lift her off her feet so that he could deposit her onto the bed, as though she weighed nothing at all.

Rose was expecting something fast and furious but instead he pinned her hands above her head, ordered her not to move a muscle and then sat back on his haunches to gaze at her with open admiration.

If this was how he was in bed with a woman, she thought in a heated daze, then she was surprised that there wasn't a demanding queue of ex-lovers banging on her front door, braying for him to return to bed with them.

'Just for the moment,' he said huskily, 'indulge me and allow me to take charge.'

With her hands still above her head, burrowed underneath the pillow, Rose half smiled.

'Are you trying to tell me that you don't take charge in everything you do?' she teased, 'because if you are then I don't believe you.'

'It's true. Some people have accused me of occasionally being somewhat…assertive.'

He seemed determined to assert himself right now. Starting with her breasts.

He kissed them, nuzzled their softness, making her writhe and stretch underneath him, her movements feline and sensuous. He licked one nipple with his tongue and then sucked on it, drawing it into his mouth and teasing the sensitive tip with his tongue. As he ministered to her breast, he dipped down to rest his hand between her thighs, lightly covering her mound with the palm of his hand and then pressing down in lazy circular movements.

Bliss.

Rose was dripping wet and she didn't care. She was explosively turned on. Something about the position of her arms heightened the sensitivity of her breasts and each flick of his tongue and caress of his hand made her want to cry out loud.

He trailed a path of kisses along her stomach and she inhaled sharply, wanting more than anything for him to taste her *down there* again, there between her legs where the ache desperately craved his touch.

As he found that place and began, once again, to tease her with his tongue, she arched up, spread her legs wider and bucked against his questing mouth.

Sensation started with an electric ripple that spread outwards with the force of a tsunami until she was lost in a world dictated by her physical response to his mouth. She could no more have strung a coherent thought together than she could have grown wings and taken flight.

When she came against his mouth it was with such force that she cried out, hands clutching the bed linen, her whole body arching, stiffening and then shuddering as everything exploded inside her.

She eventually subsided on a wave of mind-blowing contentment.

'Felt good?' Arturo lay alongside her, then curved her against him, pushing his thigh between her legs.

Rose linked her fingers around his neck and darted some kisses over his face. 'I'm sorry.' She looked at him with such genuine apology that he winced.

'Sorry about what?'

'Just lying there and…um…enjoying myself…'

'You have no idea how much enjoyment I got from pleasuring you.'

Rose smiled and curved against him, taking the initiative this time, adoring the hard, muscled lines of his body as she ran her hands over it. Along his shoulders, over his hard, sinewy chest, taking time to tease his flattened brown nipples.

His erection was thick and pulsing and she lowered herself into a position where she could take him into her mouth and he, manoeuvring her, could take her into his.

An exchange of intense pleasure that brought her right back up to the edge from which she had only recently descended.

Rose had never experienced such a lack of inhibition. She had always approached the opposite sex from a position of caution, a place where mechanisms were in place to prevent her from being too hurt. She'd never let go with anyone, not that her life had been cluttered with an abundance of men, and it astounded her that, of all the people in the world, she should be so free and open with one who wasn't destined to play any kind of permanent role in her life.

It didn't make sense.

But wonderfully open was exactly what she was feeling as she licked and teased and sucked him, as she felt him move between her thighs, tickling her with his tongue, their bodies fused as one.

They both knew when the time was right for the foreplay to end before it cascaded into orgasm.

Arturo eased her off him, groaning as their bodies broke contact. It was a matter of a few fumbling seconds and then, protection in place, he positioned himself over her.

Rose could barely contain her excitement. Her whole

body ached for the ultimate satisfaction of having him inside her and when he drove into her, thrusting hard and firm, she groaned long and low.

He filled her up and with each thrust she came closer and closer to the brink.

Art had never been with anyone as responsive as she was. It was as though he was tuned in to her, sensitive to just how far he could take her before she came, able to time his own orgasm to match hers, and when they came it was mind-blowing.

Deep inside her, embedded to the hilt, he drove hard and felt her shudder and cry out just as he rocked with waves of such intense pleasure that he couldn't contain his own guttural cry of satisfaction.

It was a few moments before they could unglue their bodies from one another. Unusually, Art didn't immediately feel the urge to break the connection by escaping to have a shower.

Instead, he slid off her and held her. What the hell had he done? He'd come here on a mission and this most definitely had *not* been any part of his mission.

But he looked down at her flushed face, her parted mouth, felt the warmth of her beautiful body pressed against his, and all he wanted to do was have her all over again.

Art knew that this was a weakness. In fact, sleeping with her at all had been a weakness. Since when had *any* woman taken precedence over common sense and, more importantly, work?

And what happened now?

Art knew what *should* happen. He should walk away. He should walk away and keep on walking until he hit London and the reality of his life there. He should put an immediate end to this charade and conduct whatever business needed conducting through his lawyers and accountants. The land belonged to him and tiptoeing around that stark fact was a matter of choice rather than necessity.

Okay, so maybe if she got stuck in and took a stand, the community would view his development as a blot on their landscape and react accordingly to the newcomers buying properties, but that wouldn't last. Within six months everything would settle down and life would carry on as normal.

His presence here and his willingness to do his best to ease the process would bear testimony to his capacity for goodwill.

It would also be useful because, in due course, he would be putting in another planning application and a hostile community would make that more difficult.

But in the end he would get what he wanted because he always did.

And, in the meantime, this…was a complication.

'What are you thinking?' Rose asked drowsily, opening her eyes to look directly at him. 'No,' she continued, 'I know what you're thinking.'

'Mind reader, are you?' Art smiled and kissed the tip of her nose. He cupped her naked breast with his hand and marvelled at how nicely it fitted. Not too big, not too small.

'You're thinking that it's time you went back to your

bedroom and you'd be right because it's late and I want to go to sleep.'

'Is that the sound of you kicking me out of your bedroom?' he murmured, moving in to nibble her ear and then licking the side of her neck so that she squirmed and giggled softly.

'It's the sound of a woman who needs her beauty sleep.' She wriggled away from him so that she could head for the bathroom.

'But what,' Art heard himself ask, 'does a red-blooded man do if he wakes in the early hours of the morning and needs his woman by his side?'

Rose stilled but when she answered her voice was still light and teasing. 'He goes downstairs for a glass of milk?'

'Wrong answer.' Art heaved himself into a sitting position and pulled her towards him. 'I never thought I'd hear myself say this, but let's spend the night together…and, by the way… I'd like it if you called me Art. Not Arthur…not Arturo. Art.'

CHAPTER SIX

ART GAZED AT the vast swathes of empty land around
him. Open fields. The very same open fields that had
confronted him on day one when he had arrived with
a plan and a deadline.

Slight difference now. The plan and the deadline
had both taken a battering. He'd slept with Rose over
a week and a half ago and even as his head had urged
him to turn his back and walk away, his body had argued against that course of action and had won.

They'd shared a bed every night since then. He
couldn't see her without wanting her. It was insane but
whatever attraction kept pulling him towards her, it was
bigger than all the reserves of willpower at his disposal.

And the land…

Art strolled to the very spot where the protesters had
set up camp. There were some stragglers but most had
left. He'd been busy arguing his corner whilst making sure not to stand on any soapboxes bellowing his
opinions. He'd listened to everything that had been said
and had quickly sussed that, however fervent they were
about the abstract notion of the land being developed,

when it came down to basics, the offer of those very same heartless developers doing some good for their community had won the day.

Financial assistance for the primary school; a fund towards the local library, which also served as a meeting place for most of the senior citizens; playing fields to be included on some of his land which, as it happened, suited Art very well indeed, bearing in mind his future plans for the site.

Art had advised them to contact the team of lawyers working for DC Logistics.

'There's always a solution when it comes to sorting problems,' he had asserted, safe in the knowledge that they would find no hindrance to their requests. Not only was he happy to ease the situation but he was positively pleased to be able to do so because he had grown fond of all of them, had seen for himself, first-hand, how strongly they felt about the land.

In London, community spirit of that kind was noticeably absent and he'd been impressed by what he'd seen.

And, crucially, Rose had more or less conceded that it was the best solution because, like it or not, those tractors and cranes would move in sooner or later.

His job here was done and satisfactorily so.

He could be pleased with himself. He could start thinking about step two. He knew in his gut that there would be no obstacles in his way and step two had always been top of the agenda. Art might have been cynical when it came to the romantic notion of love, but familial love, discovered in the most unexpected of places, had settled in his heart and filled the space there.

He'd thought outside the box and it had paid off. Now, as he looked at his land, he realised that thinking outside the box and getting what he'd wanted had come at an unexpected cost.

Rose.

He abruptly turned away, headed for the battered Land Rover which couldn't have been more different from his own fleet of super-charged, high-performance cars.

She'd temporarily loaned him her car.

'I'll be buried in case files for the next week or so.' She had laughed, her arms wound around his neck, her eyes sparkling, her half-clad body pressed against his. 'You'll want to be out and about. Lord knows you've become some kind of mentor to half the protesters...with that promise of yours that the developers are going to meet their extravagant demands! Mind you, I'll be pleased to have my kitchen table back.'

Art would have to come clean. There was no way around it. He couldn't believe that he had been disingenuous enough, when thoughts had entered his head about sleeping with her, to believe that he could have a fling and walk away.

Two adults, he had argued to himself. Two consenting adults who fancied one another. What was the problem? All he had to do was make it clear to her from the very start that he wasn't going to be hanging around and his conscience would be clear.

He'd approached all his relationships with the opposite sex like that. With honesty and no promises. If some of them had become distraught when he'd walked away because they'd been pointlessly looking for more than he had in him to give, then so be it. Not his fault. How could it have been when he'd done nothing but warned them off going down that road?

But the situation with Rose was different and that was something he had failed to factor in.

He'd conveniently whitewashed the whole business of *why* he had turned up, unannounced, on her doorstep into something that wasn't really relevant—he wasn't going to be sticking around so she would never actually discover his true identity. Therefore, why did it matter *who* he was?

Except it did.

And now he would have to pay the price for his not-so-innocent deception.

It was not quite six in the evening. He had spent the day partly in the library, where he had worked in pleasurable peace, and partly in a five-star hotel near Oxford, where a high-level meeting had been arranged with the CEO of a company he intended to buy.

He wondered whether his attack of conscience had been kick-started by that return to the reality of his high-powered city life. Sitting at that table, back in his comfort zone of work, business and making money... had it brought him back down to earth with a bump? Reminded him of the single tenet he had always lived by—work was the only thing upon which a person could rely?

Art didn't know. He just knew that he owed Rose more than a disappearing act.

He made it back to her house within fifteen minutes, to find her still in her office alone, Phil having gone for the day.

Rose looked up and smiled.

He'd told her that he didn't do commitment and he didn't do domesticity and yet they'd cooked together and discussed everything under the sun from world politics to village gossip.

'You're just in time,' she said, standing up and stretching. 'If I read any more of this file I'm going to end up banging my head on the desk in frustration. You wouldn't believe the spurious arguments this company is using to get rid of one of their longest-serving employees just because it would be cheaper for them to get a young person on board.'

'The world of the underdog would be nothing without you...' Art framed that light-hearted rejoinder in a voice that lacked his customary self-assurance.

He clenched his fists, walked towards the double-fronted bay window, sat down on the ledge and stared out for a few silent seconds.

'Are you disappointed in the outcome of the protest?' he asked abruptly, swinging around to look at her but remaining where he was by the window, perched on the broad ledge, his legs loosely crossed.

He had no idea how to begin this conversation and even less idea as to where it was going to end. For once in his life he was freefalling without a safety net and he loathed the sensation.

For a man to whom control was vitally important, this lack of control was his worst nightmare.

Rose tilted her head to one side. The smile with which she had greeted him had faded because she was sensing that something was out of kilter, although she wasn't sure what.

'Not disappointed, no…' She gave his question consideration. 'I always knew it was going to be a token protest because the land had been bought and all the channels had been navigated with planning permission, but I do think it's a result if the developers consent to all the things they've made noises about.'

'They will.'

'You seem very sure about that.' Rose laughed because this sort of assertiveness was just typical of him and it was something she really…

For a few seconds her heart stopped beating and she could feel the prickle of perspiration break out over her body. Something she *really found amusing*. Not something she *loved*, but something she found *amusing*.

'I am.'

'Well, I must say, it would be fantastic for the community as a whole. Naturally, I still stand by my guns when I say that I hate big developers who think they can descend and gobble up whatever slice of land they want, but it's fair to say that not many would go the extra mile to appease disgruntled locals.'

Art didn't say anything. He'd slept with her and done a hundred small things with her that he'd never done with anyone else. That, in itself, was unsettling and he latched onto that sentiment with some relief because it made him realise that he was clearing off in the nick of time. Sharing cosy suppers and painting bedrooms wasn't in his genetic make-up and never would be! He wasn't cut out for anything like that and had he stayed on he knew that the inevitable boredom with her would have set in.

She invigorated him *at this moment in time*, but it wouldn't have lasted.

He would have become restless, got itchy feet. It never failed to happen.

Which was *why*, he thought with conviction, it was imperative he left. Rose, underneath the tough veneer, had risen above the odds dealt to her in her background and turned out to be endearingly romantic. Were he to stay on, there was a chance that she would have fallen for him.

And then what? A broken heart when he vanished? A life in need of being rebuilt? Looking at the bigger picture, he was doing her a favour.

'That's because,' Art told her patiently, 'there's always more to people than meets the eye, and that includes billionaire developers.'

'Really? I hadn't noticed. Do you want to tell me what's going on here, Art, or shall I make it easier for you by bringing it out into the open myself?'

'What do you mean?' He frowned.

'I mean you…*this atmosphere*…' She breathed in deeply and exhaled slowly. 'Something's off and I'll spare you the discomfort of spelling it out in words of one syllable, shall I? You're leaving. Your time here is up. You came for a protest that ended up a damp squib. Perhaps you were hoping for more fireworks.'

'The opposite,' Art told her quietly.

'You're...not off?'

'No, that bit you got right. I... It's time for me to pack my bags and leave.'

Rose stared at him, horrified at how painful it was to hear those words. Everywhere hurt. He was going. She'd known he'd be off but, now that he'd confirmed it, it felt as though she'd been hit head-on by a train. Her legs had turned to jelly but she kept standing, holding her ground and hoping with everything inside her that the pain tearing her apart wasn't reflected in her face.

'Of course,' she said politely.

'You always knew I'd be leaving.'

'Because you're a wanderer in search of a cause.'

'Not entirely.'

'What do you mean? What are you talking about?'

'I think this is a conversation better conducted with you sitting down.'

'Why?' Rose wondered whether she would be able to move at all without falling to the ground in an undignified heap. That was what jelly legs did to a person.

'Because...you might find what I'm about to say somewhat surprising.'

Rose looked at him uncertainly, then galvanised her body into action. She wasn't going to sit at her desk. She wasn't conducting an interview! Although the atmosphere felt hardly less formal.

She walked towards the sitting room, which was the only room downstairs, aside from the large cloakroom, that hadn't been converted into something useful that could be modified and used as a source of income.

Like all the other rooms in the house, it was high-ceilinged and gracious in proportions. It was painted in soothing shades of grey and cream and lavender and the furniture was well-made and tasteful.

Rose flopped down onto the sofa and then watched in tense silence as he prowled the room, his beautiful lean body jerky as he darted thoughtful glances in her direction.

'Are you going to spare us both the drama and just say what you have to say? It's not as though you haven't warned me in advance and you needn't worry that I'm going to do anything silly like break down and cry.'

'It might be better if I show you,' Art said slowly. He pulled out his phone, found what he was looking for on the screen and handed it to her. And waited, eyes glued to her expressive face. Every nerve in his body twanged with the sort of tension he had seldom experienced in his life before.

He watched as bewilderment turned to confusion, as confusion turned to disbelief and then, finally, as disbelief morphed into appalled horror.

Long after she should have finished reading the article about him, just one of many to be found online, she kept staring at the phone as though hopeful that it might deliver something that would make sense of what he'd shown her.

His biography. Succinct. Replete with his success stories. Sycophantic in its adoration of the man who had made his first billion before the ripe old age of thirty-five.

She finally looked up with a dazed expression.

'*You're* DC Logistics…?'

Art flushed darkly but he wasn't going to start justifying himself.

'Yes,' he said flatly.

'*You're* the guy we've been fighting…'

'Yes.'

'You came here… You pretended to be… *Why*?' She shot up, trembling, as thousands of implications clearly began sinking in. 'You *bastard*.' She edged away from him, recoiling as though he was contagious, and took up position by the large Victorian fireplace, leaning against it and staring at him with huge round eyes.

'You came here with a plan, didn't you? You came here so that you could infiltrate and get us onside. You didn't like the fact that we were protesting about you putting up a bunch of houses that no one wants!'

Art's jaw hardened but there was nothing he could say to refute her accusations since they were all spot on. 'I owned the land. I was going to build, whether you stood in the way or not. I thought it diplomatic to try to persuade you to see sense before the bulldozers moved in and trying to persuade you within the walls of my London offices wasn't going to work.'

'You *used* me.'

'I…' Art raked his fingers through his hair. 'There was no need for me to come clean. And I did not *use* you. We both enjoyed what happened between us. I could have walked away without saying anything.'

'Are you asking for a medal because you finally decided to tell the truth?'

'There was also no need for me to grant the concessions that I have.'

'No wonder you were so confident that the big, bad developers were going to accept our terms and conditions. Because *you* were the big, bad developer.'

'I played fair.'

'You lied!'

'A small amount of subterfuge.'

'You came here…you…' She turned away because she needed to gather herself. Everything was rushing in on her and she was beginning to feel giddy. She took a few deep breaths and forced herself to look at him. To her fury, he met her gaze squarely, as if he was as pure as the driven snow!

'I let you stay in my house.' Rose laughed bitterly. 'No wonder you insisted on paying rent! You're worth a small fortune. It must have troubled your conscience that you were sponging off someone who couldn't hope to come close to matching you in the financial stakes. Someone with rooms in need of decorating and plumbing on the verge of waving a white flag and giving up! I bet you've never painted anything in your life before or done anything manual *at all*!'

'Going through each and every detail of the ways you feel deceived isn't going to progress this.'

'I slept with you.'

Those four words, delivered without any expression

whatsoever, dropped like stones into a quiet pond and silence settled between them, thick and uncomfortable.

'I'm guessing...' Rose kept her voice level but the blood was rushing through her veins like lava '...that that was all part of the game plan? To get me onside?'

'That's outrageous!'

'Really? Is it? Why? You conned your way into my home!'

'I was more than happy to go stay in a hotel.'

'You accepted my hospitality and you *used it* to get what you wanted out of me! I can't believe I was stupid enough to actually think that you were a man of integrity.'

'Sleeping with you was never part of any plan.' Art shook his head and dropped down on the sofa, legs apart. She walked towards him and stood in front of him with her arms folded. 'You doubt me?' he growled, staring at her, and even in the height of this scorching argument, when she was burning with rage, those fabulous dark eyes still had the power to do things to her body. Rose's lips thinned.

'Do you honestly believe that I could make love with you the way I have if I wasn't seriously attracted to you?'

Hot colour flooded her cheeks. Rose remembered the intensity of their lovemaking, the flaring passion in his eyes. She remembered the way he had touched her, his fingers as they'd explored her body and the urgency of those times when he just couldn't wait to have her.

No, he hadn't been faking *that*. Somehow that was

something she just knew. He'd come here on a mission but going to bed with her had never been part of the plan. Should she feel better for that? Maybe, but then, with a bitter twist, she also remembered the way *she* had felt about *him* and her stupidity in actually thinking that there might have been more to what they had than just a romp in the sack.

It was *always* going to be just a romp in the sack, had she but known, because she had *always* just been an enjoyable add-on to the main reason he was there, a pleasant side dish but never the main meal.

Humiliation roared through her, stiffening her backbone and settling like venom in her veins.

How on earth could she have been so stupid? She, of all people! Always cautious, always watchful...how could she have thrown herself in the path of a speeding train and actually thought that it would be okay?

'You need to leave,' she said coldly.

'I was honest with you.' Art rose to his feet, a towering, dominant presence that made her step back in alarm.

He sucked the oxygen out of the room, left her feeling as though she needed to gasp for air, and the strength of her reaction terrified her because she knew that, mixed in with the rage, the hatred and the bitter disillusionment, was something else...something she didn't want to put her finger on.

'And now that I'm weeping with gratitude at your terrific display of honesty, are you going to renege on all the things you said you'd do for the village?'

'Dammit, Rose!' Art roared. 'I could have just disappeared. Instead, I came clean. Why can't you cut me some slack?' He stepped towards her, ignoring her crab-like shuffle away from him, until he had cornered her without her even realising it was happening.

She collided with the wall and he placed both hands squarely on either side of her so that she had nowhere to run.

'I didn't come here to—' he looked away and clenched his jaw in frustration '—mess you or anyone else around.'

'You came here to get on our good side so that we would get off your case and make things easier for you!'

'Where's the crime in that? I purchased the land going through all the proper channels. Okay, yes, I admit I figured that life would be a lot smoother if I didn't have to steamroller my way through protesters waving placards, but I can't think of many *big, bad wolves* who would have given a damn about the pro-testers *or* their placards.'

'You could have done the decent thing and been hon-est from the start!'

'You would have had the sheriff run me out of town before I got the first sentence out.'

'That's not true.'

'Isn't it?'

Rose flushed. She could breathe him in and it was doing all sorts of crazy and unacceptable things to her nervous system.

'I thought,' Art said heavily, 'that this would be fairly straightforward. How hard could it be to talk sense into a group of people who were never going to win the war?

I never banked on really engaging with anyone here and I certainly never entertained the idea that...'

Rose tilted her chin and stared at him in hostile defiance. 'That what? That you'd break that code of yours and start sharing space in a kitchen with a woman?'

To think that she had actually entertained the idea that having him do all that domesticated stuff might be an indication of feelings that ran deeper and truer than they had both originally predicted.

'Something like that,' Art muttered, glancing away for a few taut seconds before returning his dark gaze to her face. 'You're hurt and I get that,' he continued in a low, driven voice.

Rose raised her eyebrows. She was keeping it together by a thread, determined not to let him see just how devastated she was, but it was so, so very hard, especially when he was standing so, so very close to her, when, with barely any effort, she could just reach out and touch that body she had come to feel so much for. Too much.

'Thanks. I feel so much better for that,' she said with thick sarcasm.

'I'm no good for you.' He gave her a crooked smile and pushed himself away, although he remained standing in front of her.

'No, you're not,' Rose said shortly.

'You deserve a far better man.'

'I do.' She tossed her hair and for a few seconds her expression changed from anger to on-the-edge-of-tears disappointment. 'I always knew that guys with money were unscrupulous and I proved myself right.'

'I refuse to get into a debate about this. I don't think

your fellow locals will agree when they find themselves the recipients of some spanking-new additions to the village. I don't think they'll be gnashing their teeth and shaking their fists and cursing my generosity.'

'You can wave money around but that doesn't make you an honourable man. It doesn't mean that you've got any sense of...of *spirituality.*'

'I didn't think you were paying too much attention to my fascinating lack of a spiritual side when we were in bed together.'

'How dare you bring that up?' The silence that greeted this was electric. Her nostrils flared and her pupils dilated and every pore in her body burned with humiliation because the warmth between her legs wouldn't let her forget the shameful truth that she still found him unbearably sexy even though she absolutely loathed him for how he had played her.

She breathed deep and closed her eyes and wasn't aware that he was reaching out until he was. Reaching out to lightly stroke the side of her face.

'You still want me,' he murmured and Rose glared at him furiously. 'You still want me and you can't deny it.'

Rose opened her mouth to utter an instant denial of any such thing. How dared he? Her skin burnt from where he had touched her. *How dared he?*

'Are you going to lie?' Art asked in a low, sexy undertone. 'You can't possibly stand there and accuse me of being a monster of deceit only to lie about something that's so obvious.'

'Well, it doesn't matter,' she said on a sharply indrawn breath. 'So what if I'm attracted to you? You're an attractive man. But I will never be tempted to act on that attraction again, not that the situation is ever likely to arise.' She took a deep breath. 'I can't fault you for being honest and telling me from the start that you weren't going to be sticking around. Fair enough. But you hurt me with your deceit, whether that deceit was intended or not. I'll never, ever forgive you for that.'

Art's lips thinned.

'Forgiveness has never been high on the list I've striven for.'

'Can I ask you something before you disappear back to that jet-set life of yours?' Rose folded her arms, proud of the fact that her voice continued to betray nothing of what was going on inside her, the roil of tumultuous emotions tearing her up.

'I'm guessing that's a question you will ask whatever my response.'

'If we'd stood firm, would you have steamrolled us all away? So that you could have your acres and acres of land for the sake of a handful of flash houses?'

'Yes.'

Rose frowned because she had sensed something behind that flat monosyllabic reply. A curious shadow had crossed his face but then she wondered whether she'd imagined it because when he fixed his deep, dark eyes on her they were as remote as hers were. Two people who had shared intimacies she had never dreamed of and now here they were, standing opposite one another with a huge unsurmountable wall between them.

Rose looked away quickly because she could feel the treacherous onset of tears.

She put distance between them and gathered herself.

'I'll get my things,' Art said abruptly. 'I'll be fifteen minutes, tops.'

'I expect you won't need to borrow my battered car to get you to the station? Maybe you could call your personal chauffeur to swing by for you. Or, if that's not efficient enough, I'm sure you could find a corner of your field to land a private jet.'

'My driver is on his way.'

'Of course he is,' Rose said acidly. 'I'll leave you to get on with your packing. You know where the front door is.'

She didn't look back. She headed straight to her office and she made sure to close and lock the door behind her. But she didn't cry. She knew how to contain the tears. She'd learned that trick at a very young age.

CHAPTER SEVEN

SITTING AT THE head of the conference table, around which twenty people were all looking to him, Art could feel nothing but a certain amount of apathy even though a deal that would harvest several million was on the verge of completion.

With some surprise, he realised that he had doodled Rose's company logo onto his legal pad, a detail he wasn't even aware he had stored in his memory bank.

He'd last seen her three weeks ago and the memory of that final encounter was one that he rehashed on a daily basis.

It was getting on his nerves.

His concentration levels were down. His focus was erratic. He'd made two dates with women. The first he'd managed to stick out for an hour or so before admitting defeat and making up an excuse to leave early. The second he'd simply bailed on before subjecting himself to the possibility of another evening of torturous banalities.

He dreamed of Rose.

Not only did the memory of her haunt his waking

hours, but it didn't have the decency to allow him to get a good night's sleep when he fell into bed in the early hours of the morning.

Art had come around to thinking that she had taken up residence in his head because things had not ended *properly* between them.

He'd left still wanting her and, like an itch that needed to be scratched, that *want* kept clamouring for satisfaction.

It didn't help that he'd also left knowing that *she* still wanted *him*.

It was frustrating because he had never had any area of his life over which he was unable to exercise complete control. In this instance it had gradually dawned on him that he would never get her out of his system unless he took her to bed once again.

Pride dictated that he drop all seditious thoughts along those lines. Common sense warned him away. The litany of complications if they ended up in bed again was too long to catalogue and it beggared belief that she would actually *want* to sleep with him anyway. Yes, she fancied him. She'd admitted that much. But her amazing eyes had been full of scorn even as the admission had been leaving her lips.

When Art thought about that, he felt a spurt of raw frustration that left him confused and at odds with himself. He wondered whether this was what it felt like to be dumped, a situation he had never personally had to endure.

He went through the motions for the remainder of the

morning. The deal was signed. His company's bank account was inflated to even more impossible proportions.

None of that touched him. What *did* affect him was when, two and a half hours later, he dialled Rose's number and sat back in his office chair, waiting to see whether she would ignore his call or pick up. His name would flash on her screen, warning her of his identity. Whatever she did now would dictate the way he responded. He would leave it to fate.

For the first time in weeks, Art felt comfortable. He was doing *something*. Circumstances hadn't simply conspired to yank the rug from under his feet and leave him feeling at odds with himself, restless and unable to concentrate.

The slate had been wiped clean. There were no more half-truths between them. He would see her. He would feel out the situation and then, who knew...?

Life was an unfolding mystery.

He heard her voice and automatically straightened, all senses on full alert, every primitive instinct honing in to what he wanted to do, where he wanted to go with this...

'Been a while,' he drawled, relaxing back in his chair and swivelling it so that he could stretch his legs out.

Rose had debated whether or not to take the call. His name had flashed up on the screen and her insides had immediately turned to mush even though, over the past long three weeks, she had played and replayed in her mind how she would react if he got in touch.

'What can I do for you?' she asked coolly.

'Surprised to hear from me?'

'Are you phoning about anything in particular, Art? Because I'm quite busy at the moment.'

'I'm almost there, finalising the details of my investment in your community.'

'I wouldn't know. I've handed that over to a property lawyer in Oxford, who is a close friend of mine. I'm sure he would be happy to supply details of the ongoing process but I've told him that there's no need to fill me in until everything's sorted.' Images of Art jumped into her head, sickly reminding her of the powerful and dramatic effect he had on her body. Even the sound of his voice was enough to make her breasts tingle and her breath shorten.

'I rather think,' Art drawled, 'that I would like *you* to be personally involved in the closure of all of this.'

'Me? What? *Why?*'

'You started it, in a manner of speaking. It's only fair that you should finish it. Aside from which, if I'm to sink a vast sum of money into the community, it would benefit from someone knowing the place first-hand, knowing where best to divide the cash and how to put it to the best possible use. I may be generous, but I'm not a pushover. I have no intention of seeing my money ineptly spent on whatever takes some councillor's fancy. So handing over the file to someone else to tie up all the loose ends isn't doing it for me.'

'I haven't got time.'

What would it involve? She surely wouldn't have to meet him again! She couldn't face it. It was bad enough hearing the deep, dark, sexy timbre of his voice down the end of a phone line. She couldn't get her head around the possibility of actually ever seeing him in the flesh. He'd deceived her and he'd slept with her, knowing all the time that whilst she had been opening up to him, which was a big deal for her, she'd been opening up to a stranger.

'Well, then, you'll have to make time.' Art sliced through that objection swiftly and conclusively. 'You've turned caring for the community into an art form, Rose. It's not asking too much for you to step up to the plate and finish the job. When can you get to London so that we can discuss this?'

'We?' Rose queried faintly, as her stomach fell away and her mouth dried.

'Why, me and you, of course,' Art said in a tone of incredulity that she should even have thought to ask such an obvious question. 'I can't very well ask you to finish the job when I don't do likewise, can I? My people have handled all the formalities. We can agree the sign-off. And I think it would be beneficial for you to have a look at the details of the houses I intend to build on the land.'

'But I don't see why.' Rose cleared her throat, anxiously wondering what would happen if she flat-out refused. Would he renege on the deal? No! She knew he wasn't that sort but the possibility still niggled. It would be a disaster because he now had the complete, enthusiastic backing of everyone in the community and if it all collapsed because of her then she would be mortified.

'I don't see the point of another lengthy explanation. Now, when can you get down here? I wouldn't suggest commuting—I think you should plan on having a couple of days in London. There are legalities we can iron out between us and I will need to see some plans for the distribution of my money. In fact, it wouldn't be remiss of me to suggest a week. I can arrange for a makeshift office to be set up at my headquarters in the city if you need to spend some time communicating with clients. Or you could always take a bit of holiday. Enjoy the sights. It's quite different to the countryside.'

'Get down there? London? And yes, Art, I *do* realise that the big city is a little different to a field of cows and a village with a post office, a corner shop and a pub in case anyone wants a nightlife.'

'Not my thoughts and certainly not my words. I have my diary to hand. I could block out some time from the day after tomorrow. It won't be easy but the sooner this business is wrapped up the better, and construction can start on the land. And I won't remind you that any delay to the work beginning is a mere formality and a courtesy to you.'

Rose detected the crispness in his voice and pictured him glancing at his watch, raring to get on with more important business. He was doing what he felt was the right thing, involving her in the final process, and what he said made sense. She had supported the protesters and it was only fair to them and to the community that she take an active part in deciding how the money should be distributed to best benefit everyone.

She was overreacting because of the tumult of emotions that still coursed through her at the thought of him.

It wasn't like that for Art. He had taken a bit of time out with her but he was back where he belonged and she would be no more than a fast-fading memory for him. If she did what she wanted to do, namely launch into a thousand reasons why she had no intention of having anything further to do with a man who had deceived her, he wouldn't understand. He had given her his reasons for having done what he had, he had come clean and frankly, as far as he was concerned, had elevated himself to the position of self-proclaimed saint because he could have just walked away, leaving her none the wiser. What was the big deal now? All water under the bridge.

Playing it as cool as he was, she thought, was the only way to deal with the situation and maybe, just maybe, seeing him again and in a different environment would kill off the effect he continued to have on her, against all reason.

He would be in his natural habitat. He would be surrounded by all those trappings of wealth that she had never had time for in the past. Plus, speed would be of the essence for him. He wanted the whole business sorted fast. A couple of days in his company might be just the thing for clearing her head because ever since he'd disappeared she'd done nothing but think of him and the longing, the anger, the disenchantment and the regret were wreaking havoc with her sleep and distracting her from her work.

Bucked up by this process of reasoning, Rose felt a little calmer when she answered.

'If you hold for a minute, I'll check my schedule…'

* * *

Art held. For a minute, two minutes…when he looked at his watch with some impatience it was to find that she had kept him hanging on for five minutes. Inconceivable. He gritted his teeth and wondered what he would do if she turned him down flat, as she had every right to do. He could waffle on about the importance of both of them jointly putting the finishing touches to the deal that had been brokered to ease acceptance of the construction of his development, but any close inspection would reveal more holes in that argument than a colander.

'Well?' he pressed.

'Okay.'

'Okay?' Art straightened, a slashing smile of intense satisfaction softening his lean face. 'Good. Tell me when, exactly, you will be arriving and I will make sure that suitable accommodation is sorted for you.'

'I can sort my own accommodation,' Rose asserted hurriedly.

'You're not paying for a hotel.'

'No way am I…'

'I believe this is a favour it is within my remit to return,' Art said flatly, cutting her off in mid-protest, 'and, just in case you're thinking of a speech about accepting favours from me, let me assure you that no money will leave my hands.'

'What do you mean?'

'I own the hotel.'

'Of course you do,' Rose snapped. 'I wonder why I'm not surprised at that. I did look you up online but the list of things you owned was so long that I fell asleep before I could get to the end. I didn't get to the hotel.'

'Chain.'

'I beg your pardon?'

'Hotel *chain*. A little sideline I invested in some years ago that has ended up exceeding all expectations.'

'Good for you. I shudder to think what must have gone through your head when you were confronted with a paintbrush, a can of paint and four walls with peeling plaster.'

Art burst out laughing. 'It was an unforeseen challenge. Now, back to business. Do you require somewhere to work? And, before you say no, I'll tell you again that it would be no trouble for me to have someone arrange an office for you.'

'It would be helpful,' Rose said through her no doubt gritted teeth. 'With a bit of juggling, I shall try to arrange a couple of client visits while I'm in London. It would work if I could have somewhere to go with them. And, of course, at some point I'll have to see Anton.'

'Anton?' Art's ears pricked up and he frowned.

'Anton Davies. He's the lawyer who has been handling the formalities in Oxford. If there's going to be a transition of duties then we'll have to get together to discuss that and to work out his fee accordingly. Although…he's not the sort to quibble.'

Art heard the smile in her voice, the softening of her tone, and his hackles rose accordingly.

But, he thought, if she was working under his roof, so to speak, then he could easily find his way to whatever space had been allocated to her and meet the guy.

It was a taste of jealousy rarely experienced and he moved on from that to conclude the conversation.

Less than five minutes later, everything had been sorted. It took one phone call to his PA for the hotel room to be arranged and a work space sorted.

She was going to experience the joy of five-star luxury and the seclusion of an office in one of the most prestigious buildings in the city.

He sat back and luxuriated in a feeling of pure satisfaction that was very far from the cool, forbidding and controlled exterior he showed the world.

Rose had no idea really what to expect of her time in London. She had been all cool logic and common sense ever since she had agreed to Art's proposal but now, standing in front of the daunting glass tower where his headquarters was housed, her heart plummeted faster than a boulder dropped from a great height.

At her side was her pull-along case, neatly packed with essentials. Work clothes. Prim, proper work clothes which were nothing like the relaxed, informal stuff she was accustomed to wearing in her own house. The image she wanted to project was one of inaccessible businesslike efficiency. There was no way she wanted him to think for a passing minute that she was the same woman who had hopped into bed with him, breathless and girly and excited.

To that end, she had actually bought two reasonably priced grey skirts and a jacket, two white blouses and a pair of black pumps. The perfect wardrobe for a woman who was in London for business.

She was wearing a sensible white bra which matched her sensible white knickers and bolstered her self-confidence as she continued to gaze at the aggressively thrusting glass facade with a racing heart.

She had asked for a schedule and a schedule she had duly received. Arrival at ten. She would then be shown to her temporary working quarters and then taken to the hotel, where she would deposit her belongings. At that point she could choose to return to the office to work if she liked. In all events, she wouldn't be seeing Art until early evening in his office, where they would briefly discuss some of the details of the projects that lay ahead for the village.

She had liaised with his personal assistant by email for all of this and, reading between the lines, she had got the message that Arturo da Costa, billionaire and legend in the world of business and finance, was a man who had precious little time to spare so what she was getting would be his leftover free time, a few snatched moments here and there when he happened not to be closing an important deal or entertaining important big shots.

Rose had held her tongue and refrained from pointing out the obvious. Why on earth was he bothering to see her at all if he was *that* busy? But then she remembered that he was the guy who had gone the extra mile to appease the natives and this was just a duty-bound finishing touch to his benevolence.

Anyway, she thought now, taking a deep breath and propelling herself into the glass tower, it was great that he was only going to be around now and again.

That way, she would see enough of him to kill all the foolish, nostalgic, whimsical memories that seemed to have dogged her, against all her better judgement. She would have a world class view of the real man and he wasn't going to be the easy-going, sexy, laid-back guy who had painted a room in her house and stood by her side in the kitchen pretending that he knew what to do when it came to food preparation, joking and teasing and turning her on just by being *him*.

A little disorientated, she found herself in a vast marble-floored foyer, manned by an army of receptionists who would not have looked out of place in *Vogue* magazine and, just in case anyone might think that there was an unfair proportion of female models in front of those silver terminals and where the heck was feminism when you wanted it, then they'd have to think again because there was a fair sprinkling of men alongside them who also looked as though they'd have been quite at home on a catwalk. People were coming and going. There was an air of purpose about the place. This was what the business of vast money-making looked like. It was as far removed from her own workplace as an igloo was from a hut on a tropical beach.

She had no idea who would be meeting her but she was expecting the helpful PA.

She was certainly not expecting Art and, indeed, was unaware of him until she heard his voice behind her, deep and dark and sexy.

'You're here.'

Rose spun around. She'd gone from ice cold to

scorching hot in the space of two seconds. Dazed, she focused on him and the heat pouring through her body almost made her pass out.

'I wasn't sure whether you were going to come or not,' Art remarked, already turned on even though the deliberately uninspiring office outfit should have been enough to snuff out any stirrings of ardour.

It was her face. It had haunted him and one look at her revived every single image that had been floating around in his head and every single lustful thought that had accompanied those images.

He was pleased that he had been proactive. He could have sat around thinking of her. Sooner or later the memories would have vanished into the ether but he wasn't a man to rely on a *sooner or later* scenario.

The interruption to the smooth flow of his work life had been intolerable and the solution he had engineered had been worth the trouble.

Art hadn't known how he was going to play his cards when she arrived. He'd acted on impulse in engineering the situation in the first place, had ceded to the demands of his body.

Now, for the first time in his life, he was taking a chance and venturing into unknown territory. At an age when he should have been having fun, Art had had to grow up fast to deal with his father's unpredictable behaviour and the emotional and financial fallout each relationship had left in its wake. Before he had had a chance to plot his own life, he had already concluded that the only safe course was to hold tight to his emotions and to his money. Lose control and he could end up like his father. Adrift and ripped off.

This was the biggest chance he had ever taken. At least he wasn't going to be ripped off and she would be gone just as soon as he got this *thing* out of his system.

He still wanted her. He accepted that as his body surged into hot arousal. Didn't make sense but there you had it. What they had required a natural conclusion and looking at her now, seeing the way her cheeks reddened and noting the slight tremble in her hands, Art knew that she felt the same.

Even if she didn't know it. Yet.

He dealt her a slow smile of utter charm and Rose's mouth tightened.

'Well, here I am,' she replied neutrally. She wondered whether that remark of his had hinted at a suspicion that she might have tried to avoid meeting him because of the effect he still had on her. Had he thought that she had hesitated because she'd been scared of seeing him again? Or was that just being fanciful?

The way he was looking at her…

She dropped her eyes and resisted the temptation to fidget. 'I was under the impression that your secretary would be meeting me.'

'Change of plan.'

'Why?' She looked at him and it took a lot of will-power not to instantly look away because gazing into those fathomless dark eyes was the equivalent of having a shock delivered to her nervous system.

'Call it respect for the fact that what we had was bigger than the sum total of what I'm going to contribute to your community.'

Rose felt the sting of colour creep into her cheeks. She didn't want the past recalled. She wanted the brief time they'd shared neatly boxed up and shoved somewhere out of sight.

'There was no need,' she said tightly. 'I'm not here to have a stroll down memory lane, Art. It's not appropriate. I'm here to sort whatever details need sorting and then I'm heading back home. The quicker we can deal with what we need to decide the better.'

'In which case,' Art said briskly, 'let's start with your work space...'

It was the same size as the room which she shared with Phil and their assistant and all the various people who came and went at will. Compared with the clutter of the office in her house, the clean white modernist vision she had been allocated made her jaw drop.

She thought of the warm chaos of her own house and the familiar sounds of occupied rooms and felt a pang of longing so great that it took her breath away.

Life pre-Art had been simple. Making ends meet as she'd buried herself in her worthwhile causes had been a walk in the park because, when it came to stress, there was nothing more stressful than dealing with emotions. She had managed to avoid that for her entire life because no one had ever penetrated the protective wall she had built around herself.

'What is it?'

'Nothing,' Rose muttered, looking down at her feet.

'Don't you like the office space?'

He'd moved directly in front of her and Rose only managed to stand her ground through sheer willpower and a driving urge not to feel intimidated.

'It's very…nice.'

'Very *nice*?' Art looked away briefly, then returned his dark searching gaze to her face.

'It's not what I'm used to.' Rose cleared her throat and gathered herself. 'It really makes me see the gaping chasm between us.'

Art flushed darkly. 'We've been over this. Let me take you to the hotel. You can drop your bag and then we'll go for lunch.'

'Art, there's no need to put yourself out for me. I don't expect you to take me to lunch or anywhere else, for that matter. Your PA gave me the impression that I wouldn't actually be seeing a great deal of you.'

'Like I said, plans change. You'll be thrilled to hear that I've cleared my diary for you.'

Rose looked at him wryly, eyebrows raised. 'Do I look thrilled?'

'I've missed your sense of humour. Some men might be turned off because you're not simpering, but not me.' Art held her gaze and raked his fingers through his dark hair, his lean body taut and tense.

Rose stilled. Her whole body froze and for a few seconds she wondered whether she had heard correctly. His fabulous eyes were giving nothing away but there was something there that made her mouth go dry.

'You *missed* me?'

Her body came to life. Her nipples pinched and a

spreading dampness between her legs was a painful reminder of the dramatic effect he still had on her.

She'd hoped that seeing him in his gilded surroundings would kill off what remnants of idiotic sexual attraction lingered inside her, but looking at him now...

She was no expert but that suit looked handmade, to match the shoes which also looked handmade. His smooth, ridiculously sophisticated attire would probably have cost the equivalent of what most normal earthlings earned in a year. It should have got up her nose, been a massive turn-off, and yet she had a sudden urge to swoon.

'Well, I have not missed *you*,' she croaked and he looked at her steadily, eyes pinned to her flustered face. 'And I don't appreciate you...bringing this up. What happened between us...happened and I'm not here to rake up the past. As I've already told you.'

'I know. I'm crashing through all those barriers and voicing what you don't want to hear.'

'Shall I be honest with you?' He dropped the loaded question into the lengthening silence and waited.

'No,' she whispered.

'I still want you, Rose. Just standing here is doing all sorts of things to my body, turning it on in ways you couldn't begin to imagine. You're in my system and, I won't lie, you're screwing up my working life because I can't get you out of my head.'

'Art, don't...' Rose heard the weak tremble in her voice with horror. She glanced at him and her breath hitched in her throat.

'I still want you in my bed,' he continued roughly.

'It's the only way I can think of to get you out of my system. I won't lay a finger on you but…every time you look at me, you should know that I'm thinking about touching you.' He stared away.

'I should never have come here!'

'But you're here now. Do you want to leave?' His smouldering dark eyes fastened on her, pinning her to the spot.

Rose hesitated. As he said, she was here now and she would sort out all the fine detail he had summoned her to London to sort out. She had promised all those loyal protestors that she would return with plans in place for them to start thinking long-term about improvements to the community. She wasn't going to let them down.

'I'll do what I came here to do,' she replied, breathing in deep and not looking away. 'I told everyone I would have details for them to pick over and I have no intention of going back empty-handed. What you think when you look at me is your business.'

CHAPTER EIGHT

IF ART HAD planned on dropping a bomb in her life then he'd succeeded.

He still wanted her. He still wanted to take her to his bed. He still wanted to do all those things to her that she still wanted to do to him.

When Rose thought about that she felt giddy. She knew that, by being honest, he had deliberately dropped that bomb to wreak havoc with her peace of mind. Honest or selfish? Did he really care if he ended up getting what he wanted? He'd got her to London under false pretences and now he was playing a waiting game.

It had only been forty-eight hours but already her nerves were shredded. She felt like a minnow being slowly circled by a shark and, worse, the minnow was finding it hard to stop fantasising about its predator.

Now, he was taking her out to an elaborate dinner.

'Networking,' he had explained succinctly, having earlier dropped by her office, which had also turned into her sanctuary, where she could find a brief reprieve from his overwhelming personality.

She had looked up and given him a perplexed frown,

which had clearly done nothing to dampen his high spirits.

'I'm not here to network.'

'Granted, but this is a charity event hosted by some fairly prominent members of the international legal community. All those causes you take such an interest in? Well, they'll be represented across the board. Several people you'll have heard of will also be giving speeches and, for the intrepid, I gather there will be an opportunity to go abroad to places where civil liberties are at risk. You may not want to personally vanish to the opposite side of the globe on a crusade to eradicate injustice, but you might be interested in meeting fellow like-minded citizens who are.'

'A charity event?'

'Reasonably smart, I should point out, as these things invariably are. A few degrees off black tie.'

'I haven't brought any smart clothes with me, Art.'

'Nothing but the *hands-off* suits that could have been designed to deter roving eyes and repel curious hands,' he murmured, in his first departure from the perfectly well-behaved gentleman he had been since his warning of intent. 'Why don't you get yourself something? You can charge it to my company account. Elaine, my PA, will sort that out for you.'

'I couldn't...'

He'd shrugged but he'd dropped the bait and she'd taken it.

How could she not?

Rose immediately told herself that it didn't mean anything. She'd been presented with an opportunity to

meet people she admired so why shouldn't she grab the
chance just because Art had arranged it? She could pat
herself on the back for not letting his suffocating presence plunge her into a state of permanent confusion.
And since he seemed convinced that she wouldn't take
him up on his offer to subsidise an evening dress for
the event, then why shouldn't she prove him wrong and
do what he least expected?

Rose wasn't stupid. She knew how to sift through
the deceit and ferret out the truth. Art had descended on
their village with one thing in mind and that had been
to persuade her to stop the protests that were slowing
up development of the land he'd bought. He could have
run roughshod over all of them because he had the law
on his side but he was clever enough to know that a diplomatic solution would have been preferable and so that
was the road he had decided to go down.

He hadn't banked on her being a nuisance and getting in his way but he'd found her attractive and she
knew why. It was because she represented everything
he wasn't accustomed to. From the way she dressed to
the person that she was, she was a woman far removed
from the stereotypes he was used to dating and he had
found that appealing.

He went out with catwalk models. Nothing could
have been further than a pro bono lawyer whose wardrobe consisted of flowing skirts, baggy tops, faded jeans
and waterproof anoraks.

She'd been a trip down novelty lane and that hurt.

When Rose tried to equate that to her own feelings

towards him she drew a blank because she had been drawn to him against all good reason.

It didn't make sense but everything about his personality had appealed to her. She'd been cautious but in the end she hadn't been able to resist the pull of his intelligence, his easy wit, his charm. Was she more like her mother than she realised? It didn't matter whether her mother had been a loyal wife. When her husband had died she had behaved in a way that had had lasting consequences for her daughter. She had been promiscuous and eventually she had ended up with a guy who had been so out of her league that it was a mystery that they had lasted as long as they had. Rose had been careful all her life not to repeat any of the mistakes her mother had made and it frightened her when she thought of where she was now.

She had opened up to Art. Even before he had shown his true colours, she had *known* that he wasn't the kind of man who should have registered on her radar, but she had *still* fallen for him and she had actually fooled herself into thinking that *he* might have had similar feelings for her.

Not so.

For Art, it was all about the sex, hence his openness in telling her straight off the bat that he still wanted her. Had she given off some kind of pheromone that had alerted him to the fact that she still fancied him?

That horrified her but she was honest enough to realise that it had probably been the case because, the second she was in his presence, her head and her body took off in two different directions and she was left rudderless and floundering and he was a guy who could pick up on things like that in a heartbeat.

With her thoughts all over the place and her body threatening to go its own way and let the side down, Rose had gone to town shopping for something to wear to the charity event.

Part of her was determined to show him that she was more than just a country bumpkin lawyer with no dress sense.

Another part was curious to see whether, exposed to the sort of gathering that didn't frequently occur in her life out in the sticks, she would find that there were other interesting men out there. That Art hadn't netted all her attention to the exclusion of everyone else. Had he been as much of a novelty for her as she had been for him? Was she giving him too much credit for having burrowed into the heart of her when, in fact, she had just been vulnerable to a charming man because she'd been out of the dating scene for too long?

To this end, she had gone all out and now, with a mere forty minutes to go before Art's driver called for her, Rose contemplated her reflection in the floor-to-ceiling mirror with satisfaction.

In the background, she absently took in the sumptuous surroundings that had made her gasp the first time she had entered the hotel room. The lush curtains, the blonde wood, the pale marbled bathroom...the decadent chandelier that should have been over the top but wasn't...the handmade desk on which was stacked fine quality personalised stationery and a comprehensive collection of London guidebooks which she had had precious little time to peruse.

She refocused on her reflection.

She had gone for drama and chosen a figure-hugging dress in a striking shade of raspberry. The narrowness of her waist was emphasised by a silver corded belt that lent the outfit a Roman appeal and the dress fell elegantly to mid-calf. In nude heels, her legs looked longer and her body more willowy than she had ever noticed before.

And her hair. It fell in tousled waves along her shoulders and down her back and was as soft as silk because she had managed to squeeze in an appointment with a hairdresser, who had done some wonderful things with highlights and blow-dried it in a way she couldn't possibly have done herself.

She'd also bought a shawl in the same nude shade as the heels and she slung that over her shoulders and smiled, excited.

She felt like an exotic bird of paradise.

For the first time in her life, Rose wasn't being cautious. No, she amended, gathering all her stuff as her cell phone buzzed, alerting her to the arrival of the driver...

She'd already thrown caution to the winds when she'd jumped into bed with Art. She was just carrying on in a similar vein and enjoying herself in the process.

It was sufficient to bring a guilty tinge to her cheeks but she was composed as she slid into the back of the glossy Mercedes and she maintained that composure all the way to the venue and right up to the moment she spied Art, who was waiting for her, as arranged, in the lobby of the hotel.

Stepping out of the car, with the door held open by one of the parking attendants who had sprung into action the second the car had pulled up, made her feel like a movie star.

This was more than just *fancy*. There were journalists snapping pictures of the arriving guests. In a daze, she realised that she recognised faces from the world of movies and television and one or two prominent politicians and their other halves.

But all those faces faded into a blur alongside Art, who had begun moving towards her and, in the process, created a bubble of excitement around him.

He looked magnificent. The whiteness of his dress shirt emphasised his bronzed complexion. The black bow tie looked ridiculously sexy instead of stuffy, as did the very proper black suit.

Rose was barely aware of him moving to politely usher her inside.

'You look,' he breathed without looking at her and only inclining slightly so that he couldn't be overheard, 'sensational. Was that the intention?'

'Thank you. That's very kind.' But her pulse raced and she shivered with wild pleasure at his husky undertone.

Art laughed as they strolled away from the lobby and into the impressive ballroom, which was buzzing with the great and the good. 'Not a description that's been used much about me but I'll take it.'

'I mean it. Look at the women here.' She was holding onto him for dear life, very much aware that they were being stared at. 'I recognise some of them from fashion magazines.'

'And I thought that you never read anything as frivolous as a fashion magazine.'

'But thank you for pretending that I look okay,' Rose said distractedly.

'Where's this sudden attack of modesty sprung from?' They'd left the paparazzi outside; there was still a sea of people but without the gawping of the public and the reporters. Art drew her to the side and looked down at her. 'You're the most self-confident woman I've ever met.'

'When it comes to work…'

'You knock spots off every woman in this place.'

Rose burst out laughing. If he wanted to put her at ease, then he was doing a good job of it. 'I don't. But thanks.'

'You're fishing.'

'Of course I'm not!'

'You know how I feel about you. The only thing I want to do right now is get you out of here and into a bed so that I can make love to you until we're both too exhausted to carry on. I want to peel that dress off your luscious body and touch you in all the places I know you like being touched. So when I tell you that you put every other woman in the shade here, then trust me. I'm not kidding.'

'Stop!' Her blood was boiling and she was so very aware of him that she could barely think. 'You know I don't want you saying things like that…to me.'

'Say that like you mean it.'

'I *do* mean it. I'm just a little…nervous.'

'No need. Look around you. If you were hoping to attract some glances, then you've succeeded.' Art heard the edge in his voice and knew that it was a few degrees off the light, amused tone he had intended. *She* might not have noticed, but *he* had seen the way men had turned to have a second look. Most women were dressed to kill in black. Rose was a splash of exotic colour, a bird of paradise with her long wild hair and her strong intelligent face. She announced to the world that she was *different* and that was a very sexy trait. And not just to him.

Halfway through the evening, he realised that she had disappeared into the crowd. The man who was accustomed to a high level of irritation with women clinging like limpets to him at functions like this found that his irritation level was skyrocketing now and for a different reason.

Where the hell was she *now*? And why was he having to hunt for her?

It got on his nerves. She was a flash of red but, before he could pin her down, she was gone. Nursing a whisky while a blonde tried to get his attention, Art decided that, for Rose's own good, he would take her back to the hotel.

'Got to go.' He interrupted the blonde abruptly. Pushing himself away from the wall, against which he had been leaning, he ignored a couple of MPs who had been trying to gain his attention.

Rose was laughing at something some guy was telling her. Art wasn't born yesterday. He could recognise a man on the make a mile away.

He came to an abrupt towering halt in front of them and Rose blinked and frowned at him.

'Mind if I interrupt?' Art interrupted anyway. 'I've barely seen you all evening...'

'That's because I've been chatting to all the interesting people here,' Rose returned gaily, swiping a glass of wine from a passing waitress. 'For instance, this is Steve and he does some amazing work for the UN.'

Steve reddened and straightened and stuck out his hand, clearly awed by Art, who felt ancient and cynical beyond his years in comparison. He politely asked a couple of interested questions but his attention was focused on Rose and his body language dismissed the young fair-haired man, who duly evaporated into the crowd after boldly exchanging phone numbers with Rose.

Which made Art's teeth snap together with annoyance.

'I think it's time to go,' he said without preamble.

'But I'm not ready to leave yet.'

'Tough. It's been over four hours, which is two hours longer than I usually stay at these things.'

'I'm having fun. There's no need for us to leave together, is there?' Rose squinted at his darkly disapproving expression. 'I know,' she pressed on, 'we came together, in a manner of speaking, but it's not as though we're on a date and there are so many more interesting people I still want to meet.'

'Repeat. Tough. Anyway, don't you think you've had

your fill of interesting people? Or is the entire room interesting after a few glasses of Chablis?'

'Not fair.'

Art shifted uncomfortably, recognising that she had a point. He raked his fingers through his hair and shot her a frowning glance. 'I apologise.' He tugged and undid the bow tie. 'But you've had a few drinks and you're not accustomed to that. I wouldn't feel comfortable leaving you here on your own to get on with the rest of what remains of the evening.'

'Do you think the poor little country girl might end up making a fool of herself? These shoes are killing me, by the way. Are there any chairs around here?'

'I think the poor little country girl might end up finding herself in slightly more hot water than she bargained for. And not many chairs, no. The expectation is for networking, not falling asleep in an armchair.'

'What do you mean about me finding myself in hot water?'

'You're sexy when you get angry.'

Rose blushed and pouted. 'Don't try to change the subject. What do you mean? I'm more than capable of taking care of myself. I've been doing it most of my life.'

'This isn't a quiet, sleepy village in the middle of nowhere.' Art didn't care how this sounded. There was no way he was going to leave her here on her own. The thought of predators circling her, moving in for the kill, made him see red. She was stunning and part of her appeal was the fact that she was so natural, so utterly without pretence, so patently open and honest. Aligned to her intelligence and her dramatic looks...well, it was a recipe for disaster in the big, bad city. If she didn't see that, then it was just as well that she had him around to see it on her behalf.

'I'd noticed, now that you mention it.'

'Have you paid any attention to the number of lechers who have been hanging around you all evening?'

'Have *you*?'

Art flushed. 'You came with me. I can't be blamed for wanting to look out for you.'

Rose's mouth twitched.

Art noted the way her pupils dilated and her eyes widened. He clocked the way her breath hitched and was suddenly turned on in a way that shocked him in its ferocity.

'Should I be grateful?' Rose breathed huskily.

'Don't.'

'Don't what?' The entire roomful of people could have evaporated. There was just the two of them, locked in a bubble in which he was acutely sensitive to every fleeting expression on her face, to the rasping of her breath and the deep, deep longing in her eyes.

'Don't look at me as though you want to touch me. Do that and you're playing with fire.'

'I started playing with fire the minute you came into my life,' Rose said in a tone of complete honesty.

'We should go,' Art told her roughly, leading the way, his hand cupping her elbow.

She was coming on to him. He felt it and, much as he would have liked nothing better than to have followed up on those hot little signals she was giving off, a tipsy Rose wasn't going to do. He wanted her sober and desperate for him, the way he was desperate for her. Nothing else would do.

It was cool and crisp outside and his car was waiting. Art propelled her into it and slid alongside her in the back seat.

'Do you think you have to show me to my door just in case I get waylaid by some of those lecherous men you seem to think are waiting around every corner for a country bumpkin like me?'

'How did you guess?'

'It's the dress. It stands out. When you said that it was going to be smart I had no idea what to buy. I didn't think that everyone would show up in black.'

'I could have warned you. Those functions are usually deadly. Black is an appropriate colour. Anyway, it's not the dress.'

'You don't think so?' Their eyes tangled and she didn't look away. She licked her lips, shivering in the burning intensity of his stare.

'We're here,' Art murmured, relieved.

'So we are. And just when I was beginning to enjoy the car ride.'

'I take it you're enjoying yourself,' he responded once they were out of the car and making their way up to her suite.

'What do you mean?'

'Enjoying playing with me.' Art shot her a wry smile. 'You must know what you're doing to me... I don't play games when it comes to sex...'

'You played a game with me when you slept with me.' She slid the card key into the slot and pushed open the door to her room. When she walked in she didn't push it shut behind her and she didn't tell him that it was fine for him to leave now that he had done the gentlemanly thing and seen her safely to her door. She looked over her shoulder, face serious.

'No game,' Art muttered in a strangled voice. 'The sex was for real. Stop looking at me like that... I'm not going to do anything, Rose. You...you've had a bit to drink. You don't know what you're doing. You don't know what you're playing with.'

'Fire. You've told me that already. I'm playing with fire.' The bed beckoned, oversized, draped in the finest Egyptian cottons and silk.

Rose turned to face him. The lighting in the room was mellow and forgiving. 'I've had a bit to drink,' she admitted without skipping a beat, 'but I'm not the worse for wear. I've been drinking a lot of water in between the wine and I've also eaten for England. Those canapés were to die for.' She walked towards him, kicking off the heels on the way. 'Want me to walk a straight line for you?'

'There's a lot I want you to do for me and walking a straight line doesn't figure.'

'What? What would you like me to do for you? What about this?' She reached down to cup the bulge between his legs and felt his swift intake of breath. Now or never.

Art pressed his hand over hers. He had to because, if he didn't, he wasn't sure what his body was going to do at the pressure she was exerting on his arousal.

'I want you.' Rose maintained eye contact. She'd never seemed more sober. 'When you told me who you really were I felt betrayed and deceived and I never, ever wanted to see you again.' She moved her hand and reached up to link fingers behind his neck. It was as if she'd given herself permission to touch and it was all she wanted to do now. 'I thought that it would be easy to put you behind me. How could I carry on wanting a guy who had used me?'

'Rose…'

'I know you're going to go into a long spiel about why you did what you did but that doesn't matter. What matters is I *couldn't* put you behind me. It didn't matter what you'd done, you'd still managed to get to me in ways…in ways I just never thought possible.'

'You underestimated the power of sex,' Art murmured, resting his hands on her narrow waist.

'I thought that if I saw the real you, the unscrupulous billionaire, then I would be so turned off that this stupid attraction would wither and die.'

Art inclined his head and knew that he had felt something similar, that if he saw her out of her surroundings and in his own terrain then common sense would reassert itself. 'No luck?' He ran his fingers along her back then over her ribcage, leaving them tantalisingly close to her breasts, close enough for her to shiver and half close her eyes.

'It doesn't make sense,' Rose practically wailed.

'Some things don't.' Art hadn't planned on taking her to bed, not tonight. But this wasn't a Rose who was not in control of her faculties. This was a Rose who was so in control that she could vocalise why she was doing what she was doing. This was the Rose he knew—open, honest, forthright and willing to confront a difficult decision head-on.

She couldn't have been a bigger turn-on.

Sex. The power of it. Never more than now was he forced to recognise the strength of body over mind. For someone always in control, this was like being thrown into a raging current without the benefit of a lifebelt. He looked forward to the challenge of battling against that current and emerging the victor.

He hooked his fingers beneath the straps of the sexy red dress and slid them down. She was wearing a silky bra that cupped her breasts like a film of gauze. Art groaned at the sight. The circular discs of her nipples were clearly visible, as was the stiffened bud tipping each pink sphere.

'You gave your phone number to another man,' he said illogically.

'Were you jealous?'

'I wanted to punch him straight into another continent.'

'But you told me I should network...'

'I can't stand the thought of another man touching you.'

'Take me,' she breathed, reaching behind her to unhook the bra, which she shrugged off, stepping back then to unzip the dress at the side and then wriggling out of it so that she was standing in front of him in just her lacy panties.

'Is this the wine talking?' Art was close to the point of no return. She wasn't tripping over her feet but there was no way he was going to get up close and personal with her, only to find himself pushed to one side because she'd fallen asleep on him. He intended to hear groans of pleasure as opposed to the snores of someone who'd had a glass too many.

He smiled at the image because if there was one woman alive who would fall asleep on him it was Rose.

'You're grinning.' Rose began undressing him, clearly trying her best not to rush.

'I'm grinning because I'm busy picturing you falling asleep on me and snoring like a trooper, leaving me with the consolation prize of a cold shower.'

'No chance of that,' Rose said huskily. 'You don't have to worry that I'm under the influence.' She shot him a wicked look from under her lashes. 'Don't tell me that you're so lacking in self-confidence that you think a woman will only sleep with you if she's had one too many.'

'Wench...' But he burst out laughing and propelled her gently back in the direction of the bed, simultaneously completing the job she had begun of getting rid of his clothes. 'Shall I show you how timid and lacking in confidence I am when it comes to pleasuring a woman?'

Rose hit the bed and flopped back onto it, laughing and pulling him down towards her.

'Please,' she breathed, arching up to kiss him. 'Please, please, please... That's exactly what I want...'

CHAPTER NINE

ROSE HAD FANTASISED about those nights when she and Art had made love. She'd delved deep into her memory banks and closed her eyes and tasted, in the emptiness of her bed after he'd disappeared in a puff of treacherous smoke, the touch of his mouth on hers, the feel of his hands tracing the contours of her body, the heavy weight of him on top of her and the way her legs had parted for him, welcoming him into the very core of her.

Now, touching him again, she realised that no amount of recall could ever have done justice to the reality of him.

Running her hands over his lean, hard body was like tasting nectar after a diet of vinegar.

He felt so good.

She traced the corded muscles of his back and then squirmed so that she was taking charge of proceedings, flattening him against the bed and angling her body in such a way that she could devote all her attention to his vibrant arousal whilst, at the same time, he could pleasure her between her legs.

She'd forgotten how well their bodies meshed, as

though created to fit one against the other. She moved against his questing tongue, her breathing fast and furious, making little guttural noises as she licked and tasted him, feasting on his hardness and playing with his erection while she explored it with her mouth.

Her long hair was everywhere and she flipped it over her shoulder and then arched up, her whole body quivering as ripples of an orgasm began coursing slowly through her.

'Art…' she gasped, not wanting to come.

Not yet.

This time it was Art who took control. With one easy move, he flipped her so that she was now facing him and he edged her up so that there was next to no pause in his ministrations.

She was sitting over him, allowing him the greatest intimacy as he continued to flick his tongue over the stiffened bud of her core. Hands firmly on her waist so that he was keeping her in position, he teased her with his mouth and when her breathing quickened and her body began to stiffen he concentrated on bringing her to a shuddering explosive orgasm.

She spasmed against his mouth and he revelled in the honeyed moistness of her orgasm.

He'd missed this.

He'd missed more than this. It felt so good that he had to reach down and hold his own erection firm because he felt on the very edge of tipping over even though he wasn't inside her, which was where he wanted to be.

Rose subsided, temporarily spent. She lay down next

to him and wrapped her legs over his and, as one, they turned to one another so that their naked bodies were pressed up tight, hot and perspiring.

'Not fair,' she said shakily, but there was a smile in her voice as she wriggled against him, nudging her wetness against his arousal.

'No, it's not,' Art murmured indistinctly. Decidedly unfair that she had this dramatic effect on him, that she was capable of derailing his life the way she had. Just as well that he was putting it back on track. 'Dump the hotel,' he heard himself say, 'and move in with me for the rest of your stay in London.'

'Dump the hotel?'

'It's inconvenient.' He'd never asked any woman to stay in his penthouse apartment but he was comfortable with this decision because a precedent had already been set. He'd shared her space with her so no big deal if she were to share his space with him.

He wanted to be able to reach out and touch her in the middle of the night. He wanted to feel her, warm and aroused, lying next to him. He curved his hand between her thighs and stroked her soft, silky skin, nudging up to feel her wetness graze his knuckles.

He stepped away to fetch a condom from his wallet.

'I guess I could,' Rose murmured as he slipped back into bed to pull her against him. 'I guess it could work...' She parted her legs and sighed as her body began to get excited all over again. 'I mean,' she continued, voice hitched, 'I hadn't banked on any of this happening.'

'That's been the story of my life from the second I saw you,' Art agreed with heartfelt sincerity. 'You may well have converted me to the pleasures of the unforeseen.'

'We both have the same goal.'

Art caressed her breast then levered himself into a position where he could taste it. He flicked his tongue over her nipple and then took it into his mouth so that he could suckle on it while he played with her other nipple, teasing it into tight arousal.

'The same goal...' Her words registered and he slowly kissed his way up to nuzzle against her neck before settling alongside her in a lovely, comfortable position where he could carry on teasing her nipple between his fingers.

'I don't want to want you.' Rose imagined that his next girlfriend might have brains, might have more staying power, might be the woman he let into his life because he had now seen for himself that being in a kitchen together and sharing a meal and then doing the washing-up whilst talking about anything and everything was not something to be feared and reviled. She had done him a favour in pointing him in a different direction and her heart twisted because when he left her behind and walked away it would be into a relationship that might prove to be *the one*.

'And,' she continued, tugging him up because she couldn't focus on anything when he was doing what he'd been doing, 'I know you feel the same.' She paused, a fractional little pause during which he could have jumped in with a denial or said something that might have indicated an interest in more than just *getting her out of his system.* He failed to take the bait. 'So, yes, perhaps if I moved in with you for a couple of days... well, while I'm here, then this thing we have going on... well, we can get it out of our systems faster.'

Art frowned. 'My way of thinking,' he said, on cue.

'There's something about familiarity...'

'You certainly know how to massage a guy's ego. In a minute you'll start comparing me to a virus.'

'Well, it *is* a bit like that.' Rose laughed shakily.

'And what if it doesn't conveniently blow over in a couple of days?'

Rose knew that he was playing devil's advocate. 'It will,' she said firmly. 'We don't have anything in common, Art. We don't have what it takes to have a proper relationship, which is the only thing that would stop this *thing* from blowing over.'

Art frowned. 'Define a *proper* relationship. Is there a checklist for something like that?'

'More or less, if I'm being honest.'

'So now you're saying I tick none of the boxes.'

'There's still one box that gets a very big tick.'

'Glad to hear it.'

'But for me,' Rose said on a sigh, 'a relationship is so much more than just sex.'

'And yet sex, like it or not, is so much a part of any relationship. Too much talking. I get the picture. We're here and this is something we have to do and I can't tell you how much I'm going to enjoy doing it.'

He'd just never mentioned a timeline...

Rose lay in bed, half dozing, drinking him in as he

strolled through the bedroom of his penthouse apartment, completely naked, hunting down his laptop computer because, even though it was still only six in the morning, he was up and ready to work.

She was warm and replete and contented. He'd roused her an hour earlier, nudging her into compliant wakefulness, and they had made love oh, so slowly. Caught in that hazy, half asleep place, Rose had let him take her to places that had left her crying out with pleasure. When, after touching her everywhere, after exploring her soft, warm body, he had finally thrust into her, filling her up, she had felt tears leak down her cheeks and had had to surreptitiously wipe them away because that definitely wasn't part of the deal.

The package deal had kicked off three days previously, when she had fallen into his arms like a starving woman deprived of food who suddenly found herself with a ticket to an all-you-can-eat banquet.

They had made love and then, after a handful of hours' sleep, had made love again and the very next morning she had moved in with him.

They hadn't discussed how long this arrangement was going to last. How did you talk about something like that? How did you work out the length of time it would take for one person to get sick of the other?

How long would it take for him to get bored with her?

Rose knew that that was the way it was going to play out because she wasn't close to getting him out of her system. Indeed, with every passing minute spent together, he became more embedded in her bloodstream.

They'd talked about sex. He did that a lot. When they

made love he would whisper things in her ear that made her whole body burn. He would tell her, in a husky, shaky voice, how much he wanted her and what he wanted to do with her.

He was ruled by lust. He couldn't keep his hands off her and the more he showed that want, the more she needed something more. Something more powerful than *want*.

But that was off the cards and it was always going to be off the cards.

Except…now…looking at him and his careless elegance, Rose felt her heart twist and she knew with an awful sense of despair that she was powerless to initiate the necessary break-up.

She was held in place by something far bigger than lust.

Somehow, against all odds, she had fallen in love with him and she was as powerless now as a speck of flotsam being tossed around this way and that on an unpredictable, fast-flowing current.

She could only make sure he never saw her vulnerability because if he did he would run for the hills.

Love was not on his radar. Not with her. And it never would be. The novelty value that had drawn him to her might not have yet released him from its hold but, now that she was immersed in his life, she knew with dreadful certainty that she was only ever going to be a distraction for him.

He didn't do love. The highs and lows of emotion were things he would seek to avoid. Above everything, he enjoyed the power of control and that included control of his emotional life. He would find someone but she knew in her heart that he would not want someone who was as emotional as she had turned out to be.

Far from being the level-headed woman she'd imagined she was, love had turned her to mush and she wasn't ashamed of it.

Even though she knew that hurt was lurking around the corner, waiting for her.

He produced the laptop from where it had been residing under a bundle of discarded clothes on a chair in his bedroom with a grin of triumph and turned to her. 'First time this hasn't been at my fingertips.'

'You were in a hurry last night.' She forced herself to grin back, keeping it light.

'So I was,' he murmured, dumping the computer and making his way back towards the bed to lean over her, then dropping a kiss on her forehead. 'You do that to me.'

'Make you want to run?' Rose teased, playing with words.

'I can't get to you fast enough.'

Art looked at her for a few serious seconds and Rose had the feeling that there was something he wanted to tell her. A cold chill spread through her but she kept smiling, keeping it light. There could only be one thing he could have wanted to tell her that would have put that serious expression on his face and those words were not ones she wanted to hear. She swallowed down the nasty lump of desperation.

'Stay in bed with me,' she urged. 'Surely work can wait.'

'Not this.' He was still looking at her with that expression on his face.

'Big deal you have to close? I can't imagine there's any deal big enough that you can't ignore it for a few more minutes.'

His expression lightened. 'And to think I've always prided myself on being the kind of guy who can hold out for longer than a couple of minutes…although,' he mused, 'fast and furious does hold a certain appeal, I have to admit.' He sighed, glanced at his cell phone and looked at her again with that pensive expression, thinking thoughts she couldn't begin to fathom. 'Unfortunately, this has nothing to do with work, as such…'

'Why am I getting the feeling that you're speaking in riddles?'

For a few seconds Art remained silent and during those few seconds Rose felt her heart clench tightly, painfully in her chest. Now was the time for her to voice her thoughts and either give him permission to walk away or else pre-empt his departure by announcing hers first.

She was spared any decision because just at that moment his phone buzzed. He looked at the number, then at her.

'Private call,' he said lightly, turning away.

He'd never done that before. Fighting down a wave of nausea, Rose hurriedly leapt out of the bed the second he had left the bedroom, shutting the door quietly behind him. She flew into the bathroom and had a very quick shower. She was dressed and ready for the day and he still had not returned.

Was the call so important that he had to take it at

this ungodly hour, without even taking time out to get dressed?

Was it another woman?

She knew that he had conference calls at strange hours from people in a different time zone, but he had always been fully prepped for those. He'd always conducted them in front of his computer, accessing information while talking to whoever might be on the line.

This was...different.

Rose couldn't credit that he might sleep with her whilst having something going on with someone else. He just wasn't that kind of guy, but then maybe, quite by chance, he had met someone in the last day or so. Was that so tough to believe? Hadn't she already come to the conclusion that he was a changed man, even though he might not see it for himself? A man more open to the possibility of letting someone into his life? A suitable woman.

People gave out vibes without even realising it. Had he projected some sort of availability-to-the-right-woman vibe?

Tense with anxiety, she stood back and looked at her reflection in the mirror. She was nothing special, however much he might wax lyrical about her sexiness.

She was tall and rangy and her looks, such as they were, were unconventional.

Was his private call with a woman with more to offer in the looks department? Was he returning to his comfort zone after his brush with a girl from the wrong side of the tracks?

She found him in the kitchen and he was no longer

on the phone. He was also no longer buck naked but had a towel slung around his lean hips. He must have nabbed it from the spare bathroom while he had been strolling to the kitchen.

Coffee was on the go.

He was so drop-dead gorgeous. So sinfully sexy. So horribly addictive. She remembered that she had fallen for him within five minutes of meeting him. So much for her much-prized defence system when it came to the opposite sex!

'What was that about?'

Art stilled. He'd been reaching for a couple of mugs and he paused for a fraction of a second.

'Coffee?'

'You're not going to answer?'

Rose was dismayed at the shrill, demanding tone of her voice. She had aimed for banter mingled with amused curiosity. She had ended up with shrewish nag but she couldn't claw her way back from the question and she wasn't sure she wanted to. If he was going to break it off with her because of some other woman then he should have the decency to come right out and tell her.

She shouldn't have to second-guess.

'I didn't think that sharing my private phone calls was part and parcel of what we had.'

Rose flushed. 'Who was it?' she was horrified to hear herself ask.

'I think this is a conversation best put on hold,' Art said coolly.

'And I happen to think that I deserve an answer. If it was a personal call with another woman, then I deserve to know. I realise this isn't anything serious but I'm not interested in sleeping with anyone who's seeing someone else on the side.'

'Is that what you think?' he asked quietly.

Rose hesitated but, like someone who had crossed a certain line, she was now doomed to carry on walking that road. And besides, she roused herself to a place of self-righteous justification, she *did* deserve to know if he was thinking about ditching her for someone else!

'How do I know what to think if you won't tell me what's going on?' she muttered.

'I'm going to get changed.'

'You're walking away from an uncomfortable conversation,' she challenged but he was already heading back to the bedroom and after a while she tripped along behind him.

Art stopped dead in his tracks and looked at her, eyes flint-hard. 'I don't do this,' he said calmly.

Rose returned that gaze with one that was equally cool. 'Do what, Art?' She folded her arms, determined to brave out what she knew was going to be their final conversation. 'Discuss anything you might find a little awkward? I know this isn't about love and commitment, but it should be about respect and if you respected me you wouldn't baulk at having this conversation.'

Rose hoped that he would read nothing in her eyes that gave the lie to that statement because when it came to love she was drowning under the weight of it. Pride would never allow her to admit that, however. She was going to leave but she would leave without him ever having cause to think that he had had a narrow escape from yet another needy woman who had foolishly disobeyed his *Do Not Trespass* signs and developed unacceptable feelings towards him.

He had let slip in conversation the headaches he had had with a couple of previous girlfriends who had wanted him to meet the parents, who had mentioned the possibility of making plans further ahead than the next couple of hours.

Rose had absorbed those passing comments and was not going to be bracketed in the same category, to become yet another irritating ex to be produced during some future conversation with some future woman.

Art's eyebrows shot up but something made him hesitate before heading back to the bedroom.

'I'm not going to have this conversation,' he said abruptly. 'If you feel that I am the sort of man who disrespects women, who has somehow disrespected *you*, then it's clear that we should not be together.'

'Art...'

'I'll be back but don't wait up.'

'Is that your way of saying that you'd like me to be gone by the time you return? Because if it is then why don't you have the guts to come right out and say so?'

'No one speaks to me like that!'

Rose folded her arms and stared at him mutinously. On the inside she was breaking up into pieces. On the outside she refused to show him just how much she was hurting. 'Then you're right,' she said gruffly. 'It's clear that we shouldn't be together if I'm only allowed to speak to you in a certain way!'

The tense silence between them stretched on and on and on...stretched until she could feel all her wretchedness washing over her in a painful tidal wave.

'Like I said,' Art drawled, 'don't wait up.'

Rose watched in silence as he threw aside the towel to get dressed. She found that she couldn't look at him. Even at the height of this toxic argument, she could still be moved by his sheer animal beauty. She didn't want to be moved.

He left the room without a backward glance and for a while she actually hoped that he would have second thoughts and return.

He didn't.

She had no idea where he'd gone and her feverish imagination provided her with all sorts of unwelcome scenarios. Had he disappeared into the waiting arms of some other woman? Had he somehow manoeuvred a situation in which she would react in a way that would give him an out?

She wasn't going to hang around to find out and there was nothing more to be said.

She gathered her things in record time. She hadn't brought much with her and what little she *had* brought took ten minutes to toss into her case.

She paused to look at the wonderful dress she had worn for the charity event that had been so memorable for so many reasons.

No way was she taking it with her.

It took her half an hour and then she was out of the mansion block and casting one last look behind her from the back of a black cab.

* * *

Art returned to an empty apartment. Of course he knew that she would be gone by the time he got back. He'd disappeared for over four hours. No explanation. What would have possessed her to hang around?

He flipped on the lights and went straight to his computer and switched it on. In his peripheral vision, he could tell that all her belongings had gone with her. There was no need for him to waste his energy hunting for evidence of her departure.

The screen opened up and he stared at it and realised that it really was possible to look at numbers and letters and symbols and see absolutely nothing whatsoever.

She would have caught a taxi to the station and would be heading back to her house by train. He was tempted to look up the possible departure times of the trains and resisted.

He'd done the right thing. That reaction was sufficient to harden his resolve. He had been weak once, had engineered a situation because he had still wanted her and had been unable to resist the demands of his body, but that weakness was something that had to be overcome.

He had seen where emotional weakness could lead. Those lessons had been learned when he had been too young but they were lessons he would never forget.

His indecision had been getting on his nerves and so he'd killed it fast. He hadn't signed up to a querulous woman throwing a hissy fit because he refused to be subjected to a cross-examination.

So what if that phone call had had nothing to do with a woman?

He scowled, mood plummeting faster than the speed of light. Right about now she should be winding her arms around him, warm and naked and distracting.

Right about now he should be forgetting about work and climbing right back into bed with her because he couldn't do anything *but* climb into bed with her whenever they were in this room.

Art envisaged what her reaction would be in a couple of months, when the full extent of that phone call became common knowledge.

He'd deceived her once but she had returned to him and he knew that it had been something she would not have undertaken lightly.

Sex was all well and good but she would have had to square it with her conscience and he'd never met any woman with a more lively conscience. Her conscience practically bounced off the walls.

To discover what she inevitably would, to find out without benefit of any explanation…

He abandoned all attempts to focus on work, sat back and wearily rubbed his eyes with the pads of his thumbs.

He'd never thought himself to have a particularly active or vivid imagination but he was imagining now, in a very vivid fashion indeed, the horror that would engulf her were she to discover, as she would in due course, that there would be more going on that vast acreage of land than a handful of tasteful houses.

It would be the ultimate deception for her because she would know that he would have had countless opportunities to raise the issue. To be deceived once was forgivable. To be deceived twice would be the ultimate sin in her eyes.

He should have broached the subject. That phone call would have provided the perfect opportunity to raise it. Instead, the shutters had slammed shut on her. Habit. He had never been a man to be nagged or cajoled into saying or doing anything he didn't want to say or do. He had reacted with stunning predictability.

And it had been a mistake.

The truth was that she deserved honesty—and that was exactly what he was going to give her.

The slate would then be wiped clean.

Mind made up, Art didn't bother consulting anything as pedestrian as train timetables. Why would he? He had two options. His private helicopter or his driver. Or he could take any one of his fast cars and drive himself.

Which was exactly what he chose to do.

He didn't know whether he would reach her house before her but it didn't matter. What mattered, and mattered with an urgency he couldn't quite put into words, was that they talked.

He'd say what he had to say and then leave.

Traffic was light as he left London. A Ferrari was built to eat up the miles with silent efficiency and it did.

Under normal circumstances, he would have kicked back and enjoyed the dynamic horsepower of a car he rarely got to drive but his mind was too busy projecting the conversation that was going to take place.

He made it to her house in record time and knew, without even having to ring the doorbell, that she wasn't yet there.

With any luck, she was going to show up soon and hadn't decided to do a spot of sightseeing before catching the train back.

Art positioned the powerful car at the perfect angle to see her just as she entered her drive. He wasn't going to let her run away this time.

Rose was spent by the time she made it to the local out-post where trains arrived in their own sweet time. The slow journey would have got on her nerves at any other time but on this occasion she relished the unhurried tempo of the trip. Her head felt as though it was burst-ing with thoughts, too many thoughts to be contained, just as her heart was bursting with too many feelings.

And at the very centre of all those thoughts and feel-ings was the dark, throbbing knowledge that she was not going to see Art again. The void that opened up in-side her when she thought about that was so big that it threatened to swallow her up like a sinkhole.

At the station she hailed a taxi, which exited the small car park as though urgency was a concept that didn't exist. She knew the taxi driver. She had done some pro bono work for his father two years previ-ously, and she heard herself chatting to him but from a long way away.

She was so tired.

Lapsing into silence, she closed her eyes and wasn't aware that she was approaching her house until the taxi began to slow, until it swerved slowly into the drive, and only then did she open her eyes and stir herself into wakefulness.

Only then did she see the red car in the drive, sleek and elegant and so, *so* sexy.

CHAPTER TEN

ART WAS OUT of the car before the passenger door of the taxi had opened. He'd been hanging around for over an hour. He'd stretched his legs a couple of times but he still felt cramped and restless.

Watching through narrowed eyes as she emerged, he felt at peace for the first time since he had left London.

No…since she had re-entered his life, if not before.

His thoughts were so clear he felt washed clean.

He could see the wariness in her eyes and he strode towards her before that wariness could persuade her to get back into the taxi and disappear, leaving him stranded on her doorstep.

'What are you doing here?' Rose's voice was curt as she paid the taxi driver, who was watching proceedings with keen interest. 'Thanks, Stephen—' she said to the driver through the window of the car, eyebrows raised '—I won't keep you. I expect Jenny and the kids would like to have you home.'

'That the big-shot she's been banging on about for weeks?'

'No idea, Steve. I don't know how many big-shots

Jenny's met recently...' She slammed shut the door and leaned towards him. 'Give her my love and the thumbs-up that everything's in place for the changes to the library. She can start picking out colours for the new kids' space.'

Rose was playing for time but, with no distraction left, she remained where she was as Steve headed away. Her case was on the ground at her feet.

'I've been waiting here for over an hour.' For the first time in living memory, Art was nervous. He almost failed to recognise the sensation. He couldn't take his eyes off her. He wanted to climb into her head and read what she was thinking but her expression was cool and remote and he wondered...where did he go from here?

Scowling and ill at ease, he walked towards her and was pleased to note that, almost indiscernibly, she flinched. He was having some kind of effect on her and that was good because, going by her expression, he could have been a wind-up toy.

'So sorry to have kept you waiting,' Rose said coolly, tilting her head at a mutinous angle and refusing to back away. 'And you still haven't told me what you're doing here.'

'I...' He shook his head, looked away, raked his fingers through his hair and then returned his dark gaze to her pale, cool face. 'I...shouldn't have...let you leave... with the wrong idea...' was pretty much all he could find to say.

'Not interested,' Rose muttered, looking away. 'You're a free agent and you can do what you want. You're right. You don't owe me any explanations.'

'Are we going to carry on this conversation out here?'

'I didn't think we were having a conversation. You came here to explain whatever it is you feel you should explain and I'm liberating you from that responsibility. So there's no conversation to be had.'

'It was about the land.'

'Sorry?'

'I was on the phone to someone about the land. The land you were protecting from greedy developers like me. I wanted to tell you...' Art looked away but only momentarily.

'The land?' Rose looked at him in confusion because this was the last thing she'd been expecting to hear. 'You weren't on the phone to a woman?'

'I'm monogamous.' His lips quirked in a dry smile but he had no idea how this was going to play out and the smile only lasted a second. His usual panache and easy self-assurance were nowhere in evidence. 'And when would I have had time to think about frolicking with another woman? You've kept me pretty busy...'

'What about the land?'

Lengthening silence greeted this and eventually Rose spun around and began walking towards the house.

'Tell me you haven't been keeping more from me about the land,' she said quietly as soon as the front door was shut behind them. She clearly hadn't wanted to invite him into the house but he'd left her with no choice.

'You don't have the complete picture,' Art said flatly. Cold dread was gripping him and he knew now that full disclosure should have been his approach. But events had moved swiftly and now...

He was going to lose her and if that happened he had

no idea what he was going to do because he couldn't contemplate a life without her in it. He'd screwed up.

'Start small, end up big. Is that the complete picture?' They were in the kitchen. Rose felt as if she could do with a stiff drink but instead she began the business of making herself a cup of coffee—anything to still her nerves, which were running amok as she gradually worked out that he had deceived her once again.

Had he slept with her the second time round so that he could build up to yet more revelations about what he intended to do with the acres of land he had bought?

Had he sweet-talked her into phase one with the intention of sweet-talking her into phase two, except she'd scuppered his plans by overhearing that conversation, jumping to the wrong conclusion and then walking out on him before he could complete what he had set out to do?

She felt sick.

'You didn't want a handful of tasteful mansions with lots of spare land, did you? That wouldn't have made financial sense. What you wanted was to start with a handful of tasteful mansions and then what, Art? A housing estate? Mass housing that would mean more profits for you? As if you aren't rich enough already.'

She managed to make it to the kitchen table, now free from placards and posters and cardboard with rousing slogans, and she sank into one of the chairs.

'Way too rich.' Art drew a chair up close to hers, as if to stop her from somehow fleeing the room. She didn't like his positioning and automatically drew back into herself, freezing him out as her defences came down. When he leaned forward, elbows resting loosely on his thighs, he was practically touching her.

'Too rich to think about whether putting up a hundred houses is going to net me more money than putting up ten.' He sighed heavily, caught her eye and held her gaze. 'But you're right. I haven't been entirely honest with you.'

'I don't want to hear.'

'And normally that would work for me,' Art returned. 'Normally justifying myself in any way, shape or form isn't something I would see the need to do, but in this instance...'

'Am I supposed to think that you have a conscience?' Rose questioned painfully.

'I don't suppose I've given you a lot of reason to trust anything I have to say.'

'Spot on.'

'But...' He shook his head. 'I'll try to start at the beginning. I... You'll have to bear with me. I don't... know how this is done.'

'How what is done?'

'This talking business.'

'This *talking business*? What does that even *mean*?' But there was an air of vulnerability about him that she'd never seen before and it did something to her even though she fought hard to resist the pull and tried to remember that this wasn't going to end up in a good place.

'I... I've never had much time for talking, Rose. Not when it came to women. When it came to women, things were very clear-cut. It was all about mutual pleasure.

Nothing lasted and nothing was meant to. It was the way I liked it. When I met you, I had an agenda, but in no way was sleeping with you part of that agenda, and of course that should have set the alarm bells ringing. The fact that sleeping with you made no sense and yet I had to do it, had to get you into bed. It was as though something bigger and stronger than me had taken charge and was dictating how I behaved when it came to you.'

Rose looked at him with a jaundiced expression and wondered whether she was supposed to melt at that admission. She wished he'd back away a bit. His proximity was suffocating her.

'You need to just tell me what else you've been hiding from me,' she said quietly. 'I don't want to hear about…how much you wanted me…'

Art sat back and half closed his eyes, then he looked at her for a while in silence.

'There was always an agenda for that land. I had to have it. Had to make sure that everything went through and I had to get the residents of the village onside. Yes, for the expensive houses that were going to be built but also, in due course, for more building work that I had planned.'

'I thought as much.' Rose looked away, heart pounding, bile in her mouth.

'You really don't.' He turned her face to his, finger lightly under her chin, compelling them to lock eyes, and Rose gazed helplessly at him.

'I can't bear the thought of being used, Art. All my life, the one thing I've taken away from what happened to my mum is that I would never allow myself to be used by any man. She abandoned me for a man she met and knew for five seconds! Yes, she came back but I'd lost a lot in that time that she'd been away and I'd grown up and learned lessons. Lesson one was that when it came to my heart, common sense was always going to be more valuable than stupid, crazy *lust.*'

'We're singing from the same song sheet,' Art murmured. 'We both had lessons ingrained into us thanks to our backgrounds. Rich or poor, our experiences made us the cautious people we ended up being. I was happy to be ruled by lust. I just resisted anything more than that. Until you. Until you came along.'

'What do you mean?' Rose found that she was holding her breath and she exhaled slowly, hoping that her calm, detached exterior was still in place, making no assumptions even though her heart was beating fast now but with forbidden excitement.

'I told myself that it was a mistake to sleep with you. I didn't want the waters to be muddied. I had come for a specific reason and I naturally assumed that a minor temptation wasn't going to confuse the issue. How wrong I was. I decided where was the harm? There wouldn't be any fallout because I was always, had always been and always would be, in control of my choices. We were both consenting adults and, if anything, getting you into bed would give me an added advantage in persuading you to listen to reason when it came to the protest.' She looked away sharply and Art tilted her stubborn face back to his.

'The truth of the matter was that I couldn't resist you. You did something to me and you carried on doing it even when I left and returned to London. I couldn't get you out of my mind. I kept drifting off into inappropriate fantasies at inappropriate times. In the middle of conversations, in the thick of an important meeting, just as I was about to sink my teeth into the finest food money could buy. And yet I still didn't wake up to what should have been blindingly obvious.'

'Which is what?'

'Somewhere along the line I fell in love with you. Please don't say anything because I need to tell you about the land. After you've heard what I have to say I'll leave, but I felt you needed to know...how I felt.'

'Art...'

He'd fallen in love with her? Did he really mean that?

Her heart had migrated to her mouth so when she spoke her voice was muffled and she had to clear her throat. 'Do you mean that?'

'I wasn't looking for love. I've never been looking for love. My father had so many ex-wives that so-called *love* was always in plentiful supply and always, without fail, ended up in the divorce courts, where each and every one would wrangle until they went blue in the face for a slice of his money. I was jaded beyond belief by the time I left my teens behind. Love was for idiots and I was never going to be an idiot. The truth is that I just never fell in love and I never realised that love makes idiots of us all.'

'Why didn't you say something?' Rose whispered.

'How could I,' Art asked wryly, 'when I didn't recognise the symptoms?'

Symptoms? Never had that single word held such thrilling promise.

'Please tell me about the land.' Everything should have been perfect. The man of her dreams had just declared his love for her and yet the rest of his story cast a long shadow, even though she couldn't see what could possibly spoil the moment. She just knew that a fly in the ointment could turn out to be a lot more toxic than it might first appear. If she was going to get toxic, then she wanted to get it straight away.

'I targeted that land because I want to build an equestrian centre there,' Art said heavily. 'And not just an equestrian centre, but something of a farming complex. You won't be getting the neat arrangement of polite, high-spec houses you signed up for and there's no other way of putting it but to tell it like it is.' His mouth twisted crookedly. 'In hindsight, if I could have predicted how circumstances would unravel, I would have taken the plunge from the very start but hindsight, as I've discovered to my cost, is a wonderful thing. And, like I've said—' he smiled with self-mockery '—hindsight isn't something I've ever had time for. My predictive talents had never been challenged and when you know what's coming you're not glancing over your shoulder and shaking your head because you took the wrong turning.'

'Sorry? You want to build *a farm*?' Rose was finding it hard to get past that stark announcement.

'Long story, but… I have a stepbrother, José. He's severely autistic and currently in a home in the New

Forest. He's not yet twenty-two but the home, good as it is, really can't deal with the needs of a young adult.'

'You have a brother...'

'Stepbrother. And the only step-sibling I've ever had time for. Ironic, given his mother had very *little* time for him. In fact, my father had no idea he existed at all until after the marriage had ended. Eliza kept her son's existence under wraps, just in case it jeopardised the pot of gold at the end of the rainbow. At the time, José had been shoved in a mixed bag home and practically forgotten. I met him and felt sorry for him. No, more than that. I wanted to protect him and then I grew to love him. He was honest and trusting and incredibly talented in certain areas but he'd been hung out to dry by his scheming mother, who had no time for him. To her credit, she did pop her head into the home now and again but where she left off, I found that I was taking over. Years after she disappeared from my father's life, she was killed in a road accident, at which point I took José under my wing. I was climbing the ladder of success. It became my mission to ensure that he got the best that money could buy. I saved José but, in a strange way, I think José also saved me.'

'Art, my head is spinning.'

'There's no concise way to explain all of this. I just need you to understand that my dilemma was finding a place where I could develop a centre for José and for other kids like him. A handful. He is soothed by horses and enjoys being outdoors. He has a way with them. The farm would be something of a therapeutic centre.

Some arts and crafts could be incorporated. You'd be surprised at how talented some of these kids are.'

'But why on earth didn't you say anything about this?'

'To the council?' His eyebrows shot up. 'People can be strange when it comes to having anyone different as their neighbours. It took a long time to find a suitable location, somewhere commutable for me, a convenient middle ground for other occupants. I wasn't going to risk jeopardising the project by introducing it from the beginning. I thought that by the time the community got accustomed to the notion of the land being developed they would be more open to my future plans for the place.'

'I love you,' Rose said simply, because all of this showed her a side to him that she'd known was there, a caring, thoughtful side lurking underneath the ruthless billionaire exterior.

It was the side that had sucked her in and, even when he'd confessed to his deception, had kept her sucked in because deep down she had known him for the good guy he was. She'd seen the moral integrity underneath the tough *love is for the birds* exterior.

'You're not upset that I lied to you yet again?' Art looked as though his heart was soaring.

'I'd like to meet your stepbrother one day.'

Art reached out but he didn't tug her towards him. Instead, he held her hands in his. It was a chaste gesture that made her smile.

'You will,' he said gruffly. 'But first you have to promise me one thing.'

'What?' She nudged closer to him and played with his fingers. She couldn't help herself. She reached out and stroked the side of his face with the back of her hand, then she traced the contours of his mouth.

She leaned into him and kissed him, a slow, tender, melting kiss and it felt good to have her love out in the open, to be as vulnerable as he was.

'Promise me that you'll marry me,' Art said in a muffled voice. 'Because I can't imagine a life without you in it. I want to go to sleep with you and wake up to you. I don't want to ever let you go.'

'Yes.' Rose smiled. 'A thousand times *yes*.'

They were married just as the finishing touches were being put to the local library.

It had been planned as a quiet wedding but it turned out to be rather larger than either of them had expected. Once one person had been invited others had to be included, and Rose discovered that she had done a lot more for the residents of her quiet community than she had ever dreamed.

Everyone wanted to come.

Everyone knew her story and the wedding was almost as much of a fairy tale for them as for her.

She wore a simple cream dress and little silk buds were woven into her long hair, and the look on Art's face when he turned to look at her as she walked up the aisle of the little country church was something she would take with her for as long as she lived.

And now...

Six months later, life couldn't be better and so much had changed. For starters, the house had no more leaks in need of fixing. It had been renovated to its original splendour but, with all the right planning permission in place, was now a fully functioning office catering for several start-up companies as well as the legal practice which Phil, Rose's partner, had taken over in its entirety.

Rose no longer lived there but whenever she returned she marvelled at its wonderful transformation.

'I don't think,' she confided to Art a few weeks after she had moved out and shortly before their wedding, 'that I ever really saw it as *my* house. Even though, technically, it was. And even though I always, always knew it to be a real blessing. I guess I always somehow associated it with a time in my life that brought back bad memories so, whilst I'm happy it's renovated, I'm pleased I no longer live in it.'

Where she lived now could not have been more wonderful. Not the sprawling modernist vision in London which Art had occupied but, he also admitted, never actually viewed as anything other than a handy space in a useful location, but a country cottage that was the perfect blend of ancient and modern.

It was just outside London, convenient for commuting both back to London by train and to the centre in the Cotswolds where José would be eventually located.

Rose had fallen in love with the cottage at first sight.

With the husband of her dreams and the house to match, she hadn't thought that life could get any better but it had.

She started as she heard the front door open and her heart quickened, as it always did at the arrival of her husband.

She rose to greet him and smiled at the naked love and desire etched on his lean face.

He was so beautiful and he was *hers*. She smiled at the thrill of possession that swelled inside her.

Art smiled back, moving smoothly towards her while undoing the top couple of buttons of his shirt.

'You don't get to look like that without accepting that there'll be consequences.' He pulled her towards him, cupped her rounded bottom and crushed her against him so that she could feel the tell-tale stirring of his desire.

'Look like what?' Rose burst out laughing, drawing back and capturing his face between her hands.

'Oh, you know…pair of jeans, tee shirt, flip-flops…'

'Oh, you mean my *fancy* outfit.'

'You've gone all out on the dinner, I see.' Art peered around her to see the kitchen table, which was candlelit and set in some style. 'What have I forgotten? It's not a birthday and it's definitely not our anniversary, unless it's the anniversary of the first time you decided that I was the best thing that ever happened to you, which would have been, hmm, about five minutes after we met?'

'Time's done nothing to dim that ego of yours, Arturo da Costa, has it?'

Art burst out laughing. 'Don't keep me in suspense. With any other woman, I'd be inclined to think that you're bracing me for some wildly extravagant purchase, but then, my darling, you're not any other woman and I thank my lucky stars for that every day.'

Rose tugged him into the huge open-plan kitchen with its granite countertops and its wonderful state-of-the-art built-in appliances.

'Champagne,' Art murmured, glancing at the counter. 'Now I'm really beginning to get worried.'

'Then don't. I actually would have dressed up for the occasion but I opted for comfortable over glamorous.'

'Don't distract me.'

'The champagne is for you. I'll be sticking to mineral water for the moment and for the next, oh, let's say... nine months or so...'

'Are you telling me what I think you're telling me?'

'I'm pregnant.'

Art wrapped his arms around her and held her tight to him for several long minutes. 'I couldn't have asked for a better end to my day, my darling. I love you so very much.'

'And I love you too. Now and for ever.'

* * * * *

THE TYCOON'S STOWAWAY

STEFANIE LONDON

To my wonderful husband for supporting me from the very first time I wrote 'Chapter One'. Thank you for always understanding my need to write, for keeping me sane through the ups and downs, and for holding my hand when I took the biggest leap of my life.

I love you.

Always.

PROLOGUE

Hot. Loud. Crushing.

The dance floor at the Weeping Reef resort bar was the perfect way to shake off the work day, and for Chantal Turner it was the perfect place to practise her moves. She swung her hips to the pulsating beat of the music, her hands raking through her hair and pushing damp strands from her forehead. A drop of perspiration ran in a rivulet down her back but she wouldn't stop. At midnight, the night was still in its infancy, and she would dance until her feet gave out.

She was enjoying a brief interlude away from her life plan in order to soak up the rays while earning a little money in the glorious Whitsundays. But the second she was done she'd be back on the mainland, working her butt off to secure a place at a contemporary dance company. She smiled to herself. The life in front of her was bright and brimming with opportunity.

Tonight the majority of her crew hadn't come out. Since Chantal's boyfriend wasn't much of a dancer he stood at the bar, sipping a drink and chatting to another resort employee. No matter—the music's beat flowing through her body was the only companion she needed. Her black dress clung to damp skin. The holiday crowd had peaked for the season, which meant the dance floor was even more densely packed than usual.

'Pretty girls shouldn't have to dance on their own.'

A low, masculine voice rumbled close to her ear and the scent of ocean spray and coconut surfboard wax hit her nostrils, sending a shot of heat down to her belly.

She would know that smell anywhere. A hand rested lightly on her hip, but she didn't cease the gentle rolling of her pelvis until the beat slowed down.

'Don't waste your pick-up lines on me, Brodie.' She turned and stepped out of his grip. 'There are plenty of other ladies in holiday mode who would appreciate your cheesy come-ons.'

'Cheesy?' He pressed a hand against his well-muscled chest. 'You're a harsh woman, Chantal.'

The tanned expanse of his shoulders stretched out from under a loose-fitting black tank top, a tattoo peeking out at the neckline. Another tattoo of an anchor stretched down his inner forearm. He stared at her, shaggy sun-bleached hair falling around his lady-killer face and light green eyes.

He's off-limits, Chantal. Super off-limits. Don't touch him...don't even think *about it.*

Brodie Mitchell stepped forward to avoid the flailing arms of another dancer, who'd apparently indulged in a few too many of the resort's signature cocktails. He bumped his hip against hers, and their arms brushed as Chantal continued to dance. She wasn't going to let Brodie and his amazing body prevent her from having a good time.

The song changed and she thrust her hands into the air, swinging her hips again, bumping Brodie gently. His fingertips gripped her hips like a magnet had forced them together. Every touch caused awareness to surge through her veins.

'You can't dance like that and expect me not to join in.'

His breath was hot against her ear. Her whole body tingled as the effects of the cocktails she'd downed before hitting the dance floor descended. The alcohol warmed her, giving her limbs a languid fluidity. Head spinning, she tried to step out of his grip, but stumbled when another dancer knocked into her. She landed hard up against Brodie, her hands flat against his rock-hard chest. He smelled good. So. *Damn*. Good.

Against her better judgment she ran her palms up and down his chest, swinging her hips and rolling her head back. The music flowed through her, its heavy bass thundering in her chest. She probably shouldn't have had so many Blue Hawaiians—all that rum and blue curaçao had made her head fuzzy.

'I can dance however I like,' she said, tilting her chin up at him defiantly. 'Mr Cheese.'

'You're going to pay for that.' He grinned, snaking his arm around her waist and drawing her even closer. 'There's a difference between charming and cheesy, you know.'

'You think you're *charming*?' she teased, ignoring the building tension that caused her centre to throb mercilessly. It was the alcohol—it always made her horny. It was absolutely *nothing* to do with Brodie.

'I do happen to think I'm charming.'

His lips brushed against her ear, and each bump of his thighs sent shivers down her spine.

'I've had it confirmed on a number of occasions too.'

'How *many* women have confirmed it?' She bit back a grin, curious as to the number of notches on his bedpost. Brodie had a bit of a reputation and, as much as she hated to admit it, Chantal could see why.

It wasn't just that he had a gorgeous face and a body that looked as if it belonged in a men's underwear commercial. Hot guys were a dime a dozen at the resort. Brodie had something extra: a cheeky sense of humour coupled with the innate ability to make people feel comfortable around him. He had people eating out of the palm of his hand.

'I don't kiss and tell.'

'Come on—I'll even let you round up to the nearest hundred.' She pulled back to look him in the eye while she traced a cross over her heart with one finger.

He grabbed her wrist and pulled her hand behind his back, forcing her face close to his. 'I'm not as bad as you think, Little Miss Perfect.'

'I doubt that very much.'

The music switched to a slow, dirty grind and Brodie nudged his thigh between hers. A gasp escaped her lips as her body fused to his. She should stop now. This was *so wrong.* But it felt better than anything else could have right at that moment. Better than chocolate martinis and Sunday sleep-ins…even better than dancing on a stage. A hum of pleasure reverberated in her throat.

'I bet you're even worse.'

'Ha!' His hand came up to cup the side of her jaw. 'You want to know for sure, don't you?'

Her body cried out in agreement, her breath hitching as his face hovered close to hers. The sweet smell of rum on his lips mingled with earthy maleness, hitting her with a force powerful enough to make her knees buckle.

Realisation slammed into her, her jaw dropping as she jerked backwards. His eyes reflected the same shock. Reality dawned on them both. This was more than a little harmless teasing—in fact it didn't feel harmless at all.

How could she possibly have fallen for Brodie? He was a slacker—an idle charmer who talked his way through life instead of working hard to get what he wanted. He was her opposite—a guy so totally wrong for her it was almost comical. Yet the feel of his hands on her face, the bump of his pelvis against hers, and the whisper of his breath at her cheek was the most intoxicating thing she'd ever experienced.

Oh, no! This is not happening... This is not *happening.*

'You feel it, don't you?' Worry streaked across his face

and his hands released her as quickly as if he'd touched a boiling pot. 'Don't lie to me, Chantal.'

'I—'

Her response was cut short when something flashed at the corner of her eye. *Scott.*

'What the *hell* is going on?' he roared. His cheeks were flushed scarlet, his mouth set into a grim line.

'It's nothing, man.' Brodie held up his hands in surrender and stepped back.

He was bigger than Scott, but he wasn't a fighter. The guilt in his eyes mirrored that in Chantal's heart. How could she have done this? How could she have fallen for her boyfriend's best friend?

'Didn't look like nothing to me. You had your hands all over her!'

'It's nothing, Scott,' Chantal said, grabbing his arm. But he shook her off. 'We were just dancing.'

'Ha!' The laugh was a sharp stab of a sound—a laugh without a hint of humour. 'Tell me you don't feel anything for Brodie. Because it sure as hell didn't look like a platonic dance between friends.'

She tried to find the words to explain how she felt, but she couldn't. She closed her eyes and pressed her palm to her forehead. She opened them in time to see Scott's fist flying at Brodie's face.

'No!'

CHAPTER ONE

REJECTION WAS HARD ENOUGH for the average person, and for a dancer it was constant. The half-hearted 'Thanks, but no thanks' after an unsuccessful audition? Yep, she'd had those. Bad write-up from the arts section of a local paper? Inevitable. An unenthusiastic audience? Unpleasant, but there'd be at least one in every dancer's career.

Chantal Turner had been told it got easier, but it didn't feel easy now to keep her chin in the air and her lips from trembling. Standing in the middle of the stage, with spotlights glaring down at her, she shifted from one bare foot to the other. The faded velvet of the theatre seats looked like a sea of red in front of her, while the stage lights caused spots to dance in her vision.

The stage was her favourite place in the whole world, but today it felt like a visual representation of her failure.

'I'm afraid your style is not quite what we're looking for,' the director said, toying with his phone. 'It's very...'

He looked at his partner and they both shook their heads.

'Traditional,' he offered with a gentle smile. 'We're looking for dancers with a more modern, gritty style for this show.'

Chantal contemplated arguing—telling him that she could learn, she could adapt her style. But the thought of them saying no all over again was too much to deal with.

'Thanks, anyway.'

At least she'd been allocated the last solo spot for the day, so no one was left to witness her rejection. She stopped for a moment to scuff her feet into a pair of sneakers and throw a hoodie over her tank top and shorts.

The last place had told her she was too abstract. Now she was too traditional. She bit down on her lower lip to keep the protest from spilling out. Some feedback was better than none, no matter how infuriatingly contradictory it was. Besides, it wasn't professional to argue with directors—and she was, if nothing else, a professional. A professional who couldn't seem to book any decent jobs of late...

This was the fourth audition she'd flunked in a month. Not even a glimmer of interest. They'd watched her with poker faces, their feedback delivered with surgical efficiency. The reasons had varied, but the results were the same. She knew her dancing was better than that.

At least it had used to be...

Her sneakers crunched on the gravel of the theatre car park as she walked to her beat-up old car. She was lucky the damn thing still ran; it had rust spots, and the red paint had flaked all over the place. It was so old it had a cassette player, and the gearbox *always* stuck in second gear. But it was probably the most reliable thing in her life, since all the time she'd invested in her dance study didn't seem to be paying off. Not to mention her bank accounts were looking frighteningly lean.

No doubt her ex-husband, Derek, would be pleased to know that.

Ugh—she was *not* going to think about that stuffy control freak, or the shambles that had been her marriage.

Sliding into the driver's seat, she checked her phone. A text from her mother wished her luck for her audition. She cringed; this was just another opportunity to prove she'd wasted all the sacrifices her mother had made for her dancing.

Staring at herself in the rearview mirror, Chantal pursed her lips. She would *not* let this beat her. It was a setback, but only a minor one. She'd been told she was a gifted dancer on many occasions. Hell, she'd even been filmed for a documentary on contemporary dance a few years back. She *would* get into one of these companies, even if it took every last ounce of her resolve.

Despite the positive affirmation, doubt crept through her, winding its way around her heart and lungs and stomach. Why was everything going so wrong now?

Panic rose in her chest, the bubble of anxiety swelling and making it hard to breathe. She closed her eyes and forced a long breath, calming herself. Panicking would not help. Thankfully, she'd finally managed to book a short-term dancing job in a small establishment just outside of Sydney. It wasn't prestigious. But it didn't have to be forever.

A small job would give her enough money to get herself through the next few weeks—*and* there was accommodation on site. She *would* fix this situation. No matter what.

She clenched and unclenched her fists—a technique she'd learned once to help relax her muscles whenever panic swelled. It had become a technique she relied on more and more. Thankfully the panic attacks were less like tidal waves these days, and more like the slosh of a pool after someone had dive-bombed. It wasn't ideal, but she could manage it.

Baby steps... Every little bit of progress counts.

Shoving the dark thoughts aside, she pulled out of the car park and put her phone into the holder stuck to the window. As if on cue the phone buzzed to life with the smiling face of her old friend Willa. Chantal paused before answering. She wasn't in the mood to talk, but she had a two-hour drive to get to her gig and music would only keep her amused for so long.

Besides, since her divorce Chantal had realised that real friends were few and far between, so she'd been making more of an effort to keep in touch with Willa. Ignoring her call now would go completely against that.

She tapped the screen of her phone and summoned her most cheerful voice. 'Hey, Willa.'

'How's our favourite dancer?'

Willa's bubbly greeting made a wave of nostalgia wash over her.

'Taking the arts world by storm, I hope?'

Chantal forced a laugh. 'Yeah, something like that. It's a slow process, but I'm working on it.'

'You'll get there. I know it. That time I saw you dance at the Sydney Opera House was incredible. We're all so proud of you for following your dream.'

Chantal's stomach rocked. She knew not everyone Willa referred to would be proud of her—especially since it was her dancing that had caused their group to fall apart eight years ago.

Besides, they only saw what she wanted them to see. If you took her social media pages and her website at face value then she was living the creative dream. What they *didn't* know was that Chantal cut out all the dark, unseemly bits she wasn't proud of: her nasty divorce, her empty bank account, the reasons why she'd booked into some small-time gig on the coast when she should be concentrating on getting back into a proper dance company...

'Thanks, Willa. How's that brother of yours? Is he still overseas?' She hoped the change of topic wasn't too noticeable.

'Luke texted me today. He's working on some big deal, but it looks like he might be coming home soon.' Willa

sighed. 'We might be able to get the whole gang back together after all.'

The 'whole gang' was the tight-knit crew that had
formed when they'd all worked together at the magical
Weeping Reef resort in the Whitsundays. Had it really
been eight years ago? She still remembered it as vividly
as if it were yesterday. The ocean had been so blue it
had seemed otherworldly, the sand had been almost pure
white, and she'd loved every second of it... Right until
she'd screwed it all up.

'Maybe,' Chantal said.

'I think we might even be getting some of the group
together tonight.' There was a meaningful pause on the
other end of the line. 'If you're free, we'd love to see you.'

'Sorry, Willa, I'm actually working tonight.'

Chantal checked the road signs and took the on-ramp
leading out of the city. Sydney sparkled in her rearview
mirror as she sped away.

'Oh? Anywhere close by?'

'I'm afraid not. I'm off to Newcastle for this one.'

'Oh, right. Any place I would know?'

'Not likely, it's called Nine East. It's a small theatre—
very intimate.'

She forced herself to sound excited when really she
wanted to find a secluded island and hide until her dancing ability came back. God only knew why she'd given
Willa the place's name. She prayed her friend wouldn't
look it up online.

'Look, Willa, I'll have to cut you short. I'm on the road
and I need my full concentration to deal with these crazy
Sydney drivers.'

Willa chuckled. 'I forget sometimes that you didn't grow
up in the city. Hopefully we'll catch up soon?'

The hope in her voice caused a twinge of guilt in Chantal's stomach. She didn't want to see the group. Rather, she

didn't want them to see how her life was not what she'd made it out to be.

'Yeah, hopefully.'

There was nothing like being surrounded by friends, with the sea air running over your skin and a cold drink in your hand. Add to that the city lights bouncing off the water's surface and a view of the Sydney Harbour Bridge against an inky night and you had a damn near perfect evening.

Brodie Mitchell leant back against the railing of his yacht and surveyed the group in front of him. Champagne flowed, music wafted up into the air and the group was laughing and reminiscing animatedly about their time working at the Weeping Reef resort. A long time had passed, but it made Brodie smile to think the group was no less lively now than when they'd all been fresh-faced kids, drunk on the freedom and beauty of resort life.

'Hey, man.' Scott Knight dropped down beside him, beer in hand. 'Aren't you drinking tonight?'

'I'm trying to be good for once.' Brodie grinned and held up his bottle of water in salute. 'I'm training for a half marathon.'

'Really?' Scott raised a brow.

Brodie shoved his friend and laughed. 'Yes, really.'

As much as he wanted to be annoyed that his friends would assume him incapable of running a half marathon, he kind of saw their point. Running competitively required a certain kind of routine and dedication that wasn't Brodie's style. He was a laid-back kind of guy: he thrived on surf, sand, and girls in bikinis. Abstaining from alcohol and waking up at the crack of dawn for training... Not so much.

'You have to admit it doesn't seem to fit in with the yachting lifestyle.' Scott gestured to the scenery around them.

The boat was a sight to behold—luxury in every sense of the word from its classy interior design to the quality craftsmanship out on the deck.

Growing up in a big family had meant the Mitchells' weekly grocery shop had needed to stretch across many mouths, and schoolbooks had always been passed down the line. They hadn't been poor, but he'd never been exposed to fineries such as yachts. Now he owned a yacht charter business and had several boats to his name.

'I didn't exactly come up with the idea myself,' Brodie admitted, taking a swig of his water. 'There's a guy at the marina back home and he's always on my back about taking up running. He bet me a hundred bucks I couldn't train for a race.'

'So you started with a half marathon?' Scott shook his head, laughing. 'Why not attempt a lazy ten k to begin with?'

Brodie shrugged and grinned at his friend. 'If I'm going to waste a perfectly good sleep-in, it might as well be for something big.'

'Says the guy who once chose sleep over judging a bikini contest.'

'And lived to regret it.'

Scott interlocked his fingers behind his head and leant back against the boat's railings. 'Those were the days.'

'You look like you're living the dream now.' Brodie fought to keep a note of envy out of his voice.

A slow grin spread over Scott's face as his fiancée, Kate, waved from the makeshift dance floor where she was shaking her hips with Willa, Amy, and Amy's friend Jessica. The girls were laughing and dancing, champagne in hand. *Just like old times.*

'I am.' Scott nodded solemnly.

Just as Brodie was about to change the topic of conversation Willa broke away from the group and joined the boys. She dropped down next to Brodie and slung her arm around his shoulders, giving him a sisterly squeeze as she pushed her dark hair out of her face.

'I'm so glad you're back down in Sydney,' Willa said.

'And where's your man tonight?' Brodie asked.

'Working.' She pouted. 'But he promised he'd be here next time. In fact I think he was a little pissed to miss out on the yacht experience.'

Brodie chuckled. 'It's an experience, indeed. My clients pay an arm and a leg to be sailed around in this boat, and she's an absolute beauty. Worth every cent.'

The *Princess 56* certainly fitted her name, and although she was the oldest of the yachts his company owned she'd aged as gracefully as a silver-screen starlet. He patted the railing affectionately.

'Guess who I spoke to this afternoon,' Willa said, cutting into his thoughts with a faux innocent smile.

Brodie quirked a brow. 'Who?'

'Chantal.'

Hearing her name was enough to set Brodie's blood pumping harder. Chantal Turner was the only girl ever to have held his attention for longer than five minutes. She'd been the life of the party during their time at the Whitsundays, and she'd had a magnetic force that had drawn people to her like flies to honey. And, boy, had he been sucked in! The only problem was, she'd been Scott's girl back then. He'd gotten too close to her, played with fire, and earned a black eye for it. Worse still, he'd lost his friend for the better part of eight years over the incident.

Brodie's eyes flicked to Scott, but there was no tension in his face. He was too busy perving on Kate to be worrying about what Willa said.

'She's got a show on tonight,' Willa continued. 'Just up the coast.'

Brodie swallowed. The last thing he needed was to see Chantal Turner dance. The way she moved was enough to bring grown men to their knees, and he had a particular weakness for girls who knew how to move.

'We could head there—since we have the boat.' Willa grinned and nudged him with her elbow.

'How do you know where she's performing?' he asked, taking another swig of his water to alleviate the dryness in his mouth.

'She told me.'

'I don't know if we should…' Brodie forced a slow breath, trying to shut down images of his almost-kiss with Chantal.

It was the last time he'd seen her—though there had been a few nights when he'd been home alone and he'd looked her performances up online. He wasn't sure what seeing her in person would do to his resolve to leave the past in the past.

The friend zone was something to be respected, and girls who landed themselves in that zone never came out. But with Chantal he seemed to lose control over his ability to think straight.

'We should go,' Scott said, patting Brodie on the shoulder as if to reassure him once again that there were no hard feelings about that night. 'I'm sure she'd appreciate the crowd support.'

By this time Amy, Jessica, and Kate had wandered over for a refill. Scott, ever the gentleman, grabbed the bottle of vintage brut and topped everyone up.

'We were just talking about taking a little trip up the coast,' Scott said. 'Chantal has a show on.'

'Oh, we should definitely go!' Amy said, and the other girls nodded their agreement.

All eyes lay expectantly on him. He could manage a simple reunion. Couldn't he…?

'Why the hell not?' he said, pushing up from his chair.

* * *

When Chantal pulled into the car park of the location specified on her email confirmation her heart sank. The job had been booked last-minute—*they'd* contacted *her*, with praise for the performance snippets she had on her website and an offer of work for a few nights a week over the next month.

A cursory look at their website hadn't given her much: it seemed they did a mix of dance and music, including an open mike night once per week. Not exactly ideal, but she was desperate. So she'd accepted the offer and put her focus back on her auditions, thinking nothing of it.

Except it didn't look like the quietly elegant bar on their website. The sign was neon red, for starters, and there were several rough-looking men hanging out at the front, smoking. Chantal bit down on her lip. Everything in her gut told her to turn around and head home—but how could she do that when it was the only gig she'd been able to book in weeks? Make that months.

Sighing, she straightened her shoulders. *Don't be such a snob. You know the arts industry includes all types. They're probably not criminals at all.*

But the feeling of dismay grew stronger with each step she took towards the entrance. She hitched her bag higher on her shoulder and fought back the wave of negativity. She *had* to take this job. Her ex had finally sold the apartment—meaning she had to find a new place to live—and this job included on-site accommodation. It would leave her days free to pursue more auditions, *and* it was money that she desperately needed right now.

One of the men hanging out at the front of the bar leered at her as she hurried past, and Chantal wished she'd thrown on a pair of tracksuit pants over her dancing shorts. The sun was setting in the distance but the air was still heavy and warm. She ignored the wolf-whistling and continued on, head held high, into the bar.

The stench of cheap alcohol hit her first, forcing her stomach to dip and dive. A stage sat in the middle of a room and three men in all-black outfits fiddled with the sound equipment. Chantal looked around, surveying the sorry sight that was to be her home for the next month. The soles of her sneakers sucked with each step along the tattered, faded carpet—as if years of grime had left behind an adhesive layer. Though smoking had long been banned inside bars, a faint whiff of stale cigarette smoke still hung in the air. A small boot-sized hole had broken the plaster of one wall and a cracked light flickered overhead.

Delightful.

She approached the bar, mustering a smile as she tried to catch the attention of the older man drying wineglasses and hanging them in a rack above his head. 'Excuse me, I'm here—'

'Dancers go upstairs,' he said, without even looking up from his work.

'Thanks,' she muttered, turning on her heel and making her way towards the stairs at the end of the bar.

Upstairs can't possibly be any worse than downstairs. Perhaps the downstairs was for bands only? Maybe the dancers' section would be a little more…hygienic?

Chantal trod up the last few steps, trying her utmost to be positive. But upstairs *wasn't* any better.

'Oh, crap.'

The stage in the middle of the room sported a large silver pole. The stage itself was round with seats encircling it; a faded red curtain hung at the back, parted only where the dancers would enter and exit from. It was a bloody strip club!

'Chantal?'

A voice caught her attention. She contemplated lying

for a second, but the recognition on the guy's face told her he knew *exactly* who she was.

'Hi.'

'I've got your room key, but I don't have time to show you where it is now.' He looked her up and down, the heavy lines at the corners of his eyes crinkling slightly. 'Just head out back and get ready with the other girls.'

'Uh…I think there's been some kind of mistake. I'm not a stripper.'

'Sure you're not, darlin',' he said with a raspy chuckle. 'I get it—you're an *artist*. Most of the girls say they're paying their way through university, but whatever floats your boat.'

'I'm serious. I don't take my clothes off.' She shook her head, fighting the rising pressure in her chest.

'And we're not technically a strip club. Think of it more as…burlesque.' He thrust the room key into her hand. 'You'll fit right in.'

Chantal bit down on her lip. Perhaps it wouldn't be as bad as she thought.

But, no matter how hard she tried to convince herself, her gut pleaded with her to leave.

'I really don't think this is going to work,' she said, holding the key out to him.

'You *really* should have thought of that before sending back our contract with your signature on it.' His eyes hardened, thin lips pressing into a harsh line. 'But I can have our lawyer settle this, if you still think this isn't going to work.'

The thinly veiled threat made Chantal's heartbeat kick up a notch. There was no way she could afford a lawyer if they decided to take her to court. How could she have made such a colossal mistake?

Her head pounded, signalling a migraine that would no doubt materialise at some point. What kind of club had a lawyer on call, anyway? *The dangerous kind...the kind that has enough work for a lawyer.*

'Fine.' She dropped her hand by her side and forced away the desire to slap the club owner across his smarmy, wrinkled face.

She was a big girl—she could handle this. Besides, she'd had her fair share of promo girl gigs whilst trying out for dance schools the first time. She'd strutted around in tiny shorts to sell energy drinks and race-car merchandise on more than one occasion. This wouldn't be so different...would it?

Sighing, she made her way to the change room where the other dancers were getting ready. She still had that funny, niggling feeling that something wasn't quite right... and it wasn't *just* that she'd somehow landed herself in a strip club.

She concentrated for a moment, analysing the feeling. It had grown stronger since her audition—an incessant tugging of her senses that wouldn't abate. She unpacked her make-up and plucked a face wipe from her bag. Smoothing the cloth over her face, she thought back to the director. He'd looked so familiar, and he hadn't seemed to be able to look her in the eye.

A memory crashed into her with such force she stopped in her tracks, hand in midair. An old photo, taken a few years before she'd first started dating Derek—*that* was where she'd seen his face before. He was a friend of her ex-husband's, and that *couldn't* be a coincidence.

Rage surged through her. Her hands trembling, she sorted through her make-up for foundation. That smarmy, good-for-nothing ex-husband of hers had put her name forward for this skanky bar. He probably found the idea hilarious.

If I ever come across that spiteful SOB again I'm going to kill him!

* * *

An hour and a half later Chantal prepared to go on stage. She looked at herself in the mirror, hoping to hell that it was the fluorescent lighting which made her look white as a ghost and just as sickly. But the alarming contrast against her dark eye make-up and glossed lips would look great under the stage lighting. She'd seem alluring, mysterious.

Not that any of the patrons of such a bar would be interested in 'mysterious'. No, she assumed it was a 'more is more' kind of place.

She sighed, smoothing her hair out of her face and adding a touch of hairspray to the front so it didn't fall into her eyes. The other dancers seemed friendly, and there *were* actually two burlesque performers—though they didn't look as if they danced on the mainstream circuit. When she'd asked if all the dancers stripped down she'd received a wink and an unexpected view of the older lady's 'pasties'.

Well, *she* wouldn't be taking off her clothes—though her outfit wasn't exactly covering much of her body anyway. She looked down at the top which wrapped around her bust and rib cage in thick black strips, and at the matching shorts that barely came down to her thighs. She might as well have been naked for how exposed she felt.

It wasn't normal for her to be so filled with nerves before going onstage. But butterflies warmed her stomach and her every breath was more ragged than the last. She pressed her fingertips to her temples and shut her eyes, concentrating on relaxing her breathing. After a few attempts her heart rate slowed, and the air was coming more easily into her lungs.

Her act would be different—and she wouldn't be dancing for the audience…she would be dancing for herself. Taking a deep breath, she hovered at the entrance to the stage, waiting for the dancer before her to finish.

It was now or never.

CHAPTER TWO

'ARE YOU SURE we're in the right place?' Brodie looked around the run-down bar and shook his head. 'She can't be dancing *here*.'

'I double-checked the address,' Willa said, her dark brows pinched into a frown. 'This is definitely it.'

'Looks like there's an upstairs section to this place.' Kate pointed to a set of stairs on the other side of the room.

A single guy sat in the middle of the stage, playing old country-and-western hits, his voice not quite up to par. The bottom half of the bar was crowded and Brodie stayed close to the girls, given a few of the patrons were looking at them a little too closely for his liking. The group wove through the crowd until they reached the staircase at the back of the room, filing one by one up to the next level.

The music changed from the twangy country-and-western songs to a more sensual bass-heavy grind. The crowd—all men—encircled the stage and were enthusiastically cheering on a blonde dancer performing on a pole. She wore little more than a glittering turquoise bikini and her feet were balanced precariously on the highest pair of heels Brodie had ever seen.

'We *must* be in the wrong place.' Brodie rubbed his fingers to his temple, forcing down the worry bubbling in his chest.

Willa shrugged, looking as confused as he felt.

Chantal was a magnificent dancer—he'd often sneaked away from his duties at the Weeping Reef resort when he'd known she'd be using her time off to practise. She had innate skill and passion when she danced, no matter if it was in a studio or on the resort's packed dance floor. He couldn't understand why on earth she would be wasting her talent performing at some dingy dive bar.

The blonde left the stage to a roar of approval from the crowd and the music faded from one song to the next. His eyes were riveted to the space between the red curtains at the back of the stage. Heart in his throat, he willed the next dancer to be anyone else in the world other than Chantal. But the second a figure emerged from the darkness he knew it was her. He felt her before his eyes confirmed it.

No one else had a pair of legs like hers—so long and lean and mouth-wateringly flexible. She took her time coming to the front of the stage, her hips swinging in time to the music. Each step forward revealed a little more as she approached the spotlight. Long dark hair tumbled in messy waves around her shoulders, swishing as she moved. The ends were lightened from too much sun and her limbs were bronzed, without a tan line in sight.

Her eyes seemed to focus on nothing, and the dark make-up made her look like every dirty, sexy, disturbing fantasy he'd ever had. A jolt of arousal shot through him, burning and making his skin prickle with awareness.

He was in a dream—that *had* to be it. It was the only plausible explanation for how he'd ended up in this hellish alternative universe where he was forced to watch his deepest fantasy come to life right in front of him. He'd never been able to keep his mind off Chantal at the resort, but now she was here, the ultimate temptation, and he had to watch a hundred other men ogle her as though she were a piece of meat offered up for their dining pleasure.

His fists balled by his sides as he fought the urge to

rush up onto the stage and carry her away. She wasn't his responsibility, and the more distance he kept the better. He'd learnt that lesson already.

A wolf-whistle erupted from the crowd, snatching Brodie's attention away from his inner turmoil. Chantal had one hand on the pole, and though she wasn't using it as a prop, the way her fingers slid up and down the silver length made the front of his pants tighten. He shut his eyes for a moment, willing the excitement to stop. He shouldn't be feeling as if he wanted to steal her away and devour her whole...but he did.

When he dared to open his eyes he found himself looking straight into the endless depths of Chantal's luminous olive-green gaze. Emotion flickered across her face and her mouth snapped shut as she continued to dance, her eyes locked straight onto him.

Was it his imagination or were her cheeks a little pinker than before? For a moment he let himself believe she danced only for him, each gentle curve of movement designed to bring him undone.

In that moment she was *his*.

Dancing barefoot, she moved about the stage as though she owned it. Her feet pointed and flexed, creating lines and artful movement. Her arms floated above her head, crossing at the wrists before opening out into a graceful arc. Brodie's body hummed as though she played him with each step, with each look, each flick of her hair.

Her eyes remained on him. She seduced him. Broke apart every brick of resolve that he'd put in place until the wall crumbled around him like a house crushed by a tidal wave.

She capsized him. Bewitched him.

Her eyes glimmered under the spotlight, energy building with the climax of her performance. His body tensed and excitement wound tight within him. A coil of wanting, ready to be released at any moment. It was so wrong. He'd thought he'd moved on. Forgotten her. What a joke. He'd never get Chantal out of his head. *Never.*

The spell was broken as soon as her song finished. Her eyes locked on him for one final moment before she retreated behind the red curtain. The catcalls and cheering only made Brodie's pulse increase and tension tighten in his limbs. She should *not* be dancing in a place like this. Wasn't she supposed to be married? Where the hell was her husband and why wasn't he protecting her?

'That wasn't quite what I expected,' Willa said, looking from Amy to Brodie and back again. 'I mean, she's a gorgeous dancer—but this place is…'

'Wrong.' Brodie gritted his teeth together.

'Don't be so judgmental, you two.' Amy folded her arms across her chest. 'I'm going to see if I can find out what time she finishes.'

She wandered off in the direction of the stage but Brodie hung back with the others. Scott and Kate were chatting and laughing amongst themselves; Willa and Jessica were discussing the outfit of the next performer. Brodie leant back against the wall and ran a hand through his hair. His heart thudded an erratic beat and he wasn't sure if it was from the desire to protect Chantal or from the fact that her skimpy black outfit had worked his libido into overdrive.

No, it had to be concern over her safety. He had four little sisters, and the need to protect was ingrained in him as deep as his need to breathe. Sure he was attracted to Chantal—what red-blooded man wouldn't be? But it was nothing more than that. It had *never* been more than that.

Somehow the lie was no more believable now than it had been eight years ago.

Chantal had thought it wasn't possible for the night to get any worse. Dancing in front of a room full of people who wouldn't know art if it hit them over the head was bad enough, and the catcalls and leering were the proverbial cherry. But then she'd spotted Brodie and a good chunk of the Weeping Reef gang. Her stomach had felt as if it had dropped straight through the stage floor.

She braced her hands at the edge of the make-up bench and looked at herself in the mirror. All she wanted was to wash off her make-up and lock herself away until humiliation lost its brutal edge…though it was possible that would take a while. The shock on his face had been enough to destroy whatever confidence she'd managed to build up. He'd looked at her with an unnerving combination of disbelief and hunger.

She was about to remove her false lashes when her name rang out amongst the backstage hustle and bustle. Amy bounded towards her, arms outstretched and shiny blond hair flying around her face.

'You were fantastic!' Amy threw her arms around Chantal and gave her a friendly squeeze.

'Thanks.' Chantal forced a smile, wishing for possibly the hundredth time since she'd met Amy that she could have even an ounce of her vivacious confidence. 'It's a small gig in between a few bigger things.'

She hoped the lie didn't sound as hollow out in the open as it did in her head, but she couldn't let go of the false image she'd constructed. If they knew how bad things were right now… She wouldn't be able to handle the pity. Pity was the thing she detested most in life—possibly due to the fact that it had been doled out in epic proportions throughout her childhood.

The teachers had pitied her and her borrowed schoolbooks, the other mums and their suit-and-tie husbands had pitied the way she'd had to wear the same clothes week after week, and as for the students…pity from her peers had always stung the most.

'No judgment here.' Amy held up her hands. 'You have to come for a drink with us, though. We've got everyone together...well, almost everyone.'

'Oh, I would love to, but...' Chantal's smile wavered. 'It's been a long day and I've got an audition tomorrow.'

She scrambled for an excuse—something that Amy wouldn't question. There was no way she could go out there and face them—no way she could keep her head held high after what they'd seen. Heat crawled up her neck, squeezing the air from her throat. *Not now, please don't fall apart now.*

'Is your audition in Newcastle?'

'No, Sydney. So I've got quite a long drive.'

Amy grinned and grabbed her hand, tugging her towards the door. 'I've got the perfect solution then. Brodie got us here on his yacht, but he's supposed to be docking at The Rocks. If your rehearsal is in the city it would be perfect. You won't have to drive there, and Brodie can sail you back here after your audition.'

'I really *am* tired.' She shook her head and pulled her hand from Amy's grasp.

'You just need a drink or five.' Amy winked. 'Come on—it'll be like old times.'

Chantal stole a glance at her reflection. She'd have to change. There was no way she'd go out there and stand in front of Brodie wearing mere scraps of Lycra. *It's not like he didn't notice you dancing half-naked on that stage.*

'Just one drink,' she said, sighing. 'I need to be on good form tomorrow.'

'Great.' Amy bounced on the spot. 'I'll let you get changed. Meet us out the front in a few minutes?'

'Sure.'

With Amy gone, Chantal could let the fake smile slide from her lips. Why the hell had she agreed to a drink with the old gang? She was supposed to be keeping her distance—at least until her life had started to match the image she'd presented online. No doubt they'd ask about her marriage: fail number one. They'd want to know about her career: fail number two. And she'd have to act as if it wasn't awkward at *all* being around Scott and Brodie: fail number three.

Willa had told her that they'd recently repaired the rift she'd caused, but that didn't make her any less squeamish about having the two of them in the same room as her.

She contemplated looking for a back exit to slip out of. Maybe if she disappeared they might get the hint that she wasn't feeling social right now.

You can't do that. These people are your friends...possibly your only friends.

Since her divorce her other acquaintances had been mysteriously absent. Perhaps being friends with Derek the talent agent was of more value to them than being friends with Chantal the out-of-work dancer.

She frowned at herself in the mirror, taking in the fake lashes and dark, sultry make-up. What a fraud. Sighing, she stripped out of her outfit and threw on her denim shorts, white tank top and sneakers from earlier. She didn't have time to remove all of her make-up—that tedious task would have to wait for later.

Swinging her overnight bag over one shoulder, she decided against dumping it in her room first. If she found the comfort of a private room it would be unlikely she'd come back out. *Suck it up, Chantal. You've made your bed, now lie in it!*

Outside the crowd heaved, and she had to dodge the patrons who thought their ticket to the show meant they had a right to paw at her. This was *not* the dream she'd had in mind when she'd first stepped into a dance studio at the age of seven.

Her skin crawled. She wanted out of this damn filthy

bar. Perhaps a potential lawsuit was worth the risk if it meant she never had to come back.

She was midthought when she spotted Brodie, standing alone by the stairs. Where had everyone else gone? Her blood pumped harder, fuelling her limbs with nervous energy.

As always, his presence unnerved her. His broad shoulders and muscular arms were barely contained in a fitted white T-shirt; his tanned skin beckoned to be touched. His shaggy blond hair sat slightly shorter than it had used to, though the ends were still sun-bleached and he wore it as though he'd spent the day windsurfing. Messy. Touchable.

But it was his eyes that always got her. Crystal green, like the colour of polished jade, they managed to seem scorching hot and ice-cold at the same time. When he looked at her it was easy to pretend the rest of the world didn't exist.

'The others have gone to the boat,' he said, motioning for her to join him. 'I didn't want you to walk on your own.'

She followed him, watching the way his butt moved beneath a pair of well-worn jeans. He'd filled out since she'd seen him last—traded his boy's body for one which was undeniably adult. She licked her lips, hating the attraction that flared in her and threatened to burn wild, like a fire out of control.

It was strange to be attracted to someone again. She hadn't felt that way in a long time...possibly not since Weeping Reef. Her marriage hadn't been about attraction— it had been about safety, security... Until that security had started to feel like walls crushing in on her.

They made their way out of the bar and into the cool night air. The breeze caught her sweat-dampened skin and caused goosebumps to ripple across her arms. She folded them tight, feeling vulnerable and exposed in the sudden quiet of the outdoors.

'You didn't have to wait,' she said, falling into step with him.

Their steps echoed in the quiet night air, their strides perfectly matched.

He turned to her and shook his head. 'Of course I did. I was worried you wouldn't make it out of the bar on your own, let alone down the street.'

The disapproving tone in his voice made her stomach twist. The last thing she needed was another over-protective man in her life.

'I can take care of myself.'

'Your bravado is admirable, but pointless. Even the smallest guy in there would have at least a head on you.'

His face softened into a smile—he never had been the kind of guy who could stay in a bad mood for long.

'Not to mention those skinny little chicken legs of yours.'

'I do *not* have chicken legs.' She gave him a shove and he barely broke stride, instead throwing his head back and laughing.

The bubble of anxiety in her chest dissolved. Brodie *always* had that effect on her. He was an irritating, lazy charmer, who talked his way through life, but he was *fun*. She often found herself smiling at him even when she wanted to be annoyed—much to her chagrin.

'No, you don't have chicken legs…not any more.' He grinned, his perfect teeth flashing in the night. 'You grew up.'

'So did you,' she said, but the words were lost as a motorcycle raced down the road.

They had eight years and a lot of issues between them. *Issues*, of course, was a code word for attraction. But *issues* sounded a little more benign and a little less like a prelude to something she would regret.

'I thought your husband would be here to watch out

for you.' He was back to being stern again. 'He should be keeping you safe.'

'I think he's keeping someone else safe these days.' She sighed. Why did all guys think it was their job to be the protector? She'd been happy to see the back of her ex-husband and his stifling, control-freak ways.

'So that means you're single?'

She nodded. 'Free as a bird and loving it.'

'All the more reason to have someone look out for you.'

Chantal bit her down on her lip and kept her mouth shut. No sense in firing him up by debating her ability to look out for herself. She wasn't stupid, her mother had made her take self-defence classes in high school, and she was quite sure she could hit a guy where it hurt most should the need arise.

They walked in silence for a moment, the thumping bass from the bar fading as they moved farther away. The yacht club glowed up ahead, with one large boat sticking out amongst a row of much smaller ones. She didn't have to ask. Of *course* he had the biggest boat there.

'Are you over-compensating?' Chantal asked, using sarcasm to hide her nervousness at being so close to him…at being alone with him.

'Huh?'

'The boat.' She pointed. 'It's rather…large.'

'You know what they say about men with large boats.' He grinned, his perfect teeth gleaming against the inky darkness.

She stifled a wicked smile. 'They have large steering wheels?'

He threw his head back and laughed again, slinging an arm around her shoulder.

The sudden closeness of him unsettled her, but his presence was wonderfully intoxicating when he wasn't waxing lyrical about her need for protection. He smelled

exactly the same as she remembered: ocean spray and coconut. That scent had haunted her for months after she'd
left Weeping Reef, and any time she smelled a hint of coconut it would thrust her right back onto that dance floor
with him.

Her hip bumped against his with each step. The hard
muscles of his arm pressed around her shoulder, making
her insides curl and jump.

'It's not my personal boat. My company owns it.'

'Your company?' Chantal looked up, surprised.

Brodie was not the kind of guy to start a company; he'd
never had an entrepreneurial bone in his body. In fact she
distinctly remembered the time Scott had threatened to
fire him for going over time on his windsurfing lessons
because his students had been having so much fun. He
had a generosity of spirit that didn't exactly match bottom-
line profits.

'After I left Weeping Reef I bummed around for a while
until I got work with a yacht charter company off the Sunshine Coast. It was a lot of fun. I got promoted, and eventually the owners offered me a stake in the company. I
bought the controlling share about a year ago, when they
were ready to retire.'

'And now you run a yacht tour company?'

He nodded as their conversation was interrupted by a
loud shriek as they strolled onto the marina. The girls had
clearly got into the champagne and were dancing on deck,
with an amused Scott watching from the sidelines. Willa
waved down to her and motioned for them to join the party.

Chantal's old doubts and fears crept back, their dark
claws hooking into the parts of her not yet healed. She
was not the person she claimed to be, and they would all
know that now. They would know what a *fraud* she was.

Her breath caught in her throat, the familiar shallow
breathing returning and forcing her heart rate up. She had

a sudden desire to flee, to return to the dingy bar where she probably looked as if she belonged.

She didn't fit in here. Not with these classy girls and their beautiful hair. Not with Brodie, who'd made a success of himself, and not with Scott, whom she'd betrayed.

She sucked in a deep breath, her feet rooted to the ground. Panic clutched at her chest, clawing up her neck and closing its cold hands around her windpipe. She couldn't do it.

'Chantal?' Brodie looked down at her, his hand at the small of her back, pushing gently.

She bit down on her lip, shame seeping through her every limb until they were so heavy she couldn't move. *Why did you come? You're only setting yourself up to be laughed at. You're a failure.*

'Come on.' Brodie grabbed her hand and tugged her forward. 'We don't want to get left behind.'

CHAPTER THREE

BRODIE WANTED TO look anywhere but at Chantal, yet her dancing held him captive. Her undulating figure, moving perfectly to the beat, looked even more amazing than it had at the bar. In casual clothes, with her face relaxed, her limbs loose, she looked completely at ease with the world.

Unable to deal with the lust flooding his veins, he'd caved in and had a beer. The alcohol had hit him a little harder since he'd been abstaining the past few weeks. But he needed to dull the edges of his feelings—dull the roaring awareness of her. He'd hoped the uncontrollable desire to possess her had disappeared when he'd left the reef. However, it had only been dormant, waiting quietly in the background, until she'd brought it to full-colour, surround-sound, 3-D life.

When they'd first stepped onto the yacht Chantal had hesitated, almost as if she wasn't sure she should be there. But Scott had given her a friendly pat on the shoulder and a playful shove towards the girls. They'd brought her into the fold and she'd relaxed, dancing and giggling as though she'd been there all night. Every so often Brodie caught her eye: a quick glance here or there that neither of them acknowledged.

'You should get out there and dance with her.' Scott dropped down next to him, another beer in his hand.

Brodie's eyes shifted to Scott and he waited to see what

would come next. He'd harboured a lot of guilt over the
way things had ended between them at Weeping Reef—
not just because he'd hurt Scott, but because he'd hurt
Chantal as well.

'Come on, man. You know there's no hard feelings.'
Scott slapped him on the back. 'We talked about this already.'

'It's not your feelings I'm worried about.'

'Since when do you worry about anything?'

Brodie frowned. People often took his breezy attitude
and laissez-faire approach to mean he didn't care about
things. He knew when Scott was teasing him, but still...

'Some things are meant to be left in the past.' Some
people were meant to be left in the past...especially when
he couldn't possibly give her what she deserved. Not long-
term anyway.

'You sound like a girl.' Scott laughed. 'Don't be such
a wuss.'

He *was* being a wuss, hiding behind excuses. Besides,
it was only a dance. How much harm could it do?

*Keep telling yourself it's harmless—maybe one day
you'll believe it.*

Brodie pushed aside his gut feeling and joined the girls.
Loud music pumped from the yacht's premium speakers
and the girls cheered when he joined their little circle.
His eyes caught Chantal's—a flicker of inquisitive olive
as she looked him over and then turned her head so that
she faced Amy.

He took a long swig of his beer, draining the bottle
and setting it out of the way. Moving closer to Chantal,
he brushed his hand gently over her hip as he danced. She
turned, a shy smile curving on her lips. She wasn't performing now—this was her and only her. Green eyes seemed to
glow amidst the smudgy black make-up... Her tanned limbs
were moving subtly and effortlessly to the beat.

'Want a refill?' Brodie nodded to the empty champagne flute she'd yet to discard.

She hesitated, looking from the glass to him. Was it his imagination, or had Willa given her a little nudge with her elbow?

'Why not?' She smiled and followed him into the cabin. The music seemed to throb and pulsate around them, even at a distance from the speakers. But that was how music felt when she moved to it. It came to life.

'I'm sad to say this yacht is bigger than my apartment.' She held out her champagne flute. 'Well, my old apartment anyway.'

Brodie reached for a fresh bottle of Veuve Cliquot and wrapped his hand around the cork, easing it out with a satisfying pop. He topped up her glass, the fizzing liquid bubbling and racing towards the top a little too quickly.

She bent her head and caught the bubbles before they spilled. 'You're a terrible pourer.'

He watched, mesmerised, as the pink tip of her tongue darted out to swipe her lips. Her mouth glistened, tempting and ripe as summer fruit.

'I'm normally too busy driving the boat to be in charge of drinks. But I'll make an exception for you.'

'How kind.' She smirked and leant against the white leather sofa that curved around the wall. 'Are you always on the boats?'

'No, I have to run the business, which keeps me from being out on the water as much as I'd like. I have a town-house on the Sunshine Coast, but it's a bit of a tourist trap up there. Sometimes I stay with the family in Brisbane, and then other times I stay on the yacht.'

'What a life.' Her voice was soft, tinged with wonder. 'You float along and stop where you feel like it.'

'It has a little more structure than that...but essentially, yeah.'

'Now, *that* sounds a little more like the Brodie I know.'

Her words needled him. He *wasn't* the surfer bum loser she'd labelled him in Weeping Reef. Sure, he might have dropped out of his degree and taken his time to find his groove, but he was a business owner now...a successful one at that.

'How's the arts world treating you?' It could have sounded like a swipe, given what he'd seen tonight, but he was genuinely interested.

She managed a stiff smile. 'Like any creative industry, it can be a little up and down.'

A perfectly generic response. Perhaps her situation was worse than he'd thought. He stayed silent, waiting for her to continue. For a moment she only nodded, her head bobbing, as if that would be enough of an answer. But he wanted more.

'I'm waiting to hear back from a big company,' she continued, her voice tight.

He suspected it wasn't true, or that she'd coloured the truth.

'Tonight was one of those fill-the-gap things. I'm sure it wasn't what you were expecting to see.'

Her eyes dipped and her lashes, thick and sultry, fanned out, casting feathery shadows against her cheekbones. She gathered herself and looked up, determined once more.

'It *wasn't* what I expected,' Brodie said, watching her face for subtle movements. Any key to whether or not she would let him in. 'But that's not to say I didn't enjoy it.'

How could he possibly have felt any other way? Watching her work that stage as if she owned the place had unsettled him to his core. A thousand years wouldn't dull that picture from his memory. Even thinking about it now heated up his skin and sent a rush of blood south, hardening him instantaneously.

'I could have done without the men ogling you.'

Her lips curved ever so slightly. 'You say that like you have some kind of claim over me.'

It was a taunt, delivered in her soft way. She hit him hardest when she used that breathy little voice of hers. It sounded like sin and punishment and all kinds of heavenly temptation rolled into one.

Brodie stepped forward, indulging himself in the sight of her widening eyes and parted lips. She didn't step back. Instead she stilled, and the air between them was charged with untameable electricity—wild and crackling and furious as a stormy ocean. She tilted her head up, looking him directly in the eye.

Brodie leant forward. 'I did see you first.'

'It doesn't work like that.' Her voice was a mere whisper, and she said it as though convincing herself. 'It's not finders keepers.'

'What is it, then?'

'It's *nothing*.'

He grabbed her wrist, his fingers wrapping around the delicate joint so that his fingertips lay over the tender flesh on the inside of her arm. He could feel her pulse hammering like a pump working at full speed, the beats furious and insistent.

'It's not nothing.'

She tried to pull her wrist back. 'It's the champagne.'

'Liar.'

A wicked smile broke out across her face as she downed her entire drink. A stray droplet escaped the corner of her mouth and she caught it with her tongue. God, he wanted to kiss her.

'It's the *champagne*.'

'Well, if you keep drinking it like that...'

'I might get myself into trouble?' She pulled a serious face, her cheeks flushed with the alcohol.

She'd looked like this the night he'd danced with her at

Weeping Reef. Chantal had always been the serious type—studious and sensible until she'd had a drink or two. Then the hardness seemed to melt away, she loosened up, and the playful side came out. If she'd been tempting before, she was damn near impossible to resist now.

'You always seem to treat trouble like it's a bad idea.' He divested her of her champagne flute before tugging her to him.

'Isn't that the definition of trouble?' Her hands hovered at his chest, barely touching him.

He shouldn't be pulling her strings the way he usually did when he wanted a girl. He liked to wind them up first. Tease them...get them to laugh. Relax their boundaries. He was treating Chantal as if he wanted to sleep with her...and he did.

He was in for a world of pain, but he couldn't stop himself.

'Bad ideas are the most fun.'

She stepped backwards, cheeks flushed, lips pursed. 'Come on—we're missing all the action out there. I want to dance.'

Only someone like Brodie would think bad ideas were fun. She could list her bad ideas like a how-to guide for stuffing up your life—have the hots for your boyfriend's BFF, pick the wrong guy to marry, lose focus on your career.

No, bad ideas were most definitely *not* fun.

Brodie was smoking hot, and it was clear that their chemistry still sizzled like nothing else, but that didn't mean she could indulge herself. He was *still* a bad idea, and she'd established that bad ideas were a thing of the past... well, once she'd got out of her current contract anyway.

If only she could tell her heart to stop thudding as if a dubstep track ran through her body, then she would be on her way to being fine. The throbbing between her legs was another matter entirely.

She stepped onto the deck, wondering for a moment if she'd dreamed herself onto his boat. The ocean had been engulfed by the night, but the air still held a salty tang. The smell reminded her of home…and of Brodie.

Shaking her head, she approached the girls. Kate extended her hand to Chantal and drew her in. She had decided almost immediately that she liked the gorgeous, witty redhead, and it was clear neither she nor Scott held any ill feelings towards her. It was a relief, all things considered.

'And where were *you*?' Willa eyed her with a salacious grin, her cheeks pink from champagne and dancing. She brushed her heavy fringe out of her eyes and swayed to the music.

'Just getting a refill.' The champagne was still fresh on her tongue…her mind was blurred pleasantly around the edges.

'Riiiight.' Willa smirked.

Chantal could feel Brodie close behind her, his hands brushing her hips every so often. Everything about the moment replicated *that* dance eight years ago. The alcohol rushed to her head, weakening the bonds of her control. The heat from his body drew her in, forcing her to him as if by magnetic force.

'I always said pretty girls shouldn't have to dance on their own,' he murmured into her ear.

'And *I* always said I would never fall for your cheesy lines.' She turned her head slightly, meaning to give him the brush-off, but his arm snaked around her waist and closed the gap between them. Her butt pressed against his pelvis and she resisted the urge to rock against him. 'Besides, I'm not on my own.'

'I know. You're with me.'

He spun her around and drew her to him. In sneakers, she could almost reach his collarbone with her lips, and she had an urge to kiss the tattoo that peeked out of his top. She was always fascinated by ink. The idea of permanence appealed to her. But life had taught her that everything was fleeting: money, success, love…

'I'm not *with* you, Brodie. You should stop confusing fantasy with reality.'

'It's hard to do when you have all that black make-up on.'

Her cheeks flamed and he laughed, holding her tight. It was all she could do to remain upright. With each knock of his hips, his knees, his thighs, her resolve weakened. Maybe one kiss wouldn't hurt—just so she could see if it was as good as she'd always imagined. Just so she could see if he tasted as amazing as he smelled.

His hand skated around her hip, a finger slipping under the hem of her tank top to trace the line of skin above her shorts. She squeezed her legs together and willed the throbbing to stop. Clearly she had a little pent-up frustration to deal with, but that wasn't an excuse to let Brodie unravel her.

Chantal spun back around and stepped out of his grip. The others had started to drift away. Kate and Scott had retired into the cabin; Amy and Jessica were finishing off the last of the bubbles and sat with their legs dangling over the edge of the boat. Willa was sitting next to them, her phone tucked between her shoulder and her ear.

'What are you going to do now, Little Miss Perfect?' Brodie's lips brushed her ear. 'It's just us.'

His fingertip traced from the base of her ear down her neck, until he plucked at the strap of her tank top. She burned all over with hot, achy, unfulfilled need. The music had been turned down but the bass still rumbled inside her, urging her to swing her hips and brush against him.

'I'm dancing.'

'You're taunting me.'

The unabashed arousal in his voice tore at the last shreds of her sanity, and with each throaty word she came further undone.

It had been so long since she'd been with anyone—so long since she'd experienced any kind of pleasure like this. Just one kiss…just one taste.

She turned, gathering all her energy to say no, but when his hands cupped her face the protest died on her lips. He came down to her with agonising slowness, and rather than crushing his mouth against hers he teased her with a feather-light touch.

'All that teasing isn't nice, is it?'

'I never teased you.' She frowned, but her body cried out for more.

'Back then your every step teased me, Chantal. You were the epitome of wanting what I couldn't have.'

His tongue flicked out against hers, his teeth tugging ever so gently on her lower lip. So close, but not enough. Nowhere near enough.

'You should have got in first.'

His green eyes glinted, the black of his pupils expanding with each heavy breath. 'I thought it wasn't finders keepers?'

'Sometimes you have to take what you want,' she whispered.

So he did.

His lips came down on hers as he thrust his hands into the tangled length of her hair, pulling her into place. She offered no resistance, opening to him as one might offer a gift. His scent invaded her, making her head swim and her knees weaken.

One large hand crept around her waist and crushed her to him. The hard length of his arousal pressed against her. Unable to stop herself, she slipped her hands under his shirt, smoothing up the chiselled flesh beneath. The feel of each stone-like ridge shot fire through her as their tongues melded. His knee nudged her thighs apart and she gasped as though she were about to come on the spot.

What happened to banishing bad choices and focusing on your career? Abs do not give you a free pass.

She jerked back, and the cool night air rushed to fill the void between them. She shook her head, though in response to what she wasn't sure. Her head should have been in the game, focusing on getting her into a proper dance company. Instead she was gallivanting around on a yacht, kissing a man she should have stayed the hell away from the first time.

'I'm sorry. That shouldn't have…' She struggled to catch her breath, emotions tangling the words in her head.

He waved his hand, ever the cool customer. 'Alcohol and sea air—it's a dangerous combination.'

The stood barely a foot apart, unmoving. The muscles corded in his neck as he swallowed, his Adam's apple bobbing, pupils flaring. He might look calm on the outside, but his eyes gave a glimpse to the storm within.

Around them the night was inky and dark. The breeze rolled past them, caressing her skin as he had done moments ago.

'Very dangerous.'

Brodie woke with a start, the feel of Chantal's lips lingering in his consciousness. Had he dreamed it? He rubbed his hands over his face, pushing his hair out of his eyes. White cotton sheets were tangled around his limbs like a python, holding him hostage lest he get out of bed and do something stupid.

Groaning, he sat up and stretched. His mouth was dry and he desperately wanted a shower. The digital clock beside his bed told him it was barely seven-thirty—why was he up at this ungodly hour? He listened to see if a noise had woken him. Were his guests up already? But the only sound that greeted him was the gentle slosh of waves against the boat and the occasional cry of a seagull.

Brodie showered, relishing the cool water on his over-heated skin, and then made his way to the kitchen. He didn't drink much coffee, but there was something about being awake before eight in the morning that necessitated a little caffeine.

He fired up the luxurious silver espresso machine; it had been chosen specifically to balance the champagne tastes of the company's clientele with ease of use. Within seconds hot, dark liquid made its way into his cup and he added only the smallest splash of milk before wandering outside.

He stopped at the edge of the cabin, realising he wasn't the only early bird this morning.

Chantal stood in the middle of the deck, balancing on one leg with the other bent outwards, the sole of her foot pressed against her inner thigh, hands above her head. She stayed there for a moment before lowering her foot and bending forward until her hands were flattened to the ground, her butt high in the air. Brodie gulped, unable to tear his eyes away from the fluid movement that looked as though it should have been performed to music.

Flexibility didn't even begin to describe some of the shapes that Chantal could form with her body. Her legs were encased in the tiny black shorts, leaving miles of tanned skin to tempt him. Her hair was free flowing, the dark strands fading into a deep gold at their ends, bleached by hours in the sun.

As if she could sense him she looked up sharply and caught his eye. Unfolding herself, she gave her limbs a shake and made her way over to him.

'Enjoy the show?' A smile twitched on her lips.

'Always.'

She leant forward and breathed in the billowing tendrils of steam from his coffee. 'Got any more of that?'

He motioned for her to follow him and they walked in silence into the cabin. She climbed up onto the chrome and white leather stool at the bench near the kitchenette, her long legs dangling, swinging slightly as she propped her elbows up on the polished benchtop.

'What was that you were doing outside?'

'Yoga,' she said. 'It's part of my stretching routine—keeps me nice and limber.'

'I could see that.' And he had a feeling he would never *unsee* it.

'It's good for relaxation too—helps to quieten the mind.' A flicker of emotion passed over her face, but it was gone as instantly as it had appeared. 'Are we all set to sail back to Sydney soon?'

'We sure are. Scott and Kate have plans this afternoon. I promised I'd get them back before lunchtime.' Brodie filled another cup with coffee and handed it to Chantal. 'Are you performing again tonight?'

'No, I have an audition today.' Her face brightened, a hopeful gleam washing over her eyes.

'Oh, yeah. Amy said. In Sydney, right?'

She nodded. 'This is a big one.'

'I'm sure you'll ace it.'

'Let's hope so.'

The doubt in her voice twisted in his chest. Someone with talent like hers should never be in a position to doubt herself, but she seemed less confident than he remembered. Even last night there had been a hesitancy about her that had felt new—as if she'd learned to fear in the eight years since he'd seen her last.

'How come you're not with a dance company at the moment?'

Brodie studied her, and saw the exact moment her mask slid firmly into place as if she'd flicked a switch.

'I'm waiting for the right opportunity. No sense in taking the first thing that comes along if it doesn't tick all the boxes.'

He chuckled. 'You always were one of *those* girls.'

'What's that supposed to mean?'

'You're a check boxes girl. Everything has to fit your criteria or it doesn't even come up on your radar.'

She tipped her nose up at him. 'It's called having standards.'

'It's narrow-minded.' He sipped his coffee, watching as her cheeks coloured. Her lips pursed as she contemplated her response.

'And I suppose you think it's better to drift through life unanchored by responsibility or silly things such as priorities or commitments?'

'You always thought I was such a layabout, didn't you?'

If only she knew what had brought him to the resort in the first place. Most of the kids working there had been on their gap year, looking for a little fun before hunkering down to study at university. He'd been there because he'd devoted himself entirely to taking care of his sister Lydia after a car accident had stolen her ability to walk.

His mother had pushed him to go, and in truth he'd needed the break—needed some space for himself.

'It wasn't just my opinion, Brodie. That's the kind of guy you are—fun-loving and carefree...'

'You underestimate me.' He narrowed his eyes.

'I didn't mean it as an insult.' She sighed and squeezed his hand. 'We're different people, that's all.'

He swallowed. Whatever they had in common, beneath the surface she would never see him as anyone but Brodie the lazy, talk-his-way-into-anything kid at heart. Would she?

'What are you doing for the rest of the weekend?' he asked, an idea forming. 'Do you have to go back to the bar?'

'Not until Sunday. I think they save the Saturday spot for top-billing dancers.' She rolled her eyes, as if trying to hide her embarrassment that he'd brought up her crappy job. 'I was going to hang around in the accommodation there…work on a new routine. That kind of thing.'

'Stay on the yacht with me. The gang will be back tonight and we can hang out some more.' He smiled. 'This would be better than the bar's accommodation. And safer.'

'I don't know if that's a good idea…' She sucked on her lower lip, her eyes downcast. 'I need to focus on dancing right now.'

'Well, you hardly need practice in that department. I've seen you move.' He reached out and grabbed her hand, wanting to soothe the doubt from her mind. 'Stay tonight, and if you're sick of me by the morning then I'll take you back. No hard feelings.'

'No hard feelings?' She looked up at him through curling lashes.

'None whatsoever.'

'Okay.' She nodded. 'I'll stay.'

CHAPTER FOUR

ONCE THEY WERE back in Sydney, and the rest of group had gone their separate ways, Chantal couldn't help but notice how alone she and Brodie were. Nervous energy crackled through her body, lighting up all her senses as though she were experiencing adrenaline for the first time.

It wasn't good. She needed to be calm for her audition—she *couldn't* stuff it up. If she did then she was fast running out of dance companies and productions to approach. What if she couldn't find a real job? Would she be stuck working a pole like those other women at the bar? No, she wouldn't let that happen.

She needed to focus on herself—*just* herself—no messy emotional entanglements, no betrayal, no disappointment. Just her and the stage.

Closing her eyes, she drew a long breath and held it for a moment before letting the air whoosh out. *Breathe in, hold, breathe out. Repeat.*

Staying on the yacht with Brodie was a terrible idea—she needed *all* her focus right now. And Brodie was the kind of guy who could take a woman's sanity and blow it to smithereens with a single look. He'd done it at Weeping Reef, he'd done it last night, and he would do it again.

But that kiss…

Chantal's body tingled at the memory. Brodie's kiss had been exactly what she'd thought kissing would be like as a teenager, before the reality of one too many slobbery guys had shattered the fantasy. Brodie had the kind of kiss that could make a girl's bones melt.

That's because he's had a lot of practice.

'What's with the frown?'

Brodie's voice cut through Chantal's musings. He stood above her, holding out a hand to help her up from her Lotus Position.

A pair of faded jeans hugged his strong legs and a soft white T-shirt skimmed over the muscles in his shoulders and chest. A leather cuff encircled his right wrist—it looked as though he'd worn it for years. The leather was faded and smooth, and it accentuated the muscles in his arm. But Chantal's eyes were drawn to the anchor tattoo on the inside of his forearm, as always. She had to resist the urge to reach out and trace it with her fingertip.

'Where are we going?' he asked.

'Huh?'

'Your audition. Where is it?'

'Right over there,' Chantal said, pointing across the Sydney Harbour Bridge. 'It's about ten minutes on foot.'

'Great—let's go.' Brodie turned and made his way off the yacht.

'You don't need to come with me.'

She grabbed her bag and scrambled after him, her blood pressure shooting up. Having him watch her last night had been humiliating enough. The last thing she needed was for him to witness a more serious rejection today!

'Don't you want a little moral support?'

'No.' She hitched her dancing bag higher on her shoulder and looked Brodie squarely in the eye. 'I've been doing this on my own for quite a while. I like it that way.'

'What if I want to watch?'

He said it in such a way that Chantal almost lost her footing on the jetty.

'You only get to watch when I say so.'

Her blood pulsed hot and fast, flooding her centre with an uncomfortable and entirely distracting throbbing sensation. She didn't have time to be horny. She had an audition to nail and he was getting in her way.

'Brodie, I don't have time to argue.' She waved him off. 'Can't I just meet you afterwards?'

'If you insist.' He shrugged and fell into step with her.

The sun beat down on Chantal's bare shoulders, making her skin sizzle on the outside as much as Brodie was making her sizzle on the inside. Humid air made her skin glisten and frizzed her hair. She yanked the length behind her head and fastened it with a hair tie... Anything to keep her hands busy.

They walked past other yachts, most of them matching the size of Brodie's boat. It was definitely more upscale than the place where they'd been docked last night. A family to their right boarded a boat that looked twice as big as the house Chantal had grown up in. The mother and daughter had identical long blond ponytails and carried matching designer bags.

'Do your clientele look like that?' She nodded towards the family.

'Rich?' Brodie gave them a cursory glance and shrugged. 'Yeah, I guess. People who charter a private yacht tend to have money.'

'More money than sense,' she muttered under her breath.

'It's certainly not the kind of life I had growing up, that's for sure.'

Chantal's curiosity was piqued. Brodie hadn't shared too much about his family while they'd all lived on the Whitsundays. She'd seen a picture of him with a group of younger girls whom she'd presumed to be his family. It had been pinned up on the wall in the room he'd shared with Scott. But other than that she knew little about his family, or where he was from...

'I always got the impression you were well off.'

'Why did you think that?'

She shrugged. 'I don't know... You always seemed so relaxed—so...at peace with the world. It seemed like you'd had an easy life.'

Brodie's blond brows crinkled and they walked in silence for a few minutes. Had she hurt his feelings? She hadn't intended it, but he seemed to lack the tough outer shell of someone who'd struggled their whole lives failing to keep up with everybody else. Someone like her.

'We had our ups and downs,' he said, talking slowly, as though he chose each word with care. 'My family wasn't different to anyone else's.'

'You never talked about your family much while we were working together.'

'You and I never had a serious conversation about anything.' He grinned. 'Too busy playing cat and mouse.'

'We did *not* play cat and mouse.' She shook her head, but her cheeks filled with roaring heat.

'You don't think so? I used to do anything to rile you up, to get your attention. I'd drive you crazy by teasing you about being a stuck-up ballerina.'

'And I'd try to correct you by explaining the difference between ballet and contemporary dance. But I don't think that's a game of cat and mouse.'

'Why do you think I teased you?'

They hovered under the expressway, enjoying the cool reprieve of the shade while people milled around. Sunlight sparkled on the water and laughter floated up into the air as the crowd filtered past. Everywhere people soaked up the rays, ate ice cream and held hands. The Sydney Harbour Bridge stretched out above, the Opera House in the distance, with the sun coating everything in a golden gleam.

Chantal had to admit it. As much as she found the hustle and bustle of a big city overwhelming, Sydney *was* beautiful.

'I thought you were hot.' He slung an arm around her shoulder.

'You shouldn't have thought that.'

He leant down until his lips were close to her ear. 'I *still* think you're hot.'

Caring about his opinion was a mistake, but his words made something flutter low down in her belly. She'd never wanted to be attracted to Brodie, but he had this *thing* about him. It was indescribable, intangible, invisible… but it was there.

She said, 'I think you're full of crap.'

He threw his head back and laughed. 'Prickly as ever, Chantal. Good to see some things don't change.'

'I have to get to my audition.'

She shrugged off his arm and strode in the direction of the Harbour Dance Company's building at the other end of the wharf.

You cannot stuff this up. Focus, focus, focus.

As much as she hated to admit it to herself—and she would *never* admit it to another living soul—Brodie rattled her. He was the only person who could knock her off course with such effortless efficiency. She needed a little distance from him, and tonight she would ask him to take her back to the bar. The feelings he evoked were confusing, confrontational, and she didn't have time for them.

Not now, not ever.

Perhaps if Chantal wasn't so hot when she was mad he wouldn't be tempted to tease her all the time. He loved it when she got all pink cheeked and pursed lipped. Eight years hadn't dulled or lengthened her fuse—she still lit up like a firecracker when he baited her. Hot *damn* if he didn't love it.

Up ahead, he saw her stride quicken, her full ponytail flicking with each step like the tail of an agitated cat. In all his years, through all the women he'd taken to bed, he'd never found a girl who got his pulse racing the way she did.

But he had to get it out of his head—had to get *her* out of his head. Sex with friends was a no-go zone. Normally he had enough choice that steering clear of any women he wanted to keep in his life was a piece of cake. Normally he could resist temptation... But Chantal was testing his limits.

Falling into a jog, he caught up with her. She counted the pier numbers, her gaze scanning the buildings until a soft, 'Aha!' left her lips.

'I'll be in there, but you really don't need to wait,' she said. 'I'm quite equipped to manage this on my own.'

'I've got nowhere else to be. Besides, I might spy a few hot dancers while I wait around for you.'

'Don't forget to leave a sock on the door if you get lucky,' she quipped.

Her eyes flicked over his face, her lips set into a hard line. Was it his imagination or was there a note of jealousy in her voice? *Wishful thinking.*

'You're the only one coming home with me.'

She licked her lips, the sudden dart of her tongue catching him by surprise. He hardened, the ache for her strong and familiar as ever. How was it that she could reduce him to a hormone-riddled teenage boy with the simplest of actions?

He *had* to get it out of his system—otherwise she'd haunt him forever.

'I'm coming back to the yacht with you—not coming home with you. Those two things are quite different.'

'They don't have to be different.'

'Brodie…'

Her voice warned him, as it had done in the past. *Stay away, hands off, do not get any closer.*

'Fine.' He leant down and planted a kiss on her forehead, enjoying the way she sucked in a breath. 'Good luck. I know you'll kill it.'

'Don't jinx me.' She mustered a smile and then turned towards the building marked 'Harbour Dance Company'.

He hated to see her doubt herself. She had no cause to. If the people holding the audition couldn't see her talent then they were blind. Perhaps he should follow her, just in case they needed convincing…

No. She was not his responsibility. He would wait for her, but he wouldn't get involved. He wouldn't get invested.

Brodie settled in to the café on the ground floor of the building, ordered a drink and set up at a small table by the window. Views of the pier with a backdrop of the bridge filled it. Sydney always made him feel small, but in a good way. As if he was only a tiny fleck on the face of the earth and his actions didn't matter so much in the scheme of things. As if he could be anyone he wanted to be…could sail away and no one would notice.

He envied Chantal and the freedom she had. She was beholden to no one. He, on the other hand, was stuck in the constant clashing of his desire to be his own person and his obligation to his family. He would *always* look after his sisters, but sometimes he wanted a break without feeling as though he were abandoning them. Even holidaying in Sydney was tough. What if something happened with Lydia while he was away? What if she got stuck in the house on her own and couldn't call for help?

He shoved aside the worry and reached for a newspaper, making sure to offer a charming smile to the waitress as she set down his coffee. She was cute—early twenties, blonde. But he didn't feel the usual zing of excitement when she smiled back, lingering before heading to her station. Something was definitely amiss.

Several articles and a sports section later Brodie looked up. He'd downed his coffee and then switched to green tea—which tasted like crap—and a bottle of water. A beer would have hit the spot, but he'd skipped training that morning and tomorrow's session would be hell if he didn't get his act together. Ah, discipline…it was kind of overrated.

Chantal still hadn't returned. How long had it been? Time had ticked by reluctantly, but she must have been gone an hour…maybe two. Was that a good sign? He hoped so.

The phone vibrating on the café table pulled his attention away from thoughts of Chantal. A photo of his youngest sister, Ellen, flashed up on screen. She looked so much like him. Shaggy blond hair that couldn't be controlled, light green eyes, and skin that tanned at the mere mention of sun.

'Ellie-pie, what's happening?'

'Not much.' She sighed—the universal signal that there *was*, in fact, something happening. 'Boy stuff.'

'You know how I deal with that.' Brodie frowned.

Trouble related to boys was squarely *not* in the realm of brotherly duties. Unless, of course, the solution to said boy problem involved him putting the fear of God into whichever pimply-faced rat had upset his little sister.

'Yeah, I know. I wasn't calling about that.' Pause. 'When are you coming home?'

'I only left a couple of days ago.' Not that it stopped the guilt from churning.

'I know.' She sighed again. 'Hey, can I come and stay with you when you get back?'

He smiled. 'Are the twins driving you crazy again?'

'No. Lydia's being difficult today.'

The relationship between his oldest and youngest sister had always been tense. And Lydia's mood changes seemed to affect Ellen more than anyone; she was often the one at home, taking on the role of parent when Brodie and their mother were working and the twins were out living their lives.

It might have been easier with another parental figure around, but his dad was best described as an 'absentee parent'. Even before the divorce his father had shunned responsibility, favouring activities that allowed him to 'find his creativity' over supporting his kids or his wife.

'Lydia can't help it. Her situation is tough—you know that.'

'You *always* take her side,' Ellen whined.

'No, I don't.' He sighed, pressing his fingers to his temple.

'You do—just like everyone else!' The wobble in her voice signalled that tears were imminent.

'I'm not taking sides, Ellen, and I understand you cop the brunt of it.'

That seemed to appease her. 'I want to get out of the house for a bit. And I can't go to Jamie's… We broke up.'

Oh, boy. 'Do I need to pay him a visit?'

'No. It was mutual. We weren't ready to settle down with one another.'

Not surprising—she was only nineteen. Brodie rolled his eyes. 'I'll call you when I get home. Then you can come and crash for the weekend.'

Chantal had arrived at the table, and a soft smile tugged at her lips. Was that because she'd had good news, or because she'd caught him playing big brother? He finished up his call with Ellen and shoved the phone into his pocket.

'You're still here.'

Her voice broke through the ambient noise of the café.

'Of course I'm still here. I said I would be.'

She hovered by the edge of the table, hands twisting in front of her.

'You don't need an invitation,' he said, but he stood anyway and drew back the seat next to him so she could sit down. 'How did it go?'

'I don't know. It felt good.' She shook her head and sat, tucking her feet up underneath her. 'But that doesn't always mean anything. They said they'll get back to me.'

'I'm sure you were amazing.' He reached out and grabbed her hand, giving it a soft squeeze.

'*Amazing* doesn't always cut it.'

'It doesn't?'

'No. You can't just be a great dancer—you have to look right, have the right style...' Her cheeks were stained pink and she rubbed her hands over her face. 'These are the big guns too. They didn't even open up for auditions last year.'

Her breath came out irregular—too fast, too shallow. He could see her mind whirring behind those beautiful soulful eyes. He could see the doubt painted across her face. He could imagine the words she didn't say aloud. *I hope it was enough. I hope I was enough.*

Instead she said, 'Some days I wonder if it's worth it.'

'Of course it's worth it.'

How could she say something like that? People would kill for her talent.

'Easy for you to say—you're not the one up there, putting yourself out for every man and his dog to judge you.'

'People judge each other every day,' Brodie pointed out. 'You don't need a stage for that.'

She smiled, her shoulders relaxing as she loosened her hair. The dark strands fell around her shoulders, golden ends glinting in the sun streaming through the café's window. 'Is that a dig at me?'

'It might be.'

He flagged down a waitress and ordered Chantal a coffee. They watched each other for a moment like two dogs circling. Wary. Charged.

'Because I think you lead a charmed life?'

'Because you don't think I work for it.' He took a long swig from his water bottle. 'I do.'

'I know you work for it. But you have to admit you seem to land on your feet, no matter what.'

'And you don't?' He raked a hand through his hair.

'No, I don't.'

She let out a hollow laugh and the sound made him want to pull her tight against him.

'You have no idea what it's been like the last few years.'

'So tell me?'

Silence. Perhaps she didn't expect him to care. Chantal paused while the waitress set down her coffee. She cradled the cup in her small hands, blowing at the steam.

When she stayed quiet he changed tactic. 'How come you never called?'

'You never called either.'

She sipped her drink and set the cup down on the table. For a moment the view of the pier had her attention, and the tension melted from her face.

'I wasn't exactly keen to share that my career was going down the gurgler. Why else would I have called?'

'Because we're friends, Chantal, despite how it ended.'

'You're right.' She nodded. 'Friends.'

God, he wanted to kiss her. She was sex on legs. Perfection.

'Friends who have the hots for each other.'

'I don't have the hots for you,' she protested, but her cheeks flamed crimson and her gaze locked onto some invisible spot on the ground.

'How about you look me in the eye when you say that?'

'Okay—fine. You're kind of a hottie.' Red, redder, reddest. She still didn't look up. 'But you're not my type.'

'What's your type?'

'Tall, dark and handsome?' she quipped with a wave of her hand. '*No* guys are my type at the moment. I have this little thing called a career that needs saving.'

'It's not that you don't have time for guys—you just don't have time for relationships.' Brodie rolled the idea around in his head. 'Maybe what you need is a little no-strings tension-reliever.'

'Is *that* what the kids are calling it these days?' She raised a brow at him and traced the edge of her coffee cup with a fingertip.

'Doesn't matter what it's called so long as it feels good.'

'I'm not a hedonist like you, Brodie. There are more important things in life than pleasure. I need my focus at the moment.'

'Perhaps… But don't you think you could do with a little pleasure right now?'

He reached out and cupped the side of her face. Their knees touched under the table and he could feel the heat radiating from her.

Her dark lashes fluttered. He wasn't going to kiss her again—not yet. She'd run scared if he pushed too hard too soon… But he would draw her in. Relax her boundaries. Give her space to let her guard drop.

Then he would have her.

CHAPTER FIVE

LATER THAT EVENING Chantal and Brodie wandered around The Rocks. To anyone else they might have looked like two people who'd been together forever. Behind the bridge the sun had set, streaking the sky with rich shades of gold, pink and red. Sydney was ready for a night out, glittering and looking its absolute best in the balmy air.

Brodie looked as though he belonged with the glamorous city crowd—as he did with any scene he joined. He had the ability to melt into a group of people no matter who they were. Rich clients, hard-working staff, children—he charmed them all. She'd seen it first hand at Weeping Reef. No wonder he'd done so well with his business.

Women were his forte. He knew exactly what to say to charm them straight out of their panties. Sometimes he could do it without saying a thing. Now she couldn't help but notice the way other women stared at him as they strolled back to the yacht. And why wouldn't they?

His hips rolled in a sensuous, languid gait. He had that loose-limbed, laid-back sexiness that was impossible to fake. You either had it or you didn't. And, *boy*, did he have it!

What is it about focus that you don't understand? Hands off, lips off, eyes off...everything off. Ugh, stop thinking about him!

'You're quiet,' he said as they returned to the boat.

The rest of the Weeping Reef crew would be joining them in an hour or so, and Chantal planned to enjoy her night off. The audition played on her mind, but if she thought about it any more she'd surely go crazy. No, tonight would be an opportunity to let her hair down and relax before she had to go back to the bar.

'My mind isn't,' Chantal muttered.

'Anything in particular bothering you?'

'Just thinking about work stuff.'

It wasn't a total lie, and she wasn't going to encourage him by revealing her inner monologue about his hotness.

'You can't be all work and no play.' He walked to the fridge on deck and pulled out a bottle of champagne, popping the cork and pouring her a glass.

'I think you have enough play for both of us.'

'I'd be happy to share it with you.'

He handed her the flute, her fingers grazing his as she grasped the stem. Goosebumps skittered across her skin and she wondered if perhaps her slinky, skin-tight dress had been a dangerous choice. She'd bought the dress after her audition because it was the exact blue-green of the ocean in the Whitsundays—a fitting choice for catching up with the old gang.

But her arms and legs were exposed to the night air, along with a portion of her back beneath the thick bands of fabric criss-crossing their way down her spine.

It would be fine. The others would arrive soon, and she'd make sure that she and Brodie weren't left alone. Piece of cake.

Yeah, right.

'So what did you do after you left the reef?' she asked, sipping her drink.

'A bit of this and that. There's not much to tell.' He shrugged, dropping down into a seat and stretching his long, muscular legs out in front of him. 'Went to university, dropped out of university, got a job sailing yachts.'

'That's it? Come on—I'm sure a lot more happened in eight years.' She dropped down next to him, resisting the desire to ease against him as he automatically slung his arm along the back of her seat.

'There was a girl.'

'Just one?' she teased, hating herself for the clutch of jealousy deep in her chest.

His eyes darkened, the pale green glowing in the dimming light. 'One relationship. It didn't end well and I don't have any desire to revisit the experience.'

'Why did you break up?' Colour her curious, but she'd never known Brodie to have a relationship with *anyone*. Unless you called repeated booty calls a relationship.

'It was a combination of things.' He shook his head, tilting his gaze up to the darkening sky. 'I was away a lot with work. I had my family to look after. She needed a *lot* of attention. Nothing more than incompatibility, pure and simple.'

'You always struck me as the attentive type.'

'No one is *that* attentive. She wanted us to be joined at the hip.' His voice tightened. 'I don't do inseparability. I need my space—the open waters and all that.'

'How did you meet?'

'She was a friend.' His mouth twisted into a grimace. 'I met her at university but we didn't get together until after I dropped out.'

'I guess she's not a friend any more?'

'No.'

'Sounds like you made the right call.'

'The right call would have been not going there in the first place.' Brodie sighed. 'Some people aren't cut out for relationships.'

It sounded like a warning. Not that she needed it. She

had no intention of getting sucked into Brodie's sex vortex the way other girls did. She knew he was a love 'em and leave 'em kind of guy… It was why she'd stayed away from him in the first place.

But she didn't exactly want a relationship right now either. Didn't that make them perfectly compatible for one night?

Heart thudding against her rib cage, she took a long swig of her champagne. Brodie's arm moved from the seat to her shoulders and his intoxicating coconut-and-sea-air smell made her mouth water.

Would it be so bad to have a little 'no-strings tension-reliever', as he'd called it? Surely she could afford to be unfocused for one day…just a night, really. Not even a whole day.

She was only working at the crappy bar tomorrow, so it wasn't as if she needed to be on her A-game. Maybe it wouldn't hurt. But could she walk away after a single night? Weeping Reef had taught her that Brodie's powers of seduction were second to none. What if he wanted more and she couldn't say no? The last thing she needed was to get sucked into a situation where she had another man trying to overpower her, trying to control her decisions.

She couldn't let that happen.

'What about you? Was it all about the dancing after you left?'

'I stayed a while longer on the resort, actually.'

After watching the Weeping Reef friendships disintegrate she'd wanted to flee. But dance school wouldn't pay for itself and she'd refused to ask her mother for anything else. It had been her time to prove what she was made of. Prove how determined she was.

'But it wasn't the same.'

'We had a great year together, didn't we?'

'We did.'

'I couldn't keep my eyes off you.' His voice was low, rough.

Chantal turned and his arm tightened around her. Her fingers ached to touch him. The now inky sky glittered with city lights. Magical. Surreal. He leant forward, his eyes drinking in every detail.

'Perv,' she said.

Her shaky laugh failed to diffuse the tension.

'I was so jealous of Scott. He had you to himself night after night.'

She tried to shrug his arm away but he held tight. 'And *you* had every other girl on the resort.'

'None of them compared to you, Chantal.' He brushed his lips against her temple, the soft kiss sending electric sensations through her. 'They didn't even come close.'

'Why didn't you say anything?'

She asked it so quietly that she couldn't be sure he'd heard it. Not till his pupils flared and his breath came in short bursts did she dare think about that night. About that *dance*.

'It was wrong being so attracted to you when you were Scott's girl.' Brodie shook his head, blond hair falling about his face.

'Is that why you left?' She reached up and brushed the strands out of his eyes.

His hand caught her wrist, turning it so he could press his lips to the tender skin on the inside. 'Of course it's why I left.'

Breathing was a struggle. Thinking was…impossible. Kissing him was all she could focus on.

'You were *everything*. All I could think about…all I could dream about.' He drew her arm around his neck and leaned in, lips at her ear. 'All I could fantasise about.'

Each word nudged her body temperature higher. Her

hand curled in the length of his hair, gripping, tugging. Resisting.

'Brodie...'

'I've wanted you from the second I saw you at that resort. You were dancing. I'd never seen anyone move like that before.'

'We shouldn't do this...' *Should we?*

His eyes were engulfed by the onyx of his pupils. 'Stay with me tonight.'

'I am staying here.'

'Stay with *me*. In my bed.'

'Brodie...' His name was a warning on her lips, but temptation spiralled out of control. Where was her resolve? Her focus?

'Just for tonight. Then tomorrow we can pretend it never happened.'

He stood and turned, waving to the rest of the Weeping Reef gang as they approached the yacht.

Chantal hadn't heard them. But with Brodie about to kiss her, a bomb might have been dropped and she wouldn't have noticed a damn thing.

'You two looked pretty cosy before,' Scott said.

The boys had separated from the girls and they hung out on the deck, port side. After dancing their feet off—and putting on quite the show—the girls were taking a break in the cabin, a fresh bottle of champagne flowing and peals of laughter piercing the night air.

'No idea what you're talking about, mate.' Brodie put on his best poker face—which, if his track record was anything to go on, was terrible.

'You're so full of it.' Scott laughed.

'You're a bit of an open book, aren't you?' said Rob Hanson, Willa's partner, in his distinctive South African accent. He eyed Brodie with an amused smile that crinkled the corners of his eyes.

Just because Scott and Rob had sorted their love-lives out it didn't given them licence to have a dig at his. Not that he *wanted* a love-life—he was happy with a gratifying and varied sex-life, thank you very much.

'Are you going to get it over with?' Scott took a swig of his beer.

Brodie rolled his eyes and looked out to the water. 'Nothing's going on.'

'Maybe not yet.' Rob smirked. 'But you're better off getting it out of your system.'

Brodie's pocket vibrated and he pulled out his phone. *Saved by the bell!* A text from Jenny—aka twin number one. She'd had a fight with twin number two and wanted a place to crash.

No can do, Jen. I'm in Sydney. Stop giving your sister a hard time.

He toyed with the phone, knowing that there would be an immediate response from his serial-texting younger sister.

'Family?' Scott asked with a knowing look. 'They still driving you crazy?'

'Are they ever?' He shook his head. 'I hope for your sake you and Kate only have boys.'

Brodie's phone vibrated again.

You always take her side.

I do not.

'Is your sister a bit of a handful?' Rob asked.

'Sisters,' Brodie corrected. 'I've got four of them—all younger.'

'Jeez.' Rob let out a low whistle. 'Your parents must have been gluttons for punishment.'

'Not really,' Scott chipped in. 'Brodie always did most of the work with them.'

'Just doing my job.' Brodie waved off the comment. He'd done what any big brother would have. His father's absence had left a gaping hole in his sisters' lives. If he hadn't looked after them who would have?

'Family comes first, but you have to find some balance,' Rob said.

Brodie shrugged. 'The rest of my life is pretty carefree. I sail when I feel like it, work on my business, cruise around the country. Meet lots of interesting people.'

'Brodie has never had any trouble meeting *interesting people*.' Scott rolled his eyes and turned to Rob. 'He used to have the girls falling at his feet when we were all at the reef.'

'It's the tatts,' Brodie replied. 'Something about a little ink makes them go crazy.'

'What's that about tattoos?' Willa wandered over and immediately tucked herself against Rob.

Rob gave her a squeeze and grinned. 'Apparently girls go gaga for Brodie's ink. What do you think, Willa?'

'I don't think it's just the ink,' she said, smirking.

'Should I be getting jealous?' There wasn't a hint of jealousy in Rob's voice, but Willa shook her head anyway. She only had eyes for Rob, anyone could see that.

The rest of the girls had filtered out of the cabin and now joined the discussion. Rob took the opportunity to make Brodie squirm.

'What do you think, Chantal? Tatts or no tatts?' His eyes glittered and he fought back a smile when Brodie shot daggers at him.

'On the right guy it looks good,' she responded carefully, her eyes flicking from Brodie to Rob and back again, as though she were trying to work out who'd instigated the suggestive discussion. 'Though looks aren't everything.'

'Aren't they?' joked Kate, flipping her long red pony-tail over one shoulder as she laughed at Scott's serious face. 'Joking!'

This time the group wasn't crashing on the yacht. Scott and Kate were staying at a hotel for the night, Amy and Jessica were going to continue the festivities at a local bar, and Willa and Rob were retiring back to their newly rented penthouse.

But what about Chantal?

'Are you sure you don't want to join us, Brodie?' Amy asked with a coy smile.

'I would *love* to party it up with you lovely ladies, but I have training tomorrow.' Brodie pulled Amy in for a friendly hug. 'Literally at the crack of dawn—and you know how much I hate mornings.'

She grinned. 'How about you, Chantal?'

Brodie held his breath. This was it. If she stayed then he would do everything in his power to make her come— over and over and over.

She shifted on her strappy tan heels and raked a hand through her long, wavy hair.

'I've got work tomorrow.' She smiled sweetly. 'I think I'm going to need all my energy for it.'

Amy stifled a smile and nodded.

The crew filtered off the boat, leaving Brodie and Chantal completely alone. She hovered by his side, refusing to look up at him. Not that it mattered where she looked, so long as it was his name on her lips.

'I hope you weren't serious about needing energy tomorrow,' he said as they waved the group off. 'You're not getting *any* sleep tonight.'

CHAPTER SIX

WAS SHE MAKING a colossal mistake? Her body seemed to think not. In fact her body acted as though it had been served up a certifiable slice of heaven, complete with whipped cream, cherries *and* sprinkles.

'Sleep is for the weak.'

His hands found her waist and pulled her close. Air rushed from her lungs with the delicious contact. His pelvis was hard against her, the ridge of his burgeoning erection pressing into her belly through the thin material of her dress.

His full lips curved into an impossibly sexy smile. 'I'm glad we're on the same page.'

'We will be if we never speak of this again.'

'Romantic,' he quipped. 'I like it.'

She ran her palms up the front of his chest, feeling the smooth cotton of his shirt glide against her skin. Each muscle in his chest was crisply defined, all hardness and athletic perfection. Her fingers hovered at the top button, tracing the outline in slow, deliberate circles.

'I don't want anything beyond one night. Clear?'

'Crystal.'

Chantal swallowed, Brodie had agreed more readily than she'd expected. But that was the kind of guy he was, the kind of life he led—easygoing, breezy, sans strings. She shouldn't be disappointed.

'Any more rules I should be aware of?' he asked, trailing feather-light kisses from her temple to her jaw.

In heels, she didn't feel quite so small next to him—though he still had a head on her. Perhaps she'd leave the heels on.

A wicked smile curved her lips. 'Ladies first.'

'Hmm…' The throaty growl was hot against her neck. 'A woman after my own heart.'

She thrust her hands into his hair and wrenched his face down to hers, slanting her mouth over his and stripping away any doubts, fears or reservations with a hot, combative kiss. He came back with equal force, his hands sliding down her back until they cupped her behind and forced her against him.

He was hard, salty and heavenly. She moaned, the sound lost between them.

A chorus of cheers and laughter from a neighbouring boat broke them apart.

A giggle bubbled up between her heavy breaths and Chantal pressed her hands to burning cheeks. 'Looks like we're putting on a bit of a show.'

'You *are* a performance artist.'

Brodie lifted her and she instinctively wrapped her legs around him, groaning as her centre made contact with the hard length beneath his jeans.

'But now it's time for a private show.'

He walked them into the cabin, through the lounge and to the bedroom. *His* bedroom. A huge bed dominated the centre of the room. It was a hell of a lot bigger than Chantal had imagined it would be on a boat. It was a bed not made for sleeping but for hot, *Kama Sutra*–referencing, scream-at-the-top-of-your-lungs sex.

Brodie turned and sat on the edge of the bed, still holding her so that she was in his lap. The friction of his jeans against the wispy material of her underwear drove her crazy. She bucked, rolling her hips to increase the pressure. His mouth came down on hers, lush and open and intoxicating.

'Dance for me,' he growled.

Cheeks burning, she pushed hard against his chest so he toppled back. She straddled him, grinding her hips in a slow circular motion. 'But it's so good here.'

'I want to watch you.'

'You only get to watch when I say so.' She echoed her words from earlier in the day, heat flooding her body and throbbing out of control.

His eyes blazed like green fire and darkness. 'I'll make it worth your while.'

'How?' The question escaped her lips before she could think, before she could reason. She needed to hear his answer. Needed to absorb the experience of being with him through her every sense.

Warm palms slid up her thighs, bunching blue material around her waist. His hand brushed her sex, sending a jolt of pleasure through her. Toying with the edge of her underwear, he traced the pattern on the lace with his fingertip.

'If you can walk, talk or function on any level tomorrow then I haven't done my job.'

Her lips trembled. It wasn't enough. She wanted detail. She wanted all of it with a greedy, hedonistic gluttony.

'More.'

'I'm going to take you to the point where you think there's nothing left and I'm going to make you beg.' His eyes were wild, his pulse throbbing in his neck. 'I'm going to make you forget any word you've ever spoken except for my name. I'm going to be the only thing you know. I'm going to be your everything.'

'Brodie...' she whispered, the throbbing between her legs ceaseless. She ached to the point of pain. It had been so long...so very long.

'Dance for me.' His voice was rough, scratched up and torn apart with desire.

She pushed back, balancing on her heels and taking a step away from the bed. Her hands trembled, and her mouth was suddenly devoid of moisture as her hips swayed to a non-existent beat.

She wasn't passionate…her dancing wasn't passionate. Hadn't that been Derek's parting shot as he'd walked out of their house for the last time?

'You're a technical dancer, Chantal, but you're all business. No passion. No one wants to watch that. You'll never make it without me.'

Her throat closed in on itself, her heart jackhammering against her ribs. This was *Brodie*—not her controlling, possessive ex-husband. Smoking hot, life-loving Brodie. She could be herself around him because tomorrow this wouldn't exist. This would never have happened.

Safe in the impermanence of their situation, she ran her hands up her body, over the curve of her bust, the ridges of her collarbones, the column of her neck, into her hair. Fingers divided the strands, shaking her hair out until it fell around her shoulders.

'God, Chantal…' Her name was a strangled plea on his lips. 'Your body is incredible.'

She reached for the hidden zip that ran down the side of her rib cage, drawing it open with agonising slowness. Cool air rushed in, tickling her exposed skin. Stepping closer to him, she pulled him into a sitting position and dragged his hands to her hips so he could feel the movement.

Her head tilted back. There was nothing but the invisible beat and his hands on her. He pulled her between his legs, thrusting the dress up over her hips. His lips made contact with the flat of her belly above the waistband of her black lacy underwear. His tongue flicked out, filled with the promise of what was to come.

She yanked the dress over her head and flung it away.

'Perfection,' he breathed, and the hot air caressed the apex of her thighs.

His hand slid up over her rib cage to clasp her naked breast. Deft fingers toyed with her already hardened nipple, wringing a low moan from the back of her throat.

'Your turn.' She reached for his shirt, unbuttoning him quickly, urgently.

'You're far too good at that,' he chuckled, blackened eyes looking up at her.

'Dance costumes—fiddly buttons are no match for *my* fingers.'

'You do have beautiful fingers.' He pulled one of her hands to his lips and kissed each fingertip in turn. 'Beautiful palms.'

His mouth was hot in the centre of her hand, tracing a line over her wrist and up to her elbow.

'Beautiful everything.'

'Don't distract me.' She pushed the shirt from his shoulders, exposing golden skin stretched tight over a wall of muscle.

The cross tattoo caught her eye. She bent to kiss it, her hands falling to his belt. She wrenched at the closure, making his hips jerk forward as she released the belt.

'Easy, girl.' He covered her hands with his as she lowered the zip.

Within seconds he was completely naked. Ink covered more of his body than she remembered. The cross on his chest had been joined by scrolling words down the side of his rib cage and another anchor lower down, with numbers surrounding it. The sharp V of muscle drew her eyes... then her hands, then her mouth.

Her fingers brushed over the hard length of him, tracing the tip before she sank to her knees and drew him into her mouth. The mixture of earthy masculine scents and the subtle taste of him intoxicated her.

'Didn't I say easy girl?' he moaned, his hands fisting in her hair. She wasn't sure if he meant to hold her in place or pull her away.

She ran her tongue along the length of him before looking up. 'I heard you. I just didn't listen.'

'Come here.'

He hauled her on top of him, tilting them both back so that she straddled his hips. The hard weight of his erection dug into her thigh.

'We've got the whole night. You're not rushing me.'

Stretching his hand back, he found the drawer beside his bed and produced a foil packet. He reached down, sheathed himself, and before she knew what was happening he thrust up into her. The sudden movement was the perfect blend of pleasure and shock...with the tiniest, most delicate hint of pain.

Strong arms held her flat against him, her breasts pushed up against his chest, her lips at his neck. Each moan shot fire through her, and each thrust of his hips bumped her most sensitive part, making her body hum. Orgasm welled within her, climbing, peaking and pushing.

His hands were in her hair again, yanking her face up to his so his lips could slant over hers. Teeth tugged at her mouth, the taste of him drawing her closer and closer to release. She ground against him. So close...so close.

'Come for me, Chantal. I want to feel you shake around me.' His voice was tight, his breath coming in hard bursts.

'Brodie...' Her voice trembled, release a hair's width away.

'Scream for me.'

And she did.

On and on and on she cried out his name, eyes clamped

shut, fists bunched in the pillow, face pressed against his neck. The bubble burst and she tumbled down, down, down. As she clamped around him he found his own release, groaning long and low into her hair.

Silence washed over them. The air was cool on their sweat-dampened skin. He held her close, clinging on as if he wanted to stay that way forever. She didn't move in case he let go.

He could officially die a happy man. The gentle weight of her comforted him. One of her legs had wound around his; her foot was tucked against his calf. As her breathing slowed he stroked her hair, breathing in the heady scent of her perfume mingled with perspiration and sex.

Beside his head her hands were still clutching the pillow. Outside, Saturday-night parties raged on, contrasting with inside, where a hazy silence had settled over them.

'That was okay, I guess,' she mumbled against his neck, chuckling when he turned to look her in the eye. 'If you like that kind of thing.'

Glossy dark strands of hair covered half her face and he pushed them aside, drinking in her drugged gaze with satisfaction. Her lips were swollen and parted, her cheeks bright pink. Tracing her lower lip with his thumb, he brought her head down for a slow, teasing kiss.

'And *do* you like that sort of thing?'

'Nah—orgasms are overrated.' She grinned, pushing herself up so she straddled his hips.

The view was pretty damn good from this angle.

'Blasphemy.'

'Total blasphemy.' She planted a kiss on the tip of his nose and traced the lines of his latest tattoo. 'This is new.'

'It's twelve months old.'

'"In the waves of change we find our true direction".'

She read the words that had been etched onto him forever. 'That's beautiful. Why that quote?'

'I thought it made me sound intelligent,' he joked, hiding his sudden vulnerability with a wink.

How did she do that? She had a homing beacon aimed straight for his most sensitive areas…and not the good kind!

She smirked. 'What's the real reason?'

'I felt like I needed a reminder that change is necessary…healthy.' He sighed, and rolled so that she came down and landed on the bed next to him.

He'd meant to move away, but her body immediately curled into his, finding the groove between his arm and his chest. It felt so damn good to have her by his side, to finally be able to wrap his arms around her without the guilt of the past. He only had one night—he might as well let himself enjoy it.

What if one night wasn't enough?

Bookings were piling up. He'd be sailing back to Queensland soon enough to bury himself in work and his family. Even if they did stretch this fiasco on for more than a night his time here had a solid end date. Normally that was what he liked. But he wasn't experiencing his usual sense of relief at their ring-fenced sleeping arrangements.

'Do you think you need to change?'

'Everyone needs to change,' he replied, running a fingertip up and down her arm.

'What do you want to change?'

He laughed, shaking his head. 'What's with the twenty questions? I thought I'd signed on for a night of steamy sex—not the Spanish Inquisition.'

'Is that so?' She reached for him, the brush of her fingertips hardening him. 'What if I'm done?'

'*I'll* say when you're done.'

Rolling on top of her, he mentally thanked the king-size bed for its endless space.

Pinned, she tilted her face up at him, a defiant glint in her eye. 'You're not the boss of me,' she said.

Yeah, right. He had her exactly where he wanted her. Kissing his way down her neck, he sucked on her skin, only stopping to draw a still-hard nipple into his mouth. Her breasts were perfect: smallish, but firm, topped with bronzed peaks that were oh-so-responsive to his touch. She arched, stifling a groan. He licked, nipped, tugged until she let out the heavenly sounds of pleasure.

'That's it,' he murmured against her breast. 'Don't keep that wonderful sound from me. I want to hear you.'

'Bossy boots.' Her head lolled back against the pillow. Her eyes were closed, but a wicked smile curved her lips.

'Damn straight.'

'We were *talking*.' Strong fingers gripped his hair, pulling his head up so she could look down her body at him.

'And now we're not.'

'Why are you so averse to talking?'

'I'm not averse, but I prefer touching you.' To illustrate his point he kissed a trail down to her hip, swirling his tongue over the slightly protruding bone.

'You're such a *guy*.'

With her hands still in his hair he made his way to the juncture of her thighs, blowing cool air on her heated skin. 'Want me to stop?'

'What if I say yes?'

Her voice wavered. *Victory.*

'I'll call your bluff.'

Delicate licks drew an anguished moan from her.

'Stop.'

'Okay.' He pulled his head away but she pushed him back into place.

'Damn you.'

He laughed against the inside of her thigh, nipping at the sensitive flesh before moving back to her sex. The honeyed scent of her made his head swim, made him want to ravish her. It wouldn't be right to push her over the edge too quickly. She would have to wait while he had his fill.

He drew the sensitive bud of her clitoris into his mouth, working her, teasing her, tasting her. Smooth legs draped over his shoulders; demanding hands pushed and pulled him into place. Chantal was clear about what she wanted, and that was exactly the way he liked it.

'Brodie...' she gasped. 'For the love of...'

'Want me to stop again?'

'No!' The tension built within her, tremors rippling through her legs. 'Please.'

He bore down, giving her what she wanted until orgasm ripped through her. This time there was no holding back. She cried out so loudly that the neighbouring boats were sure to hear.

He clutched at his drawer, grabbing another condom and burying himself in her, riding the final waves of her release as he lost himself in her pleasure.

CHAPTER SEVEN

CHANTAL AWOKE WRAPPED in Brodie arms. Her face was pushed against his bicep, which was far cosier than it should have been, considering the guy was a rock-hard tower of muscle. His even breathing soothed the thumping of her heart.

From her days at Weeping Reef she knew Brodie was a heavy sleeper. She'd tested it on more than one occasion by sneaking into his room with Scott so they could play pranks on him. Like the time they'd switched the clothes in his drawers for frilly girls' nightclothes, so that he had to wander down to Chantal's room in a pink leopard-print negligee.

Not that he'd been too upset. He'd strutted his stuff as he did every day and the girls had fallen at his feet anyway.

Biting down on her lower lip, Chantal watched his peaceful face. Full lips were curved into a slight smile; thick lashes cast shadows on his cheekbones. His shaggy blond hair managed to look magazine perfect. Damn him.

Flashes of last night came back in a rush of needy, achy feeling. Every part of her body throbbed in a totally satisfied, pleasure-overload kind of way. Brodie was as good in bed as she'd suspected, but there was a tenderness to him that had been a complete surprise. The way he'd stroked her hair, the comforting embrace in the middle of the night, the gentle sweep of his hand along her arm—she hadn't been prepared for that at *all*. If anything it would have been easier if he was cold and impersonal afterwards.

She couldn't do this with him. It had been so much more than scratching an itch. He'd pushed her limits, bringing her to sensual heights she'd never known existed. He'd stirred her curiosity. The words inked on him revealed that he was so much more than the shallow charmer she'd labelled him. How could she look into those beautiful green eyes again without wanting to learn more? To dig deeper?

It was supposed to be about sex.

It is *about sex. You don't owe him anything. You got what you wanted—now move on and focus on your career. Playtime is over.*

Careful not to wake him, Chantal extracted herself from his muscular hold. She slipped out of the bed, holding her breath as her feet touched the polished boards. It was like playing a game of Sleeping Giant—except that the giant was a hunky guy with whom she didn't want to have awkward after-sex conversation.

How was she going to get back to Newcastle for her shift at the job from hell? Cringing, she tiptoed around the room. More importantly, where the hell was her dress? She'd managed to find every single one of Brodie's clothing items from their stripping frenzy, but the little blue dress was nowhere to be seen. Normally she was a leave-nothing-behind kind of girl when it came to her clothes, but the blue dress would have to be sacrificed.

Changing slowly, and as silently as possible, Chantal pulled on the clothes she'd arrived in on the first night, grabbed her phone and slung her overnight bag over one shoulder.

Now she had to make her way to Newcastle without the aid of Brodie's boat or her car—which was still parked at the bar. Simple...*not*. A cab was out of the question, since her wallet was frighteningly lean. Perhaps she could ring one of the girls and beg for a lift?

She bit down on her lip. She hated to ask. What if they already had plans? They probably would, and she would be interrupting. The bed squeaked as Brodie turned in his sleep, spiking her heart rate. She had to get out of there.

Pushing down her discomfort, she made her way off the boat and dialled Willa's number. 'Hey, I know it's early, but I need a favour...'

Within twenty minutes she was in Willa's car and on her way to Newcastle. There would be a price to pay for Willa's generosity in giving up brunch with Rob...and it wasn't going to be monetary.

'So,' Willa began, not bothering to hide the curiosity sparkling all over her face, 'how was he?'

Chantal pretended to study an email on her phone. 'I don't know what you're talking about.'

'Oh, come on! I did *not* miss out on baked ricotta and eggs to have you BS me, Chantal.'

'Nothing happened.'

Willa chuckled. 'Then why is your face the same shade as a tomato?'

'Sunburn?' Chantal offered weakly. 'Okay—fine. I slept with him.'

'Thank you, Captain Obvious. I'd figured that out already.' Willa leant forward to watch the traffic as she merged onto the Bradfield Highway. 'I don't want confirmation—I want *details*.'

Where to begin? Images of last night flashed in front of Chantal's eyes, snippets of sounds, feelings, sensations... Her body reacted as though he were right there in front of her. Damn him!

'It was...satisfying.'

'Just satisfying?' Willa narrowed her eyes at Chantal.

'Either you dish or it's going to be a long walk to New-castle.'

'He was amazing.'

Shaking her head, she willed her heart to stop thumping and her core to stop throbbing. She should be satiated, considering he'd woken her up twice during the night to continue wringing as many orgasms from her as possible.

'I'm sure he's had plenty of practice,' Chantal added, folding her arms across her chest.

'Don't go using that as a way to put distance between you. I can see what you're doing there.'

'I am not.'

'That's one thing I like about you, Chantal. You're a *terrible* liar.'

She huffed. Perhaps she would have been better walking. 'I don't need to put any distance between us because we agreed that it would be a one-night-only thing. Then we'd pretend it had never happened.'

'Gee, that sounds healthy.' Willa rolled her eyes.

'Why not? It's just sex—nothing more.' *I don't need any more, and I don't need him.*

'If it was just sex then why do you need to pretend it didn't happen?'

As much as she hated to admit it, Willa had a point. What was so bad about admitting that she'd had a one-night stand with Brodie?

Even thinking the words set a hard lump in her stomach. She'd been down this path before—men always started out fun, till the over-protectiveness stirred, control followed, and smothering wasn't far behind.

'Well, we don't want to upset Scott...'

'That's not it. Scott is totally head over heels for Kate. She's it for him. So I can guarantee he wouldn't care about you and Brodie hooking up.'

Why *did* she feel so funny about it? Perhaps admitting

it aloud meant it was real, and if it was real then it might happen again.

It's a slippery slope to disaster—remember that.

'Eight years is a long time to harbour feelings for someone. No wonder you're scared.'

'I'm *not* scared.' Chantal's lips pursed. 'And I have most certainly *not* been harbouring feelings for Brodie Mitchell for the last eight years.'

'I think the lady doth protest too much.' Willa stole a quick glance at Chantal, her amusement barely contained in a cheeky smile. 'You know, it *is* okay for you to like people—even annoyingly handsome men like Brodie.'

'I don't like him. I only wanted his body.' Her lip twitched.

Feelings for his body were a little easier to deal with than the possibility of feelings for him as a person. She had to shut this down right now. She did *not* have feelings for Brodie and she most certainly didn't want to start something permanent with him. It was a simple case of primitive, animalistic need. Relationships were not something on her horizon.

But no one had said anything about relationships, had they? Crap, why did it have to be so damn confusing? Head space came at a premium, and she could not afford to waste any spare energy on men, no matter how incredible their hands or mouth were.

'Uh, Chantal? I asked you a question.'

'Did you?' Great—now she'd lost her ability to even sustain basic conversation.

'Yes, I asked if you'd heard back after your audition.'

Sore point number two. 'Not yet. But it was only yesterday. They could take a little while to get back to me.'

'Do you think it went well?'

'Who the hell knows?' She sighed, rubbing her hands over her eyes. 'I can't tell any more.'

'I'm sure you'll land on your feet.' Willa reached over and squeezed her hand.

For a moment Chantal was terrified that she might cry. She hadn't allowed herself to shed any tears over her marriage or her failing career, and she didn't plan on opening the floodgates now. All that emotion was packed down tight. There would be time to cry when she'd secured herself a position with a dance company. For the time being tears were a waste of time and energy.

Thankfully Chantal was able to steer Willa to a safer topic. She was all too happy to talk about how things were going with Rob. Other people's lives were preferable talking points over the tricky, icky state of her career and her unwanted feelings towards Brodie.

Willa dropped Chantal off at the bar's parking lot, and she was almost surprised to find her car was still there. It was too crappy to steal, apparently.

Hitching her overnight bag higher on her shoulder, Chantal made her way around the back of the bar to the staff accommodation. She needed a hot shower, a cup of coffee and a lie down before she even attempted to get herself ready for another night of humiliation.

Her unit was number four. The metal number hung upside down on the door, one of its nails having rusted and fallen out. Holding her breath, she shoved the key into the lock and turned. The room didn't smell quite as bad as the bar, but the stale air still made her recoil as she entered the room.

'Home sweet home,' she muttered, dumping her bag onto the bed. *'Not.'*

The small room was almost entirely filled with an ancient-looking double bed covered in a faded floral quilt. A light flickered overhead, casting an eerie yellow glow over walls that were badly in need of a new paint job. A crack stretched down one wall, partially covered by a photo frame containing a generic scenery print. It was probably the picture that had come with the frame.

A quick peek at the bathroom revealed chipped blue tiles, a shower adorned with a torn plastic curtain and a sink that looked as though it needed a hardcore bleach application.

Chantal dropped down onto the bed and checked her phone. Nothing. What was she expecting? Brodie to be calling? Asking her to come back?

Something dark scuttled across the floor by her feet. Chantal drew her knees up to her chest and wrapped her arms around her legs.

She would not cry. She would *not* cry.

Brodie woke to the sound of his phone vibrating against the nightstand. He stretched, palm smoothing over the space next to him in the bed. The *empty* space.

Grinding a fist into his eyes, he forced the fogginess away. What time was it? He groped for his phone, fumbling with the passcode. It was a text from Scott.

Bro, I thought we were going for a run? Where are you?

Run? It was three o'clock in the afternoon. Crap, how had *that* happened?

Sorry, got caught up. Will have to reschedule.

The bed sheets were tangled around his legs and he caught a brief flash of Chantal's ocean-coloured dress peeking out from underneath his jeans in the corner of the room—a sure sign that the lavish images of losing himself in her body over and over weren't from a dream.

His phone immediately pinged with a new message.

Got caught up with what? Or should I say who?

Ugh. Where was Chantal? His feet hit the ground, thighs protesting as he stood. Yep, that was a sign of one hell of a night. He stretched, forcing his arms up overhead and pressing against the tightness in his muscles. Damn, he felt good.

He poked his head into the en-suite bathroom. No Chantal there. Padding out to the kitchen, he typed a message back to Scott.

No comment.

She wasn't in the kitchen either. Why hadn't she woken him? He wandered out onto the deck to see if she was doing any of her yoga stuff. Nope, nothing there either.

He raked a hand through his hair, coming back to the kitchen and flicking the coffee machine on. It whirred, grinding beans and then flooding the room with its delicious, fresh-brewed coffee scent.

Weak. Not that it takes a genius to figure it out...

Scott had a point. It had been bound to happen between him and Chantal. Their tension had been through the roof back then, and eight years hadn't dampened it at all. It had been a special kind of torture having Chantal back in his life...even if only for a short period of time.

Last night had been easily the best night of his life. But only because she was insanely hot and did things with her mouth that would make the most experienced of men blush. It was a conquest thing—a very long-awaited notch on his belt.

Yeah, right.

Okay, so maybe he normally woke up *hoping* the girl

had made a quick exit…if he'd even brought her back to his place. Normally he opted to go to hers, so he had control over a quick getaway.

But something about Chantal's leaving didn't sit well with him. He felt the absence of her keenly—almost as if he wasn't ready for it to be over. Understandable, since he'd been lusting after her for such a long time. He needed a little while longer to get it out of his system. Like forever.

So much for the 'hands off your mates' rule.

Frowning, he plucked his espresso cup from the coffee machine and breathed deeply. Where could she have disappeared to? Surely she hadn't gone back to that crappy bar on her own? His chest clenched, fingers tightening around the china cup.

The thought of her getting back up on that stage, dancing in front of those men… It was enough to unsettle even the most relaxed guy. He sipped the coffee, relishing the rich flavour on his tongue, but it didn't satisfy him as much as usual. After tasting Chantal all other flavours would pale in comparison, of that he was sure.

Perhaps the dance company had called her in for another audition? Not likely, since she'd only auditioned yesterday. She *couldn't* be back at that bar. How would she have got there on her own? Her car had never come back to Sydney.

His phone vibrated again, and he was about to curse Scott's name when Willa's photo flashed up.

'Hello?'

'Hey, Brodes.'

The traffic in the background told him she was calling from the road.

'I wanted to let you know I drove Chantal back to Newcastle.'

Dammit. 'When?'

'I dropped her off about an hour ago—I'm still on my way back. It's a long drive! Thought you might want to know, since I got the impression she hadn't said anything to you this morning.'

'She hadn't.'

'I don't like the idea of her staying at that place.'

He let out a sharp breath. 'Neither do I. I wouldn't have let her go…'

'That's probably why she didn't tell you.' She sighed. 'I only took her because I knew she'd find her own way if I said no. I didn't want her hitchhiking or anything like that.'

He swore under his breath. 'She makes me lose my cool, Willa.'

'She must be the only girl ever.'

He ignored the jibe. 'I'll go get her.'

'Good.'

By the time Brodie had sailed back up the coast, the sun had dipped low in the sky and his blood had reached boiling point. He wasn't sure what made him angrier: the fact that she'd left him the morning after or that she'd returned to a crappy job that was not only beneath her but a possible threat to her safety.

Okay, maybe he was overreacting, but that bar *was* shady. The guys who hung around it were rough. He could only imagine what the on-site accommodation looked like. The thought of one of those men following her after she'd finished her shift…

His fists clenched. He *had* to get her out of there.

He strode across the car park, ignoring the catcalls from a group of scantily clad girls leaning against a souped-up ute with neon lights and chrome rims. Inside, a band belted out metal music, the screaming vocals grating on his nerves.

Bypassing the growing crowd, he took the stairs up to the second floor. Would he be able to grab her before she performed or would he have to sit through the sweet torture of watching her up on that stage again?

The bass thumped deep in his chest as he climbed the stairs. Chantal wasn't on stage. Instead the crowd was cheering for an older woman wearing sparkling hearts over her nipples. Brodie squinted. Were those *tassels*? The stage was littered with a pair of silk gloves, a feather boa, and something that looked like a giant fan made of peacock feathers. The woman shook her chest, sending the tassels flying in all directions.

Find Chantal now! Otherwise she might be the next one on stage, shaking her tassels.

Two girls who sat at the bar looked as though they might be dancers. Their sparkly make-up, elaborate outfits and styled hair certainly seemed to suggest it.

'Excuse me ladies,' he said, approaching them. 'I'm looking for a friend of mine who dances here.'

'*I* can be your friend who dances here.' The blonde batted her false lashes at him, silver glitter sparkling with each blink.

'We come as a pair.' The redhead chuckled, tossing her hair over one shoulder.

'That's tempting,' he said, turning on a charming smile. 'And I'm sure you're both a lot of fun. But I need to find a girl called Chantal.'

'You can call me whatever you like, sugar.' Red winked, blowing him a kiss from her highly glossed crimson lips.

'Are you her boyfriend?' asked Blonde, tracing a lacquered finger up the length of his shirt. 'Most of the girls here don't stick to one guy. They get too jealous.'

'The guys?'

Blonde nodded. 'They start fights. You're not going to start a fight, are you?'

'I'm a lover, not a fighter.'

He watched the bartender eyeing him. The guy was old,

but his arms were covered in faded prison tattoos. Brodie directed his eyes back to the girls.

'You sure look like a lover.' Red licked her lips. 'A good one, too. But all guys go crazy for the right girl.'

'Chantal is a friend. So, have you seen her?'

'A friend? Right.' Blonde laughed. 'If she was just a friend you wouldn't be here with that puppy love face, looking for her.'

He opened his mouth to argue but snapped it shut. Trying to reason with these two would be a waste of time—time that could be better spent looking for Chantal and getting her the hell out of this hole.

'Thanks for your time, ladies.'

'Good luck, lover boy.' Red chortled as he walked away.

He stood by the bar and scanned the room. Mostly men, a few women who might or might not be dancers, muscle stationed by the stairwell and by an exit on the other side of the stage. That must be where the dancers went backstage.

He was about to attempt to get past the muscle when he spotted Chantal. In denim shorts and a white tank top, she looked dressed for the beach rather than a bar. But her face and hair were made up for the stage. She had a bag over one shoulder. Perhaps she'd already danced?

As she attempted to weave through the crowd someone stopped her. A guy much bigger than her put his hands on her arms and she tried to wriggle out of his grasp. The bouncer looked on with mild amusement, but made no attempt to step in and protect Chantal.

Brodie rushed forward, grabbing her by the arm and yanking her back against him. She yelped in surprise, but relief flooded her face when she realised it was him. She stepped back, standing partially behind him.

'Is there a problem, mate?' The guy towered over Brodie, and he saw a snake tattoo peeking out of the edge of his dark T-shirt.

'Yeah, you had your hands on my girl.' He looked the guy dead in the eye, ready to fight if it came to that.

A wave of guilt washed over him. Was this how Scott had felt that night at Weeping Reef?

He shoved the thought aside and pushed Chantal farther behind him. Nothing mattered now but getting her out safely.

'Maybe you shouldn't be letting her parade around in next to nothing, then.' He leered, exposing an aggressive gap-toothed smile. 'Some of the guys here aren't as easy-going as me.'

Brodie turned, wrapped his arm around Chantal's shoulders and steered her towards the stairs. They moved through the throng of people and he didn't let go of her. Not once.

'What are you doing here?' she asked as they exited the bar. Her brows were narrowed, and her face was streaked with conflicting emotions.

It wasn't dark yet. An orb of gold sat low on the horizon while the inky shades of night bled into the sky. Chantal hovered at the entrance of the bar, her eyes darting from the driveway to the accommodation and back to him. The red neon sign from the bar flickered at odd intervals.

'I'm saving your butt—that's what I'm doing.' He raked a hand through his hair, tremors of adrenaline still running through him. 'I'm giving you a place to stay.'

'I have a place to stay.' The defiance in her voice rang out in the night air, and her fists were balled by her sides.

'And how is it? I'm assuming you came back here after you hauled arse this morning?'

The breeze ruffled her dark hair, sending a few strands into her eyes. She blew them away. 'I did.'

'And?'

She folded her arms across her chest. 'It's serviceable.'

'And you'd take "serviceable" over a luxury yacht? Or would that just be to spite me?'

Why was he even worried? She either wanted to stay or she didn't. They weren't in a relationship. So why was the thought of her staying here alone like a stake through his gut?

Too many years playing big brother—that's all it is.

'I'm not trying to spite you, Brodie.' She sighed. 'But I don't need you following me around playing macho protector.'

'What would have happened if I hadn't been here?' He threw his hands up in the air, the mere thought of anyone harming her sending his instincts into overdrive.

'I would have handled it.'

'Oh, yeah? How?'

She waved a hand at him. 'I can look after myself, Brodie. I've done it without your help for the last eight years.'

'I would have been here the second you asked.'

Her face softened, but she didn't uncross her arms. 'But I didn't ask, did I? That's because I'm fine on my own.'

'It didn't look like you were going to be fine tonight.'

'That's *your* perception.'

How could she not see the danger? Was she actually that blind or was it all a ruse so he'd believe her strong and capable? He *did* think she was strong and capable, but the facts still stood. A huge guy would easily overpower her petite frame, no matter what skills she had. Her refusal to accept his help made him worry more.

'Only an idiot couldn't see the path that you almost went down.'

'Only *this* idiot?' She rolled her eyes, flattening her palm to her chest. 'I'm not a damsel in distress—no matter how much you fantasise about it.'

'You think I fantasise about you being in trouble?' Rage tore through him. If only she knew the fear that had coursed through him when he'd realised where she was today.

She opened her mouth to retort, but changed her mind. 'I don't think that, Brodie. But I want you to understand that this thing between us is just sex. You're not obligated to be my bodyguard.'

The words hit him like a sledge-hammer to his solar plexus. *Just sex.* Of course that was all it was. That was what they'd agreed last night... So why did he feel as if she was tearing something away from him?

'Come back to the boat.' He set a hard stare on her, challenging her. 'For *just sex.*'

'I don't want you coming back into the bar.' She loosened her arms, pursing her lips. Her eyes were blackened and heavy, her lips full. 'You don't need to rescue me.'

'Fine.'

It went against every fibre of his being, but he would have agreed to anything to get her away from the bar at that point. He would deal with the consequences next time he turned up to rescue her—because hell would freeze over before he let her put herself in danger. She could get as mad as she liked.

She eyed him warily. 'Okay, then. Let's go.'

CHAPTER EIGHT

THEY WALKED AROUND the side of the bar to the staff accommodation so she could retrieve her bag. Going back to his boat felt like giving in, which seemed spineless after her great escape that morning. But the guy from the bar *had* shaken her. His disgusting words whispered into her ear along with the sickly scent of cheap whisky and Coke had made her stomach churn. Brodie had showed up at the right time and, though she would *never* admit it, she wasn't quite sure how she would have got herself out of that situation.

But it was a slippery slope from accepting help to being controlled, and she would never go there again.

A pale yellow beam from an outside security light spilled into the tiny motel-like room, causing shadows to stretch and claw at the walls. She wanted to be here about as much as she wanted to stab herself in the eye with a stiletto. But the alternative wasn't exactly peachy. Another night on Brodie's boat…another night of searing temptation and slowly losing her mind.

True to his word, he hadn't mentioned them sleeping together, but the evening was young. Something about the way he watched her pack told her he wasn't here out of friendly concern alone.

'How many more shifts do you have?' he asked, hovering by the door.

He stayed close but didn't touch her. Still, she was fully

aware of the heat and intensity radiating off him. He wore a shirt tonight, soft white cotton with sleeves rolled up to his elbows. A thin strip of leather hung around his neck, weighted with a small silver anchor. A silver watch sat on one wrist, contrasting against his deep tan.

'I've got a month in total,' she replied. 'They're pushing for more, though.'

'You're not going to stay, are you?'

'If I don't find something else I might not have a choice.' She faced away from him, stuffing the few items she'd unpacked back into her overnight bag. 'A girl's gotta eat.'

He frowned. 'There must be something else you could do.'

'Yeah, I could wait tables or work as a checkout chick at a supermarket. No matter how bad this is, it's *still* dancing. It means I haven't given up.'

Slinging her bag over one shoulder, she walked out of the room and slammed the door shut behind her.

Silence. She sensed a begrudging acceptance from him.

'No word on the audition?'

'Not yet.'

Once on the yacht, Chantal stashed her things in the guest room, hoping it signalled to Brodie that she had no intention of sleeping with him again. Incredible as they were together, it was clear she needed to focus on her current situation. She was already taking way too much from Brodie. She couldn't rely on him, his yacht or his money. She'd made this mess—she needed to get herself out of it.

'Why don't you grab a shower and I'll get dinner on the go?' he said, already pulling a frying pan from the kitchenette cupboard.

'Are you trying to tell me I smell?' She smirked, leaning against the breakfast bar.

Soft denim stretched over the most magnificent butt she'd ever laid eyes on as he bent down. He was the perfect shape. Muscular, but not OTT bulky. Broad, masculine, powerful. She swallowed, her mouth dry and scratchy.

'If I thought you smelled I would come right out and say it.' He looked over his shoulder, blond hair falling into his eyes.

He mustn't have shaved this morning. Blond stubble peppered his strong jaw, making the lines look even sharper and more devastating. Golden hair dusted his forearms, and she knew that his chest was mostly bare except for a light smattering around his nipples and the trail from his belly button down. She couldn't get that image out of her head.

'Hurry up—before I drag you there myself.'

He said the words without turning around, and Chantal thanked her lucky stars that he didn't. The words alone were potent enough, without the cheeky smile or glint she knew would be in his eyes.

'Then you'll be in trouble.'

The steam and hot water did nothing to wash away the tension in her limbs, nor the aching between her thighs. Wasn't a shower supposed to be cleansing? The quiet sound of rushing water only gave her time to replay the most delicious parts of last night, and she stepped out onto the tiles feeling more wound up than before.

A mouth-watering scent wafted in the air as she slipped into a loose black dress, and padded barefoot into the kitchen. The table was set for two. Intimate...personal.

Two glasses held white wine the colour of pale gold. White china rimmed in silver sported a faint criss-cross pattern—simple, but undeniably luxurious. A bowl of salad sat in the middle of the table.

'Pan-fried salmon with roasted potatoes and baby carrots.' He brought two plates to the table. 'Not fancy, but it *is* healthy—and pretty darn tasty, if I do say so myself.'

'I didn't know you could cook.'

'I'm a man of many talents, Chantal.' He set the plates down and dropped into the seat across from her. 'I thought you would have figured that out by now.'

She rolled her eyes, cutting into the salmon steak and sighing at the sight of the perfectly cooked fish. 'Does it get annoying, being good at everything?'

'No.' He grinned and speared a potato.

They picked up their glasses and clinked them together. The bell-like sound rang softly in the air. Crystal glasses. *Of course they're crystal—this is a boat for rich people... not people like you.*

Chantal shoved the thought aside and sipped her wine. 'Did you do a lot of cooking at home?'

'I did, actually. I was probably the only fifteen-year-old kid who cooked dinner for the family most nights of the week.'

'Really?'

She couldn't hide her surprise. He hardly seemed like the kind of guy who would be in charge of a household. But the salmon melted on her tongue, and the tangy aromatics of a lemon and ginger marinade danced in sensational delight. He didn't cook in the way most people did, where the food was functional first and foremost. He had talent—a knack for flavour and texture.

'Yep. Mum was a nurse and she often worked afternoons and nights. The cooking was left up to me.'

'What about your dad?'

'He wasn't around.' Brodie frowned. 'Dad was an artist, and he had a lot more passion for painting than he did for his family.'

'That's sad.'

'Yeah... I was fine, but the girls really needed him—especially Lydia. She remembered him more than the twins and Ellen.' He reached for his wine, looking as though he were about to continue the thread of conversation but changing his mind at the last minute. 'What about you? Were you the house chef?'

'I can do the basics. My mum worked long hours too, so I had to fend for myself a fair bit.' She swallowed down the guilt that curled in her stomach whenever she thought about her mother. 'I can do a basic pasta…salads. That kind of thing.'

'What does your mother do?'

'She's a cleaner.' Chantal bit down on her lip, wishing the memories weren't still so vivid. 'I don't think she's ever worked less than two jobs her whole life.'

His eyes softened. Damn him. She didn't want his sympathy.

'What about your dad?'

'He left when I was ten.' She shrugged, stabbing her fork at a lettuce leaf more forcefully than she needed to.

'Siblings?'

'None. Probably sounds strange to someone with such a big family.' *Good—turn the conversation back to him.*

'Yep—four sisters and never a moment of peace.'

She envied the contented smile on his lips. It was obvious his family was important to him. She'd bet they would be close, despite his father's absence. The kind of family who had big, raucous Christmas gatherings and loads of funny traditions. So different from her. They'd been so poor at one point that her mother had wrapped her Christmas present—a Barbie doll from the local second-hand shop—in week-old newspaper. The memory stabbed at her heart, scything through the softest part of her. The part she kept under lock and key.

'It drove me nuts, growing up,' he continued. 'But I became amazingly proficient at hair braids and reading bedtime stories.'

Her stomach churned. 'You'll make a great dad one day.'

A dark shadow passed over his face. The wall dropped

down in front of him so fast and so resolutely that Chantal wondered what she'd said. A sardonic smile twitched the corner of his lips. Okay, so there *were* some things that put Brodie in a bad mood.

'I don't want the white-picket-fence deal.' He drained the rest of his wine and reached for the bottle to empty the remaining contents into his glass. 'Marriage, kids, pets… not for me. I've got enough responsibility now.'

'Cheers to that.' They clinked glasses again.

He quirked a brow. 'But you got married.'

'Just because I did it once it doesn't mean I'll do it again.' Her cheeks burned. '*That* debacle is over for good.'

The wine had loosened her limbs a little, and it seemed her tongue as well. She probably shouldn't have accepted the shot of whisky one of the other dancers had offered her before she went onstage. But she'd so desperately needed Dutch courage to force her back onstage.

'Sounds like there's a story there.'

'Maybe.' She shrugged.

Could she claw back her words? Brodie didn't need to see the ugly bits of her life…especially not after she'd gone to such efforts to hide them. Then again, did it really matter?

'I've seen you naked, remember.' He grinned.

How could she possibly forget?

'No point keeping secrets from me now.'

She took a deep breath and decided to throw caution to the wind. After all, he knew her most devastating secret: that her career had turned to crap. What harm could another failure do if it was out in the open?

'The short version is that I was young, naive and I married the wrong guy.'

'And the full version?'

'I married my agent,' she said, rolling her eyes and

taking another sip of her wine. 'What a bloody cliché. He seemed so worldly, and I was a wide-eyed baby. We met a month after I left Weeping Reef, and he promised he'd make me a star. He did—for a while—but then he started treating me like his student rather than his wife. He wanted everything his way, all the time.'

Brodie held his breath… *Dammit*. If she asked, wild horses wouldn't keep him from finding the dude and teaching him a very painful, very permanent lesson. Fists clenched, he drew in a slow breath.

'I couldn't take it. The constant criticism, the arguing…' Her olive eyes glittered and she shook her head. 'Nothing I did met his expectations—he smothered me. Pushed all my friends away until I could only rely on him. I couldn't forgive that.'

'Good.' The word came out through clenched teeth and Brodie realised his jaw had started to ache. 'A guy like that doesn't deserve your forgiveness. What an arse.'

'Yeah, *major* arse.' Her lips twisted into a grimace. 'We ended up separating, and the divorce went through about six months ago. I've been trying to find work but I keep bombing out.'

'Why do you think that is?'

'I don't know.' She shook her head, despair etched into her face. 'Maybe after being told for so long that I don't work hard enough, that I'm not disciplined enough, I've started to believe it…'

'That's complete crap and you know it.' He gripped the edge of his seat, knuckles white from lack of circulation. How could anyone not see the lengths that she went to in order to achieve her goals? She deserved every success in the world.

She managed a wan smile. 'So there you have it: the failings of the not-so-great Chantal Turner. I can't keep a career and I can't keep a man. I can't even book a god-damn dancing job without getting myself into trouble.'

'It's not your fault,' he ground out. His stomach pitched, and the need to bundle her up in his arms thrashed like a wild beast inside him.

'Oh, but it is.'

She drained another glass of wine. Was that two or three? Not that it mattered. He'd keep her safe on the boat tonight. He'd protect her.

'I've done all these things myself. My judgment—my errors.'

'You *can* ask for help.'

She shook her head, dark locks flicking around her shoulders. 'No. I got myself in trouble—I'll get myself out. Besides, I'd need to trust people. I can't do that.'

Her vulnerability shattered him. She'd worked for everything she had—chased it and made sacrifices for it. It wasn't fair that she was here, feeling as if she'd stuffed everything up. He wanted to erase the pain from her voice, smooth the tension from her limbs and barricade her from the dangers of the world.

'You can't go back to that accommodation.' It wasn't a question, and it wasn't a suggestion.

'I need to stay somewhere, Brodie. I need to find a damn supermarket and cook myself a meal.' She shook her head. 'I need to get my life together.'

He wondered if, in her head, she'd told herself that she couldn't rely on him. But he wanted her to... Against his better judgment, he *wanted* her to lean on him.

'Stay here—at least for now. That will give you time to find something else...something safer.' He grabbed her hand across the table, cursing internally when his blood pulsed hard and hot at the contact. 'I'll keep the boat docked here and you'll be close to the bar. Then we can wander around during the day. Have fun. Pretend life isn't such a pain in the butt.'

A small smile pulled at her lips as she retracted her hand from his grip. 'I don't know...'

'You don't have to trust me.'

Her eyes roamed his face before she shrugged her acceptance. 'So that's days and evenings sorted. What did you have planned for nights?'

He swallowed. It would be easy to come up with a list of things they could do at night, and most of them would make excellent use of her yoga flexibility. Hell, how would he keep his distance after what they'd shared last night? He didn't need things getting messy between them, and he certainly didn't want to do anything that would make him lose her again.

'What *about* nights? We can watch movies, chill out on the deck. Keep it PG-13.'

Totally chivalrous—he was simply being a good friend. Keeping an eye out for her. *Yeah, right.*

She smirked. 'Does PG-13 include kissing?'

'It might.'

'Heavy petting?'

'That sounds like it could lead to something a little more X-rated.'

'I want to know what kind of tricks you might try to pull—what loopholes you might use.'

'If I want something I make it happen. Loopholes or no loopholes.'

'Yes, you certainly do.' Her eyes flashed, pupils widening as she shifted in her seat.

Her foot brushed his leg under the table. Had she done it on purpose? He couldn't read her face—couldn't tell whether her flirtatious tone was meant to bait him or mock him. She pushed her plate away and leant back in her chair.

One bronzed leg crossed over the other and the hem of her dress crept up to reveal precious inches of thigh.

'But you can't blame a girl for trying to protect herself,' she said.

'Why do you think you need to protect yourself around me?'

'To make sure history doesn't repeat itself.' She stretched her arms, dragging the dress farther up her thighs. If she kept up the pace she'd be naked soon, and he'd be on his knees. Not a bad thing, given the way she'd cried his name last night.

Cut it out. You're supposed to be helping her—not plotting her future orgasms.

'No more dancing?'

'You're far too tempting on the dance floor. All the girls at the resort thought so,' she said. Her eyes focused on something distant, something lost in memory. 'You're a magnet for the ladies.'

He hadn't cared too much what the other girls thought of him. Only Chantal's opinion had stuck like a thorn in his side.

'That was then.'

'And it's not the case now?' She threw him a derisive look. 'I see the way women look at you, Brodie.'

'Are you jealous?'

'Hardly.' Her brows narrowed, pink flaring across the apples of her cheeks.

He stood, collected the dishes and carried them to the kitchen. He returned moments later with a tub of ice cream and two spoons. No bowls, which would save some washing up. It was only a bonus that they'd need to sit close to share the tub.

'Anything else off-limits?'

He opened the tub and stuck his spoon in, scooping a

small portion of the salted caramel and macadamia ice cream and shoving it into his mouth.

His eyes shut as the sensations danced on his tongue. Sweet, creamy vanilla ice cream, swirls of sticky, salty caramel, and the crunch of toasted nuts. It was heavenly.

It would taste even better if he was able to eat it off that deliciously flat stomach of hers.

Pleasure sounds came from the back of her throat as her lips wrapped around the other spoon. She dragged it out of her mouth slowly and Brodie salivated watching her. If the ice cream was delicious, then *she* was the dessert of the heavens.

'I might have to make this ice cream off-limits. I don't think I'll be able to stop myself polishing off the whole damn tub.' She sighed and dug her spoon back in. 'But we can't let it go to waste—that wouldn't be right.'

'I'll take you for a run tomorrow morning.'

He sucked another tasty morsel from his spoon, focusing on it rather than on Chantal and how her lips looked as if they were made for every kind of X-rated fantasy he'd ever had.

'That should restore some balance.'

'I don't know if I could keep up with you,' she said, tilting her head and toying with her spoon.

'You can definitely keep up.'

Were they still talking about running? She stabbed the ice cream with her spoon, leaving the silver handle sticking straight up like an antenna.

'Tell me more about your family,' she said. 'And please take that ice cream away before I eat myself into oblivion.'

He grabbed the tub, pulled out her spoon and replaced the lid before wandering into the kitchen with her close on his heels. As she climbed up onto a bar stool at the kitchen bench, her legs not quite touching the ground, he felt walls shoot up around him. *Good.* At least some of his defences remained intact. He'd been sure she'd somehow dismantled them.

'Why the sudden interest in my family?'

'I don't know.' She shrugged. 'I felt like you were a bit of a mystery while we were at the reef...and you *did* say we were friends. I know most of my other friends better than I know you.'

'I think we've had enough talking tonight.' He shut the freezer door a little more forcefully than he needed to.

Images of her naked, bending into those damn yoga positions, trailing her hair across his stomach, all invaded him with equal combative power. He wanted her again... and again and again. But they *were* friends. She'd just confirmed it. Breaking the rule once was excusable—heat of the moment and all that—but twice was playing with fire.

He couldn't afford to entangle himself in another relationship, no matter how temporary. He had his priorities all worked out: build his business, take care of his family. That was it. Simple. Straightforward. Uncomplicated.

Chantal Turner was like an addictive substance, and everyone knew the first hit was the best. He'd had his taste—time to move on. She needed to be put squarely in the friend zone.

'I'm going to bed.' He stretched his arms above his head, not missing the way her eyes lingered on him. 'Got to get up early for that run.'

'Sweet dreams.' She hopped off the bar stool, her face in an unreadable mask, and headed to her room.

'Undoubtedly,' he muttered.

The digital clock in the bedroom mocked her with each hour that passed, its red glow holding sleep at an arm's length. She tossed and turned, twisting the sheets into knots around her limbs. What was wrong with her?

Brodie refused to leave her mind alone. One minute he

was hot for her and sharing things about himself, the next he was done talking and wanted to sleep.

It's a good thing he had the guts to do what you couldn't.

Was it possible that now he'd got what he wanted, she was out of his system? That thought shouldn't have rankled, but it did—and with surprising force. Surely eight years of unrequited sexual tension couldn't be over in one night?

Why should she care?

Shaking her head, she turned over onto her side and huffed. It was clear that she'd become unhinged. Perhaps her inability to find a real job was slowly driving her insane, making her more sensitive to things that should have meant nothing. Only Brodie didn't mean nothing...did he?

The bedroom suddenly felt too confined, too tight for her to breathe. Chantal swung her legs out of the bed and stood, relishing the feeling of the smooth floorboards on her bare soles.

She padded out to the deck and tipped her face up, her breath catching at the sight of the full, ripe moon hanging in a cloudless sky dotted with stars. In Sydney the city lights illuminated everything twenty-four-seven and the stars weren't visible. She'd missed them.

Growing up in a small coastal town had meant night after night of sparkling sky—endless opportunities to place a wish on the first one that winked at her. Perhaps that was why everything was falling to pieces now? It had been a long time since she'd made a wish. She closed her eyes, but her mind couldn't seem to form a coherent thought. She knew what she wanted to wish for...didn't she? Her stomach twisted itself into a knot and her breath shortened to shallow puffs.

What if things didn't turn around? What if the dive bar was her best option? *Don't think like that, you* have *to be positive. You have to keep trying...try harder!*

Alone, she felt tears prickle her eyes. The sadness was pushing its way to the surface, mingling with her ever-present panic like blood curling in water. She needed to hang on a little while longer—long enough to get some-thing—*anything*—which would prove she hadn't wasted her mother's sacrifices and her own hard work. Then she could deal with the bad stuff.

'What are you doing up?'

Brodie's sleep-roughened voice caught her off guard. She whirled around, blinking back the tears and pleading with herself to calm down. She didn't want him to see her like this—not when she felt she was about to fall apart at the seams.

'Are you okay?'

She nodded, unable to speak for fear that releasing words might open the floodgates of all she held back. Her breathing was so shallow and fast that the world tilted at her feet. She pressed a palm to her cheek, mentally willing him to leave her. Her face was as warm as if she'd spent the night sleeping next to an open fire, and her skin prick-led uncomfortably.

'You don't look okay.' He stepped closer and captured her face in his hands, studying her with his emerald eyes.

That only made it worse. By now her palms were slick with perspiration and her stomach swished like the ocean during a storm. Tremors racked her hands and her dig-nity was slipping away faster than she could control it. She was drowning, and once again she was relying on him to save her.

'Hey, it's all right,' he soothed, moving his hands to her shoulders and rubbing slowly up and down her arms. 'Let's get you a glass of water.'

He pulled her against his side, wrapping an arm around her shoulder and guiding her into the cabin. Setting her down on a stool, he grabbed a glass and pressed it against the ice machine on the fridge. Loud clinking noises filled the room as the ice tumbled into the glass, followed by the glug of water from a bottle in the fridge.

Breathe in—one, two, three. Out—one, two, three.

'Drink it slowly—don't gulp.' He handed her the glass and smoothed her hair back from her face.

No doubt she looked like a crazy person, huffing and puffing like the wolf from that nursery rhyme. Her hair would be all over the place, sticking out like a mad professor's. It was only then she realised that she was practically naked, with a pair of white lace panties her only keeper of modesty. She hadn't thought it possible for her face to get any hotter, but it did.

'Thanks,' she mumbled, shaking her hair so it fell in front of her, covering her bare breasts.

She must have ditched her T-shirt while she was trying to get to sleep. Stress overheated her. Most of the time she slept in nothing at all—unless it was the dead of winter, and then she wore her favourite llama-print pyjamas. But it was warm on the boat and her body was reaching boiling point. She pressed the cool glass to her burning cheek.

You're rambling in your head—not a good sign. Calm. Down. Now.

'Do you want me to grab you something to wear?'

Brodie's voice cut into her inner monologue and she nodded mutely, switching the glass of water to her other cheek. Her whole body flamed. Shame tended to do that. This was exactly why she should have said no to the invitation to Brodie's boat in the first place! Now he knew... He knew what a mess she was. She couldn't even fall asleep without working herself up.

'Here.'

He took the glass from her hand and set it down, helping her weakened limbs into the armholes of a T-shirt and guiding her head through the neck opening.

The fabric swam on her, smoothing over her curves and giving her protection. The T-shirt was his—it smelled of him. Smelled of ocean air and soap and earthy maleness.

'Are these panic attacks a recent thing?' He leant against the bench, his face neutral.

'No, I've had them a while.' She couldn't look him in the eye.

'They suck,' he said. 'My little sister gets them pretty bad too. Water usually works for her.'

Chantal bit down on her lip, toying with the glass before taking another sip. Could she be any more humiliated right now?

'It's nothing to be ashamed of. You know that, right?'

He touched her arm, the gentle brush making her stomach flip. Her breathing slowed a little.

'Ellen gets them a lot. She's only nineteen, but she puts a lot of pressure on herself to do well. She wants to get into a performing arts school.'

'What does she do?' Curiosity piqued, she looked up.

Brodie dropped down onto the stool next to her, his knees inches from her thighs. 'She plays piano pretty damn well, if I do say so myself. I used to run her to practise when I lived at home—went to all her recitals too. She's ace.'

The pride in his voice was unmistakable. Chantal had often wondered what it would be like to have siblings—to look after someone other than herself, to worry about people all the time. She would have been a terrible sister—she couldn't even keep her own life together, let alone help anyone else.

'Then there's the twins: Jenny and Adriana. They're twenty-two, and as different as two people can be. Jenny is the loud one. She got into modelling a while ago and has done a fair bit of travelling with it. Adriana is still studying. She's going to end up being a doctor of some-

thing one day.' He smiled. 'Then Lydia is the oldest...
she's twenty-four.'

His eyes darkened for a moment and she wondered if
he was going to continue. His lips pulled into a flat line
as he raked a hand through his hair, stopping to rub the
back of his neck.

'Lydia is in a wheelchair. She was in a car accident some
years ago and she was paralysed from the waist down.'

'That's awful.'

'Yeah.' A sad smiled passed over his lips. 'She wanted
to be a dancer.'

Emotion ran through her—grief for this poor girl whom
she didn't even know, for the sadness on Brodie's face and
for what their family must have gone through. At least she
could still dance. Her heart swelled. He cared so deeply
about his family. For all her jokes about his carefree attitude, he was a good person.

He drew a breath, steadying his gaze on her. 'So there
you go. You wanted to know something else about my
family—it's not all sunshine and roses.'

'I guess we've all got our stuff to deal with.' She downed
the rest of her water. 'I nearly gave up dancing once.'

'Really?' His blond brows arched.

'It wasn't long after my dad left. We didn't have a lot
of money and Mum had lost her job cleaning one of the
local motels.' The memory flowed through her, singeing
her heart with the same scorching hurt that came every
time she remembered what life had been like back then.
'She picked up cleaning work at my school. The kids used
to tease me, so I told her that I wanted her to find another
job...but there aren't a lot of jobs in little beach towns.'

Why was she telling him this? She hadn't told *anyone*
this story—not because she was ashamed of having grown
up with no money, but because she'd been so horrible to

her mother. More than a decade and a half later, guilt over her behaviour lingered.

'She gave me a choice. Give up dancing and she would quit her job at the school—because that's what it was paying for. Otherwise, if I wanted to keep dancing, she had to keep working two jobs.' She squeezed her eyes shut for a moment. 'So I gave up dancing for a week.'

'You can't blame yourself that. How old were you? Ten? You were just a kid.'

'I don't think I've ever hurt her as much as I did then.' She shook her head, amazed that it felt as though a weight had been lifted from her shoulders. 'I wish I could take it back.'

'I'm sure she knows how you feel.'

'I hope so. She gave up so much for me to be able to continue dancing. She hardly ever came to my competitions or exams because she was always working, but she never complained.' She let out a hollow laugh. 'Not once.'

'She never gave up?'

'Nope.' She shook her head. 'Which means *I* can't give up.'

'Sounds like you got a lot of your tenacity from her.'

The tenderness in his voice sparked her insides, lighting up her whole body—as if he had a direct 'on' switch to her nervous system. Her hands were fluttering in her lap. The desire to reach out and touch him made her fingers tingle. If she didn't put some distance between them—and fast—she'd do something stupid.

'Thanks for the drink.'

She went to hop off her stool but Brodie's hand came down on her bare thigh. His fingers skimmed over her knee, touching the hem of the T-shirt. The touch was so light she could easily convince herself that she was imagining things. Despite her brain shouting out warnings, she didn't want this to be a dream.

'Is it wrong that I couldn't sleep because I was thinking about you?' he asked.

His bare torso was the only thing she could look at. Broad shoulders, the ripple of muscle at his abdomen, the V that dipped below his cotton pyjama bottoms. He would be naked underneath them. She could tell from the inadequate way the thin fabric concealed the length of him.

Her breath hitched, and the sudden flutter of her heart had nothing to do with panic. 'You were the one who wanted to go to sleep.'

His hand inched up, the tips of his fingers slipping under her hem of the T-shirt. Each millimetre his hand travelled stoked the fire low in her belly, stirred the tension in her centre. She pressed her thighs together, rocking gently against the stool in the hope that it would ease the need in her.

It didn't.

Nothing would ease the need except him. He was the only solution to her problem, the only cure for her ailments. In that moment she was raw. Exposing her past had opened up something within her—a cavernous hunger long buried by insecurities and fear. He'd shown her it was safe to be who she was, to open up and allow herself to be vulnerable. She wanted nothing more than to wipe away the old hurt with new pleasures. To erase the parts of herself that clung to bad memories, to be a new person.

'You were the one who wanted to figure out what loopholes I might use to make a move on you,' he said, eyes blackened with desire.

'Have you thought of any yet? Because I could use a loophole right about now.'

CHAPTER NINE

IT WAS ALL the invitation he needed. Willpower was a fragile thing, easily overridden by blazing attraction, pent-up sexual tension, and too many dirty dreams. Could he take her into his bed a second time, knowing that it wasn't going anywhere? Knowing that he wouldn't *let* it go anywhere because his life didn't have room for her?

'Brodie?'

A plump lower lip was being dragged through her teeth, and the desperation in her voice urged the increased thumping of his heart.

Even if he'd wanted to pretend he wasn't interested he didn't have the opportunity. She jumped down from her stool and stood between his legs, her hands finding the rigid muscles in his thighs, brushing the aching hardness of his erection.

'We're friends.' He pushed off his stool and moved into the kitchen, opening the freezer door and pretending to look for something.

'Friends who have the hots for each other.' She echoed his words with a cheeky smile.

The cold of the freezer wasn't making him any less hard or any less horny. In fact it had only drawn his eyes to a chilled bottle of vodka. He wrapped his hand around the neck, savouring the ice-cold glass against his heated palm. A cold shower would have been better, but getting naked might prove dangerous.

'Tell you what,' she said, reaching past him and grabbing the bottle out of his hand. 'If you can drink a shot of this off me and still not want to sleep with me, I'll let you go back to bed.'

He slammed the freezer door shut and turned, resting his back against it. 'You'll *let* me?'

'Yes.' She unscrewed the bottle. 'I'll let you. And I won't mention it in the morning—or ever again.'

'Why are you suddenly trying to seduce me with body shots when before you were more concerned about setting up barriers?' He raked a hand through his hair and tried not to think about how naked she was under his T-shirt.

'Why the psychoanalysis?' She raised a brow. 'Can't a girl change her mind?'

'I have a rule about sleeping with my friends.'

'What happened to that rule last night?' She smirked. 'You didn't seem to be too worried about rules then. Or are you afraid that you won't be able to say no after your little drink?'

She knew how to fire up his competitive streak—and she *did* have a point. He hadn't been all that worried about his rule last night. But the rule existed for a reason. Sleeping with her would be messy in both the best and worst ways. It would mean dealing with the awkward aftermath and potentially losing their friendship if things went pearshaped. He'd made an exception for Chantal because he'd wanted to get her out of his system, but now he was caught between taking the safe route and taking what he wanted.

That backfired, didn't it? Man up—do the shot and then go to bed.

'Fine.' He grabbed the bottle from her grip and located a shot glass.

As he turned around Chantal was slowly peeling off his

T-shirt. The white lace scrap covering her sex was revealed first, then a flat bronzed plane of stomach, two perfectly formed breasts, collarbones and a long mane of dark hair as she whipped the T-shirt off. He'd need a drink now. His tongue felt dry and heavy in his mouth.

'Ready?' She hoisted herself onto the bench.

'You still have to tell me why the sudden change of heart.' With a shaking hand he poured vodka into the shot glass.

'Maybe I realised that I should be grateful for the things I have, no matter how tough it is right now.' She lay back and stared intently at a spot on the roof, lower lip between her teeth.

He'd got to her with the story about his sister. Though he was hoping she'd apply it more to cutting herself some slack and persisting with her dance career—not to mention leaving that trashy bar—rather than to jumping back into bed with him.

'And you're grateful for having sex with me?'

'I'm grateful for orgasms.' Her head tilted so she could look at him. 'It's been a long time since I let myself have any fun.'

'It *is* fun, isn't it?' He stepped closer, smoothing a hand over her stomach. 'Just a bit of fun—nothing more.'

He poured the vodka into her belly button, the excess liquid spilling out onto her stomach. She let out a sharp cry at the coldness but he dropped his head and sucked, lashing his tongue across her belly and catching the liquid before it spilled onto the bench. It burned for a second, and then a smooth warmth spread through him.

The alcohol mingled with the taste of her warm skin. He ran his tongue down to the edge of her underwear, watching the slick trail he left behind. Her fingers thrust into his hair as he snapped at the waistband with his teeth, a low groan rumbling from deep inside her. He should have pulled away then, but the vodka felt good. It softened his edges, warmed his limbs. It made it easier to forget that sleeping with her was a bad idea.

A tasty, satisfying, *perfect* bad idea.

'Don't worry—I don't expect anything.' Her voice had become rough, husky. 'A bit of fun is exactly what I need. No strings, no obligation.'

'So you're not going to fall for me?'

The scratch of her lace underwear against his tongue sent a shiver through him. He pressed his lips to the peak of her sex and was rewarded with a gasp and the sharp bite of her nails against his scalp.

'You wish.'

Smooth skin beckoned to him. Hooking a finger beneath the waistband, he peeled her underwear down to mid-thigh, trapping her legs and preventing them from opening. His lips found the bare smooth skin of her centre, pressing down with agonising slowness. A quick swipe of his tongue had her hips bucking against him.

'This is cruel…and unusual.' Her hands dug deeper into his hair, wrenching his head up. 'I can't move properly.'

'Anticipation, Chantal. Just go with it.'

He grabbed her wrist and put her hand down by her hip, holding on so she couldn't move. His other hand teased her, his thumb rubbing against the sensitive bud of her clitoris in slow, circular movements. His tongue followed, parting her so he could claim her most sensitive spot between his lips. Her movement was restricted by the underwear holding her prisoner and she writhed against him in unfulfilled need.

'Please…' she panted. Her eyes had rolled back; her mouth was slack with pleasure. Her hair trailed over the side of the bench, brushing against the kitchen cupboards as she moved.

The sight of her laid out like an extravagant dessert

was almost enough to send him over. He wanted to taste every inch of her, keep her begging while he feasted. He released her from her lacy bindings and his fingers found her hot and wet. His mouth came up, capturing a bronzed nipple as she squirmed, grinding again his hand until her cries peaked.

She shouted his name over and over, until the syllables jumbled together into an incoherent decree of passion and release. Shock waves ran through her and he withdrew his hand slowly, gently. His mouth found hers, his tongue parting her lips and bringing her back to the moment.

'Still think I'm cruel?' he murmured against her mouth, sliding a hand beneath her neck to lift her into a sitting position.

She faced him, wrapping her legs around his waist. Heat enveloped him as her hand slid down the front of his pants and stroked his erection. She caressed him—long, slow movements designed to make him want something out of reach.

'I think you've got magic hands,' he said.

Hair tickled his chest as she rested her head against him, still touching him. He pressed into her hand, gasping at the sharp flare of pleasure that forced his eyes shut.

'Brodie?'

Olive eyes met his, the black of her pupils wide. Her tongue swiped along his lower lip, the taste of her tempting him.

'I want you inside me. Now.'

Her hands tugged down his pants, exposing him to the warmth of her thighs. He lifted her from the bench and carried her to the bedroom. They landed on the bed, her body pinned beneath his, and he reached out to his drawer and withdrew a condom. Sheathing himself, he plunged into her. His mouth slanted over hers, hot, demanding. He savoured her heat and tightness until she couldn't hold on.

Her muscles clenched around him—thighs around his waist, arms around his neck. He couldn't hold back, couldn't stop the desire to drown in her warm skin and open mouth. Burying his face against her hair, he brought her close to the edge again. She shook, holding on as if she were about to fly away.

'Let go,' he whispered. 'Just let go.'

And she did. Crying, shaking, gasping. Her orgasm ripped through her with an intensity that brought on his own release within seconds. He rode her slowly, until the waves of pleasure subsided.

The realisation that she wasn't in her own bed came swiftly when morning broke. Sunlight filtered into the room—Brodie's room—and the ache between her thighs confirmed that she hadn't imagined those naughty images of them in his kitchen. It wasn't a dream—it was the mind-bending truth.

Brodie was like peanut butter ice cream with extra fudge. Decadent, tasty, hard to say no to. But, like all delicious things, he wasn't the best choice she could have made. What she needed was a steady diet of apples and focus—not ice cream and orgasms.

'Morning,' he murmured against the back of her neck.

One arm was slung over her mid-section, turned slightly to expose the edge of his anchor tattoo. She traced the outline with her fingertip. Something firm dug into her lower back. She moved under the guise of stretching her back, smiling when he groaned and pressed against her.

'Don't start what you can't finish.'

She chuckled. 'You're insatiable.'

'Says you, Miss Body Shot. I was perfectly happy sleeping on my own last night.'

'Liar.' She rolled over, catching his stubble-coated jaw with her cupped hand.

He didn't hesitate to kiss her, his tongue delving and tangling with hers. A hand found her breast, fingers tugging and teasing her nipple until she gave in and let him roll on top of her.

'Weren't we supposed to be going for a run this morning?' she asked, blinking her eyes at him with faux innocence.

'I know a few other things we can do that will burn calories.'

Apples, not ice cream.

'Worried you won't be able to keep up?'

'Ha!' He grinned. 'Like I said before, don't start what you can't finish.'

'Oh, I can finish it.' She tipped her chin up at him, giving his chest a playful shove. 'Loser makes breakfast.'

'You're on.'

Chantal regretted making the challenge a few ks into the run, when it became clear that Brodie was much better at running than she was. He jogged effortlessly alongside her, breaking into a sprint every so often to prove he could. The Newcastle coast blurred past in a haze of blue skies, bluer waters and pale sand. How was it possible to be in such a beautiful place and not be able to enjoy the scenery?

'Can we take a break?' Chantal slowed to a walk and fanned her face.

'Conceding defeat already?' He jogged on the spot, a victorious grin on his face. 'You know that means you'll be making my scrambled eggs when we get back?'

'Fine. You win.' She waved him away as she took a long swig from her water bottle. 'Looks like dancing fitness doesn't translate to running fitness.'

'No need to make excuses,' he teased, and she elbowed him.

'No need to be a smug winner.'

He reached for her water bottle, tipping it to his lips and

gulping the liquid down. Muscles worked in his neck. It was hard not to stare at how he made the most regular of actions seem inherently male.

'It's not often I get one over you, so let me have my moment. Besides, I've got a long way to go if I'm going to run a half marathon.'

Her brows furrowed. 'You're training for a marathon?'

'*Half* marathon,' he corrected.

'How far is that?'

'Just over twenty-one k.'

'Funny how you didn't tell me that when you let me challenge you to a run.' She narrowed her eyes at him. 'Cheater.'

A booming laugh erupted, startling a woman jogging past with her small dog. 'That's not cheating.'

'Why on earth do you want to run that far?'

He shrugged. 'To see if I can do it. A buddy challenged me, and you know how I am with challenges.'

'It just seems…' She took in the gleam of his tanned skin, the T-shirt that hugged his full biceps, the golden hair on his athletic legs. 'Out of character.'

'Why? Because I don't have the discipline to be a runner?' A bitter tone tainted the words.

'No, I meant because you're more of a water sports kinda guy.' She cocked her head, studying him. 'Windsurfing, sailing boats, water-skiing…that kind of thing.'

'Oh.' A smile tugged at the corner of his lips.

'I always wondered if you were half dolphin, since you spend so much time in the water.'

'Wouldn't that make me a mermaid?'

'Mer*man*,' Chantal corrected, gesturing with her water bottle.

'That's not manly.' He crossed his arms. 'What about half shark?'

'Whatever floats your boat, Mr Cheese.'

Strong hands grabbed her arms and hauled her to him. His mouth came down near her ear. Hot breath sent goose-bumps skittering across her skin.

'Looks like you finally fell for my cheesy lines after all.'

Uneasy waves rocked her stomach. She'd certainly fallen for something. Her attraction to Brodie had always been physical...at least that was what she'd told herself. She was attracted to him *in spite* of his joker, take-nothing-seriously personality. At least it had *used* to be in spite of that...

Now she was the one convincing him to pour vodka on her, challenging him to a competition, teasing him about being a merman. This wasn't *her*. She was never this... relaxed.

'I haven't fallen for anything, Brodie. You're just good in bed.'

'Just sex.' His eyes avoided hers and he bent to inspect his shoelaces. 'That's all I was aiming for.'

An awkward silence settled over them. Could the exchange have felt as hollow to him as it did to her? Could he sense the fear in her voice as she tried her hardest to pull a barrier up between them?

'Let's head back,' he said, turning in the direction from which they'd come. 'I'm ready for my winner's breakfast.'

The tinkling of cutlery mingled with the rush of waves on the shoreline below. Tea light candles flickered in the gentle ocean breeze, and the smell of sea air mixed with the mouth-watering smells of steak and freshly cooked seafood.

'What's up?' Scott took a swig of his beer. 'You seem tense.'

Brodie had almost forgotten that Scott and Kate had agreed to make the trek up to Newcastle for a drink that night, at one of the beach hotels run by Brodie's friend.

Once Kate had caught wind that Chantal was staying on the boat she'd insisted they make it a double date of sorts. Having Chantal there meant he couldn't forget their run earlier that day—couldn't stop her comment swirling around in his head, kicking up all the memories and feelings he'd buried long ago.

I haven't fallen for you, Brodie. You're just good in bed.

In no possible situation should that have upset him… but he was off-kilter. Agitation flowed through him like a disruptive current, causing him to drum his fingers at the edge of the table where the group sat. Since when was being good in bed a *bad* thing?

'Maybe all this water is turning your brain to sludge.' Scott gestured towards Brodie's tall glass of mineral water. 'Why don't you have a beer?'

'The race is next week and I've reached my quota of indulgence.' He put on a fake smile and hoped that Scott had consumed enough beers not to look too hard. 'I'm winning that bet.'

The girls had gone to the bar for more refreshments. They stood side by side, giggling and chatting animatedly. Chantal's short black skirt skimmed the backs of her thighs, leaving miles of long tanned legs gleaming in the golden early-evening light. Her shoulders were barely contained in a flowing white top with small gold flowers. A small tug would be all it would take to free her, to expose her breasts to his mouth.

Brodie watched as they fended off an enthusiastic approach from a group of guys who appeared to be on a bucks' night.

'Maybe I should see if the girls need a hand,' Brodie said, frowning.

'She's got to you again, hasn't she?'

'Huh?'

Scott laughed, slapping him hard on the back. 'Oh, man, I didn't realise how bad it was. You get this look on your face when she's around—don't know how I missed it back at the reef.'

'You're full of crap.'

'*You're* an open book.' Scott's fist landed hard on his bicep. 'And when it comes to Chantal—'

'It's just sex.' *Good* sex, according to Chantal, but *just* sex.

'Yeah, and a half marathon is *just* a run.' Scott narrowed his eyes, studying Brodie in that analytical way of his.

'You know me. I don't do relationships. Surf, sand, bikinis—that's what it's all about.'

'Maybe before.' Scott shrugged. 'Doesn't explain why you look like you're about to snap the table in two because some guys are talking to her.'

Brodie looked down. Sure enough, his white-knuckled grip on the table was a little unusual. 'Says you. I thought you were going to deck me that time I danced with Kate.'

'I thought I was too. And why was that, huh?' Scott chuckled. 'Anyway, I'm not letting you get away with changing the subject. You helped me and now it's my turn to help you.'

'I don't need help.' Brodie let go of the table and ran his palms down the front of his jeans.

'You don't want help, but you damn well need it.'

The girls arrived back at the table, champagne in hand, plus a beer for Scott and another mineral water for Brodie.

'How does it feel, being a teetotaller?' Kate asked, flipping her long red hair over one shoulder.

'It's temporary. I don't think I could handle it long-term.' Brodie twisted the cap on his bottle, waiting for the rush of bubbles to die down before removing it. 'But temporarily it's okay. I can handle temporary things.'

Scott kicked him under the table and rolled his eyes. Okay, so maybe subtlety wasn't his strong suit. Nervous energy coursed through him, making the words in his head stumble and trip over one another. Kate eyed him curiously and Chantal pretended to be deeply involved in something on her phone.

Brodie contemplated smoothing things over, but his own phone vibrated against the table. Home.

'Hello?'

'Hey, Brodie.' The voice of his youngest sister, Ellen, came through the line. Her voice was pinched—a sure-fire sign that she was about a hair's breadth away from flipping out about something.

'What's up, Ellie-pie?'

'It's Lydia, she's had a down day. She won't eat her dinner. Mum's at work, but she said I had to make sure Lydia eats.'

The words ran into one another, and the wobble in her voice twisted like a knife in his stomach.

'Where are the twins?'

Sniffle. 'Jenny's at a party and Adriana hasn't come home from uni.'

'Put Lydia on the phone. I'll get her to eat.'

Within moments he'd convinced his sister to have at least a salad, even if she didn't want a full meal. It was hard for all of them to look after Lydia on her down days. There were times when she point-blank refused food and water for hours on end…sometimes days. He remembered a particularly bad patch when she'd ended up so dehydrated he'd had to rush her to the emergency ward. All she'd wanted was her dad—but of course they hadn't been able to get hold of him. Typical.

Perhaps he should sail home early. It was hard for him to be away. Normally he spent more time in the office running his business than on a boat. This was the longest he'd been away for some time. His stomach curled.

He hung up the phone, receiving a text almost immediately from Ellen with THANK YOU! xx in big capital letters. He loved his sisters more than anything, and right now he felt as if he was being a terrible big brother by taking time off for himself.

'Family emergency sorted,' he said, forcing a jovial tone as he returned to the table.

Chantal sipped her champagne, watching him quietly. 'Everything okay?'

'Fine.'

He looked out to the picture-perfect view of the beach slowly being drowned in darkness. Vulnerability wasn't something he did well—he didn't want her to see that he was anything but his usual cool, calm self. 'Just sex' didn't involve feelings or spilling your guts about family stuff... no more than he had already, anyway. In his defence, that had been to comfort her—not because he'd needed to get it off his chest.

'I should probably head off,' Chantal said, downing the rest of her drink and reaching out to give Kate a friendly hug. 'Thanks for the company.'

'Are you still dancing at the bar?' Scott asked, looking from her to Brodie and back again.

'Yep—I still need to make a living, don't I?' She seemed more comfortable about it than she had previously, there was light at the end of the tunnel. Her contract would run out eventually, and Brodie would make sure she didn't sign on for more work there.

'Don't let the creeps get you down,' Kate said.

'Creeps?' Brodie asked, his protective sensors going off.

'It's nothing.' Chantal shot Kate a look. 'You've seen the place. The clientele isn't exactly the picture of genteel politeness.'

'I'll meet you out the front when you finish,' Brodie said.

Chantal shook her head, shooting him a warning look as if to remind him of their argument last night. 'I'll be fine.'

'I'll meet you out the front.'

CHAPTER TEN

THOUGH SUMMER HAD drawn to a close a few weeks back, the air still hung heavy with humidity. Brodie stood by the railing outside the bar, waiting for Chantal to appear. He'd spent a good five minutes deciding whether or not to go in, but the temptation of hauling her off the stage had been too much to bear, and he didn't want to show her he was having doubts about his feelings towards the temporary nature of their arrangement.

Instead he waited outside, fending off requests for cigarettes, wishing that somehow Chantal had wriggled her way out of the contract. He wasted the time away by texting Ellen, hoping that she didn't hold his absence against him.

'I'm with someone.'

Chantal's voice caught him by surprise. He whipped around and saw her backing away from a big guy whose tank top said 'Team Bogan'. The guy looked at Brodie, sizing him up.

'See.' Chantal gestured to Brodie. 'This is my boyfriend—Axl.'

Brodie raised a brow. *Axl...really?* The guy lumbered away, distracted by a group of girls who didn't appear to have boyfriends waiting for them. Chantal used the opportunity to jog over to him, and sling her arm around his waist.

'Axl was the best you could do?' He shook his head. 'Never picked you for a Guns N' Roses fan.'

'Sorry.' She laughed, holding on to him as they made their way out of the bar's parking lot. 'The band was playing one of their songs as I was walking out. Mum used to listen to them all the time when I was young.'

'Better than the music *I* listened to growing up. Mum was a huge country fan—I hated it.'

Stars winked at them from the inky sky. Away from the hustle and bustle of Sydney the darkness wasn't diluted by the glow from skyscrapers and headlights. It reminded him of home—of the outdoorsy beauty of Queensland he'd grown to love after returning home from Weeping Reef.

'Have you talked to the guy who runs the bar about skipping out early?'

Chantal shook her head. 'No, and I haven't heard back about my audition yet, so I'm not giving up a paying job if there isn't something else to go to.'

'I'll lend you some money.'

'Over my dead body.' She tucked close against him as they walked, melting into him though her tone still revealed a touch of hesitation. 'It's kind of you to offer but I don't take loans—especially when I'm unsure how long it will take me to pay it back.'

'I know you're good for it.'

'Doesn't matter. I'll finish out this contract, see where I am, and figure out my next move.'

'Why are you so against asking for help?' he asked drily.

'I don't need charity.'

They walked through the yacht club and down to where his boat was docked. On board, they sat on the cosy leather-lined seat that curved around the deck. Chantal found a spot next to him, sitting with her head and shoulders resting against his chest. He draped his arm over her and skimmed his fingers along her stomach. It was frighteningly intimate and comfortable. *Familiar.*

'Haven't you heard the saying *Many hands make light work*?'

'Some of those hands get burned,' she said. 'I prefer doing things on my own. That's how it was growing up and I like my independence. Nothing wrong with that.'

'There's a difference between being independent and being stubborn to the point of self-detriment.'

'Asking for help hasn't ever got me anywhere to date. I trust the wrong people.'

'Do you think it's wrong to trust *me*?'

'I trust you as much as I'll ever trust anyone, but I'm still my own person. I do my own thing. That's why this isn't anything but two friends enjoying one another while it lasts.'

'Right.'

Raucous laughter floated on the breeze from a neighbouring boat. Chantal shifted against him, stroking his knuckles with her fingertips. It was a light touch, casual in its intimacy, and yet it flooded him with awareness. She was far from being out of his system. If anything, she'd burrowed herself deep without even trying. Without wanting to.

He couldn't be falling for her—not when he had a life and a family in Queensland to get back to and she had a dream to follow. Different worlds. Disconnected goals. They were wrong, wrong, *wrong.*

'Was everything really okay with your family today?'

A lump lodged in his throat. He didn't want to talk about that now—not when Chantal had made it clear that there was nothing real between them. But then he would be a hypocrite, wouldn't he? He couldn't berate her for not accepting help if she was willing to lend an ear and he didn't take it.

'Nothing major. Lydia was having a bad day. It happens every so often.' He rested his cheek against the top of her head, breathing in the scent of her faded flowery perfume and his coconut shampoo in her hair. 'Ellen was on her own, trying to deal with it. But she's only a kid herself—she needed help.'

'Ellen's the youngest, right?'

'Yeah. She's a good kid—they all are.' He swallowed against the lump in his throat. 'After the accident I was the one who looked after Lydia on a day-to-day basis. She listens to me. Whereas she's big sister to the other girls and yet feels like she can't do anything for them because of her paraplegia.'

'I bet she's grateful she had a big brother to take care of her.'

'She would have preferred to have Dad around. If that didn't make him come home nothing would. But the world didn't stop turning because she couldn't walk any more.' He sighed. 'Mum still had to bring home the bacon...the girls still had to get to school. I was the one who made sure she got to her appointments, made sure she did her exercises, helped her while she was still adjusting to her wheelchair.'

'That must have been tough.' Her hand curled into his and she snuggled farther down against him.

'It's hard to be away from them. Mum's always working, and Dad just...' He shook his head. 'The guy can barely manage a call on their birthdays. He'll disappear for months at a time, then show up out of the blue—usually because he needs money.'

'Where does he disappear to?'

'Who knows? He's a painter, the creative type, and he always seems to be off somewhere unreachable. Then he comes back, tries to make amends with Mum, and it goes well for a while until he asks for money.' Brodie cursed under his breath. 'Every time it happens he breaks the girls' hearts all over again…Mum's included.'

'And your mum's okay with him coming and going?'

'Not really—she did divorce him after all. But she puts her feelings for him before the girls.' Brodie laughed, the sound sharp and hollow. 'See? I told you my family wasn't picture perfect.'

'You don't have to be the parent. You do know that, right?'

But he did have to. Whether he liked it or not, *he* was responsible for looking after those girls. They relied on him—on his advice, on his life experience, on his care. Especially Lydia.

'You shouldn't feel guilty for taking a little time away,' she continued. 'You have to live your own life.'

'I *am* living my own life. I'm here, away from home, seeing my friends and spending time with you.'

'And you feel guilty as all hell, don't you?'

How could she read him like that? Silky hair brushed against his cheek. Her body was warm beneath his hands. How could she read him as though they were far more than friends who happened to be having very casual, very *temporary* sex?

'I have a sense of obligation to my family. What kind of person would I be if I didn't care?'

'I'm not saying you should stop caring. But there are varying levels—it's not all or nothing.' She pushed up, leaning out of his grip. 'Your dad is the one who needs to step up, here—he needs to commit to being a father.'

'Only when hell freezes over.'

'Have you ever talked to him about it?'

'No point.' He shook his head, tightening his grip on her.

In that moment she anchored him. Her questions were digging deep within him. Unlocking the emotion he'd tried to keep buried, allowing him to feel angry about his father.

To see that he'd been suppressing the hurt in order to be a rock for his sisters and his mother.

'Why? Do you think he deserves to shirk his responsibilities and have you pick up the pieces?'

'Of course not. But that doesn't mean I can let the girls go without.'

'No, but maybe you're in a position to try and push your father in the right direction.' She sighed. 'It might allow you to have a little more breathing room…to have the life that you want.'

'I have everything I want.' He gestured to the air. 'Got my boat, got my business. I don't want anything else.'

'Don't you?'

Pink flashed in front of his eyes as her tongue darted out to moisten her lips. She played with the ends of her hair, twirling the strands into a bun and then letting them spiral out around her shoulders.

'Is that all you want out of life?'

Wrapping her arms around herself, she shivered. Tiny ridges of goosebumps patterned her skin.

'Let's go inside. I don't want you getting sick.' He held out a hand and she took it without hesitation. 'Although maybe that would be a good way to get you out of that contract.'

'I'm not getting out of the contract.' She followed him to the kitchen, perching herself on a bar stool. 'I have a sense of obligation too, you know.'

'There's no doubt in my mind about *that*.'

'Why do you say it like that?'

'Your career before everything else. I have no doubt it's the most important thing in your life.'

'It is.' She tilted her head, watching him as he flicked on the coffee machine and pulled two cups from the cupboard. 'What's wrong with that?'

'I think your career is like my family. It's important... sometimes *too* important.'

'So you agree you need space from your family?' She grinned, swinging her legs.

'That's about as much agreement as you'll get from me.'

'You're so stubborn!'

'Ha! You should take a look in the mirror some time.'

The coffee machine hissed, steam billowing out of the nozzle in coils of white condensation. Black liquid ran into the cups, filling the air with a rich, roasted scent. He splashed milk into the first cup and handed it to Chantal. A grin spread over her lips and she blew on the steam, waiting for him to make the first move.

She wore the black skirt and white top she'd had on at drinks earlier that evening, but she'd ditched her shoes and jewellery. The gold threads in her top glinted under the light, making it seem as if she were glowing. It wasn't possible for her to look any more at home on the boat. He wondered what it would be like if they both tossed their obligations overboard and set sail. They had a boat—he had money. It could be the two of them. Together. Alone.

What is it about 'just sex' that you don't understand? She doesn't want you like that. You're just a body. A good lay.

'Are we going to keep dancing around like this or are you going to invite me to bed?'

She looked over the edge of her cup, the white porcelain barely hiding a cheeky smile. Her dark lashes fluttered and warm pink heat spread through her cheeks.

'Who's insatiable now?'

'Time's ticking. I want to enjoy this arrangement while I still can.'

It doesn't have to stop.

The words teetered on the edge of his tongue, willing his lips to open so they could pour out. But he couldn't

let them. Instead he walked around to the other side of
the breakfast bar and pulled her into his arms. His lips
crushed down on hers, seeking out the hot, open delight
of her mouth. The taste of fresh coffee mingled with the
honeyed sweetness of her.

'As you wish.'

Chantal woke to the sound of something vibrating, but
the haze of slumber refused to release her. Groggy, she
pushed herself into a sitting position, smiling as Brodie
reached for her in his sleep. Fingertips brushed her thigh
and he sighed, rolling over. Blond lashes threw feathered
shadows across his cheekbones and his full lips melted
into a gentle smile.

'You look so damn innocent,' she muttered, brushing a
lock of hair from his forehead. He didn't stir. 'But I know
better.'

The vibrating stopped and a loud ping signalled a text
message. Removing Brodie's hand from her leg, she set off
in search of her phone. It wasn't in the bedroom, though everything else of hers appeared to be—a lacy thong, matching bra, white and gold top, stretchy black skirt.

A laugh bubbled in her throat. Her clothes were strewn
so far around the room it looked almost staged. But her
aching limbs told the truth. They'd spent another amazing,
pulse-racing, heart-fluttering, boundary-breaking night
together.

Danger! Emotions approaching—full speed ahead.

It was just sex…wasn't it? She could stop any time. *Spoken like a true addict, Turner.*

Huffing, she stomped out to the kitchen. She didn't want
to be having thoughts like this. Brodie was a bit of fun.
A friend, yes, but nothing more. She couldn't let it be any
more…not when he'd already shown that he had the same

protective urges as her ex. No matter how well intentioned he was, she would *not* let herself be smothered again.

A flashing blue light caught her attention. One new voicemail. It had better not be the bar, pushing her to extend her contract. She'd officially be admitting defeat if she signed with them for another month. Then again, it wasn't as if she had other offers to consider, and this thing with Brodie had to come to an end. He'd be sailing home at some point, and she couldn't exactly stow away on his boat to avoid her problems. No, she needed an apartment, a job...a *better* job. She needed her independence back.

She tapped in her password and dialled the voicemail number. Her pulse shot up as the caller introduced himself as being from the Harbour Dance Company. They wanted her to come in for a chat about the company and a second audition. She hadn't flunked it!

By the time she hung up the phone Brodie had ambled into the kitchen. Cotton pyjama pants hung low on his hips. A trail of blond hair dipped below the waistband. He was a god—a tattooed, tanned, six-pack-adorned god.

'Good news?'

'How could you tell?' She put her phone back on the table and bounded over to him, throwing her arms around his neck.

'Your greetings are usually a little less enthusiastic than this,' he said, chuckling, and lifted her up so that her legs instinctively wrapped around his waist. 'Not to mention you were bouncing around so much I thought you'd been stung by a jellyfish.'

'They want a second audition!' She didn't have time to counter his teasing. She was so brimming with relief that she had to let it out.

'Why wouldn't they? You're pretty damn fantastic.' He backed her up against the breakfast bar, bringing his mouth down to hers. 'So that means we'll be heading back to Sydney?'

'*I'll* be heading back to Sydney. The audition isn't till the end of the week, and you're taking off then...aren't you?'

He hesitated, the jovial grin slipping from his lips as he avoided her eyes. 'Yeah, I'll be heading back soon.'

Had he been thinking about staying? For *her*? That was too confusing a thought to process, so she pushed a hand through his hair and kissed the tip of his nose.

'No more swanning around on yachts for me.'

'No.'

'All good things must come to an end, as they say.' She wished the cheerful tone of her voice mirrored her thoughts. But the words had as much substance as fairy floss.

What was wrong with her? This was *Brodie*. Beach bum. Playboy. Dreamer. Drifter. Flake.

Only he wasn't any of those things in reality. He was a successful businessman. A friend, a great cook, a family man, the best sex of her life. He was complex, layered, and not at all as she'd labelled him. Could it get any worse?

'We should celebrate,' he said, cutting through her thoughts by setting her down. 'How about I take you out on the water and we'll have lunch?'

'I have to be back for a shift tonight, but that would be great.'

'Of course,' he said, a hint of bitterness tainting his voice. 'How could I forget about the bar?'

'Don't start, Brodie...it won't go on forever.' She wasn't going to let that scummy bar ruin their celebration.

'Why don't you have a shower and I'll get us underway.'

'Are you trying to tell me I smell again?' She shoved him in the shoulder and his smile returned...almost.

'You smell like sex.'

'Gee, I wonder why.' She rolled her eyes and skipped off towards his room.

Some time later she emerged, having spent longer than usual showering. Water helped her to think. She often did her best problem-solving under the steady stream of a showerhead. Unfortunately today seemed to be an exception to the rule. No solution to her confusion about Brodie had materialised. She was *still* stuck between wanting to enjoy their time for what it was and the niggling feeling that perhaps it was more than she wanted to admit.

Dangerous thoughts... Remember what happened last time you gave in. Remember the smothering you didn't see coming until it was too late.

She wandered to the upper area of the boat, spotting Brodie standing at the wheel and looking as though he'd been born to do exactly that. Wind whipped through his hair, tossing the blond strands around his face as the boat moved. Blond stubble had thickened along his chiselled jaw, roughening his usually charming face into something sexier and more masculine.

'Clean as a whistle,' she announced, stepping down into the driving area of the boat. 'Can I join you at the wheel, Captain?'

'You may.'

'Wow, there are a lot of dials.' Chantal hadn't yet been up to this area of the boat. It looked like the cockpit of a plane.

'It's a fairly sophisticated piece of machinery. A slight step up from your average tugboat.' He winked.

'It feels like you're free up here, doesn't it?'

The sparkling blue of the ocean stretched for miles around, and the sun glinted off the waves like a scattering of tiny diamonds.

'That's what I love most about it. I can think out here.'

A shadow crossed over his face. 'It's like I have no problems at all.'

'Do you ever wonder what would happen if you sailed away and never came back?'

'Are you trying to tell me something?' His smile didn't ring true, the crinkle not quite reaching his eyes.

'I'm serious. Don't you think it would be great to go somewhere new? Start over?' That sounded like the most appealing idea she'd ever come up with. A fresh start. No baggage. A clean slate unmarked by her previous mistakes.

He shrugged. 'Yeah, I think about it for five seconds and then I realise what a stupid idea it is.'

'Why?'

'I couldn't leave my family.'

'Even if it was the thing you wanted to do most in the world?'

'It would take something pretty spectacular to make me seriously consider it. To date, nothing has come close.'

Chantal bit down on her lip, hating herself for allowing his words to sting. He was clearly drawing a line in the sand, defining their relationship...or lack thereof. She should be happy. He'd absolved her of any guilt about leaving him at the end of the week. But the words cut into her as real and painful as any blade.

'Doesn't hurt to fantasise,' she said wistfully.

'Sometimes it does.' He looked as though he were about to continue but his face changed suddenly. 'We're going to stop soon, but you might want to head portside in a minute.'

Chantal looked from left to right. 'Portside?'

'Sorry—boat-speak.' Brodie pointed to a section of the railing to his left. 'Stand over there.'

'You're not going to tip me overboard, are you?'

He smirked. 'Don't tempt me.'

Chantal went to the railing, holding on to the metal bar with both hands. 'What am I looking for?'

'You'll know it when you see it.'

Beautiful as the view was, she couldn't see anything much. They were clearly approaching land, but the fuzzy green mounds still looked a while away. She shielded her eyes with her hand, searching.

Something glimmered below the water—a shadow. Holy crap, was that a *shark*? Moments later the water broke, and a group of a dozen dolphins raced alongside the boat in a blur of grey and splashing blue.

'Did you see that?' Chantal shouted, leaning over the railing to watch the majestic creatures leap out of the water over and over.

They were so sleek. So fast and playful.

'Careful!' Brodie called out with a smile on his face. 'Don't fall in.'

'There's so many of them.'

She watched, mesmerised by the fluid way the dolphins moved—as if they were trying to keep up with the boat. Their smooth bodies sliced through the water, their beaked faces appearing to smile. They looked joyful. Uninhibited.

Chantal could feel the heat of Brodie's gaze on her, boring holes through the thin layer of her ankle-length dress. Right now his boat was the most amazing place in the world. How would she ever leave it at the end of the week?

CHAPTER ELEVEN

SEEING CHANTAL'S FACE when she discovered the dolphins had melted his insides. The sparkle in her eye, her squeak of delight, the way she'd hung over the railing as though she was desperate to jump into the water with them…it had been too much.

After the dolphins had moved on he'd steered them to Nelson Bay and moored in the spot normally reserved for one of the dolphin and whale-watching companies. After ordering Chantal off to the shower that morning he'd called in a favour with a friend who ran the mooring services for the Port Stephens region. Now they had a couple of hours for lunch before he'd need to leave the area and head back to Newcastle.

A spread of smoked salmon, bagels with cream cheese and fresh fruit covered the table that sat in front of the curved leather and wood seat. He'd also popped a bottle of champagne, which sat in a silver ice bucket.

'Did you know the dolphins were going to be there?' Chantal asked, taking a hearty bite out of a bagel. Cream cheese spilled forward, coating her upper lip, and her pink tongue darted out to capture it.

He remembered her obsession with bagels back from when they were at Weeping Reef together. Despite being slim as a rail, she'd devoured the doughy delights every morning for breakfast. Always with cream cheese. God, he had to stop looking at her mouth. She dived in for another bite, her eyes fluttering shut as she savoured the flavour.

'You never know for sure. But there is a group of dolphins who live in the area, so it's common to see them.' He took a swig of his water.

'They live here?'

'Not specifically in Nelson Bay, but in the general Port Stephens area. It's a big pod too—about eighty dolphins, I think.'

'Wow.' She sighed. 'They're so beautiful. I've always wanted to do one of those swim-with-the-dolphins things.'

'They're a lot of fun. The bottlenecks especially—they're very playful.'

Her eyes widened. 'You've done it? I'm so jealous.'

'Yeah.' Brodie nodded, a memory flickering. 'We did it as kids once…me and Lydia. Before her accident.'

For a moment he wondered if she would dig further, ask about Lydia's accident. Instead she said, 'What do they feel like?'

'They're smooth—kind of rubbery.'

'What do they eat?'

He laughed, taken by her intense curiosity. 'Fish, squid…that kind of thing.'

Lying back on her chair, she kicked her legs out and crossed her ankles. A contented sigh escaped her lips. 'I'm so full. That salmon was amazing.'

'You're welcome.'

She turned her head, shielding her eyes with her hand. 'This is the best celebration I could have asked for… although it's not a done deal. I might flunk the next audition.'

'Always thinking positive—that's what I like about you,' he teased.

'Nothing wrong with being realistic.' She sighed. 'I'm

trying to protect myself, I guess. I don't want to be disappointed if I don't get it.'

'If they want a second audition then they obviously saw something they liked.'

'That's true.' She twirled a strand of hair around one finger.

'You're immensely talented—you know that, right?' He chewed on his own bagel, concentrating on the food so that he could hide the conflicting emotions doing battle within him.

'Let's just hope the Harbour Dance Company agree with you.' She paused. 'I've had fun staying on the boat.'

He'd hoped to hear *with you* emerge from her lips, but she stopped short. *Stop waiting to hear that she's fallen for you. She hasn't.*

'I've had *fun* too.'

He half-heartedly waggled his brows and she swatted at him, laughing.

'I don't just mean the sex, Brodie. I mean I've had fun… hanging out.'

'Hanging out? What are we? Teenagers?' he teased.

She shook her head. 'Way to make a girl feel awkward. Can't a friend give another friend a compliment?'

Friend. There it was again—the invisible barrier between them. He'd broken his rule by sleeping with her in the first place. Funny thing was, that rule had always been in place to preserve the friendship, so that when he rejected any serious advances the other person wouldn't get hurt. He'd never counted on it going the other way—not when he had his priorities sorted out and they certainly didn't include a serious relationship.

'I prefer my compliments to be of the physical variety.'

'You're not nearly as sleazy as you try to be,' she said.

'I'm not *trying* to be anything.' It came out way too defensive. Why didn't he just hold up a flag that said *Emotional sore point. Proceed with caution.*

'Yes, you are. You're hell-bent on being the casual, laid-back, cool-as-a-cucumber fun-time guy.'

'You seemed to believe I *was* that guy.'

'I didn't know you then.' Her olive eyes glowed in the bright afternoon light, the golden edges of her hair glinting like precious metal. 'But I do now.'

'You know what I want you to know.'

'No way.' Her lips pursed. 'You sailed a yacht out here to show me dolphins…you packed a champagne lunch for me. All because I got a second audition—not even a proper job. That's not a fun-time guy.'

'What is it, then?'

He was giving her a chance to be honest, to open up to him. But the shutters went down over her eyes and colour seeped into her cheeks. Her hands folded into a neat parcel in her lap. Shutdown mode enabled.

'You're a good person, Brodie. I wish we'd got to be real friends sooner.'

There was that F-word again. If he heard it come out of her mouth one more time he was going to throw something. Clearly he was going out of his mind. Girls didn't rattle him—that wasn't how he acted. On the scale of annoyance, girl problems ranked somewhere between lining up at the supermarket and typos. In other words it fell into the bundle of crap he didn't care about.

'We should probably head back.' He pushed up from his chair, feeling the burn of the afternoon sun on his legs. 'Don't want to make you late for work.'

'Yeah, that thorn in my side.' She sighed.

She followed him around as he prepared the boat to return to Newcastle. Her anxious energy irritated him—partially because he felt she had no reason to be anxious, and partially because it made him want to bundle her up and kiss her until she relaxed. The woman had an emotional stronghold over him that was both dangerous and stupid. He already had four women to take care of—five if he counted his mother. He didn't need a sixth.

'You don't need to pick me up from the bar tonight,' she said once they were back at the helm, with the boat cruising out of the marina.

'I'll be there.' No way he'd let her walk back to the boat on her own.

'I can stay at the accommodation, if you like.'

'You're welcome to stay on the boat until I have to sail back. That hasn't changed.'

He didn't look at her, but her nervousness permeated the air. She knew he was angry with her. He had to keep his emotions in check.

'I want you to stay.'

'Okay.' She put her hand over his. 'Thanks.'

Don't grab her hand...don't grab her hand. 'No worries.'

'I'll be happy when I finish up at the bar. It's certainly been a learning experience.' She let out a small laugh. 'Although the crowd is a bit rough for my liking.'

'A *bit*?' He stole a glance at her and regretted it immediately. Make-up-free, hair flowing, she looked young and vulnerable. *You're weak, Mitchell, absolutely weak.*

'Okay, a lot. It wouldn't be so bad if the guys weren't so handsy.'

'What do you mean, *handsy*?'

'You know—some guys seem to think by buying a few drinks they can have free handling of the dancers.' She rolled her eyes. 'Pigs.'

White-hot rage brewed in his stomach. 'Dammit, Chantal. Why didn't you tell me?'

'Because it's not your problem—it's *mine*.' She spoke

calmly, but she crossed her arms and stepped backwards. 'Besides, last time you came into the bar you flipped out.'

'Of course I did!' He fought to wrangle the frustration and anger warring inside him. 'It's like you refuse to look after yourself just to prove a point.'

'I'm not trying to prove a point.' She gritted her teeth. 'Anyway, I had a word with them and told them to back off.'

'Jeez, you had *a word* with them? I'm sure that will make *all* the difference.' He shook his head, gritting his teeth at the thought of these grubby morons touching her. 'You need to tell me these things.'

'I don't *need* to tell you anything.' Her eyes flashed like two green flames. Her lips were pressed into a flat line and her breath came in short, irritated stutters. 'It's not your job to protect me.'

'What if they attacked you? What if you stayed at the accommodation and they followed you?' Nausea rocked his stomach. If anything ever happened to her...

'You're not my knight in shining armour, Brodie.' She spoke through gritted teeth, her hands balled by her sides. 'I can look after myself. Don't you get that?'

'All I see is someone who's too damn stubborn to ask for help.'

She folded her arms across her chest. The air pulsed around her as she narrowed her eyes at him. 'Independence is important to me.'

'At the cost of intelligence, it seems.'

'Oh, that's rich coming from you.'

'What the hell is *that* supposed to mean?' His blood boiled. He couldn't remember the last time he'd felt this... this *everything*. Emotions collided inside him, strong and flying at full speed.

'You won't live your life because you think it's your job to take care of every tiny thing for your family. You live in guilt because your father left but you won't even confront him about it. You're scared.'

'I'm not scared.'

'Yes, you *are*.' She jabbed a finger at him.

With her composure out of the window, Chantal let frustration and anger flow out of her unchecked.

'You won't let yourself feel anything for anyone outside your family.'

'Oh, and that's as bad as dancing at some skanky bar where you're not safe?' He shook his head. 'Yeah—real smart.'

'Dancing at that bar might seem stupid to you, but I need to make it on my own. I will *not* let someone else tell me what to do.' *Least of all someone who's supposed to be a 'no-strings tension-reliever'.*

'Who would try, Chantal? It's clear you won't listen to anyone else. You're so goddamn bull-headed.'

'Try looking in a mirror some time.'

In a rush, tears welled up with the force of a tidal wave. She had to get out. *Now!*

She flew down the stairs to the lower deck and didn't stop until she reached the kitchen. Her chest heaved, and she was dragging in each breath as though it resisted her with the force of an army. Cheeks burning, she felt the toxic warmth seeping down her neck and closing around her windpipe. She would *not* have a meltdown in front of him…not again.

The smooth marble bench was cool against her palms. Was he coming after her? *And who would sail the boat then? Idiot. Of course he's not coming after you.*

Twisting the kitchen tap with a shaking hand, she bent down to splash some water onto her face before filling a glass. Brodie's yacht had made her feel free when they'd sailed out of Newcastle that morning, but now…now it was as if the walls were closing in, crushing her, trapping her. She sipped, savouring the sensation of the cold liquid slipping down the back of her throat.

It was time to end things with Brodie. Chantal only ever got mad when she cared—she only ever lost her temper when something important was on the line. Even when Scott had left Weeping Reef she hadn't been angry…just guilty because it had all ended so suddenly and because of her inability to control herself. But she'd known deep down that Scott wasn't the man for her.

What did that say about Brodie and the way she was feeling now?

It's nothing. You had a great time with him, he provided you a nice place to stay, but now it's back to reality. No more messing around. You've got an audition to nail and a job to finish.

When they arrived back at Newcastle, Brodie didn't materialise on the lower deck. Chantal decided to avoid him by getting ready for her shift. Smoky shadow made her eyes look wide and alluring…a clear gloss played up her natural pout. The make-up gave her something to hide behind—another persona to help her get through the shift. The patrons of the bar saw only the image she wanted them to see, not the real her.

But Brodie had seen the real her. The scared girl with too-high expectations, a faltering career and a predisposition for panic attacks. Appealing stuff.

She bit down on her lip so hard the metallic tang of blood seeped onto her tongue. She couldn't afford to lose it now. A second audition with the Harbour Dance Company was a sign that she was heading in the right direction. A sign that perhaps everything would turn out the way she wanted it to. Or did she want more than that?

Her packed bags sat by the kitchen bench. How long had she been living out of a bag now? Too long. The rest of her belongings had been stashed at her mother's place, with a few extra essentials in the back of her car...if it was still in the bar's car park after all this time.

Oddly, she didn't care. Numbness had taken over the anger, smoothing down the edges of her emotions until she felt smooth and cold. Closed off...the way she preferred it.

Hoisting her bag over her shoulder, she slipped her feet into a pair of ballet flats and made her way onto the deck. Brodie's voice floated down from the upper level. He was talking to one of his sisters. A smile tugged at the corner of her lips. He had a certain tone for his sisters. Tough, and yet so full of love it made her heart ache. No one spoke to *her* like that—not even her mother.

Should she bid him a formal goodbye? Thank him for giving her a place to stay? Probably.

Instead she left, heading towards the bar with a hard knot rocking the pit of her stomach. *Keep going...one foot in front of the other. You need distance and so does he.*

She was doing the right thing. Staying would only be prolonging the inevitable breakdown of their relationship... whatever *that* was. She didn't know how to label it.

At some point he'd been a mere acquaintance, a secret crush. Then a friend. Then a friend with benefits... And now?

She squeezed her eyes shut, willing away the persistent thumping at the base of her skull. Dancing tonight would be tough, but she had to get through it. Light was most certainly at the end of the tunnel...so long as she kept Brodie out of her head.

'What's wrong, Brodes? You sound upset.' Lydia's voice floated through the phone, her concern twisting something sharp in his chest.

'I'm fine. It's the sound of relaxation. You know how long it's been since I took a holiday.'

'Yeah.' She laughed. 'You work too hard. You don't sound relaxed, though.'

'It's nothing.'

'Swear?'

He gritted his teeth. He'd never sworn on a lie to any one of his sisters and he wasn't about to start now. Perhaps if he didn't say anything she'd get bored and move on.

Lydia audibly smirked into the silence. 'What's her name?'

Damn. 'Her name doesn't matter.'

'Oh, come on. I don't get to do the boy thing much—how about a little vicarious living?'

She said it with such calm acceptance that he wanted to hang up the phone and get to her in any way possible. It wasn't fair that she didn't have a boyfriend simply because she couldn't walk. Although with the way Chantal had left him with a permanent imbalance perhaps it was a good thing.

'Her name is Chantal. She's a friend.'

'But you want more?'

'No, I don't. We agreed to keep things...friendly.' His brow creased. He was so *not* talking about this with his little sister.

'Do you love her?'

He hesitated. 'Of course not. I only have enough love for you guys... There's only so many women a guy can have in his life before he goes crazy.'

Lydia huffed and he could practically see her rolling her green eyes at him. 'You sound like Dad.'

There was a scary image. *I take care of you girls. I don't run away from my family when the whim takes me.*

'When was the last time you heard from Dad?'

'Touché,' Lydia said with a sigh. 'Why won't you be more than friends with Chantal?'

'We're not having this conversation, Lyds.'

'But—'

'Not. Having. This. Conversation.'

'OMG, you're *so* boring.'

He could hear the laughter in her voice and he thanked the heavens that she was having a better day today.

'I miss you.'

'I miss you too.' There was a slight pause on the other end of the line. 'I *would* like it if you got married one day.'

'Marriage isn't for me.' He shook his head, wondering how on earth he'd got roped into talking about relationships. 'Besides, you already have three sisters. You don't need another one.'

'But I might not get married and I'd like to be in a wedding. Why wouldn't you want to do it?'

Brodie swallowed the lump in his throat at the thought of all the things he took for granted. Why wouldn't he want to do it? Did he even *know* why? He told himself he didn't have room in his life for a relationship…but then again Chantal was different from his ex. She wasn't clingy or needy…quite the opposite! He'd sworn off long-term relationships because he knew he'd have to choose between them and his family. What if he'd been wrong? What if he *could* have both?

'You'll get married one day, Lyds. Not until I've checked the guy out, though. I'll need to make sure he's good enough for you.'

She laughed. 'You'd better not scare any potential husbands away.'

'Watch me.'

He hung up the phone and made a mental note to pop in and see Lydia as soon as he got back to Queensland. Perhaps he'd head back earlier than planned. It wasn't as if Chantal would be coming back to the boat after their argument. Without her he didn't have a reason to stay.

And where would *she* stay? A cold tremor ran the length

of his spine, settling in the pit of his stomach. The bar accommodation wasn't safe, he believed that even more now after what she'd told him today. He'd noted the single lock on the door while Chantal had packed her bags in front of him. That door needed at least another five locks before it became remotely secure. Not that the cheap wood door would withstand a well-aimed kick or the swing of a crowbar...

He dropped onto a sun lounger and put his head in his hands. How had it gone downhill so quickly? One minute they were out on the ocean, racing the dolphins, and the next they were yelling at one another. That was definitely not in the vein of their friends-with-benefits arrangement.

Maybe he could convince her to let him pay for a hotel room. There was a suitable beach resort down the road from the bar. It wasn't anything fancy, but it would be more secure than her room. He could give her a couple hundred bucks, make sure she was safe, and then leave her the hell alone.

Would she take the money from him? Not likely, but he had to try. The thought of anything happening to her filled him with cold, hard dread. He cared about her. She was a friend—of *course* he cared about her. That was normal, wasn't it?

He paced the length of the helm, his muscles tightening with each agitated step. Chantal valued her independence, that was for sure, but he had a right to step in if she was endangering herself. It was his duty...as a friend.

Jogging down the stairs to the lower deck, he went on the hunt for his wallet and phone. She was gone. Her bags were nowhere to be found and the bedroom was so tidy it was as if she'd never been there. But her presence hung in the air like perfume—sweet and memory-triggering. All the scraps of lace that had littered the floor after their various escapades had been removed, and the small pile of her jewellery on his bedside table had vanished too.

He snatched up his keys from the hook on his bedroom wall and jammed his wallet into the pocket of his shorts. She was going to be royally pissed at him trying to buy her a room, but he didn't care. Having her angry at him was better than any of the other alternatives. She'd have to deal with her anger. He wasn't going to take no for an answer.

CHAPTER TWELVE

BACKSTAGE AT THE BAR, Chantal tried to psych herself up for her performance. Truth was she wanted to run away with her tail between her legs and never come back. But she was a professional, a trooper. She never backed down.

Part of her wanted to get out there on that stage to prove a point. Brodie had treated her as if she was made of crystal—as if she'd break with the slightest knock. But she didn't break. She'd been through her share of tough times and she *always* kept going. No matter what.

'Don't look so down, honey.' A blonde girl in a sparkling corset pouted at her. 'If I had natural boobs like that *I* wouldn't be frowning.'

Chantal instinctively crossed her arms over her chest. 'I'm fine.'

'Is this your first time dancing?'

'No, not at all.' Did she look *that* nervous? Hell, what had Brodie done to her? She was wound up tighter than a spring.

'It'll be okay.' The blonde nodded and gave her shoulder a light pat. The woman's long silver nails glinted like tiny blades. 'Don't let the audience frighten you. They're big old lugs. Only here for the tits and the booze, never mind that fabulous dancing we all do.'

Chantal couldn't help but smile. The blonde gave a little shimmy, flicking the black fringe edging her corset back and forth. Her stockings stopped at mid-thigh, biting into her generous flesh, and she wore black gloves that stretched up over her elbows. She looked at ease with herself...with what she was doing.

'Just have fun. Leave your worries behind!' She sang the last few words, twirling and shaking her ample booty.

'I think I need to take a leaf out of your book,' Chantal said, smiling.

'Good idea. I always get a little tipsy before I dance.' The blonde leaned in conspiratorially. 'A couple of shots of tequila. *Boom!* Loose hips.'

Chantal practised her routine in the small space next to the mirror-lined bench. Sure, this wasn't the best place on earth, and it wasn't what she wanted for her career, but she could get through it. To hell with Brodie. She'd be fine and she didn't need anyone else to take care of her. She *would* stand on her own two feet.

The dancer before her gyrated on stage, using the pole to complete some gravity-defying tricks. The audience roared, catcalls and wolf-whistles drowning out all but the heavy thump of the bass. Then it was her turn. She peeked out as the other dancer finished up. The crowd had swelled considerably since she'd first arrived.

Then she spotted Brodie. He was unmistakable. Sitting in the front row, arms folded across his chest, biceps on display...most likely on purpose. The blood drained from her face and her confidence followed it until the world tilted beneath her feet.

What the hell was he doing here?

Her music started but her feet were rooted to the ground. Someone shoved her in the back and she stumbled a little as she walked on stage. The audience didn't seem to notice. They cheered and hooted as she swung her hips, pivoting on one foot with a dainty flick of her hair. Under Brodie's intense stare she might as well have been naked. His eyes seemed to penetrate her, seeing all that she wanted to conceal.

He didn't smile, and his eyes certainly didn't sparkle the way they normally did. Had *she* turned him into this hardened lump? Where was the free and easy Brodie she'd fallen for?

And had she really fallen for him…even after everything that had happened today?

Confusion made her head fuzzy, the thoughts clashing in her mind. It was nothing—just a fling. She shook her head, trying to dislodge the warring emotions.

The steps of her choreography eluded her, but she had to keep going. Close to the edge of the stage she felt a hand brush by her—not Brodie's. A portly man with a heavy beard and mean eyes leered up at her. Her skin crawled and she backed away, still clinging to her stage presence though she was sure she'd never danced so terribly in all her life.

Brodie had leant over to the man, his face red and indecipherable words falling from his lips. For a moment she would have sworn a fight would break out, but it didn't. The bass thumped at odd intervals with the pounding in her head…everything unravelled. Fast.

She rushed off stage before her time was up, ducking her head at the curious stares of the other dancers and ignoring the cutting remarks from the manager as she scuffed her feet into her sneakers and grabbed her keys.

Outside the change room people swarmed the crowded space of the bar, the smell of beer and body odour making the air heavy and thick. Swallowing against the nausea, she pushed through, swatting away invasive hands and avoiding lingering stares. If she didn't get outside… Well, it wouldn't be pretty.

Brodie had got up from his chair. Chantal spotted him in her peripheral vision but didn't stop. This was all his fault! He shouldn't have come here thinking he could distract her, making her look like an idiot in front of all these people. As much as she didn't care about their opinions, she was still dancing. Forgetting her choreography was *unforgivable*.

'Chantal!'

How could she have let herself fall for him? The way he'd acted tonight *proved* he was the wrong guy for her. He was just like her ex: over-protective…ready to smother her.

She headed towards the stairs, running down them as fast as she could while dodging two people kissing up against the wall. Downstairs a heavy metal band thrashed about on stage, the drummer's double kicks resonating through her, the beat reverberating right down to her bones.

She stumbled outside, tripping over a pair of feet in her desperation for escape. The cool air rushed into her mouth, was trapped where her throat was closing in. She gasped, sucking the air in greedily and forcing each breath down like a pill without water. How could she have forgotten her choreography? *How?* She balled her shaking hands, wishing she could crawl into a crack in the ground and disappear forever.

'Chantal!' Brodie's voice rang out in the car park, muted by the music from inside the bar. 'Wait—'

The deep rumble of a motorcycle raced past and drowned out the rest of his words. For a moment she kept walking, each purposeful step slamming into the ground. What would happen if she kept going? Tempting as it was, she couldn't quit—she couldn't. Not when things were turning around.

'I'm trying to protect you.' His voice carried on the night air.

Chantal whirled around, her body tense, like a snake about to strike. She locked her arms down by her sides. 'You distracted me up there. I forgot my steps because I couldn't concentrate on anything but whether or not you were going to start a fight.'

'I'm here to make sure you're safe—not to distract you.' His brows pulled down, a crease forming in his forehead. 'I only wanted to make sure you had somewhere safe to stay.'

'I'm not coming back to the boat.'

He shook his head. 'I was planning to pay for a hotel room for you. I'm thinking about your best interests.'

For some reason his words cut right through her chest, making her head pound and her stomach turn. Safety...protection...best interests. These were all words she'd heard before—the vocabulary of a control freak.

'Why don't you trust me, Chantal?'

'You told me I didn't *have* to trust you.' Her voice wobbled and she cringed. 'That was part of the deal.'

His eyes flashed; his mouth pulled into a grim line. 'I thought you'd change your mind.'

'I haven't.'

He raked a hand through his hair, the blond strands falling straight back into place over his eyes. He'd come straight from the boat, still wearing his shorts and boat shoes from their trip to Nelson Bay. The black ink of his anchor tattoo peeked out from the rolled-up sleeve of a crisp blue shirt. Damn him for looking so utterly delectable when she wanted nothing more than to throw her shoe at his head.

What had happened to the laid-back Brodie she knew? Did all guys turn into 'me Tarzan, you Jane' types as soon as you slept with them?

'Have you changed your mind about *anything*?' He stepped forward, folding his arms across his chest.

'Like whether or not I should finish my contract here?' She shrugged, hoping she looked as though she cared a lot less than she did. 'I'm a professional dancer. I can't quit.'

'That wasn't what I was talking about.'

'What *are* you talking about, then, Brodie? Because I sure as hell have no idea.'

His jaw twitched, and the muscles in his neck corded as he drew a long breath. 'What about your desire to do everything on your own?'

'That's how I *need* to do it.'

At least that was what she'd believed most of her life. But somehow she didn't feel so convinced any more. *Remember what happened when you got married... You trusted him and look how that turned out. Mum did it all on her own—you can too.*

'Why?' He took the last few steps towards her until there was no space between them and his hands gripped her shoulders. '*Why* do you think you need to do everything on your own?'

'Because it's safer that way.' She shut her eyes, wishing her brain would stop registering the scent of him and firing up all the parts she needed to stay quiet at the moment. 'I'm sick of being a charity case. I want to do something on my own that I can be proud of. I *need* it.'

'You can be independent without pushing away everyone who feels something for you.'

Blood rushed in her ears. The roaring made it hard to think straight. 'Are you trying to tell me *you* feel something for me?'

That was exactly what he was saying, wasn't it? He *did* have feelings for her. Why would he keep chasing her if he didn't?

'What if I do?'

'That would go against our agreement.' Her olive-green eyes were wide, like two shimmering moons, begging him not to continue.

If he admitted to caring about her and she rejected him what would happen next? He'd never see her again. The thought of a life without her seemed pointless. Colourless. Dull.

'We're supposed to be friends,' she whispered.

'We are.'

'That's all I have room for. I don't want a relationship right now. I want to get my career sorted. I've worked my whole life for this. I'm not stopping now.'

'You do know you can have more than one thing in life, don't you?' He couldn't help the words coming out with a derisive tone. How could she be so narrow-minded?

Hypocrite.

'Can you? I thought family was *your* one thing.'

She stepped backwards and he let her slip out of his grip.

'Someone told me I was too scared to invest in anyone outside my family. Maybe that person was right.'

'No. Family should come first for you.' Chantal shook her head. 'Go back to Queensland, Brodie. Go home.'

'Who's scared now?' He hated himself for the waver in his voice. She'd managed to do what no other woman ever had—she'd made him feel something. She'd made him want to stay.

'*I* am, Brodie. I'm scared.' She looked at him with a blank face. 'I'm scared for my career, so that's what I'm focusing on right now. Please don't follow me.'

With that she turned and left him standing in the middle of the parking lot. Her silhouette faded into the night and every nerve ending in his body fired, telling him to go after her. But she'd made it clear her life had no room for a relationship. No room for him.

If she wasn't going to let him in there was no point hanging around. He was stupid to have even tried. Of course she wanted nothing more from him. How had he fallen into that trap? *He* was supposed to walk away—it was what he always did.

'You're a goddamn idiot,' he muttered, unsure if he were talking to himself or to her.

By Friday, Brodie was ready to sail home. His travel bag was packed, but he hadn't been able to convince himself to go. Instead he'd headed back to Sydney, in the hope that a change of scenery could pull him out of his incredible funk.

The view from the boat should have cured any bad feelings he had, and the sunlight sparkling off the water and the girls in their tiny shorts and tank tops was his definition of nirvana. Not today, though.

Humid air clung to his sweat-drenched body. He'd hoped going for a run would allow him to burn off the agitated energy that had kept him awake the last few nights. It hadn't. Since then he'd called the office, video chatted with the family, and run until his legs trembled. *Now what?*

The shower beckoned. He stripped, hoping the rush of cool water against his sizzling skin might ease the confusing thoughts in his head. But the normally soothing sound of water against tiles gave him space to think...something he needed like a hole in the head.

He was officially broken.

A noise caught his attention. The vibration of his phone against the benchtop, sounding like insects buzzing. Who would be calling him? The guy who managed his office had already told him to butt out until his holiday was officially up. Apparently things were running like clockwork, and he'd told Brodie he sounded as if he hadn't had any rest at all.

Brodie rubbed his eyes and tilted his face up to the spray. Exhaustion weighed down his limbs. No wonder... He was pretty sure he'd seen each hour tick over on his clock last night.

What if Chantal was calling?

He wrenched at the taps, shutting off the water, and stepped out of the shower. He grabbed a towel and wrapped it around his waist, checking the ID flashing up on his phone. Of course it wasn't her. She'd made it damn clear there was nothing between them. That didn't stop the way his body sprang to action at the thought of her contacting him.

Pathetic.

'Hello?'

'Hey, man.' Scott's voice boomed over the line. 'Want to grab a drink?'

The last thing he wanted was to see Scott face to face. His friend would know in an instant that things had gone south. 'I'm actually having a little time out at the moment.'

'You're back in Queensland?'

'No, not yet.' He'd been so rattled by the encounter with Chantal that he'd hightailed it back up the coast to Sydney without telling *anyone*. Not even Scott.

'Everything okay?'

'Nothing major,' he lied, padding to his bedroom.

'Work problems?'

He paused, unsure how much he wanted to reveal. But Scott's pushing meant he knew something was up. 'Not exactly.'

A chuckle came down the line. 'Let me guess—it starts with C and ends with L.'

'Spelling was never my strong suit.' He tried to make light of Scott's words but it sounded hollow, even to him.

'What happened?'

'I don't know. One minute it was fine—*we* were fine— and the next...' He dropped down onto the bed and rubbed his temple with his free hand. 'It was supposed to be convenient. Fun.'

'Love is anything *but* convenient,' Scott said sagely.

'I didn't say I loved her.'

'Didn't need to. Why else would you be hiding out?'

Scott had a point. He'd run like a scared little kid, tail between his legs, all because she'd drawn the line at sex. In what universe would he be upset by *that*? It was guilt-free—for once *he* didn't have to be the bad guy.

'I don't know if I love her.'

'Are you feeling miserable?'

'Yes.'

'Miserable' was probably a few notches down from the aching in his chest that had appeared when he'd sailed out of Newcastle that morning.

'Confused?'

'Hell, yeah.'

'Lost?' Scott didn't bother waiting for an answer. 'That's what love feels like.'

'It blows.'

Scott laughed. 'It only blows before you sort things out. Then it's pretty bloody amazing. Kinda funny how the tables have turned.'

'I'm not laughing.'

He wanted to throw something—anything that might help him release some of the deadening weight in his limbs.

'So what's your plan of attack?'

'Plan?'

'To get Chantal back. Jeez—keep up, Brodie.'

And there was the rub. 'It's hard to get someone back if you didn't have them in the first place.'

'Did you tell her how you felt?' Scott sounded as though he were explaining something to a dumb animal for the tenth time.

'Well, no.'

'Did you even try?'

Brodie groaned inwardly, this was *way* out of his comfort zone. He was used to being the one giving advice—as he'd done with Scott not that long ago. Why couldn't he seem to sort out his own situation?

'I kind of went a little…caveman.'

'Wow—and you're wondering why she didn't give you anything?'

'She didn't want it. I could tell.' He remembered the look in her eyes, almost as if she was pleading with him to leave.

'She's got a thing about being independent—you can't change that.' Scott sighed. 'She needs her space.'

'I know.'

He rubbed a hand over his face. Of course she wanted to be her own person, but that didn't stop him wanting to protect her. Was it completely hopeless?

'How did I screw it up so bad?'

'Is she worth the pain?'

'Yes.'

The word slipped out before he'd even had time to weigh up possible answers. Uttering that one little word had released the tension from his neck and lifted the heaviness from his shoulders. Was it possible that he was in *love* with Chantal Turner?

'What should I do?'

'Aren't *you* supposed to be the lady whisperer?' Scott teased.

'I'm lost, man. She makes me question everything and I've got no clue what to do next.'

'What do you do when you wipe out?'

Brodie smiled—he could always count on Scott to put something in *his* terms. 'Are you trying to tell me I need to give it another go?'

'I'm not trying to tell you—I *am* telling you. I know Chantal is tough. You need to let her know how you feel— she's not great with ambiguity.'

'What do I say?'

'You'll figure it out. But I would start with an apology. There's no excuse for going caveman.'

Brodie put the phone down and stared at it long and hard. He would figure it out... But having Chantal meant sacrificing other things. To be with her he would need to be away from his family more. He couldn't expect her to drop her dreams of being a dancer and move to Queensland with him.

If this thing between him and Chantal was going to work then other things needed to change too.

He reached for the phone and sucked in a huge breath, dialling his father's number quickly, before he could change his mind.

CHAPTER THIRTEEN

HIGHWAY SCENERY BLURRED past as Sydney faded away in Chantal's rearview mirror. Her old car struggled to keep up with the speed limit, but she was moving…and that was all that mattered.

Last night she'd stood tall in the face of criticism from the bar manager, keeping her head high and knowing that she would make it through to the end of the contract like the professional she was. Knowing that, no matter how dire her situation, she was supporting herself.

Thoughts of Brodie were insistent, but she cranked up the music to drown them out.

After spending the morning at her audition for the Harbour Dance Company she'd gone looking for a cheap apartment to rent. Luck must have been on her side. A tiny one-bedroom place had been vacant for a few weeks and the owner was desperate to get someone in. As she'd signed the paperwork a call had come from the dance company, congratulating her on a successful audition.

Now she was on her way to visit her mother and collect all the boxes she'd stored there. Everything had turned out the way she'd wanted it to—once her bar contract was over it would all be perfect. So why didn't she have a sense of accomplishment and relief?

Brodie.

He'd been the only thing on her mind since she'd walked

away. It had barely been three days and already there was a gaping hole in her life where he'd inserted himself in their short time together. She missed his cheeky smile, the way his arms felt as they squeezed her against him, his lips. The unmanageable desire that materialised whenever he was around. How could she have let herself fall so hard? So quickly and so deeply?

Her childhood home came into view as Chantal rounded the corner at Beach Road, where blue water lined the quiet coast of Batemans Bay. *Home sweet home.*

The roads were empty. Most of the tourists from Canberra would have gone home by now. Work would be slow for her mum…the motels and self-contained units that dotted the shoreline wouldn't need extra cleaning services now that summer was over. Hopefully she still had a gig with the local high school to at least cover rent and bills. Though there would be little left over after the essentials were covered.

Chantal pulled into the parking bay of the apartment block and killed the engine. Stepping out of the car, she smiled at the way the number on their letterbox still hung at a funny angle and the squat garden gnome she'd given her mother one Christmas still guarded the steps up to their second-floor apartment.

The stairs were rickety beneath her feet, and the railing's paintwork peeled off in rough chunks. She was certain it had been white at one point—now it looked closer to the colour of pale custard. The doorbell trilled and footsteps immediately sounded from within the front room. Her mother appeared and ushered Chantal inside with brisk familiarity.

'You should have called. I would have put afternoon tea on.' Her mother enveloped her in a quick hug.

Frances Turner's affection was like everything else she did: quick, efficient and with minimal fuss. She'd never been overly demonstrative while Chantal was growing up, but age had softened her edges.

'No need,' Chantal said, smiling and waving her hand. 'I'm here to visit you—not to eat.'

It was more that she hadn't wanted her mother to feel obligated to go out and buy biscuits, or the fancy tea she liked to drink when Chantal came over. It was easy to see where her desire to keep up appearances had come from.

'Sit, sit…'

Frances gestured to the couch—a tattered floral two-seater that had yellowed with age. Chantal remembered using the back of it as a substitute *barre* while practising for her ballet exams.

'How are you?'

'I'm good.' She smiled brightly, pulling her lips up into a curve and hoping her mother didn't look too closely. 'I got a call this morning. I'm joining the Harbour Dance Company.'

Frances clapped her hands together. 'I *knew* you could do it, baby girl.'

'Thanks, Mum.'

'Why the sad face?' Frances studied her with olive-green eyes identical to hers. Nothing got past those eyes. 'What's going on?'

'Oh, it's nothing,' Chantal said, but she couldn't force the tremble from her voice. 'Boy problems.'

'Derek's not giving you trouble again, is he?' Her thin lips pulled into a flat line. Her mother had hated Derek from day one—something Chantal should have paid more attention to.

'No, Derek is long gone.' She rolled her eyes. 'I've been spending some time with an old friend. It got…confusing.'

'How so?' Frances motioned for Chantal to follow her into the kitchen.

Yellow floral linoleum covered the floor, matching the

painted yellow dining chairs and the small round dining table. The kitchen was her favourite part of the unit—it was kind of garish and dated, but it had the heart of a good home.

She traced her fingertip along the length of a photo on the wall. Chantal stood with her mother, wearing a jazz dance costume they'd stayed up till midnight sequinning the night before a competition. She had a gap-toothed grin and her mother looked exhausted. She didn't remember her mother looking that way at the time. All she'd cared about was the trophy clutched in her young hand.

Guilt scythed through her.

'He doesn't get me and I don't get him. We're different people.'

'But you liked him enough to spend time with him?' Frances twisted the tap, holding the kettle under the running water with her other hand.

'I did.' *I do...*

'And you think it's not good to be different?' Her mother threw her a look she'd seen a lot growing up. She called it the *Get off your high horse* look.

'It's not that. It's just...' How could she explain it? 'He wanted to do everything for me. And I'm capable of doing things myself. I *want* to do things myself. I don't need some knight in shining armour to rescue me.'

Her mother would be the one person who would understand. She'd stood on her own two feet since Chantal's father had walked out. She knew what it meant to be independent—what it meant to achieve things on your own.

'And that bothers you?'

'It does. It's like he can't understand that I need to fix my own problems.' She sighed. 'I want to be able to say that I made my way without any hand-outs.'

'Accepting help is not the same as accepting a handout, Chantal. There's no gold medal for struggling through life on your own.'

The kettle whistled, cutting into their conversation with a loud screech. Frances lifted it from the stove and poured the piping hot water into two mugs with pictures of cats all over them.

'I know that.'

'Don't you think I would have accepted some help if it was available when you were growing up?'

The question rattled Chantal. 'But you used to tell me that it was us against the world and we had to work hard.'

'I wanted you to be strong, baby girl. I wanted you to be tough.' She dropped the teabags into the bin and handed a mug to Chantal. 'Sometimes being strong means knowing when you can't do it on your own. Accepting help doesn't make you weak.'

They moved to the table, and Chantal was glad to be sitting on something solid. Her knees had turned to jelly, and her breath was escaping her lungs in a long whoosh. Her mother had tipped all her long-held beliefs on their head.

'I would have *killed* for someone to come along and offer a hand when you were younger.' Frances blew on the curling steam from the tea. 'Though I feel like I did a pretty good job with you, considering.'

A smile tugged at the corners of Chantal's lips. 'Would it be conceited if I agree?'

'Not at all.' Frances reached across the small table and patted the back of her hand.

'I've stuffed up, haven't I?'

Realisation flooded her, running across her nerves until her whole body was alight with the knowledge that she'd thrown away something important. Something special.

Brodie.

She didn't want to have him back in her life. She didn't want to love him.

But she did.

She'd known it was more than sex from the first time she'd woken up in his arms. But it hadn't been until she'd stood at the edge of his boat, with the freedom of the open waters dancing in her hair, looking down at the dolphins, that she'd realised how much he would do for her. That he wanted to show her what she was missing out on by being so narrow-minded.

And what had she done to return the favour? She'd picked a fight with him…refused to let him in. She'd told him to go. No matter how much time passed, she'd never forget the hurt written on his face when she'd told him not to come after her.

How could she possibly fix it?

'Nothing is irreversible, baby girl.'

Could she let herself believe that? Would she be able to handle the rejection if the damage was too much? Funny how a few weeks ago the thought of another dance company rejecting her had been her driving force. Now her victory seemed hollow without Brodie in her life. She loved dance—it was in her blood—but a world without him seemed…hopeless. Grey.

'I need to get my stuff. I've got an apartment in Sydney now.' Her voice was hollow, her movements stiff and jerky, as if she were being directed by puppet strings.

'Go to him, Chantal. The stuff can wait. *Things* can wait.' Frances stood and gave Chantal a gentle shove towards the front door. 'He might not.'

'I don't know how to get to him.' There were too many variables…too many things to deal with. What if he'd already left for Queensland?

'Find a way—you always do.'

Chantal surprised her mother by pulling her in for a big hug—a *real* hug. Planting a kiss on her cheek, she grabbed her bag and headed for the front door. Canberra airport was the closest airport that would allow her to fly to Brisbane, but it was a two-hour drive away. She didn't even know the name of his company.

Her sneakers hit the steps in quick succession and didn't slow as she raced towards her car.

'Call me when you find him!' Frances called out.

'I will.'

She slammed the door too hard in her haste, the sound ringing out like a shot. Was she *doing* this?

Chantal bit down on her lip and looked at her mobile phone in its holder on the inside of her windscreen. There was one person who could help her. She had no idea if his number was still the same, or if he would protect Brodie rather than talk to her. But she had to try.

As she paused for a red light Chantal tapped the screen and dialled a number.

'Hello?' Scott's voice echoed through the car.

'Scott, it's Chantal. I'm hoping you can help me...'

Brodie stood in the helm, staring blankly out at the harbour. The moored boats were lined up in tidy rows, the *Princess 56* blending into the Sydney scene better than it had in Newcastle. He couldn't be anywhere on the boat without remembering Chantal.

Was she back in the city by now? Doubt rooted him to the deck. Not because he didn't believe in his feelings for her, but because he had no idea if she would ever reciprocate. He couldn't remember a time when a girl had left him so strung out...except for the Weeping Reef situation with Chantal the first time around.

Chantal: two. Brodie: zero.

Giggling came from a couple walking past the boat—the sound of two people in love. He looked away, focusing on the dials in the cockpit. He knew he should sail home, but something had stopped him from preparing the yacht.

The beautiful views and the freedom of sailing felt wasted without Chantal. No matter how opulent the scenery, it was marked by her absence.

He turned his phone over in his hands. He could call her, invite her for a drink. Apologise for pushing too hard. Then what?

Those three little words hung over him like a dead weight. Three. Little. Words.

They changed everything. He'd never loved any woman before—he hadn't thought he had any love left over after his family had taken their share. But she seemed to pull emotion from him that he'd never even known existed. It had forced him to do things he'd never thought he could... like confront his father.

The *Princess 56* was waiting for him, ready and willing. It sat there patiently, needing him only to make a decision. He could either find out where Chantal was or he could sail home.

No, he wasn't going home without her.

Scott was right—he *had* to try again. He *had* to be sure there wasn't a chance for them. His attraction to her had always been more than he'd admitted. More than her gorgeous legs, her dancing, the sex. It was something so frighteningly intense and real that he'd been unable to process it until it was too late.

Brodie was about to pick up his phone to dial her number when it buzzed. Lydia's smiling face flashed up on the screen.

'Hey, Lyds.'

'Hey, Brodie.' There was hesitation in his sister's voice. 'So...Dad called.'

'He did?' Something lifted in Brodie's chest. His father had ended their call earlier with a promise to get in touch with the girls more often, though Brodie still had his doubts. 'What did he say?'

'He's coming to visit,' Lydia replied. 'Well, he *says* that, but we'll see.'

'Would you *like* him to visit?'

'Yeah, I guess.' She hesitated. 'It would be good to see him.'

He sincerely hoped his father lived up to his promise. He'd got a sense that his father's attitude had changed—there'd seemed to be something more receptive about him that had been lacking in the past. Something down in his gut told him that their conversation had been a shifting point for the older man—a reality check that his family needed him. That his daughters needed him.

Brodie could get by on his own, but he had plans to make Chantal a part of his life more permanently—and that meant he couldn't always play the role of pseudo father. The girls needed to know they could rely on their real father as well. Hopefully this was the beginning of all that.

Lydia caught his attention by launching into a new problem—something to do with Ellen and how she was trying to mother her, even though she was the youngest sibling. But Brodie was no longer listening.

A figure hovered nearby on the jetty. Long legs, long dark hair.

Chantal.

'Brodie, are you listening to me?'

Lydia's indignant tone brought his attention back to the call. 'Sorry, Lyds. I have to go.'

He stepped out onto the upper deck and tried to get a better look at the figure. Was it really her?

'But I need your *help*.' His sister sounded as though she were about to cry. 'That's *why* I called you.'

'I'll help you. But I need to do something for me first.'

She sniffled. 'What's more important than talking to your sister?'

He jogged over to the stairs, taking them as quickly as his legs would allow. 'Love.'

'Is this about that girl?' Lydia asked, her voice returning to normal.

'It is.'

'You *love* her?'

'I do, Lyds. I'm going to ask her if she loves me back.'

'Dibs on being the maid of honour,' Lydia said. 'Call me later. Tell me *everything*.'

'I promise.'

Brodie rushed to the jetty and looked around. Late afternoon had given way to early evening and the sun was lowering itself into the water along the horizon. Autumn had started weeks ago but it had only now taken on its first chill of the year, and the cool air prickled his exposed forearms.

People milled about, stopping to take photos of the yachts. Dodging a father towing two small children, Brodie jogged to where he'd seen the figure standing. He couldn't locate Chantal amongst the swarming tourist crowd.

The girl with dark hair had disappeared—had it even been her?

He walked up past the yacht club entrance, past the other boats, until he neared the hotel that sprawled along the water's edge.

He was going crazy. His imagination was playing him for a fool. Why would she come to him when he'd stuffed things up? He hadn't even been able to tell her that he loved her. She deserved better than that.

He headed back to the boat, turning his phone over in his hands. His thumb hovered over the unlock button, ready to dial her number. As he walked across the boarding ramp and raked a hand through his hair he stopped to rub the tense muscles in his neck.

'Brodie?'

Chantal walked out from the cabin, hands knotted in front of her. Long dark strands tumbled around her shoulders, the messy waves scattered by the gentle breeze. A skirt with blue and green shades bleeding into one another swirled around her ankles with each step. A long gold chain weighted by a blue stone glinted around her neck. She looked like a mermaid…a siren. A fantasy.

'What are you doing here?' he asked, his heart hammering against his ribs.

'I thought you'd gone back to Queensland.'

She bundled her hair over one shoulder, toying with the ends as he'd noticed her doing whenever she was anxious. He noticed everything about her now.

'I was supposed to.'

'Why did you stay?'

Light flickered across her face—a ray of hopefulness that dug deep into his chest.

'Unfinished business.'

'With who?'

The question emerged so quietly it might have come from his imagination. But her lips had moved; her eyes were burning into his.

'With you, Chantal. Why do you have to make everything so hard?'

A smile tugged at the corner of her lips. 'I'm difficult, I guess.'

'You are.'

He rubbed at the back of his neck, wishing that his body would calm down so he could be in control of the conversation. Instead his central nervous system conspired against him by sending off signals left, right and centre. There was something about the mere presence of her that had him crackling with electricity. Those parts of him had been dead before her.

'I'm sorry I pushed you away.' She drew a deep breath.

'I'm sorry I wouldn't let you help. I've been afraid of letting anyone close—not just after my divorce but for a long time.'

'You do seem to have trouble accepting help...'

What if he didn't accept her apology? It would be her own fault. She'd been stubborn as a bull from day one, determined to keep a wall between her and the outside world. Only now she wanted to tear down anything standing between her and Brodie. She wanted to remove all barriers—even the ones that had been there so long that they had cemented themselves in.

'I'm working on it,' she said solemnly, swallowing against a rising tide of emotion. 'I thought that I needed to do everything on my own because that's what my mother did. I wanted to be strong...to be my own person.'

He rubbed a hand along his jaw. 'It's a lonely way to live.'

'It is.' She nodded. 'I've been so concerned with making everyone think I was leading this successful life that I put no time into my reality. I only cared about my career, and I almost lost the best thing that ever happened to me.'

'Which is...?' His green eyes reached hers, the burning stare making her knees shake and her limbs quiver.

'You, Brodie. You're an amazing friend, and I lost you once because I refused to acknowledge my feelings. I'm not doing it again.'

She stepped towards him, resisting the urge to reach out and flatten her palms against the soft cotton shirt covering his chest.

'I don't want your friendship, Chantal.' He ground the words out, his teeth gritted, jaw tense.

Her breath hitched. The flight response was tugging against her desire to fight. *No!* She'd come too far to turn away—she could make him see how much she cared. She could make him see that she could change. That she *had* changed already, thanks to him.

'You asked me that night if I felt something for you.' Memories flickered: the sensation of dancing in his arms. The scents. The heat. The intoxicating attraction. 'I never had the chance to answer and then you were gone. I spent eight years convincing myself I'd made an error of judgment. I'd got caught up in the emotion. But I *did* feel something.'

'And now?'

'I want you in my life, Brodie. I want to sail away with you. I *want* your friendship, but I want more than that too.' She squeezed her eyes closed for a moment so she would have the courage to speak again. 'I love you.'

In the silence of waiting for his reaction she'd never felt so vulnerable in her life. No matter how many stages she'd performed on, no matter how much rejection she'd faced before—this was it. She was at a turning point, at the edge of falling into something wonderful. Her breath caught in her throat.

'I'll protect you even when you don't think you need it—I can't help that.' His voice caught, the scratch edge telling her that he was fighting for control too. 'But I'll support you in being your own person.'

She nodded, her breath caught in her throat.

'I'll help you with everything. I will *always* be there for you.'

She sucked on her lower lip, her mind screaming out for her to touch him. But she didn't want to stop his words, didn't want to risk ruining things with him again. If only he would say those words back to her.

I love you.

'I'll make you part of my crazy needy family.' He reached forward and drew her close. 'But I know now that I don't need to be your knight in shining armour. I pushed too hard at the bar. I understand that you need your independence. So I propose that we be our own people… together.'

'Oh, Brodie.' Relief coursed through her, buckling her knees so she sagged against him. The warmth of his body relaxed her, calmed her.

'As much as I love my family, I want to be my own person too. You made me see that. I'm going to put my own needs first for a change—and that starts with loving you.'

She looked up at him, catching his mouth as it came down to hers. The taste of him sent her senses into a spin, the gentle pressure of his lips making her feel as if she'd come home. His tongue met with hers, all the relief and desire and love exploding within her like New Year's fireworks. This was it—this was how life was meant to be.

She broke away from the kiss. 'What needs might they be?'

'Specific needs,' he whispered against her ear, his warm breath sending a shiver down her spine. 'Needs that can only be met by stubborn brunette dancers who like to practise yoga.'

'I might know someone who fits the bill.' She ran her hand under his T-shirt and pressed against the hard muscles in his stomach, as if memorising every ridge and detail of him. 'But she's pretty busy these days. I heard a rumour that she finally made it into a dance company.'

His eyes lit up and he hoisted her up in the air. 'You did?'

The harbour lights blurred as he spun them around. The sky darkened as each moment passed. Somehow it felt as though the universe was cementing their decision to be together.

'I did.' She laughed as he brought her back down. Solid ground would never feel the same again.

'I never had any doubts.'

'You were the only one.' She shot him a rueful smile.

'Not true.' He cupped her face with his hands and pressed another exploratory kiss to her lips. 'But you *do* need a little help with the constant doubt.'

'Are you testing me?'

'Maybe.' A sly smile pulled at his lips.

'Well, I accept your help.' She jabbed a finger into the centre of his chest, unable to conceal a grin. 'So there.'

'Chantal, I need to be able to help you. I need to be part of your life in a way that no one else can. I'll give you everything you deserve. I'll do everything I can to give you the life you want.'

The thumping of his heart reverberated against her ear.

'I'm going to run the business from Sydney.'

'Can you do that?' Her head jerked up.

'That's the best bit about being the boss.' He grinned. 'I can do whatever I like.'

'But what about your family?'

'I put a call in to my father. He's going to start sharing the load with me.' A flash of vulnerability streaked across Brodie's eyes. ''Bout time.'

'Really? That's wonderful.'

'Besides, Queensland is only a state away, and I'm sure you'll need a break at some point. I'll have to split my time across the two states but I know I can manage it.' He chuckled. 'Besides, the girls will be desperate to meet you.'

'I'd love to meet *them*. I never had what you had growing up. I know your family isn't perfect, but I've never been part of a family like that before.'

The idea was frightening—what if his sisters hated her?

'They'll love you. I know it.' He stroked her hair, pressing his lips to her forehead. 'But you were right to point out that I hide behind my family responsibilities. I *have* been hiding.'

She smiled against his chest. 'You can't hide any more.'

'I don't want to. I love you, Chantal.'

He spoke into her hair, his arms tight around her shoulders, his hand caressing her back.

Music wafted over the night air from the boat next to them.

Brodie wrapped his arms around her waist, moving her to the music. 'And I always said pretty girls shouldn't have to dance on their own.'

'I won't dance on my own ever again.'

* * * * *

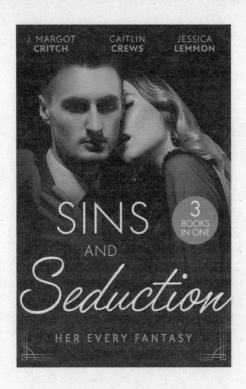

LET'S TALK

Romance

For exclusive extracts, competitions
and special offers, find us online:

f facebook.com/millsandboon

𝕏 @MillsandBoon

◉ @MillsandBoonUK

♪ @MillsandBoonUK

Get in touch on 01413 063 232